THE JACK OF SOULS

~ Book One of the Unseen Moon Series ~

by STEPHEN C. MERLINO

TORTOISE
RAMPANT

The Jack of Souls

ISBN: 978-0-9862674-1-3

Cover art and design by Jakub Rozalski @mr.werewolf.art@gmail.com
Interior layout, design, and formatting by Duvall Design
at www.duvalldesign.wordpress.com

All characters in this book are fictitious. Any resemblance to persons living or dead is coincidental, with the exception of the ghouls, which exactly resemble dead people.

If you purchase this book without a cover, you must be really desperate, so I can't fault you too much. I hope you enjoy the book. Still, I have to imagine you'd enjoy it more with a cover, and wonder if the coverless one you bought under the table could be much cheaper than a covered one you'd find in a used bookstore or Goodwill. Just saying.

For Jane, my mother, who is nothing like Harric's mom,
and who took me to my first workshop.
For Ed, my father, who taught me long patience.
For my sister Sue and brother Scott,
For the inspiration they bring by being so different from me.
For my love Kathryn, the one who didn't flee.
For Maia and Roman, my biggest fans and partners in adventure.

There is just as much of you in this as me.

Acknowledgements

My first reader is my mother, Jane, whose opinion is always insightful, smart, and, when it needs to be, gentle. She is followed by my dearest friends, Craig and Mark, who, with as much snark as my mother had gentleness, endured countless iterations of early drafts while I learned to write.

The members of Seattle Writers Cramp critique group had a huge impact on my learning as a writer. Steve, Amy, Amy, Mark, Tim, Janka, Kim, Mike, Barb, Thom, Kish, Courtland, Andrew, and Manny shared a lot of laughs with me. Their work is always a pleasure to read, and their critiques among the best writing instruction I've ever had. In that league, too, are my friends at North Seattle SFF Writers Fellowship, including Mariann, Mark, Linda, Vivian, Audrey, Kim, Yang-Yang and Sara, who took over the tradition of laughter and excellence when The Jack needed fresh eyes.

I am grateful to the pros at Fairwood Writers workshops, and I owe much to the judges of the Sandy Contest, Colorado Gold Contest, and PNWA Literary Competition, who run high quality competitions that provide new writers with a chance to break out, along with excellent coaching and feedback.

Finally, a big thank you goes to Lucienne Diver, who gave me seminal early advice about the story, and to my beta readers, Karen Duvall, Corinne O'Flynn, and Stefan Marmion, who took this to the next level with me.

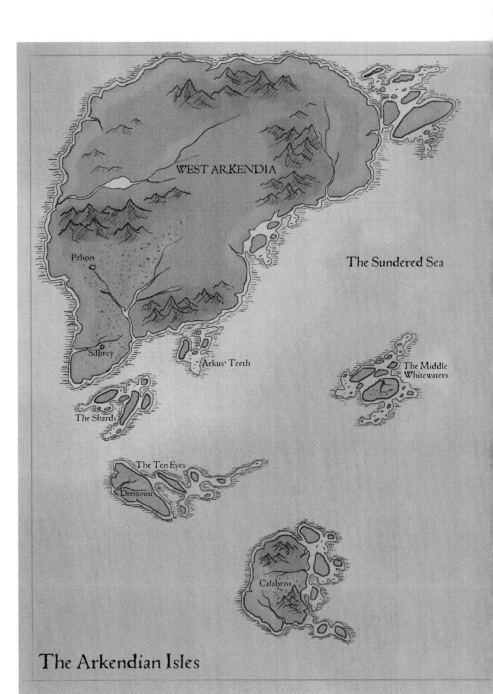

WEST ARKENDIA

The Sundered Sea

Pelion

Silbrey

Arkus' Teeth

The Middle
Whitewaters

The Shards

The Ten Eyes

Dreinousi

Calabros

The Arkendian Isles

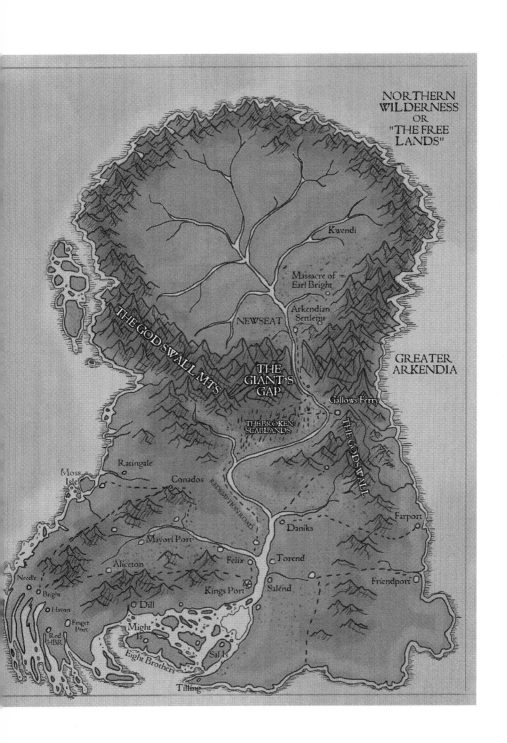

1

Cursed

"You written your will yet, lad?"

Someone shouted the words in Harric's ear over the din of the crowded barroom. He turned from the group of knights and house-girls he stood with, and found the brewer, Mags, leaning across the bar behind him. The old man fixed him with a look, drunk and earnest, and indicated the winch-clock on the bar. Five minutes to midnight. Five minutes left of Harric's nineteenth year, and his last full day of life. "You'd best write it quick," Mags said, "or Rudy'll snatch up your things before your corpse is cold."

Harric's throat tightened. He clenched his jaw against a rising rage—rage at the unfairness of his fate, at the madness that spawned it, and—

He shook it off. He would *not* end like the others, howling or blubbering for mercy.

He tipped his cup back and took a deep drink from his wine. "The night is still young."

"Don't make light of it, son. This is the day."

"You think I don't remember?"

"Just trying to help."

"You're trying to clear me out before my death spoils the party."

The old man scratched his stubbled chin. "Well, it would cramp the mood considerable…"

Harric managed a wry smile. He pointed to the winch-clock that towered above him, a column of woodwork on the bar, like a coffin on end. "When the twelfth chime sounds at midnight, my precious doom has till sunset tomorrow to find me. Plenty of time to write a will."

The brewer nodded, and grimaced as if struggling with emotion. He drew Harric close, old eyes glistening with unshed tears. "You know there isn't a one of us here who wouldn't have stopped your mother if we'd known. I'd have killed her if I had to. I swear it."

Unable to speak, Harric downed the last of his wine. "You're right about one thing," he said, pulling away. "It's time to leave the celebration to my guests." Before Mags could object, Harric stepped on a chair and onto the bar beside the winch-clock. From the back of the clock case he drew out the crowbar he'd hidden inside, and in two quick moves he wrenched out the mainspring to the accompaniment of cracking wood and outraged chimes.

"Wha—?" Mags choked. "Who's gonna pay for that?"

"Keep your hair on." Harric dropped his purse of coins on the bar, and steadied himself against the clock, forever stopped at one minute to midnight.

The clamor drew all eyes to the bar. A few present could read clocks and understood his joke; most simply saw him on the bar and fell silent, expecting a speech from their host.

Harric looked out into the smoky hall at the sea of upturned faces. In the gloom at the back of the hall, orange embers of ragleaf pipes pulsed like fireflies, and the place had fallen so silent he imagined he could hear the embers crackle with each pulse. Among the expectant faces he saw mostly locals of Gallows Ferry, familiars with whom he'd grown to manhood. Others were strangers passing through the outpost on the way to the Free Lands. He'd invited them all, and not a single enemy stood among them, for he'd drugged Rudy and his crew and left them sleeping with the hogs. A double pleasure, that.

"Almost time," he called, with a room-filling bravado he did not feel. "And it's going to stay that way for the rest of the night!" He raised the mainspring in mock triumph, to a roar of applause.

"I have no gloomy speech for you," he assured them. "We've said our farewells, and this night is for celebration. I leave you now to finish the wine and continue as if this night would never end. For you I bought up all the wine in Gallows Ferry, so it will be a great affront to my memory if a drop remains at daybreak."

Applause shook the timbered walls. Gentlemen and free men saluted with swords or raised cups. House-girls and maids threw flowers and other favors on the bar. In their faces he saw affection and curiosity and pity.

For that moment, Harric was a hero. He bowed, savoring the feeling for a single, aching heartbeat, then flung the mainspring to the crowd and departed for his chambers through the service door behind the bar.

Caris waited for him in the passage, illumined by a single candle near the door. Like all horse-touched, she was even bigger than the average man, so she filled the narrow servant's corridor, hair touching the ceiling and elbows brushing walls. If Harric hadn't expected her, he might have stepped back to give way, mistaking her in the dim light for one of the knights rooming at the inn, who sometimes got lost in its passages.

As the roar of the bar washed through the open door and past Harric, Caris flinched and clapped her hands to her ears.

He shut the door quickly and flashed a reassuring smile. "Ready? I expect they'll be on my heels."

She lowered her hands, but kept her stare on the floor between them, rocking from foot to foot. Even with the door closed, the bar's clamor distressed her horse-touched senses, so it wouldn't have surprised him if she turned and fled or—worse—curled in a ball with her hands to her ears. He'd seen it before, but he could never predict when she'd collapse and when she'd stand firm.

"Nothing I can't handle," she murmured.

"Good."

Shrill voices rose in the bar, and her eyes jumped to the door behind him.

"This here's private, folks," said Mags, on the other side. "Harric's done said his farewells."

"Aw, we can't leave him alone tonight," said a voice Harric recognized as Ana. "You *know* he's writing his will."

"Yes, and you aim to kiss your way into it," said Mags, "but I ain't letting you. So get!"

"He ain't slept alone all summer," Ana said. "Who's he got up there? Ain't that simple Lady Horse-touched, is it?"

"I said get! I got drink to pour!"

Caris's jaw clenched. She turned sideways and gestured for Harric to pass, pressing her back to the side of the passage. It made little space for him to slip by, and since she was almost two heads taller, her breasts stood level with his nose. She blushed, for though she tried to hide her feminine parts in loose-fitting men's gear, there was no denying their presence.

His skin tingled at the thought of brushing front to front, and the notion summoned the void back to his chest and a sting to his eyes. He bit the inside of his lip and turned sideways to sidle past. Before he took a step, she grasped his arms below the shoulders and lifted until his feet left the ground and his head bumped the ceiling.

"Or you could just lift me," he said.

Face dark with embarrassment, she rotated him past, set him at the foot of the stairs, and turned back to the door.

"Let me through, Magsy," said a male voice beyond it. "I'll be sure you get a share."

"*Magsy?*" The brewer snorted. "I said get!"

Caris glanced over her shoulder and frowned when she saw Harric still standing at the bottom of the stairs. "If they get by Mags, they won't get by me. You can thank me in the morning."

"You're the only one I haven't bid farewell."

"I won't let you. I'll see you in the morning."

Harric gave a weak smile. "You still think I'm crazy. You think all this fuss about my curse is for nothing?"

"I never said crazy. Just mistaken. We make our own fate."

"Ah. And all the people I grew up with here—all the people who knew my mother and her curses—they're mistaken too?"

She shrugged. "I've only been here two months. I can't say I know you or your mother like they do. But maybe that makes me see more clearly."

Harric rubbed his eyes. He knew he should go. He'd kept the boil of grief and rage well bottled all night, and he mustn't let them leak now. Of all people, Caris would know least how to receive a torrent of emotion. But she surprised him, turning toward him and lifting her gaze from the floor to meet his, a task surely harder for her horse-touched sensibilities than lifting a donkey.

"No mother would kill her child," she said, voice low, eyes bright with tears. "Not even my mother, the mother of a—" Her gaze faltered, then rose, defiant. "I'm proof. No mother could hate her child like that."

Harric smiled. "In the two months I've known you, I've only heard you mention your cob-head father, never your mother."

"Don't change the subject. Your mother didn't hate you."

Harric sighed. "Who said anything about hate?"

"You're saying she loved you?"

The ache in his chest deepened. Memories of his earliest years with his mother returned unbidden. Golden scenes of her lucid days, sitting in the sunny window above the river as she read to him, or sang. He swallowed the tightness in his throat. "She's mad. Her visions showed her that the Queen will fall because of something I do, and only my death can prevent it."

"That's ridiculous."

He nodded. "But her curses are real. I have less than a day."

The bar door flew open and banged against the wall. With a triumphant squeal, a wave of petitioners swept in, and Caris whirled to face it. Harric retreated up the lowest steps and watched as she grabbed the leader by the arms—it was Gina, the eldest barmaid—and spun her about to face the flood that followed. Pinioning Gina's arms, Caris used her as a breakwater against the rush.

Second in line was Donnal Bigs, who caught Harric's eye and waved a debt slip from the card tables. "There you are, Harric! Since you got no use for your coin anymore, be a good lad and float me—"

Donal's eagerness turned to confusion as Caris put her shoulder to Gina's back and drove her forward, mashing her into his chest as Ana collided behind. "Hey!" he cried.

"Horse-brained bitch!" Gina spat. "Brute!"

Deaf to their outrage—or perhaps fueled by it—Caris propelled them backwards, picking up speed until she ejected them into the bar, where they fell in a welter of boots and petticoats.

Their expressions as she slammed the door made Harric laugh.

Caris set her back to the door as curses rained against it. She glanced Harric's direction to be sure he'd seen the action. A rare smile parted her lips, making her quite pretty in spite of her size.

Another throb of loss in his gut. He hadn't had enough time with her. "Thanks, Caris. You've been a good friend—"

"See you in the morning." She slid down the door till she sat, knees to chest. Refusing to meet his gaze, she clapped her hands to her ears.

"Gods leave me, you can be stubborn," he said. She gave no sign of hearing, and he wondered for the hundredth time how she came to be horse-touched. Whether a careless maid had used mare's milk for her mother's tea, whether she'd been conceived in a saddle, or a dozen other explanations he'd heard, of which none might be right. The only thing anyone knew for certain about it was what could be seen: the massive body, the uncanny sympathy with horses, and the crippling incomprehension of people.

"Farewell, Caris."

No acknowledgement.

He turned up the stairs before his grief boiled over.

In the silence of his chambers, four floors above the bar, Harric inked a quill and laid it to paper.

To the lady Caris, I leave all the silver in my strongbox. May it help her find a knight brave enough to make her his squire.

To Mother Ganner, I leave my collection of painted playing cards, with all but the Jack of Souls, *which I want buried with me, and the* Maid of Blades, *which I leave to Caris, for luck.*

He leaned back in the chair to read what he'd written, and frowned. The style was too informal. He'd learned to forge wills as part of his mother's teaching, and they had always been ceremonial in their language, but somehow he hadn't thought his own will would need it, or that he'd ever value such ceremony. He set the sheet aside, bemused.

On his last sheet of paper he began anew.

I, Harric Dimoore, being of sound mind and body, do hereby bequeath unto the following people, the worldly possessions here named.

That was better. He formalized the rest. Then he added, *Item: One longsword, barely used, for Mother Ganner's mantel,* and chewed the end of the quill while he studied the words. Should he add, *with my love,* or *for being my mother when my real one was mad?* Of course. He wrote it all and swallowed an unexpected knot in his throat.

"Damn you, Mags," he hissed, rubbing a sting from his eyes. He'd already said his farewells and had his tears, and now writing the will dragged him through it again.

To Rudy, the stable master, he wrote, *my chamber pot, with contents.*

Harric chuckled, then wept.

And damn Mags for watering the wine. He'd drunk enough to lay him out, but it merely filled his bladder.

He hastily wrote off the rest, adding, *To Caris: My unrequited heart — if only it had longer to convince you to open yours.* That made him laugh again. A flirtation from beyond the grave. She'd find that perfectly in character.

Signing it for Mother Ganner as witness — as he signed for all her dealings — he set it aside.

As the sealing wax cooled on the will, he noticed the air had grown hot in his chambers. Outside, the usually ceaseless river winds had died. He tore off his shirt and dropped it to the floor, then crossed the room and threw open the wind shutters.

Silver moonlight of the Bright Mother bathed him, and he stood at the sill to let the summer air caress his skin. She watched him from across the scablands, her face full and serene as if all were well in the world. Below his window, the dark void of the river canyon sighed. He nudged a candle stub off the sill and watched it fall past five stories of inn and fifteen fathoms of cliff face toward the swirling waters. Since they'd built the inn upon the very edge of the cliff, and since the top floors jettied even farther over the river, the candle hit the surface well away from the foot of the cliff to vanish without a sound in the black waters.

The view of the broken hills across the river, which normally cheered him, only made him wistful. This was his last look. After tonight, would he ever know beauty again? Would he know anything? As the Bright Mother moon set into the scablands of the opposite shore, her low-angled light etched the rocks in stark relief, a jagged labyrinth of stone. He had always meant to explore those lands, but never had. In patches of darkness between its crags he spotted the campfires of emigrants bound for the Free Lands, another place he'd never see.

As the Bright Mother sank below the horizon, he imagined he felt her protective powers withdraw, even as the Mad Moon, which he knew rose somewhere in the east, marshaled threat and destruction.

He snorted. "Such symbolic timing, Mother."

Laughter gusted from the windows of the bar far below. His guests were probably betting on the manner of his doom again. He'd started the wagers himself, to keep things light at supper. "Hanging" had been a popular one, along with "tooken by a god," though his personal favorite was "loved to death by hoors." They all knew it was a pointless pastime, since all victims of his mother's curses died under cover of fog. The last two victims had been Harric's friends, Chacks and Remo. The day before their appointed dooms, they'd fled for the Free Lands, and the fog overtook them. Emigrants had found their bodies on the north road, without a mark on them to show how they'd died.

Harric slammed the shutters on the view, biting back a string of curses against his mother.

The room spun. His head felt heavy. Maybe the apple wine was finally doing its work. He tore off the remainder of his clothes and flopped on his bed to lie sweating in the stagnant air. If sleep would come, he'd have it; no sense watching all night for his doom. Without sleep he'd be dull and vulnerable the rest of the day, unfit for resistance.

He pulled his sword from under his bed and lay with it clasped to his breast in its scabbard. Small help, perhaps, when fighting a mystery, but its weight and edge gave comfort.

He closed his eyes, resolved at least to rest, and fell into a wine-soaked sleep, his last in Gallows Ferry.

The fog rose quickly around the cemetery island, drawing spirits from the grave cairns that crowded its stony shores. The strongest of the spirits drifted to the edge of the water. Like the rest, he was a transient citizen of the Unseen; once living, he was still bound to his bones so he might serve his kin until the next should die and take his place. Also like the rest, he hadn't seen his kin for a single night since he died, for his people feared the attentions of the dead, and placed their graves on river islands where moving water confined them.

It is here, he said of the fog. *As she promised. Soon we can cross.*

The others stood well back and watched. They were fainter souls, weak but hungry.

They gazed in hope at the fog, which had already begun to calm the violent essence of the river as a blanket stills a fire. They gazed in fear at the sky, which, like the river, had been terribly transformed from the one they knew in life. In the world of the living, the Bright Mother and the Mad Moon had dominated the heavens, while the Unseen Moon—black as the space between stars—lurked in corners, unregarded. In the unseen world of spirits, this inverted. Here the black moon dominated the sky like the hole at the center of a whirlpool, and the sky itself—which in life displayed a mantle of stars—now bore the black moon's web of souls.

Shuddering, they tore their gaze from the moon whose tides would one day draw them skyward. What happened after that, they knew not. Perhaps the creatures of that moon, which crawled the web like spiders, consumed the rising grave spirits. Or perhaps they wove the grave spirits' strands into the very web they crawled—a living network of imprisoned souls.

Neither prospect brought comfort.

The spirit at the river's edge knew better than to stare at the Web of Fate. His eyes lay on the water as he wrapped himself in fog and tested the air above the river with an outstretched hand.

Yes, he said. *The fog grows thick. It is safe to cross.*

To Gallows Ferry! a withered spirit cried. *To feed!*

To see my kin, said another.

No, said the strong one, now their leader. He glided above the sleeping waters toward the shore. *We must find Him first. That is the bargain we made with the Lady who brought the freedom of the fog.*

Across the surface of the water they sped blindly for the shore, drawn by warm blood and the breath of the living.

Tell the Lady I care not for her bargains, said another, pushing forward among them. He was nearly as strong as the leader, a butcher in life used to eating his fill. *Now that I'm free, I shall feed as I please.*

You may tell her yourself, said the leader, *for she is here.*

The Lady, as they called her, stood above the beach like a sad queen upon a platform, surveying her troops before a battle. In contrast to the starved shapes of the grave spirits, she radiated power and light. And while their soul-strands trailed miserably behind them to their graves, hers rose into the web like the flames of a signal fire. And where the spirits covered their nakedness with loops of their ragged strands, she wore hers as a gown of light. Her gaze burned. She peered from the flames of her being like a witch at the stake, mocking the fire.

What is she? one whispered in awe. *Is she not one of us? A mortal soul upon this land?*

She is, said the leader. *But she is more. She has the Sight. She knows the web. She knows its ways.*

They huddled before her on the beach, avoiding her gaze. Even the butcher faltered, but then he swelled and pushed forward beside the leader.

The leader bowed. *Lady, we have come.*

Her voice rose, pure and sad. *You know what you must do.*

We do.

Then go. She gestured in the direction of Gallows Ferry, though her sorrowful eyes rested on the butcher, as if she knew he would speak.

We must feed first. He lashed his strands angrily. *Look at us. We are weak and shriveled like corpses. There are settlers on the road; let their strands fill us first, then on to your business.*

I did not free you to feed on peasants.

I say you did not free us at all, he replied. *It was the fog that freed us, and maybe it would have come on this night without you, only you somehow saw it would come, and pretend you caused it.*

The other spirits shuffled nervously. Some moved away from him, but he stood his ground.

Perhaps it is as you say. She stepped aside and gestured to the road on the bank above. *Let us see whether you need me or no.*

He hesitated, but then puffed himself and proceeded up the bank beyond her. When she did nothing to oppose him, he raced up the road, free as air.

Several others moved to follow, but the leader pointed to the lowest strands of the web above the trees. *Look.* Something moved there. Dark shapes like crows at a gallows.

Servants of the Unseen Moon! a grave spirit hissed.

As the figures descended the web, their forms seemed to coalesce, then bleed like ink in water before coalescing again into forms varied but difficult to discern. Half shadow, half soul, they seemed to both generate and swallow the spirit light around them.

They dropped from the web onto the butcher like crows on spilled corn. The butcher cried out, brief and shrill, but his struggle quickly ceased. The moon sprites huddled around him, heads low. When they rose to perch in the web, the butcher's empty husk drifted back to his grave on its strands, formless, and fainter now than the shadow of smoke in moonlight.

Are there others who doubt I freed you? The Lady's sad gaze had never left the beach. None of the grave spirits moved. *Very well. Go before me and fulfill your half of the bargain. When it is done, you may do as you like.*

The leader followed the path the butcher had taken, and this time the moon sprites above them only watched.

Another grave spirit ventured after the leader and clung to his side. *She is truly mighty. The moon spirits do not move! They fear her too.*

She has made bargains of her own, said the leader. *One can only wonder what sacrifice she made to gain such power.*

It matters not to me what she gave, as long as I feed.

The rest of the grave spirits made themselves small and scurried beneath the watchers like rats beneath an eagle's nest. Then the Lady was behind them, bright and terrible. *Fly now, or there will be no time!* Strands of spirit lashed from her hands like whips, scoring the air above the stragglers. The spirits sped before her, and she pursued on wings like fire.

The leader of the grave spirits saw that she wept.

Harric woke in pain, bony hands around his throat. He twisted against their hold until he tore away and shot upright as his enemy dissolved into fog.

Staring about in confusion, he gulped the air. His candle had dwindled to a guttering stub, but it was enough to illumine the stream of fog sieving through the shutters and burying the floor. Already it stood as high as the top of his mattress.

He bolted from bed, sending his forgotten sword skittering to the floor, where it disappeared beneath the fog. Something cold entwined his knees. Something hard seized an ankle. He cried out and wrenched free, tripping to the door and throwing it wide to plunge down the stairs, only to find the stairwell overflowing with fog. White hands like the hands of drowned men reached from its surface to grasp at his arms.

He cried out, stumbling backward and thrashing to the window. Throwing the shutters wide, he saw the Mad Moon full on the horizon, its red skin blazing like fire. A sea of blood buried the valley to the height of his window — the fog, stained red in the crimson light of the moon.

The fog filled the valley in all directions. Only the peak of the inn and a few distant hilltops stood above the tide, tiny islands of safety.

Harric clambered through the window to stand on its sill, and grab a rung of the roof ladder beside it. Fire-red tendrils of fog slid up his knees as he stepped onto the lowest rung. He swung his other foot to the next rung, but something seized it and nearly jerked him into the void. Kicking wildly, he tore his foot free and pulled himself up with his arms.

Fear pulsed in his temples. His feet flew up the rungs. Only six more rungs to the edge of the gable above his chambers, and then he could grab the rope knot that dangled over the lip of the roof, swing a leg over, and crawl up the shingles to the roof peak above the fog.

As he clambered the last rungs and grabbed the knot securely in his fists, bony hands seized his left leg. He kicked free long enough to fling the leg over the lip of the roof, but they descended upon his right foot on the rung and wrenched it free.

Without solid purchase on the edge of the roof, his free leg slipped back, and he swung out above the void.

Harric roared. Dangling above the fog, something in him broke. The rage he'd bottled burst free and filled his limbs with fury. Stomping downward with his free foot, he broke his captor's grip. He pulled himself up, swung a leg over the lip of the roof, and hauled his body onto the shingles.

On all fours, he scrabbled up the slope. When he reached the peak above the fog, he collapsed across it and lay panting and trembling. Only then did he realize he'd screamed his voice raw, and his feet and fingers bled from the sharp slate shingles.

When he caught his breath, he stood on the pinnacle of the roof, a tiny island in a flaming sea. His naked body shivered. There was no higher point in Gallows Ferry: to the west, the crimson moon set fire to an endless sea of fog; to the east, immediately behind the inn, the fog lapped against the cliff of the Godswall, and even with a running leap it stood too far from the inn to reach, and too sheer to climb if he could. The cliff loomed above the tiny island, a granite wall a full mile high.

He was trapped. And naked. And as the fog rose, his island dwindled.

Harric shivered again and rubbed his bruised throat. So it was the fog itself that executed her curses. Or something in the fog. *And this is how Chacks and Remo must have died.* He remembered their faces as they begged for mercy at his mother's grave, the night before they fled Gallows Ferry.

"Is that what you want of me, Mother? Want me to weep and beg?"

The fog swallowed his words. Already it submerged the top of his window below, and licked at the edge of the roof. Searching tendrils twined up the slates, questing and retreating like the tongues of serpents.

The Mad Moon glared across the sea, the blistered eye of its angry god. And now beside it, like the crow-plucked socket of its twin, stared the black void of the Unseen Moon. A pulse of fear shot through him. It was rare to notice the black moon's place in the sky, and bad luck to stare when you did. Yet he found himself transfixed. It seemed not a moon but a burn-hole in the canopy of stars, blacker somehow than the night itself. It seemed to swallow the light of the nearest stars and humble even the fire of the Mad Moon beside it.

Something moved across the face of the Unseen Moon. A shimmer barely glimpsed, like a reflection from the depths of a well.

Whispers teased at the edge of Harric's mind: *We see you.*

A shiver crawled up his spine.

Fly to us. Be free.

The black moon kissed the horizon. It was setting, which meant dawn was near, for it always set before dawn. As it touched the fog, an oily stain seeped onto the surface of the sea, spilled ink on red linen. The stain meandered across its surface until it touched the shores of Harric's island. A path. In the distance he imagined huddled figures on the path, shapes as dark as the moon itself, beckoning.

Fly to us. Fly and be free.

Harric shuddered. He imagined himself stepping from the roof onto the path and plunging thirty fathoms to the river. Even if he survived the icy shock, he'd never rise from the whirlpools. No one ever did. The figures called him to his death.

Death…and then what? The black moon's belly? Oblivion? A new mother's womb and another run at happiness? *Depends on whom I ask.* Surely one must be right.

A tingle of horrible hope ran through him. Might this path to the Unseen be an offer of freedom in the afterlife—of protection from his mother's ghost, which surely waited on the other side as she waited in his nightmares? Or should he wait for the fog to reach him and then fight—weaponless and naked—against a sea of clawing hands?

The fog boiled above the eaves, near enough to touch. In it Harric glimpsed faces desperate and hollow. Its hands and tendrils grew bolder, scrabbling toward his toes. A bold arm flung from the fog and scraped his heel.

Jump. Fly.

Harric crouched, heart pounding, legs tensing to spring.

"Harric?" said a familiar voice. "What are you doing? Where are your clothes?" The voice seemed near, yet whole worlds away. *Gods take it for interrupting!*

He reset a slipping foot and tensed to spring, only to watch in dismay as the Unseen's path and figures faded from the fog. Stars winked where the Black Moon had been.

"No!" he gasped.

The Mad Moon followed its brother beneath the horizon. The sky paled. Golden sunlight glimmered on the few hilltop islands in the west, and the stagnant air finally stirred, shifting hair from Harric's eyes.

"Harric! Answer me."

Harric stared in confusion as crimson drained from the fog and Caris's head and shoulders rose through it directly before him. Big as she was, she could stand on the sill of his window with her head above the fog. Her face floated before him, a dream interrupting a nightmare.

"Harric, what in the black moon are you doing?" She clamped a strong hand around his ankle. "If you jump, you make her stupid doom come true!"

Claws erupted from the fog and seized her hair from behind, hauling her head back and peeling her away from the gable.

She yelled, twisting aside while clinging to the roof with one hand and to Harric's ankle with the other. Then she dropped as if something knocked her feet from beneath her, and her grip jerked Harric's foot from the slates.

He fell, slamming his side on the roof before she released him and he plunged over the edge into the fog. Somehow, he caught the lip of the roof with one hand and slowed his descent enough for Caris to snatch his wrist. His fingers lost hold, and this time he swung downward in her grasp and crashed against the ladder beside the window, jarring his arm in its socket.

He cried out in pain. Caris cursed steadily.

Harric groped until he found the bottom rung of the ladder, and hooked a knee over it. Before he could propel himself up, icy hands collared him and squeezed. He pried at them with his free hand, but they were bone hard and slippery. More hands grabbed his ankles and dragged him from the rung to swing free again in Caris's grasp. She groaned and tried to lift him, but the fog countered with such terrible strength that her grip slipped from his wrist to his hand.

"Grab something!" she cried.

Harric dared not release his grip on the hands at his throat, and he struggled in vain to free his legs.

Wind gusted his hair sideways and banged a shutter above. One of the claws on his ankle released him and he flung his knee back onto the rung. Another gust cut across the face of the inn, and its force seemed to literally blow the strength from the hands at his neck. He pried the fingers free and grabbed the ladder. He sucked cool air into his lungs.

As sunlight streaked the morning sky, the grasping hands withered like paper in fire. Faint screams of pain echoed around him, weirdly present yet distant. *To ground! It is done!*

In the thinning fog Harric saw Caris throw a leg over his windowsill, eyes wild and desperate. Straddling the sill, she hauled him to his feet. "Get in!" She practically shoved him through the open window, and he tumbled through.

Harric embraced the floor in relief.

Caris piled after him. She staggered to her feet and whirled to face the window, fists balled to face pursuit.

"It's all right, Caris—it's over."

She turned. Eyes wild, she grabbed him by the shoulders and hauled him to his feet. Her hair had broken free of its binding to stick out at wild angles or cling to the sweat of her face. "What in the black moon was that?" she gasped. Her eyes pleaded for explanation as if sanity depended on it.

Harric blinked. He took her hands in his to steady himself, and managed a wry smile.

"That," he said, between panted breaths, "was my mother."

...The blood of the Phyros made great knights immortal, but it also drove them mad. Countless are the tales of those who woke from black rages to find the blood of loved ones on their hands. Yet few could bear abstinence, and only one succeeded long.

—From *Lore of Ancient Arkendia,* by Sir Benfist of Sudlin

2

Blood on the Stones

Sir Willard woke from an unintended sleep in the saddle. The sound of Molly's snort had wakened him—a snort of warning, of enemies nearby— and not the first alarm she'd raised, he realized, only the first to wake him.

He cursed and peered about through the slots of his helm. At a glance he saw they were still on the road to Gallows Ferry. The two mortal ponies still plodded before them. To his relief, the ambassador remained fastened to the saddle of the smaller pony, his blanket still cloaking him, hiding his inhuman shape.

Nothing amiss there.

But it was past dawn, and their cover of fog had disintegrated in a brisk north wind, exposing their position to their pursuers. Worse, their road no longer crept along the bottom of a scabland canyon; it had climbed onto an open ridge above the river to his right, and a dry gulch on the left, where they stood skylined against the glowing mist. The river rushed below, wide and swift and cold. On its far bank, the cliffs of the Godswall erupted from the waters and soared into frosted pinnacles in blue sky.

"Something is wrong ahead?" Ambassador Brolli stirred, his weirdly fingered foot poking briefly from under the blanket.

Willard grunted, finally awakening fully to the backward cant of Molly's ears and glances. "Something behind us."

"Perhaps our pursuers did not give up as we thought."

Willard turned around in time to see the first crossbowman loose his bolt from two hundred paces on the opposite side of the dry gulch. The bolt whipped past Molly's nose and over the ambassador's head to crack against a stone.

"Willard?"

"Keep your head down!"

Willard spurred Molly hard into Brolli's pony, herding it toward the cover of a massive boulder and shielding the ambassador with Molly's bulk and his own armored back. A bolt stuck deep in Molly's neck, below her ear. She tossed her head in rage, and Willard tore the shaft away, painting the stones with immortal violet blood. Another bolt snapped upon the boulder as the ambassador reached safety, followed by a wet *thack!* and a flash of pain in Willard's thigh. A glance down confirmed a feathered bolt jutting behind the steel of the cuisse.

He cursed, and freed the shaft with an unconscious yank. White-hot pain lanced up and down his leg, and he nearly fainted. Perhaps he did faint, for he'd apparently dropped the bolt, and now he couldn't see it among the stones. Long ago he'd forgotten the crippling pain a mortal felt. How it ruled him now!

Bile welled in his throat. His vision spun.

The ambassador threw off the blanket and looked about, his gold, owlish eyes full of fear.

"You are injured!" The ambassador's long fingers flew to unfasten the straps that kept his ill-fitting body in the saddle.

"I said stay on your horse!" Willard drove Molly against Brolli's pony again, startling both pony and ambassador. "You cannot help me! Keep your head down until I return."

"You are bleed! Look!" Brolli's accent thickened in agitation. "You are fall down before you reach them!"

As if in confirmation, a line of blood tickled Willard's ankle and streamed into the dust. A qualm of nausea swept him. His bowels grew watery.

"Sir Willard, you must drink her blood."

"I cannot. My oath to Lady Anna—"

"Foolish oath! What of your oath to your queen? Your oath to return me safe home?"

Willard's head swam. He turned his eyes to the wound, and jammed a fistful of his cloak behind the cuisse to keep pressure on the wound and stanch the flow. With each fold of cloak he jammed in, the dripping slowed, but hot wires of pain shot up his legs. "You don't understand," he panted.

"If I start again, I won't stop. And the madness, Brolli. The addiction. The Blood offers no simple healing, Brolli. It changes everything. Forever. You don't know what I suffered to be rid of it."

"You wish to be rid of life, too?" The ambassador's flat face scowled, huge gold eyes burning scorn into Willard's. "You free of being Queen's Champion? You wish be free of worry her safety so long, all lost in the end? *Here* is the madness, if you not drink the Blood!"

Willard clenched his teeth against the pain. "I'll put the suggestion of cowardice down to a mistake of language, Ambassador," he growled. "But only once."

Brolli held his gaze, unflinching.

Willard sighed. "We have no time for this, Brolli." From the height of Molly's back, he laid a reassuring hand on Brolli's thick shoulder. "Trust me in this. This is my land. My people. I know how to fight them. And you must stay in that saddle, or we will not make Gallows Ferry before our enemies."

"That is not my tactics—"

"You *have* no tactics, Ambassador! Not here! You know only forest fighting. And you do not know my people. You must trust me in this, and stay as you are."

Brolli gave a curt nod of agreement, just as a bolt whizzed past his ear. He flinched and ducked as another hissed through the air where his head had been, and a third skipped off the sheltering boulder.

"Keep that head down!" Willard bellowed. Whirling, Molly launched back down the road.

The crossbowmen had made no attempt to hide themselves. Four men, four horses. They had drawn up on the opposite side of the treacherous-looking ravine around which Molly had taken him when the road bent around the head of the ravine in the shape of an elongated U. The bowmen worked the cranks of their crossbows to load another volley, watching Willard intently as he halted Molly at the edge of the ravine and assessed their position. The shortest way to the bowmen would be straight across the gully, but once Molly plunged in, the way might prove uncrossable, wasting precious time and allowing more shots at Brolli. The surest way would be the long way around the head of the ravine, on the road.

Shifting his weight, Willard turned Molly, and she exploded into the road-devouring gallop only possible for a Phyros.

As the bowmen cranked furiously at their crossbows, their horses shifted uneasily beside them, eyes on Molly. Hot-blooded stallions, Willard noted, unburdened with gear or armor. The four were scouts, sent from the main body of knights who pursued him, expressly to take potshots at the ambassador if they could catch Willard unaware.

Or sleeping. Willard ground his teeth. *Sleeping!* When immortal, he'd gone days without sleep—weeks at a time during the campaigns of the Cleansing. Now he couldn't stay awake an hour without nodding off when his mortal carcass took the notion. It made no difference that the fate of the kingdom rested upon this mad quest for the Queen or that a single bolt to the ambassador could start a war that would end it.

He roared a string of curses that left his great-helm ringing. Let them think that was his battle cry and not an anthem of frustration.

"Lady Anna, your paramour is not adapting well to mortality," he muttered to his absent love. "But I shall stay true to my oath. I will not take the Blood. I will grow old with you, I swear."

As Molly reached the head of the ravine, she cornered and accelerated, hoofbeats shattering the morning stillness. The bowmen abandoned their bow-cranks and scrambled for their horses.

Willard made no special flourish as he drew the greatsword from its sheath at his waist. It was Molly he needed them to watch: a horse so big she made their stallions seem ponies; the Mad God's own mare; a thundering, violet-black divinity with more scars than the keel of a longboat. One look at her and they'd assume that he, too, was still immortal. How could they not? In twenty generations no Phyros-rider had ever successfully abandoned the Blood and immortality.

And he still wore the impressive oversized armor. Filled as it was with pads and air around his shrunken mortal muscles, it maintained the appearance of immortal stature. The only thing that hinted at his secret was the paunch he'd hammered into his breastplate to accommodate his new belly.

And his red blood.

Gods leave me, the damned red blood on the stones. If they find the bloody bolt, the game's up. A wash of shame poured over him. To be exposed a fraud and japed at in a ballad! He could see it now: *Sir Willard Feeble Paunch. Sir Willard the Shriveled.*

Molly's blood called to him. Within easy reach, hot streams of immortality pulsed through rippling veins beneath the wine-black hide. He shut his eyes tight against temptation. How he longed to cut and drink from her! Molly cast a glance back, longing to be cut, pinning him with a violet eye and urging him with a low groan.

Willard's stomach rolled. *No.* He forced his eyes away, and she bucked in anger, but he would not look back to her. *Never more, girl. Never again.*

Roaring in frustration, Molly channeled her rage into the pursuit, iron-shod hooves hammering sparks from the stones.

The bowmen whipped their horses to an all-out run. Ahead, the road plunged over the edge of the ridge and into another scabland canyon, and they plunged down it, leaving a cloud of dust on the rim.

Only fifty strides behind, Molly sailed over the rim, and the thunder of her massive hooves compounded between the walls.

The bowmen had just reached the flat of the canyon floor when Molly flew among them. With a four-hand height advantage, and nearly two times their weight, it only took a sideways check of Molly's shoulder to shove the rearmost stallion into a stony outcrop, where he crashed from full gallop to full stop against the stone. Without breaking stride, she drove between the second and third horses, seized a rider's ankle in her jaws, and hoisted him from the saddle. She dropped him under her pounding hooves, and with the upswing of her tusk-like blood tooth opened a fountain in the neck of his horse.

The third rider tried to rein in, hoping perhaps to duck the charge and circle back for the ambassador, but Willard's blade slashed through his ribcage as they passed.

Willard sighed. It felt right, the unconscious perfection of their partnership. More right than anything he knew. Ten lifetimes in her saddle—ten lifetimes infusing Molly's blood in his veins—and how could it be otherwise?

They were one, and made for battle.

He knew she could not understand his abstinence—his repudiation of their old fellowship, his refusal of the daily ritual of drinking from her veins—and he knew she hated him for it. But unlike him, she could not release her bond. She served him rebelliously, an old lover rejected but still hopeful. Glancing back at him in challenge, she surged forward, redoubling her stride in pursuit of the remaining stallion, a sleek, crop-eared black with a fearless stride. Drawing alongside it, she seized it between her teeth at the top of its neck, behind the ears.

Willard read her signals and let her run free, adjusting his balance to her motions as Molly forced the stallion's head down and dug her hooves in for a precipitous stop. The stallion squealed in pain, twisting and juddering to a stop that launched its rider swimming through the air. Molly forced the stallion to the ground, twisting until he rolled belly up like a yielding dog. With a hoof the size of a stumper's wedge, she pressed its skull to the stones, and *leaned*.

A violet eye glared back at Willard, as if daring him to challenge her divine cruelty.

Willard grunted. "You make immortality so attractive, Molly."

The fourth bowman staggered to his feet and limped away up the road, but Molly had her toy, and Willard did not dare deprive her of it in her present mood.

They stood now in the belly of a canyon, which rose before them over a low saddle of crumbling granite, over which the road climbed and disappeared again into another nameless channel through the scablands. A glance behind confirmed all three bowmen lay motionless in the dust.

The sound of hoofbeats drew his attention back to the road ahead, where the limping bowman climbed the road toward the rise. As the man reached the crest, a thicket of pennoned lances bobbed into view beyond it, flashing spear tips angled against the winds. The bowman hailed them, waving his arms as if he would fly.

Willard sat as straight as he could manage, visor down, and drew his cloak around his waist to conceal the paunch of his breastplate, and the red blood of his wound.

Eight knights in full armor drew up on the crest. Eight squires drew up behind them, and more men behind that. Willard frowned. They'd been only half that number the day before. To grow by so much they'd have to have the support of a ship or two on the river, which was very bad news. It meant they could replace their horses with fresh ones, while he could not. Molly, of course, was tireless, but the ambassador's ponies sagged near collapse.

A knight in emerald-green armor advanced from amongst the others and signaled the ranks, from which six fresh bowmen emerged. They walked their mounts off the road among the boulders, maneuvering through the rocks until they drew even with their leader. Once there, they winched up their bowstrings. But the green knight made no further preparations for attack.

Willard grunted his approval. In the three days since Sir Green had picked up Willard's trail, he had never engaged Willard directly, only followed and sent the occasional band of snipers. Sir Green clearly knew the old rule of fifty to one for mortal-on-immortal combat, and wisely awaited reinforcements before trying anything. His short-term tactics were also sound, since his present elevated position on the crest gave him as defensible a position as he could hope for, and he knew if Willard attacked, some of the bowmen could race past and threaten the ambassador.

A *stalemate, then. Well enough.*

But something was wrong with their horses. This close to a Phyros, a mortal horse should be terrified—even the best war-trained specimens should prove difficult to manage, and the untrained mounts ought to be blind with fear. Sir Green's destriers stood on that crest as still as jades in a pasture, and even the untrained bowmen's mounts seemed nothing more than nervous.

Molly also noticed. Though she kept her hoof against the stallion's skull, she released the stallion's jaw to better view their unresponsive audience.

There was only one explanation: their horses had been conditioned to be near a Phyros, just as his ponies had. And the only way to do that was to stable them with a Phyros.

A chill slid down Willard's spine. "One of your immortal brothers has returned to Arkendia, Molly. They've got an immortal on their side."

The implications hit him like a boot in the stomach. Did the Queen know? Had she alerted the Blue Order? He would never have sworn his oath to Anna if he'd known an Old One had returned, nor would Anna have let him. *I will never drink the Blood again. I will grow old with you and die.* The oath mocked him. He bit off a curse.

Willard studied the green knight, as if he could divine from the man's appearance some clue of *which* Old One had returned without his knowing. Sir Bannus? His stomach turned at the thought. Could Sir Bannus be a day's ride behind? Might he catch them before they crossed at Gallows Ferry?

Molly snorted. She released the quivering stallion, and Willard turned her back the way they'd come.

Sitting straight and calm as any immortal, he walked her away, shifting the cloak to conceal his bloody leg. With luck, the drips on the stones would be indistinguishable from the blood of his enemies, but there was nothing he could do about the bloodied crossbow bolts. His enemies would find them both, one inked with violet divinity, the other with mortal red. And when that happened they'd know the unimagined truth: that for the first time in three hundred years, Sir Willard—their most hated enemy, chief architect of their exile—was mortal again. And they could take him at will.

At a natural bend in the road he risked a glance back, to see his enemies still watching from the rise. *Good. Stick to your strategy, Sir Green. Hold off until your immortal master arrives.*

A wave of dizziness swept him. He caught himself leaning, close to tipping from the saddle, and righted himself with a start. The wadding had shifted free and the trickle of drips returned to his ankle.

Brolli was right. I'll fall before I return to him.

Black spots crowded his vision. A humming began between his ears.

"I will not!" he snarled at the absent ambassador. "Gods leave me, I swore it, I will not!"

Yet his hands trembled as he removed a gauntlet and reached for Molly's neck to claw away the scab from the crossbow wound that had already hardened to a scar. Shuddering, he thrust the clot beneath the quilting on his leg and into the mouth of the wound.

I swore off drinking *the Blood. I never swore off plasters.*

Yet he understood too well the risk he took in touching it at all. Already the familiar fire raged in the wound, numbing as it burned. The old strength whispered briefly in his veins. But the old hunger *roared*. And the addiction that once ruled him embraced him like a possessing spirit.

More.

"No!" he gasped. "My lady!" In his delirium he could see her before him as she had been when last he saw her in court—aging away from him—now watching with pitying eyes. "I will not betray you again, Lady Anna! We will grow old and die together!"

He repeated the words like a mantra, beating his fist on his new-healed wound until he gained the bluff and cantered back up the U around the head of the ravine to the ambassador's sheltering place.

True to his word, Brolli remained fastened to the saddle on his pony. He grinned with relief and admiration. "Well done, old man!"

"Ride!" Willard gasped.

The ambassador's face fell, gold eyes searching for answers in the anguish of Willard's face.

"Ride, I say! To Gallows Ferry. And get under that blanket, or we'll be stoned by the first mob that sees you."

Red for the Peasant with dirt in his nails,
Red for the Freeman at work in the vales,
The blood of the Yeoman is red as his flock's,
And red is the Merchant's, a-counting his stocks.
Orange is for Gentlemen new to their farms,
Yellow their betters, in glittering arms,
Green for the highest a Gentle can wend,
Blues for the Nobles whose cattle we tend,
Purple the stain of the God in our Kings,
Cut deep in the veins where the Phyros blood sings.

— Didactic rhyme of the "blood ranks" of Arkendia's
ancient Blood Religion, still strong on the West Isle

3

Curse & Counterspell

Harric staggered back from Caris until he collided with the wall beside his desk. Morning light flooded the room. Wind banged the shutters, as if to frighten the fog it drove before it. A rush of relief escaped his lungs.

Caris reeled and stared, face pale with panic. "Your mother..." she murmured. Now that the crisis was past, shock seemed to squeeze in on her. The hands she'd balled for a fight now flew to her ears as if to shut out echoes of what she'd witnessed.

"Hey, it's all right, Caris," he said, her distress summoning a strength he didn't otherwise feel. He took her wrists and coaxed her hands from her ears. "She's gone. You saved me, Caris. She had me bewitched, and I was thinking I should just jump and end it when you woke me—or broke the spell, I guess."

Saying it aloud made it real for him as well, dispelling the last shreds of nightmare from his head, but Caris pulled away. Her hands snapped to her ears and she squeezed her eyes shut as if the horrors still swirled around her. "The fog—there were voices!" She crouched like she would curl up in one of her fits, but as Harric reached to put a hand on her shoulder, she sprang up and punched a hole through the plaster. With a strangled growl, she wrenched the door open and thundered down the treads, taking them three or four at a time until the sounds of her passage faded in the lower flights.

To the stables, Harric guessed, and the solace she found among horses.

He exhaled in relief. It was difficult to help her once she collapsed, and half the time when she did, his efforts at soothing were rewarded with kicks in the shins. Nevertheless, he debated whether to follow. Alone, the room seemed hollow and exposed.

His guts chilled. He imagined his mother's ghost in the shadow beside the window.

Shake it off. It's just your nerves.

A stealthy rustle drifted behind him, and he spun about, heart in his throat.

Flat against the wall beside the door stood a girl, one hand clapped to her mouth as if holding in a scream. She might have been thirteen, all willow wands and ribs in a chambermaid's dress and apron. He didn't recognize her, however, which was odd because he knew all the maids by name.

"Gods leave me," she said, in a tiny, breathless voice. "That was the curse everyone's talking about!" She sidled toward the open door, eyes wide and white.

"Don't worry. It isn't contagious."

"Almost killed that Caris lady—stay away!" she cried, as he started toward her.

He stopped.

She fixed him with eyes determined but full of fear. After several heartbeats, she said, "You don't recognize me."

He looked closer. Nothing about her mousy hair or somber mouth triggered his memory, though there was something familiar about her.

"Lyla," she said.

He exhaled slowly, his eyes searching hers.

"You won me from my master in the card game today. You freed me."

"Of course! Your face was all covered in slave paint! I see Mother Ganner took you in and got you some new clothes."

Her eyes dipped to his nakedness and bobbed back up. "You want I should fetch you some, too? The cold don't do you no favors."

Harric let out a laugh of surprise. He was bare as an egg to his toes. "I'm—ah—it's been quite a night." He grabbed his trousers from the floor and threw them on.

As he cinched up the bastard belt, she edged the rest of the way to the door, stopping only when she stood with a foot on the top step, ready to bolt. But she did not leave. She swallowed hard, as if steeling herself to speak. "I ain't here to thank you. I'm here to pay my debt."

"You don't owe me anything."

"My freedom ain't worth nothing?"

"That's not what I mean. I gave that to you freely. My payment was watching the expression on the face of that West Isle slaver while you burned the deed to your bondage. Anyway, I'm a dead man, and death cancels all debts."

"You don't have to die today. I can tell you how to beat that curse. That's how I aim to pay my debt." She took a step forward, determination giving her courage.

Harric suppressed a roll of his eyes. "Another surefire cure for curses? Look, I've seen her victims try a few dozen of those, and they don't even delay their deaths. So, thank you, but if you don't mind…" He gestured to the door to usher her out, but she stamped her foot, making a surprisingly loud bang. Her eyes blazed, wilting any remaining fear in them.

"Look, Lyla—"

"You better listen or you're gonna be dead by sunset. You survived that fog, right? Her doom didn't claim you. Why do you think that is?"

"The doom has till sunset."

She put her hands on her hips as if addressing a dense or stubborn child. "And this crawly talky fog was just normal weather around *came* here? That doom came for you this morning, but you survived, and I know why."

Harric blinked. "So do I: because Caris intervened."

"Hah! You Northies wouldn't know magic if it fell from the sky and hit you. Answer me this: all them other cursed boys had friends to help them. Mother Ganner told me all about it. But did any of them survive the fog?"

Harric frowned. She had a point. The fog had come for Davos on the foretold day that spring, and Davos had a hired company of bodyguards to protect him; the fog slipped right past and did its work all the same. Gravin's day came shortly after, and he encircled his cabin with a posse of witch hunters, who by morning lay strangled or decapitated with Gravin. Why had Harric alone survived?

Lyla stepped toward him, eyes bright and earnest. "It was the power of your nineteenth Naming Day, Master Harric. That's what I'm here to show you. You know about the Naming Day? You know about the Proof?"

Harric grimaced. "The apprentice proof? Some kind of West Isle superstition?"

She glared. "That *superstition* just saved your life, and it'll keep you alive past sunset if you make your Proof today."

"I don't understand."

"I'm here to explain it, ain't I? The nineteenth Naming Day is called the *Day of Proof* because it's the day a prentice proves he's a master by doing something only a master can do. Once he proves that, he's free, and his master has no power over him. See?"

"Yes, it works that way here, too. But how does that apply to me? I'm not an apprentice anymore. I quit two years before my training was complete, when Mother's madness got so—" His voice hitched. He swallowed and shrugged. "She chose this day for my doom because it's the day I would have completed her training. Her way of saying I brought it on myself."

"You can't quit what you already learned. You still *know* what she taught you, so you can still Prove it." She studied Harric from the corners of her eyes. "I asked Mother Ganner if your mama prenticed you as a witch, but she said your mama was never a witch. Said she was a lady of the court who went mad from visions of the future, but that your mama taught you how to be a courtier. Did I learn that right?"

Harric smiled. "As far as it goes."

She nodded. "All right then, for your Proof you have to pick a courtly art of hers—something only a master could do—and show you can perform it like a master. When you do that, you break her power over you. See?"

"And this 'Proof,' if I perform it, will somehow break my mother's curse, too?"

"Stop smiling at me like I'm some tickle-brained peasant. The curse is part of her power, ain't it? So, promise."

An ember of hope sparked in Harric. Break her curse and live? Live to see the sunrise again? Embrace Caris? Dream—

No. He snuffed it savagely. *Her dooms always come true*. Hope would only make him pathetic, scrambling after every witch charm and counter potion.

But the ember wouldn't snuff. It grew. He couldn't help it. He couldn't ignore the fact that for the first time one of his mother's dooms had stumbled, which meant there was hope. He couldn't deny it, and the hope seemed to know it, expanding from an ember to an unquenchable conflagration that reduced all his defensive walls to ashes.

"All right," he said, through grinding teeth. "You'd better be right about this."

She studied him, then nodded, evidently satisfied this qualified as acceptance, if not gratitude. "I am right." She took a tentative step forward, a flash of mischief in her eye. "So, what art will you perform your Proof in, Master Courtier: fencing, feasting, or foining?"

"You forgot *feigning*." Harric gave a barren smile. "Yes, I learned those things. But my real training was for more…*secret*…skills to serve our queen."

"It can't be a secret if it's your Proof, so you have to tell me."

He took a deep breath, trying in vain to calm the turmoil in his chest. Could he truly defeat his doom? What if he failed?

She arched an eyebrow. "Well?"

"I'll make my Proof in the art of the con. That's my strongest suit."

"I knew it! She trained you as a trickster. That's how you beat my master in poker. It's probably how she kept her magic secret all those years."

He gave a non-committal shrug. "Sadly, all of Gallows Ferry saw me trick your master. The whole outpost will be alert to anything I try now. If I want to con anyone today, I'll have to focus on new emigrants passing through the market."

"How many cons could your mother do in a day?"

"Nineteen."

"Then for your Proof you'll need twenty."

He felt the bottom drop out of his stomach. Nineteen had been a lucky day for his mother. Her best before that had been twelve.

"You can *do* it, Master Harric. You can. I saw you beat my master."

Harric nodded. He'd done well against her master, but he'd also been reckless because he didn't think he'd be alive the next day and therefore hadn't cared if he made enemies. Now, if they learned he lived, they'd try to kill him themselves if they got a chance.

"So promise you'll make your Proof."

He nodded. "All right. But if this goes wrong you should probably know I'm going to haunt you from the grave."

"I'll bury you on an island so your ghost can't cross the water."

He laughed and reached out to take her hand, but she jumped back as if he'd held out a rat, and her initial fear returned in a blink. Whirling, she flew down the stairs, but stopped at the landing and looked back. "You can do it, Master Harric. Don't forget you promised."

"I won't," he said, more to himself than her, for she had turned and continued her flight down the stairs.

He closed the door and laid his forehead against its painted wood.

His heart, which had calmed after the nightmare in the fog, had begun to flutter again like a frightened bird in his ribcage. Twenty cons in an outpost full of enemies and people who knew to watch him. He chuckled grimly. "I'm dead already."

"Doomed," said his mother, behind him. "There's a difference."

He whirled, anticipating murder, only to find her across the room, regarding him with cool amusement.

"Miss me so?" she said. She looked precisely as she did the day she died, a vision of insanity from his childhood. She wore the same threadbare ball gown she'd fled court in twenty years before, and which she'd worn almost exclusively the last ten years of her life. Scarcely more than a colorless bag now, it hung limp and stinking from bony shoulders. She smiled, cracking her mask of thick white makeup, in fans around her eyes and mouth. Blue lipstick hanging crooked on her lips. Once a subtle and delicate style of makeup in court, years of madness had made it lumpen and clownish.

He backed against the door with a thump, heart racing. Hurt and anger battled in his chest, paralyzing his tongue.

She followed his gaze to the gown, and frowned. "This is how you remember me, therefore this is how I appear to you." She swirled the skirts about her ankles, wafting the stink of urine. Her nose wrinkled. "Pah! This was but a shell I cast off at the grave. The Sight, which made me mad in life, now gives me power in the afterworld. If only you could see me as I am now. Try! Look past this memory of madness and see. Do I rave, as I once did? Do I foam at the mouth? I do not. Indeed, I come to offer you life, my son. You needn't die tonight, if only you will follow me. In the afterworld I am clear-eyed and strong. I can train you as you were meant to be trained. Follow me, and I will steer you from your doom."

Rage welled in Harric. He clamped his jaws against screaming fury and turned from her, forcing himself to breathe evenly. *She isn't real*, he told himself. *Just a vision. Part of the madness in the family blood. I mustn't engage, lest it worsen and Mother Ganner find me alone and shouting in my room again.*

Stalking past her to the wall beside his bed, he did his best to ignore her. He ran his fingers along the wainscot, searching for the latch points of the hidden closet where he kept the "bag of tricks" he'd need for his Proof.

His mother let out a careworn sigh.

"Spare me the theatrics," he growled. "I won't live as your pawn anymore."

"Then you know I must kill you. I do not wish to, but I must."

"So you say."

"I speak truth, Harric! Without my guidance, you will destroy Queen Chasia and all she has brought to our land! It is woven in the sky! You are fated to destroy the queen you love. I see it! And I cannot let it happen. That is why I cursed you. Either you must follow me that I may guide your path from harming the Queen, or to preserve her I must kill you. Oh, Harric, you break your mother's heart!"

She gazed at him, eyes soft and pleading. Tears streaked her makeup, making her even more clownish, and suddenly the whole thing seemed ridiculous, including the longing she stirred in his heart. He laughed. "You love playing the martyr, don't you, Mother? But I know it's all the same lie, your mad attempt to keep me as your puppet. And you're still jerking at my strings."

"If only that were so!"

His hands found the hidden latch points of the closet. He depressed the points, and the locks clicked. The door swiveled out on hidden hinges, revealing shelves and hangers arrayed with all the tools of a courtesan spy (or for training one). He knew the books on the shelf by heart: manuals of courtly etiquette, treatises on poison, lock crafting, subterfuge, deception. As bookend to them all stood the coded journal of his mother's secret service to the Queen.

She looked past him into the closet. A bitter scowl cracked more plaster from her nose. "Behold the glories of my arts. How can you bear to look at them, Harric? Every kit, every lock-hook, every tincture in that holy sanctum abides as a burning symbol of the greatness you rejected when you rejected your apprenticeship before it was complete. If you had finished your training, your fate would be different. Of that I am certain."

Harric clenched his jaw. He hated himself for listening, hated himself for feeling pain at her words. Why was it that nothing he said affected her as she affected him? And nothing he could do would make her leave.

He picked up his own journal of apprentice "missions" around Gallows Ferry. As he flipped through the pages, a wave of nausea rolled up his stomach. Cons, seductions, betrayals—all designed to harden his heart and wear away sentiment and petty loyalties. Each entry burned in his memory, an icon of sacrificed childhood.

He slammed the book back on its shelf and turned on her. "My only regret, Mother, is that I did not abandon you sooner."

She retreated in alarm as he advanced with steady steps. He felt the corners of his mouth draw back in a lipless smile. "I beat your doom today, Mother. You failed. I won. Why is that, do you suppose? If all the others died in your precious fog, why did I survive?"

"If I wanted you dead, you'd be dead," she snapped. "This morning was a warning, that I might offer you one last chance before sunset."

He laughed. He'd glimpsed something in her face. It took him a moment to recognize it behind the cracking mask of makeup, but when he realized it was *fear*, an ember of hope leapt to life inside him.

"Do you know why I opened the secret closet?" he said, gesturing to the open door. "So I could grab my bag of tricks and perform my Proof in the market. Do you know what that means?"

Her jaw dropped. "You fool, Harric! Queen Chasia forbids magic! In your desperation would you sneer at her? Would you disgrace and dishonor the land and your queen above all?"

"Don't try to shame me, Mother. I dedicate my life to the Queen; it's *you* I sneer at. And you question *me* about magic! That *was* your fog this morning, wasn't it? The one full of clawed hands and twining snakes?"

"In the afterworld my visions are power. I see into the Web of Fate and know its patterns—even weave them! Spirits obey me. That is not moon magic; it is power as natural there as the air is in this world. That little slut's 'Proof' is nothing but West Isle sorcery!"

His eyebrows rose at the fury in her bloodshot eyes, and he began to chuckle. "How could I have been so blind not to see it before? I've finally found something you can't control. Magic! I must fight magic with magic!"

"You leave me no choice." Her eyes rolled back in her head as the vision took hold.

"Stop it, Mother."

Her jaw went slack. She collapsed to her knees and fell on her back as if a giant invisible hand pinned her like a bug.

"Your doom approaches!" she gasped. "It comes apace! I see it before me! Oh! Flesh and blood from the very court you will one day destroy! It is woven in the sky!"

"Shut up!" he shouted. "You lie. You always lie. And I don't care what's woven anywhere. I don't care about your dooms! I'll make my own damned future!"

Grabbing the heavy carpetbag of tricks from the bottom of the closet, he heaved it almost savagely at her feet. "My Proof will destroy your doom!"

But the bag merely thumped on the floor where she'd been.

He was alone and shouting at the air again.

Harric stood in the market in the back of his grain cart, bag of tricks at his feet, as the first emigrant train poured through the south gate of Gallows Ferry.

Its herd of peasants led the procession, staring and stunned from the terrifying journey across the wild river, and up the Hanging Road across the face of the Godswall. Plainly they found Gallows Ferry no more comforting than the road had been; it must have seemed to them a mere hanging village crowded onto a wide ledge on the road.

A family at the front of the procession halted when the road plunged into the morning gloom of the Crack behind the inn. It must have reminded them of the treacherous canyons they had traversed in the scablands, only this one was artificial, made by the back of the inn on one side and the cliff face on the other. By the expressions on this family's faces, however, it was clear they'd prefer the dangers of sand cats and scorpions in the scablands to what they saw ahead in the Crack: an alley lined with frontier hucksters and peddlers in a kind of hawker's gauntlet.

A bolder family shouldered past the bewildered family, faces set, to be swallowed by the gloom, and as they trudged between the first stalls, the gauntlet of hawkers erupted.

"Fresh butter! Queen's prices!"

"Mend your shoes! Hard roads ahead!"

"Witches on the road! Protect your children! Get your witch glass here!"

To that Harric added his cry of, "Feed grain! Buy now! No grazing left on the road!"

His cart stood right in the middle of the market, with its nose tucked under the back porch of the inn. The rest of the merchants had been so delighted to see him alive that morning they'd given him the prime spot. Not only was it the narrowest point in the market, where the porch pinched the road and slowed the passing emigrants, it was also the most entertaining place in the Crack. By midday, the porch attracted revelers who watched the drama of emigrants and merchants like hecklers at a stage play. Best of all, he was safe from Lyla's master there, as the lord couldn't act against him in such a public place.

Harric studied the mass of peasants as it slid by, a brown river stinking of unwashed bodies and last night's garlic. In their eyes he saw worry and mistrust. Dozens of families trudged past in this caravan, likely a whole village being transplanted to the Free Lands. But they were not free peasants of the East Isle. Each bore a blot of orange paint in their hair, marking them the property of a West Isle lord.

Harric's jaw tightened. Among the families walked a giant and giantess who were clearly the product of some ancient Westie breeding project. He'd seen the sort before: pinched skulls with unnaturally huge mouths and tiny eyes too close together. The giant's eyes stayed fixed on the mud, as if ashamed to meet a gaze; the giantess gripped his hand and glared at everyone she passed.

"Welcome to the Not-so-Free Lands," Harric muttered. He understood the reasons why the Queen had welcomed Westies to settle the north, but he hated that political necessity. If he could achieve his Proof that day at the expense of every Westie lord that passed, it would bring an added sweetness to the day.

Soon a mounted lord emerged through the gate, attended by two retainers. Orange accents in their clothing and trappings declared the lord to be a gentleman of low rank and master of the orange-marked slaves. At the sight of him, Harric felt a spark of anxiety in his belly. His death might come with any such lord. "Flesh and blood from the court," she had pronounced in her latest doom. Though few actual courtiers came through, many visited the court for one reason or another, so that left a lot of possibilities. His death could come in the form of an unwanted duel from a drunken lord or from a simple fall on his neck when a courtier's carriage jostled his cart. How could he defend against that?

He closed his eyes and concentrated on slowing his breathing to calm his heart. *Block out the fear, or you'll make a mistake and fulfill her stupid doom for her. Just relax and enjoy the game of cons.*

Harric opened his eyes and studied his first mark. The lord was no older than Harric. He carried himself with none of the easy confidence of one well traveled or educated in court, but instead wore haughtiness as armor: his glance a sneer, his laugh too loud, as one ill at ease off his own estate. Around his neck he wore numerous witch charms, marking him as superstitious as the peasants he led.

An easy mark, yet the sight of the man opened a gulf of dread in Harric's gut, as if he were the one out of place.

A simple Bait and Switch will do, he decided. *Nothing fancy. Play it safe.*

He lifted a large but wilted paint-flower from his bag of tricks. The edges of the crimson petals overflowed both hands as he held the flower to his nose and tested its scent. Pungent. Not unpleasant. Still strong enough to drive off flies, and its familiar scent gave him a swell of confidence as he raised it above his head. He laid it carefully on his crown so the fringe of petals drooped below his brow like a bowl-cut jester's wig, and stood waiting for the lord.

"Well I'll be a horse's pizzle," said a voice behind him. "You live!"

Harric looked back to see one of the middle-aged yeomen who had been drinking and playing cards on the porch for the past two days. He and his mates had bought Harric drinks while they played a complex drinking game that took its cues from the market: when the tinker clanged his pots, someone drank; when a horse pissed, another drank; when Harric sold an ass-lily to a Westie, everyone drained their cups. A pulse of dread in Harric. The man and his comrades knew too much of Harric's games. In the last few days he'd openly shown off some of his cons, to the immense amusement of the revelers. Since he was going to die anyway, why not have a little fun? But now that he'd decided on his Proof, he wished he hadn't so freely discarded his cover. The yeomen backed him, but they were normally raging drunk by noon, and to them it was all a game; if they blabbed around the wrong person—Rudy, for instance, or some aggrieved Westie lord—Harric could be hung as a thief.

"Heard a hell of a racket last night upstairs. Figured they'd come for ye, but the fog so thick no one could see their hand in front of their face. Broke our hearts," the yeoman said, laying a hand to his breast. "Weren't nothing we could do. But you live! No one expected that."

Harric forced a smile. "It's a little awkward. But it isn't over yet. Not till sunset."

The yeoman raised one of Mags's tall wine cups to his lips. "Me and the boys did our best to make certain there wouldn't be a drop of your wine left, like you said. The cup you see before you is the last." He sipped it as if husbanding the last of a very fine vintage. "You gonna throw another party tonight?"

Harric nodded, anxiously aware that the orange lord floated nearer in the river of peasants. "If I live past sunset, you can expect one twice as big." He said it with a note of finality, but the yeoman leaned over the porch rail and beckoned to Harric with a conspiratorial grin. "You gonna sell an ass-lily to this orange-blood Westie? Me and the boys love that! No Westie ever cared much for bastards or for bastard freedom in the north."

"And we don't care much for Westies bringing slaves to the Free Lands."

"I'll drink to that."

The orange lord reined in before Harric's cart and stared at Harric's head ornament with unrestrained contempt.

"Would Your Lordship care to buy grain?" said Harric, returning his gaze as if it were perfectly normal to wear a drooping flower on one's head in Gallows Ferry.

"Bastard, there is a plant on your head."

"Yes, Your Lordship. As you can see, it keeps the flies off nicely."

The lord's mirth transformed to interest. "A paint-flower! I thought them rare in the north."

"Your lordship is wise in the ways of plants."

The lord's eyes flashed to the green and black of Harric's bastard belt. Scorn and envy glinted in his gaze. "I must have that flower, bastard. You will sell it for five silver queens."

"Ten queens, Your Lordship. I set my own price for things that are mine. On this isle, a bastard is free."

He never tired of saying those words to Westies.

The lord flushed, but hid his irritation behind a clipped laugh. "Ten queens, then. Worth twenty to be rid of the flies on this stinking road. Every slave in the Isles has shit on it."

One of the grooms paid, and Harric produced a bud as big as his hand from the bottom of his bag of cons. It looked very much like a paint-flower might look when closed, and since ass-lilies grew only in the north, the man would see no difference.

The lord lifted it to his nose and recoiled. "It's the very crack of a hog!"

The yeoman choked and coughed behind Harric. Wine had shot from his nose.

The lord studied him, eyes narrowed, as the yeoman sputtered apologies.

"The scent changes when it opens," Harric explained. "That's when it repels the flies. Just keep it in the sun on your hat till then, and soak it in water each night so it outlasts the week."

The lord examined it skeptically. "The petals are brown. Paint-flowers are red."

"They turn red once they open, my lord."

"No. I'll take the one on your head."

Harric brightened. "Same price, of course." He leaned forward so the petals fell away from his forehead. Gently slipping the edge of his hand beneath them, he lifted it free of his head. One of the petals fell off, but he scooped it up and placed it on top with a flourish. "There you are, Your Lordship. Not as fresh, but treat it kindly, and it should last a good couple days."

The lord frowned. Without Harric's hair to support the petals, they drooped like the head of a threadbare mop. "How dare you offer me such rubbish." He waved off the tired flower, and tossed the fresh bud back to Harric. "I will take the bud. Give me a pin for it."

Harric made a show of suppressing his disappointment. "But this flower is already open, Your Lordship—"

"Do you take me for a fool?"

"Yes," the yeoman muttered.

"No, Your Lordship," said Harric, as one of the lord's retainers shot the yeoman a look. The lord's eyes caught the retainer's look and followed his glare to the yeoman, but Harric handed up the bud with a pin, diverting his attention. The next moment the lord rode off with it wagging on his hat.

Harric breathed a sigh of relief, and kicked himself for letting the yeoman see too much the day before.

The yeoman laughed until he wept. "Every fly in the country will find him when it opens. It'll be a week before he knows he's been had."

"I'm sure I don't know what you mean," said Harric, and his look of blank innocence made the man laugh even harder. The laughter was good. It kept the anxiety at bay.

One down, he thought. *Nineteen to go.*

With luck, the yeomen would pass out before blowing his cover.

By noon the porch rails dripped with revelers, and the market boomed with merriment. The yeoman and his mates were still going strong, and when they told newcomers of Harric's sunset doom, everyone bought Harric drinks of apple wine.

"To your doom!" they toasted. "May it be a gentle one!"

Harric drank.

When a squire discharged a long-barreled spitfire over the crowd, one cried, "Spitfire! All drink!" and Harric joined in another.

Not an hour went by in which he didn't con at least one well-born Westie. Lyla appeared once on the porch to shake out a rug and empty a chamber pot. She managed to give Harric a conspiratorial nod before the head maid called her name and she hurried back inside. Caris never resurfaced, however, which worried Harric. After their adventure in the fog, she'd probably fled to the stables and curled up in a ball at the back of a stall. He longed to check on her, coax her back to her feet before Rudy spotted her and used it to prove her imbecility, but Harric dared not interrupt the Proof. It was just as likely she'd taken Rag for a ride up the Hanging Road. He hoped so.

Caris's absence also came as a relief, however, since he couldn't pull cons in her presence. Her ideas of nobility and honor were about as rigid as his were loose, which was why he hadn't yet dared to explain to her the true nature of his childhood training. He'd only told her part of the truth: that his mother had him trained to be a squire. The fact that he only learned enough squiring to make a convincing cover for his real arts was something he dreaded might end their friendship.

By late afternoon he scored his eighteenth and nineteenth cons, the last upon a balding Westie squire who rode off with a reduction of goat piss to rub in his scalp for new hair. With that he'd matched his mother's record, and with one more he'd have his Proof. But two hours passed after that without a suitable lord or lady passing through. Several lords passed, but they appeared to be from court; when he saw these, he held his breath and let them pass without engaging.

During those hours, too, the servants of Lyla's former master found him. The lord's men were easy to spot in their saffron-colored liveries. Four of them took stations on the porch, watching and waiting for Harric to try to leave. Harric's stomach flopped over inside him.

Worry about them later, he tutored himself. *Concentrate on nineteen.*

The inn's shadow crept steadily up the cliff wall, marking the downward path of the sun in the west, and still no suitable marks appeared. When the inn and its shadow finally reached an equal height, Harric knew the sun touched the horizon, and he had little time left. To get his twentieth con, he'd have to attempt a courtier.

"Carriage!" a reveler called, pointing to the gate. "Drink!"

A fine carriage trundled through the south gate, brass tokens flashing on the breasts of the lead horses. A knot of doubt twisted Harric's stomach, as he recognized the tokens as licenses admitting carriages into the court of the Queen.

Harric muttered a silent curse. "You think it's my doom you send in that carriage, don't you, Mother? Well, you're wrong. It's my Proof."

"Sir Bastard!" The yeoman leaned across the porch rail to offer a cup of frothing apple wine. "This your magic number? We must toast!"

Harric bowed to the yeoman, never taking his eyes from the carriage. He waved off the wine. "Keep it for after," he said. "For this I'll need my wits."

Red Moon rising, full and woode,
He bleeds fell Molly, drinks her Blood,
On every moon, he drinks again,
An ageless, wound-less, strength of ten.

— From "Immortality Becomes Him," Sir Willard ballad

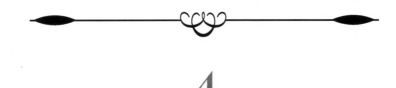

4

Of Debt & Hexes

Sir Willard followed the road down a winding canyon toward the river, herding the ponies and the ambassador before him, still concealed beneath his blanket.

If they hadn't taken a wrong turn into one of the dead-end alleys of the scablands, they should be nearing the Gallows Ferry crossing, where their flight would be over. Once there, he'd board a ferry, cross the river, and force the ferrymen to tie up for the night, stranding Sir Green on the opposite shore until morning. With his crossbow-happy pursuers off his tail, Willard could trade for fresh horses in Gallows Ferry, and still leave with a big enough lead to shake his pursuers for good.

Let's see you catch me then, Sir Green.

Relief settled in his mind. Brolli would finally be safe, and hope for a treaty with his people would be restored. Moreover, Willard needn't drink the Blood that would save him—but enslave him—once again, and shatter his oath to Anna.

He grunted, puffing on a roll of ragleaf. *Don't kid yourself, old man. Something's bound to go sideways on us. More likely it all ends on the bottom of the river.*

From a blind corner, they emerged at the head of a narrow, steep-walled valley that dropped between bluffs to the river and a graveled beach, two stone-throws below him. A wooden ferry dock jutted from the middle of the beach into the current. Beyond the dock and the wide river, the Godswall soared into the blue sky, a curtain of granite capped with sun-bright peaks of white.

He reined in sharply, surprised to see hundreds of emigrants filling the valley below him and obstructing the road all the way to the water. They were mostly simple folk, with their animals; they'd squatted or lain down on the ground in exhaustion, waiting their turn for a ferry.

The nearest travelers looked up at Willard in surprise, not ten paces away. Then their eyes widened in recognition and horror.

"Phyros!" a man screamed. A mule caught Molly's scent and kicked free of its handler to flee up the side of the gully. In the time it took to suck a breath and yell, the crowd exploded, screaming and fleeing. Goats bolted up the rocks; an ox snapped its tether and ran bellowing for the water, knocking people sideways. Some picked themselves up and fled in its wake, others scrambled up the bluffs to hide in the rocks. Mothers huddled their children for fear of trampling.

The ambassador chuckled under his blanket. "Your people love you so. It warms my heart to see."

"They think I'm an Old One," Willard said.

The furor rolled down the gulch like a wave, growing and driving the masses before it and emptying onto the dead-end beaches to either side of the dock.

Willard restrained Molly from bloody pursuit, holding fast to her reins. He'd long since stopped feeling guilt or pity for the terror she caused, but he never let her sate her bloodlust on the innocent.

Molly tossed her head, stamping sparks from the stones with her massive iron shoes.

Willard slugged her in the neck, a gesture she barely regarded. "Save it," he growled. "We'll have real foes, soon enough."

He squinted across a mile of water to the opposite side. There was no river bank over there, only sheer granite cliff for miles in either direction, but somehow the timbermen who founded Gallows Ferry had found a fault at the foot of the Godswall large enough to make a landing. From there they'd built their "Hanging Road"—a path that rose from the water and across the face of the cliffs to Gallows Ferry. The two ferries worked the passage between landings, mere toys in the distance, had just unloaded, and now churned back, wood fires blasting from the chimneys.

Willard's spirits rose at the thought that he'd be across before sunset, but sank when he watched another ship emerge from behind a bend only a mile down the opposite shore.

It was a lord's ship: sharp-nosed, with three decks of ornate railings and fancywork trimmed in brilliant sapphire paint. A *nobleman's* ship.

"Gods take them," he muttered. "It's already gone sideways on us."

"What is the troubles?"

"Sir Green's master is on that ship, I'll wager. We'll beat him to the landing, but not by enough. If we're to lose them for good, we're going to need an hour's head start at least."

Molly bared her blood tooth at the ponies she'd herded all day up the road, but the poor beasts were too weary to do more than droop their ears a little more and stagger a step away.

"We have to break free tonight, Brolli. These horses won't last another day."

"I could ride behind you on Molly, yes?"

Willard snorted. "She'd try to eat you."

"Maybe we find some help in Gallows Ferry."

Willard frowned. A mile upstream on the cliffs of the opposite shore, the tiny outpost glowed in the light of the low setting sun, bleached pink on its perch in the cliff face. To Willard it seemed little more than a snag of driftwood hung high in a crack of the Godswall.

"Don't count on it," Willard said. "We might find someone to delay our pursuers for us. But it might be a death sentence to the outpost, and we don't have enough gold to persuade anyone to take that kind of risk. But we have an expression here in Arkendia, Ambassador: *The gods help none, so help yourself.* Arkendians live and die by that motto."

Brolli laughed. "It's the 'die' part I mis-like."

"Be still, now, Ambassador. There are many eyes and ears hereabout."

"I am much tired of hiding in the blanket," Brolli sighed.

"Get used to it."

Willard urged Molly down the road, hoping a change of location might inspire a solution to their problems. Molly picked her way between abandoned handcarts and piles of toppled luggage, herding the ponies ahead. Her movement drew a chorus of fresh screams from the emigrants, who were now trapped beneath the bluffs at the either end of the beach.

Many struggled with panicked beasts near the water; several strove knee-deep in the river against a wild-eyed donkey. A pair of herders cried out in vain after a sheep swept away in the current. Most of the emigrants huddled at the foot of the bluffs, wailing like rabbits in a slaughter pen.

Willard drew in at the foot of the dock, where a knot of peasants stood their ground as if determined to keep their place at the head of the line. Some wise drover among them had put sacks over the heads of their oxen to muffle their senses and keep them still as the Phyros approached. From the peasants came the familiar chorus of fear, but there was something else there, as well—a note of defiance?—that pulled Willard from his thoughts.

A quick scan revealed the source: in the midst of the group stood a Liberator—a full-blown peasant priest—huge and hairy, and glaring at Willard.

Willard ground his teeth. The last thing he needed was some bullheaded zealot to throw a stone in the works.

Like the god he both followed and denounced, the man was a true giant. He stood chest and shoulders above the tallest peasant, and a mule's weight heavier. Also like his god, he was filthy as a boar in a pen, with a mane of beard and braids so matted it might have been a worm-eaten mantle of bear skin. He wore a smothercoat of woolen rugs that further magnified his size, and which stank so fiercely of soured wool that Willard maneuvered Molly to avoid its stench in the breeze.

A verse from "Sir Willard and the Peasant Priest" tripped into Willard's skull and stayed there long enough to annoy him:

Don't come so near, my fragrant friend,
Your beard is breeding fleas.
My sword is yours,
Sworn to defend,
But down-breeze, if you please.

"Get behind me," the priest growled to his flock. The men and women obliged, clearing the space before him to reveal his woolly shins and muddy feet. One of the priest's hands clutched the haft of an enormous Phyros ax—ancient, double-bladed, too huge for any mortal but a giant to wield. Judging by its design, Willard himself might have used that very ax during the days of the Cleansing to sever the necks of Phyros and end the reign of the Old Ones. To the peasants, and in the hand of this Liberator priest, it would be a powerful symbol of freedom.

In his other hand the priest clamped the throat of a little man in a dockmaster's uniform. The man's face had gone purple, and his eyes pleaded with the Phyros-rider for aid, but Willard made no move to acknowledge him. If the man was fool enough to deny a Liberator passage, he likely deserved everything he got.

A barefoot matron slapped at the priest's arms. "Run, ye fool!" she squeaked. "It's an Old One! Run!"

"Too late," the priest rumbled. "Can't swim." He thrust the dockmaster to arm's length and heaved the ax back as if he'd cleave him like kindling. "If I'm going to the afterworld," he growled to the dockman, "I reckon I'll send you first, you child-slaving git. And I aim to catch you there, too, and kick your scrawny arse up and down the sky."

A whisper of hope woke in Willard as he recognized the priest's voice, and then the face behind the dirty beard. "Brother Kogan." He raised a gauntleted hand in greeting. "Put your ax down. I require your help in the service of your queen."

Kogan blinked. He squinted at Sir Willard, then at the gigantic violet Phyros on which he sat, and then at Willard again. "W-Will...?" he breathed. Then louder, laughing: "I'll be hung and dried, it's Will!"

"Come here, Brother, if you please. I don't wish to disrupt your flock any further."

An exultant grin split Kogan's hairy face, exposing several cracked and missing teeth. "It's *Father* Kogan, now, Will. Father Kogan."

Kogan half carried, half dragged the dockmaster across the beach, grinning like a younger brother with a prize to show his hero. He planted the miserable man under Molly's nose like an offering, and a dark stain spread down the man's breeches.

Willard hauled Molly's head away before she gutted the man, and her fury at this latest denial of her nature was so great she nearly flung him from the saddle. A brief but backbreaking struggle ensued before he calmed her enough to reposition her, several paces removed. Kogan hooted the while, as if watching a bull-baiting. Willard glared at the grinning giant, grinding his teeth against the oaths that crowded to his lips, and the objections of his aching joints. He was never quite prepared for how dense the peasant god's priests could be. Especially Kogan. It was a factor that could complicate the escape plan taking shape in Willard's mind, but there were no other allies on that beach. Kogan would have to do.

"It's been a dog's age since I seen you, Will," said Kogan. "Molly ain't changed a bit, but I hardly knowed you with your armor all blacked. You still on the outs with the Queen?"

"Do you recall a time that I wasn't?"

Kogan laughed. "Not in my life. Thought I heard she finally forgived you and let you take your proper colors again. But now I think on it, your armor was always painted black."

"Just now I am on a quest for the Queen."

"How's that if you're out of favor?"

"Call it a redemption quest. If I succeed, she may welcome me back to court."

Kogan grinned. "Back to the Lady Anna, you mean. Better be *some* quest, Will. Her Majesty ain't famous for forgiveness."

"Just so."

Willard quelled the urge to raise his visor to speak; if Kogan saw the mortal change in his flesh, it would shock and confuse him, and there was no time for explanation. The empty ferries were more than half across the river already.

"Never got to thank you proper for holding that bridge on the West Isle whiles we escaped," said Kogan. "Thanks to you, we liberated two-score from slavery that day and lived to brag it."

"It was a fortunate meeting—"

"So is this one." Kogan shook the dockmaster by the neck till the man's false teeth flew from his lips. "You see this louse-bit, jack-a-pizzle ferry maggot?"

"Has he displeased you in some way?"

"He ain't a maker, Will, he's a breaker. Says he don't ferry lordless peasants. Aims to make us wait on this side till we run out of grub, and then sell us back to some West Isle lord—mothers, babes, and all! I was fixing to drown him like a rat when you come, but I reckon a word from you would set him straight. That'd save me from becoming a wanted man in these parts."

Willard nodded. "I'll see to your dockman. In return, you can help me."

Kogan glanced at the bound and blanketed ambassador, and cracked a conspiratorial grin. "You steal yourself a damsel, Will?"

Willard laughed in spite of himself. "Indeed not. Queen's business. A brace of knights follows me on this road. Another awaits me on that ship." He pointed to the Sapphire's ship churning up the opposite shore. "Those aboard hope to beat me to the landing."

Kogan scratched at his neck. "Don't know how I could help with that, Will. But you say the word and I'll try it; you know I owes you one."

"You owe me three."

Kogan grinned. "I always forget them first two."

The thump of the waterwheels on the first returning ferry had grown louder during their conversation. It was a simple, flat-decked vessel, with twin engines and wheels amidships on either side, and the control booth on a raised bridge spanning the deck between. It appeared the pilot had fairly raced the boat across the channel, so its chimneys glowed red, belching flame as well as wood smoke as he eased it alongside the dock. Dockhands tossed lines to deckhands. Ship bells rang, and the wheels reversed, frothing the green water to foam.

Across the river, the Sapphire's ship battled against the current, still three-quarters of a mile below the landing.

Willard leveled a finger at the dockmaster. "I shall board one ferry, sirrah. Father Kogan and his flock will board the other. You and your men will speed his loading."

The dockmaster nodded weakly.

The priest released him. "There now, Docky. That weren't so bad, were it?" The dockmaster retrieved his teeth from the mud, and slunk away. Kogan waved to the matron who'd urged him to flee. "Load 'em up, Widow Larkin. Docky here's gonna help."

She nodded, but her eyes scowled, avoiding Willard. "Don't make no bargains, Kogan. You got a flock now and can't take no fool errands."

Commotion erupted at the head of the valley above them. Six knights emerged from the canyon from which Willard had come, and bulled their way through the emigrants who had regrouped there. Once clear of the emigrants, the knights drew up within easy bow range on the slope above. Sir Green rode once again to the fore, and surveyed the scene below him. Molly snarled and pawed the gravel, sending ripples of distress through Kogan's beasts as his people struggled to wrestle them onto the ferry. Sir Green signaled, and a squire in red armor stepped his horse forward and discharged a spitfire into the air. The brilliant blue signal flare arced over the valley and water. Moments later, an answering flare rose from the Sapphire's ship across the river, confirming Willard's suspicions.

Willard kept Molly between the ambassador and the knights on the bank, his eyes wary for crossbows, but none appeared. Indeed, Willard glimpsed bowmen among the squires, but Sir Green did not give the order. He simply watched Willard, as per his original strategy of waiting for his Old One. *Green doesn't dare take shots now that he knows I can be slain by a stray bolt*, he realized. *I'll wager there's an Old One who's given the order that I am for him alone, or that I must be taken alive.*

Sir Willard leaned down and beckoned to the priest. "Listen close," he said, his voice low. "This night is our last chance at escape. I need you to hold a bridge for me, as I did for you on the West Isle. Not with arms, mind. With wagons. Stage an accident after I cross it. Jam your vehicles at the foot, so it's impassable. I need time to escape them."

"What bridge you got in mind?"

"First bridge on the Hanging Road past Gallows Ferry."

Kogan nodded, but his forehead creased in concern. His gaze wandered up past the riverbank toward the setting sun, then down to his toes.

"What's wrong, Kogan? Worried about what your woman said?"

The priest grimaced. "Widow Larkin ain't no trouble. She listens to sense. Still…she got me thinking, Will, or wondering, I guess, whether you still got that *night hex* on you…"

A stone of guilt sank in Willard's belly. Kogan knew his curse. He'd seen it that night in West Isle, so there was no denying it or playing down its hazard.

Willard nodded. "It's with me."

"Guess I knew that. No offense, Will, but I can't have my flock around you when the sun sets. That's a whopper of a hex, and it ain't nothing I can cast out—you know I tried—so it's some other kind than the sort I know." He made the sign of the heart in the air between them. "It's just that we don't need no more trouble than we already got."

"You know I don't wish to endanger you."

A chuckle from behind the knotted beard. "You never want it, but it happens anyway."

The Widow Larkin called. The flock had filled their ferry and now huddled between the houses under the control booth on the bridge. Father Kogan acknowledged her with a wave, then shrugged to Willard. "I owes you, Will. So I'll help you. That's that. But no man can slow the sunset. I reckon this oughta be worth *all three* what I owes you."

Sir Willard grinned in his helmet. Was that all he wanted? To bargain away his debts? "Done," Willard said. "I can count on you?"

Kogan hooted with laughter and strode to the dock, bare feet slapping the mud. "Be a maker, Will!" he called. He laid a good-natured smack on the dockmaster's back and vaulted onto the deck of the ferry. "We're going to the Free Lands!" he bellowed. "Free land and freedom for all!"

The tooler in the control booth sounded his bell. Bells answered from the engine houses, and the great waterwheels stirred to life, churning the river against the shore in turbid green waves. The vessel dragged from the bank and swung into the current, smoke plumes boiling from its chimneys like the wings of a mounting swan.

Willard herded the ponies onto the open deck of the remaining ferry. The shouts and scurries of its deckhands choked off the moment they sighted Molly and knew it was their fate to carry her across the water. Several retreated to the dock, while others hid in nooks behind the engine rooms; the woodmen dumped a hurried load of firewood in the holds and departed as soon as Molly's hooves drummed past them to the foredeck, where Willard reined her in with his ponies and mysterious passenger. At Willard's signal, the pilot rang his bell, the toolers engaged the engines, and the ship set out at full steam in Kogan's wake.

A glance back at shore confirmed that Sir Green and his company descended the valley for the dock.

Ahead of him, Kogan's ferry plowed along, heavy in the water with peasants and beasts. Their boarding had been rushed, or Willard would have given orders for them to follow *him* across. He hadn't expected Kogan to signal the departure.

Willard shouted to the pilot above the din of the wheels. "Pull ahead! I must land first."

The pilot's pale face appeared above the bridge rail; he nodded once and disappeared into his booth. A bell rang. More bells answered in the engine rooms, and the rhythm of the engine beams increased, churning the wheels even harder. The ferry drew up on the stern of Kogan's vessel, which labored low in the water, then veered to pass on the downstream side. As Willard's boat drew abreast, a spine-ripping shriek erupted from its starboard engine house. Brilliant steam burst up through its roof, splintering planking and blasting it into the air.

The starboard wheel halted. The ferry swerved downstream, staggering Molly and the ponies sideways. Thankfully the ponies were too weary to spook, but Molly whirled and snarled and pawed the planks.

Bells rang, men shouted, toolers ran from one engine house to the other as the ferry lost its thrust against the current, and whirled downstream among the shoals.

The pilot managed to slow the port wheel and correct with the rudders enough to halt the spin and turn it upstream. By the time he had matched speed against the current, however, they held position many boat lengths down the river, and Kogan's ferry was far ahead and nearly at the harbor landing.

Willard's pilot appeared before him on the deck, hat in hands. He bowed from a respectful distance. "Begging your pardon, Your Holiness," he said, voice trembling. "A hot-pipe blew. Lucky the whole kettle didn't go. That would've done for us all. We'll make it across, I reckon, but only just."

Willard nodded. The man bowed, backed, and scurried up the ladder to his bridge.

"Things go from bad to worse," said the ambassador. "Look. Your friend's ferry has landed, but Sir Green's master moves ahead of us."

The Sapphire's ship, which had been churning up the opposite shore as Willard's limped along, now crossed their path to the landing, at a distance of two or three bowshots ahead.

"Black Moon take it," Willard muttered. "The cards are not falling in our favor."

Brolli turned his peephole toward Willard. "Do you think this Old One is on that ship?"

Willard frowned. "I don't know. If he is and he disembarks to meet us on the shore, however, there will be only one course of action left to us: we turn this limping ferry downstream and hope to lose them under cover of darkness. You'd be safe if we could make it all the way to the court."

Brolli shuddered. "No. I did not feel safe there. That is why I left. I wish to take my chances on this road."

Willard's brow lowered in concern. "Ambassador, you may not think much of our queen or her ways, but she has brought peace to our land, and abolished slavery and many other wretched things. You must see what we are now, in the light of what came before. Before Chasia, when the Old Ones ruled, there was no peace. War is their religion. And they do not hang their enemies, Brolli. They torture and dismember, using Phyros blood plasters to heal over the amputations so their victims survive to live long lives in West Isle trophy halls and entertainment at banquets." Brolli made a small sound of surprise. Willard nodded. "Indeed. There will be no quick death by arrow for me. If I'm taken, I'll spend my days at the foot of an Old One's throne, a limbless footrest."

Brolli said nothing for many heartbeats. "I see. This also for me, if I'm caught."

"No. They don't hate you, Brolli. They just want you dead, to start a war. With me, it's personal. They can't devise punishment enough for my crime."

Brolli's head quirked to the side under the blanket. "Which crime?"

Willard heard the jest in Brolli's tone, but there was more to it than playful taunt. The ambassador wanted to understand Arkendian culture and also who he dealt with, and it wouldn't do to distort or sugar the truth. Deception was what drove Brolli from the court in the first place. "I've committed a few crimes over the course of seven lives, Brolli. Fewer, I like to think, than some commit in one. But as far as the Old Ones are concerned, my only crime is that I spilled the Blood of the God."

A pulse of guilt surprised Willard, and his lip curled in disgust. It was the Blood in his veins, absorbed through the plaster, twisting his mind, tormenting him for his ancient sin. He gave himself a shake, and Brolli must have noticed, for he grew still, watching.

"This god," said Brolli, his tone newly serious. "You call him Krato, yes? It is his blood in the Phyros? And when you immortal, it run in you?"

The Blood craving howled in Willard. If it were anyone but the ambassador, he'd have bid him hold his foolish tongue. With an effort, he said, "Yes. Krato's blood runs through Molly and all her kin. And when I was immortal..." He took a deep breath. "I bled her and drank of it regularly, as the Old Ones do of their Phyros."

"Little gods."

"Not so little, as you may see."

"And you killed them in this Cleansing your people sing on? That is your crime."

"Oh, I've killed my share, but that's not a crime to them; it's rotting hard to do, so they respect it. My crime is that I ignored all that and taught the world to slay their *Phyros*." A throb of guilt rose up, amplified by his irrational craving for Blood, and he clamped his jaw against a growl of frustration. "Moons take it, Brolli, I can't speak of it—" he began, but it was but a mutter between clenched teeth, and Brolli spoke over him.

"That thinking was wise!" Brolli said. "You slay the Phyros, and you slay Old One. They sing you for good." Brolli's head tilted sideways as if regarding Willard from the corner of his eyes through the peephole. "You are god killer. You are a complex-ated man."

Willard chewed his moustache a few times before he trusted himself to speak. "I did what had to be done. Just be sure to kill me if I'm captured."

By now they were close enough to see the nature of the harbor: a vertical fault in the granite had opened to form a wedge-shaped bay just big enough for a single ship to slip the current and land upon a little beach at its head.

Kogan's flock had already disembarked their ferry. Some of them already formed an antlike line across the Hanging Road as it rose from the beach and cut back across the wall of the harbor on its way to Gallows Ferry. Willard could see now that the Hanging Road was a natural ledge in the face of the granite, wide enough for a wagon and horseman abreast. The ledge angled steeply up from the beach and westward across the wall of the harbor. Above the mouth of the harbor, it cornered sharply northward onto the cliffs of the river proper, and from there continued above the river toward Gallows Ferry.

It was there at the point of rock above the mouth of the harbor that the locals had erected their namesake monument.

"What is that tower above the harbor?" Brolli asked.

"Must be the famous Gallows Ferry gallows."

Brolli tilted his head beneath the blanket. "A place for hangings? It is too big for that. I think it is a watchtower."

As they drew nearer, the dangling corpses became unmistakable. Six hung down from a long timber boom stretched out above the water, while lesser booms suspended iron gibbets of bleached bones. The thing was enormous, the size of a siege tower, Willard realized, though at a distance the sheer scale of the Godswall had dwarfed it to near insignificance.

"Your people are too fond of hangings," said Brolli.

The Sapphire lord's ship slowed before them, waiting, perhaps, for Kogan's ferry to clear the narrow harbor. Willard's ferry approached it from downstream, near enough to pick out individuals on the decks, though not near enough for hailing. Willard scanned the figures that appeared above the rails. *No gigantic blue-skinned immortals. So far so good.*

However, a small commotion on the bow of the ship caught his eye. A group of men had gathered on the forecastle, where they had hoisted a hanged man from a flagstaff. Willard cast a glance at Brolli, who, thankfully, was fussing with something under his blanket. He studied the hanged man. No, not a man. It didn't hang heavy enough to be a man. It was an arming manikin, adorned in orange armor.

Recognition took Willard like a hammer to the gut.

"*Tam,*" he breathed. His squire, captured only two nights before. He couldn't fail to recognize the boy's equipment: the foolish spray of victory feathers on the helm, the orange bastard belt at the waist. And he knew without studying what the armor's missing gauntlets signified. They'd taken his hands. Or wanted Willard to think so. Perhaps it was a bluff, intended to enrage him into folly.

For a moment Willard was unsure if he still sat his saddle, or if he'd fallen and was reeling about the deck. Then a grim calm descended, and his resolve returned. *Do they think to fright me with this, a mere shadow of the horrors we knew in the Cleansing?*

"Is something wrong?" Brolli twisted around to peer up at Willard through his peephole.

Willard shook his head curtly. The position of the ships altered again, and the scene on the bow disappeared from their view.

Kogan's ferry left the harbor. It churned past the bow of the Sapphire's ship and turned downstream, as Willard had instructed its pilot. The crew would find a downriver anchorage, and douse its fires, rather than return this night for Sir Green.

Shouts erupted on the decks of the Sapphire's ship as they understood the

ferry pilot's intent. Whistles sounded from the Sapphire's wheelhouse; signal
flags waved from the bow, trying to redirect the fleeing ferry. The ferry pilot
had passed them, however, and his vessel fairly flew down the current, its
chimneys belching flame.

When it was clear the ferry was lost to them, the Sapphire's ship abandoned
its whistles and flags, and made for the landing. It drew into the little wedge of
harbor and made fast to the dock at the very foot of the mile-high Godswall.

Willard's pilot held position outside the harbor as men and horses and
armored knights disembarked the Sapphire's ship and mounted on the beach.
When the ship pulled away and exited the harbor, Willard could see the entire
company milling on the steep gravel beachhead. He counted ten knights with
lances and armor, in blood ranks ranging from gentleman saffron to noble
blues.

Willard exhaled. *No immortal, gods leave us. We still have a chance.*

The Sapphire himself rode among his men, in gleaming blue armor, riding
a dapple bay stallion. He turned his horse and led his company clattering up
the Hanging Road across the sheer wall of the harbor.

"This Old One must still be on the road behind us," said Brolli.

Willard glanced back across the river, where the lack of ferries had stranded
Sir Green and his band. The Sapphire's ship now appeared to be feeling its
way across the unfamiliar channel to retrieve them. *May they run aground in
the attempt.*

"We'll take our chances passing through Gallows Ferry," Willard said.
"The Sapphire still thinks he's dealing with an immortal, so he'll pursue the
strategy of following and watching until his Old One arrives to deal with me.
However, we have to expect he'll still have his crossbowmen take shots at you."

"In Gallows Ferry?"

"Unlikely. They won't want witnesses. But if I were him I might put a few
crossbows on the upper decks of that gallows. It's the only cover I can see on
the road. More important to him, however, is getting to Gallows Ferry before
us, so he can secure the place and prevent me from raising the inhabitants
and shutting the gates against him."

"But once this Sapphire reaches Gallows Ferry, could he not shut the
gates against *us?*"

Willard smiled. "I don't think he will. It would be a simple matter for us
to turn back and board our ferry and flee downstream, prolonging this hunt
for many more days. I'm betting he won't risk having to explain such a delay
to his Old One."

Willard signaled his pilot, and the ferry turned to limp across the current and into the tiny harbor. They passed beneath the overlooking gallows, where the Sapphire lord paused to look down in triumph. Orange sunset light flashed from armor and shields. Willard noted with satisfaction that even the noble Sapphire kept his crest covered, for anonymity. The Queen's power was strong enough, even this far into the frontier, that he dare not openly oppose her. Not yet. But even that could change, since she'd allowed Westies to bring their slaves to the Free Lands. In great enough numbers, they could change the place, make it another bastion of the Old Ways.

Brolli peered up. "I hope this Sapphire shuts the gates." There was an unmistakable smile to his voice. "We would not turn around. I could open them."

Willard frowned. "With your magic? I daresay you could. And it may come to that. But I don't need to remind you what sort of folk end up at the ends of ropes here in Arkendia?"

"Oh, no. That is much clear to me. Witches, you call us. Users of moon magic."

"My people don't tolerate it." Willard scowled up at the corpses swaying from the gallows. "Those are witches, most likely. When they catch one, they throw their witch-stone in the river and hang the witch over water. Not your people, obviously," Willard added quickly. "These are witches from the Iberg Imperial Concord, across the sea."

"Your ancient enemies, yes."

"Ever since we discovered your people and your magic, Ibergs have been sneaking over here in waves hoping to get a hint of how you make your magicks, infiltrating our shores like rats from ships. Have I thanked you for that lately? Makes our whole magic-fearing population jumpy as cats in a kennel."

Brolli laughed. "You are most welcome. Our magic is magnificent. Of course they want it. And it is most strange your people do not."

Willard grunted.

Brolli sat in silence as the grisly structure above them drifted past on the port side. "I much wonder how our peoples shall live in peace together," said Brolli pensively, "for my people live by the powers of the moons. Much like these Iberg witches."

"The thought has occurred to me, as well."

"I must tell you, Sir Willard: if we are near to die, I will certainly use my magic."

Willard nodded. "If we're about to die, I give you leave to use it."

The ferry drew into the steep gravel beach, and Willard disembarked, herding the ponies before him. Up the narrow ledge of the Hanging Road, the Sapphire's entire company waited, silhouetted against the sunset fire, lance tips glinting.

Willard cursed. "What are you up to, Sir Sapphire?" Willard waited, and watched, but no move came from Sir Sapphire. At length, he exhaled loudly, drew Belle from her sheath, and rested her across the front cantle of his saddle.

"Get those weapons ready, Ambassador. You may need them sooner than I'd hoped. And remember, there may be bowmen stationed in that gallows, so stay behind me till I've had a good look."

"I am ready."

Willard nodded. He craned his neck back to peer up the mile of sheer granite above him, and felt himself shrink to the size of an insect about to storm a castle.

The frontier is haven to all manner of outcasts and swindlers. The most infamous was the Mad Lady of Gallows Ferry. Banished from the court to the edges of the frontier, the Lady made a living by seducing other outcasts, who were never seen or heard from again. Let travelers beware! The frontier has little changed since the Mad Lady's time, and visitors do well to arm themselves with wits and steel.

—From *Traveler's Guide to the Free Lands,*
Sir Arlis Craft, late reign of Chasia

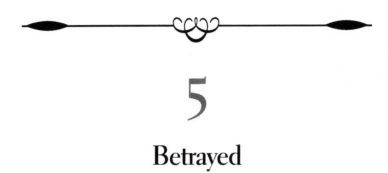

5

Betrayed

The courtier's carriage slowed to a halt in the crowded stable yard. Harric's stomach fluttered as he studied the vehicle for clues as to which con might best suit its occupants.

Either he would achieve his twentieth con on that carriage and break his mother's curse, or he would fail and…then what? His doom would find him, and it would be over.

The green paint of the carriage wasn't loud, nor its application too showy; that spoke of old money, with all its assumptions of taste and superiority. Yet this lord wasn't rich. The exterior woodwork was modest, and the vehicle leaned overmuch, suggesting a chassis meant for cobbles and courts, never refitted for the frontier. Nor could this lord afford a porter or doorman to ride outside, so the driver would double in that regard, and the team of four horses huffed as if they needed a fifth and sixth. A younger son of old gentry, Harric concluded. Landless, but used to reverence if not rich living.

A variety of suitable short cons ran through Harric's mind: the Bait Drop, the Pig-in-Poke, the Junk Sale. Nothing simple would do for this one. Then he caught a glimpse of several tiny witch-silver talismans, hanging from the bits of the lead horses, and that decided him: a Junk Sale of witch-silver charms.

He made a show of swapping out the price board on his sign pole, dropping the price from frontier market rate to Queen's price.

"Feed grain!" he cried. "No grazing left on the road! Buy now! Fair prices!"

The carriage inched to a halt in the stubborn crowd, still a stone's throw away, but its driver heard Harric's cry and squinted at the price board. Harric hadn't seen a four-horse carriage yet that didn't buy grain in Gallows Ferry, and no one else would be dropping prices at this time of night. The driver's eyes locked on the sign as if it were a mirage that might vanish if he looked away.

Bait laid. Hook set.

Harric dragged the grain sacks from the back of his cart to the front. While his back was to the carriage he counted out seven glittering witch-charm pendants from the many beneath his shirt, and lifted them outside his collar to hang in plain view. Each was a raw nugget of the white metal, polished smooth by the northern streams they once filled in abundance, and coveted by Arkendians for supposed witch-foiling powers.

"Harric." Caris spoke from the foot of his cart, interrupting his thoughts. She managed a forced smile before dropping her gaze to stare at his boots. Perspiration shone on her neck and forehead, and her cheeks flushed with sun and exertion.

Good. She hadn't balled up and hidden in the stables. She'd gone for a long ride.

He could see by the furrow in her brow and the way she pulled at the strings of the grain sacks that she wanted to talk about what had happened that morning, but her timing could not have been worse. He wasn't ready to explain to her the full nature of his mother's training, and he definitely didn't want her to learn of it by witnessing him performing a con.

He forced a smile. "What brings you from the stables?"

"I wanted to see you." Her voice remained flat, in the seemingly emotionless manner of the horse-touched. "I was wrong about your mother's curse. But I wonder if maybe it's over, and we broke it this morning."

"Sun hasn't set yet."

She looked up at the orange sunset light on the cliff. "I know. That's why I thought I'd come watch over you." A rare smile lifted one corner of her mouth, and she glanced up to meet his eyes. He noticed then the massive sword she'd strapped on her hip, and grinned in spite of himself.

The green carriage lurched to a crawl again, and his stomach flipped.

"I'm glad of your protection, Caris, but the lord in that carriage could be one of your father's spies. High enough blood rank. You want to step out of sight till the carriage passes?"

She peered at the vehicle over the heads of the crowd. "I'm sick of hiding from my father."

"When you're apprenticed to a knight, you won't have to. Until then… maybe you ought to climb up on the porch and see if you get a view of the family crest on the side door?"

She frowned and glanced up at him, an unspoken question in her eyes, then turned and climbed the stairs to the porch and peered at the carriage. Whatever family crest it was, she recognized it, and quickly retreated into the doorway of the inn.

Harric exhaled. Two strokes of luck: she'd evaded sighting, and he'd evaded the impossible task of hiding his twentieth con.

"Simple as a mule-kicked dog," said Rudy, nodding at Caris. The stableman had barged between revelers on the porch behind Harric's cart. He leaned his bare and ample belly against the rails and flashed a yellow grin. "But simple don't bother Harric," he announced to the porch at large. "He's a whore like his mama, so he'll bed a dog if there's coin in it!"

Rudy's cronies laughed, and Rudy beamed like he'd won a game of wits.

The revelers watched Caris lingering in the doorway, and Harric wondered if they saw what he saw. Tall, serious, stronger than most of them, she was also shapely, something curiously amplified by her men's garb and the plain horsetail of her hair. By the looks on several of the men's faces, he judged he wasn't alone in admiring.

"She's horse-touched, not simple," Harric returned. "So I'll wager what bothers Rudy is that she's so good with his horses she makes *him* look simple. Or maybe he's worried she'll tell us of his nighttime visits to the fillies in the back stalls."

The porch erupted in laughter, and Rudy's face distorted with rage. "Shut up! Shut up all of you all!" He turned on Harric. "Know why I'm drinking early, lord-boy? I'm celebrating because this is the day your crazy momma said we'd be rid of your fancy-talking skinny bastard ass. Think I don't know you drammed my whiskey last night? I'm gonna see you swing from the gallows tower, boy." He gestured past the gate toward the four-story gibbet on the Hanging Road. "Be the best thing ever happened, when they string your whoreson carcass up."

"Get the stable master another whiskey!" a reveler called. "He's busting a gut!"

"Go hang yourselfs!" Rudy snarled.

The revelers laughed and redoubled their heckling, until Rudy whirled and barked in reply, his pimpled back pressing through the rails. That was when Harric recognized a new face among Rudy's cronies—one of Lyla's ex-master's bodyguards. The man sat drinking, coolly watching Harric. A chill of dread in Harric's stomach. There could be no coincidence the man found Rudy, Harric's oldest enemy, in the outpost. And Lyla's master had kept *three* bodyguards; if one were here, the others were near.

The carriage creaked to a halt before Harric, making his heart jump. The distraction of Rudy and his new muscle had kept him from studying it for last-moment clues about the occupants. Worse, Rudy remained. Had the stableman got wind of Harric's games, and come to expose him? Harric clenched his teeth, trying to smile as the driver hooked his reins and clambered down to the running board to open the door for his master.

Calm down. Trust your initial read.

The driver opened the carriage door and bowed as a pampered-looking gentleman emerged from beneath the lintel and stretched to his full height in the doorframe. He breathed deeply through thin, well-plucked nostrils, as if to take in the fresh mountain air, but the stink of the market struck him in the nose like a fist.

The lord pressed a lacy handkerchief to his nose. "Gods leave us, what a place." He spoke to the driver through the scented fabric. "We'll stay only as long as we must."

"Yes, my lord."

A lady ducked her head out the door beside the lord, wrinkling her nose but peering eagerly at the tumult of the market. She was strikingly lovely, with heavy-lidded green eyes and a crop of ginger hair in the Queen's latest fashion. Harric risked a direct glance, only to find her unabashedly assaying his parts like a housewife judging dainties at the butcher. What he hoped she saw was a young man of average-to-slight frame with fine hands and features — handsome, but better suited for comfort than for land clearing in the north. He made sure his green bastard's belt was visible, displaying a gentle blood equal to hers while hinting at all the romance and rascality of bastardy. And if she saw only a bastard slave-in-free-clothing…well, he could work with that too; it just wouldn't be as fun.

"Leave soon?" she said, evidently pleased by what she saw. "I think there might be something here worth staying the night for."

Harric bowed. *If this is my doom, I could do a lot worse.*

He laid one hand over his breast in a show of gallantry that also kept his surplus charms beneath his shirt, while letting the seven he'd chosen for the carriage swing out in plain view.

Several maids-in-waiting giggled in the carriage, eyes flashing flirtatiously through the rear side window. But a second lady within sat rigid in the forward sofa, with none of their spirit. Her wide brown eyes fixed in horror upon the gallows still visible a mile back on the road, its half-dozen corpses swinging gently in the breeze. Even from here it was clear the corpses were Iberg; their olive skin and outlandish clothing cried it as loudly as it labeled them witches.

"Terrible, isn't it, my lady," said Harric, leaning toward the window so his witch charms caught her eye.

The moment she saw them, she rose to the lord's side and whispered in his ear.

He dismissed her with a sneer. "Out of the question. Those charms are rubbish."

"Please, my lord!"

The lord turned to her, exasperated, as if the subject were a persistent and vexing part of their journey thus far. He pointed at the gallows. "You see those Ibergs, my love?"

"They're witches, my lord! Ibergs are *all* witches."

"Indeed, love, they are. But they are dead witches. Dead Ibergs cannot hurt you. The fine people of this lovely settlement hang them all for your benefit, and not a one gets by."

"It's true," Harric said, as if trying to help. "And they're not after you anyway, my lady; they're after the magic the Kwendi have in the north. They say the magic's something the imperial magic schools of the Ibergs have never seen before, so they're crazy to steal it. They come creeping over by the dozen, trying to slip by, but I am certain we catch most all of them. It's hard for an Iberg to go unnoticed."

The lord made a show of strained tolerance of a bastard's interruption. "You see there, my love? These witches haven't the faintest interest in any of us."

"But the Kwendi are witches too," she said, taking the bait Harric had dangled. "And they hate us for settling their land in the north. What if we clear our land, and they come for us with magic?"

"We'll fight them, of course, and win it our way. Without magic."

The green-eyed lady laughed, a sound like tinkling chimes. "Brother dear, your lady wife is fairly dying for a witch-stone. Why don't you be a kind husband and ask the bastard if he'll sell you one of his. He appears to have stones enough to serve us all."

His sister's brash tone finally caught the lord's attention. He followed her gaze to Harric and sneered. "Really, Sister, you get more desperate with every mile from court. Or have you lost your sense of smell entirely?" He turned then to Harric, signaling the end of the discussion with the women. "We will buy twenty of your barley sacks, Bastard. Your prices are as marked?"

Harric tried a new angle, slipping out of his frontier accent to his purest accent of the court. "Indeed so, Your Grace. It will be my greatest pleasure to serve you."

The lord raised a plucked eyebrow. "You speak as one of the educated."

"Raised for court, Your Grace."

"And he don't let us forget it!" Rudy heckled from behind.

Wonderful. Rudy was listening. The lord hadn't yet noticed the stable master amidst the clamor of the market, but to Harric he sounded louder and drunker than usual. Harric stepped nearer the lord to screen his view of Rudy, and to make it harder for Rudy to hear Harric's words. "My mother was a courtesan in the first years of our queen. She educated me herself."

"Oh, how lucky of us to meet him!" said the green-eyed lady. "For this rustic bastard presents to you a very mirror of how you shall look after a year of clearing land."

The lord snorted, clearly unamused. "Gods leave me, I fear you say true. Tell me, Bastard: how does one of your breeding stand to live in this sinkhole of piss and vomit? Tell me your trick, for it will be as gold to me in the northlands."

Harric laughed as if the barb were a jest, and called a stable boy to load the grain.

As Harric leaned down to take coins from the driver, the seven witch charms swung out again from his neck, and the lord snorted. "I expect you and your mates are selling that rubbish to the ignorant? Not a very honorable sport, Sir Bastard."

"You mistake me, Your Grace; I'm not selling mine."

"Not selling? Surely you don't mean that you keep them for *protection?*"

Harric dropped his eyes as if embarrassed. "I used to sell them, Your Grace…but then when the witches started showing up—"

"You forgot your education." The lord slapped his knee as if to emphasize the point to his watching wife. "See how a court education is undone by superstition!"

Rudy blustered something like "superstition my pocky ass!" so Harric drew yet nearer to the window and directed the lord's attention to the gallows far behind on the road. "That witch on the end cursed four of us one night. One of my mates fell dead and another keeled over with a plague, but my third friend and I didn't feel a thing." Harric gave his witch-silver charms a solemn pat. "These charms saved us. I've thought about it many times, and I'm sure of it."

Harric avoided the eyes of the frightened lady in the carriage, but it was to her he now played. "You see, the friend that died had no witch-silver at all—"

"Bollocks!" Rudy cried.

"—and the friend that got sick had a charm of inferior quality," Harric continued. "But I had these *very pure* nuggets, and my friend had one too, and we both survived without a mark."

"Lies," said the lord, "or pure coincidence."

"Oh, please!" said his wife. She clung to his sleeve and went limp at the knees. "Buy one, my lord. Just one for me. Please!"

Her ladies in waiting clamored for the same, and the lord paled, apparently sensing his peril too late. "My love, he isn't selling, so that's an end of it."

"But he has so many!" Her lips went thin and pale as lines of chalk. When her chin began to quiver, the fight seemed to leave him. His shoulders sank, and he sighed as if realizing that if he did not buy them he would face this fight at every gallows they passed.

Blushing, he leaned out the door. "I'll give you twenty-five silvers for them," he muttered.

"Your Grace? I'm very sorry, as I said, I do not wish to sell—"

"Fifty, then." He made a wry smile. "You said your friend had only one of these, which proves you need only one to protect you. Keep one, and I'll take the rest."

Harric stammered, as if cornered by the logic, and Rudy bellowed something, but this time the revelers shouted him down, and sounds of a scuffle broke out on the porch behind.

"Here's fifty silvers," said the lord, handing Harric a purse and snatching six of the charms from Harric's neck. Harric acted almost too bewildered to take the coins with one hand and close the other around one remaining charm for himself.

The lord beamed in satisfaction as he withdrew with the charms into the carriage. The driver secured the door and clambered back to his seat at the reins. "A pleasure reasoning with you, Sir Bastard," said the lord from his window. "Gods leave you. And I wish you the best of luck in regaining your sense of smell."

Harric hid his jubilation in a bow of humble acceptance. He glanced at the cliff above and saw a tiny sliver of sunlight on the highest outcrop.

The sun had yet to set. He had twenty cons.

He'd done it. And the moment he realized it, something cold and hard uncoiled from around his heart and left him. A darkness left him that he'd known so long he'd forgotten it was there. His mother's curse, evaporating like morning fog. Gone. He'd done it. He was free.

Sweaty arms bear-hugged Harric from behind, pinning his arms and crushing the air from his lungs. "Wait, Your Worship!" Rudy yelled, as the carriage began to roll away.

Harric struggled in the embrace, twisting and kicking, but Rudy knew his tricks. It wasn't the first time they'd struggled. A blow to the back of Harric's head sent spots across his vision. Head butt. Rudy's specialty.

"Leave him be, ye fat guts!" a reveler called. "Ye'll spoil the party!"

"He shamed His Worship!" Rudy shouted. "Your Worship, see for yourself!"

The carriage halted before it had gone a pace. As Harric refocused his eyes, the lord appeared in the open window. Laughter from his recent triumph still lit his face. "What is this noise?"

"Your Grace," said Harric, "this man's a notorious drunk—"

Another head butt sent Harric's ears ringing. A sticky hand clapped over his mouth.

"Worship, he's been having you on. You look and see. He gots twenty of them charms under his shirt and they're as cheap as dog teeth in these parts. When you leave he'll bring 'em out and the whole porch will have a laugh."

"That's how he served my master," said one of the saffron grooms. "Cheated at cards and stole away a prime slave."

The lord's smile faltered. His eyes flicked from Harric to the faces on the porch, and whatever he saw among the revelers made him flush with color. He rapped on the door and the driver descended to open it. The lord stepped across the gap to Harric's cart, where he stood eye to eye with Harric, smoldering.

The porch fell silent.

"Is this true, bastard?" said the lord.

Rudy squeezed the voice from Harric. "Open his shirt, Your Worship, and you'll see it's true."

The lord tore Harric's shirt to expose a dozen additional charms on strings against his skin.

As if to confirm Rudy's claim, a gust of laughter burst from the revelers.

Harric twisted his face from under Rudy's hand. "These charms are of inferior quality—" he began, but Rudy bear-hugged the breath from him and left him mouthing the air like a fish.

The lord lifted the stones from Harric's chest and examined the nuggets. His lips flattened in a tight line. "They are identical to the ones I purchased," he said, very softly. Harric met the lord's eyes, and in them he saw the game was up. The lord snatched back his purse of silvers.

One of the revelers guffawed. To the man beside him he said, "Pay up! It's sunset, and he made twenty."

"No, indeed," said the other. "The fat man buggered it."

"See there, Your Worship?" said Rudy. "They all knows it."

Tears stung Harric's eyes even as a ludicrous grin overspread his face. Had he triumphed over a death curse only to be hanged as a common jack by the likes of Rudy?

A stinging slap from the lord failed to wipe the grin away.

"You dare shame me, bastard?" The lord drew near, his voice barely a whisper. "As a full blood of your rank I can mark you. Yet you dare?"

"It isn't you I gamed, Your Grace," said Harric. "It's my mother. It's complicated."

The ginger-haired lady clapped her hands. "Oh, mark him, brother! *Do* mark him." She rose with a pot of green slave paint and held it out the window to her brother. "This is turning into such fun. I hope we meet other bastards we can paint. But don't mark his hair, dear brother. He has such fine hair."

The lord took the pot and plunged the brush deep in the bright green paint it held. "I thought to mark our new peasants with this, bastard, but since the Blood Purity Laws allow me to mark a bastard…"

Harric struggled in the stableman's arms. "The Queen abolished the Purity Laws."

"This is the frontier. There are no laws."

"The *Queen's* frontier."

The lord smirked. He drew so near that Harric could see every pore in the skin of his high, sharp nose, and feel the warmth of citrus-scented breath on his cheek. "The Queen is weak, Bastard. Her reforms weaken. Maybe you haven't heard up here, but she grows old and has no heir. There is many a strong lord ready to lead us back to the Old Ways when she goes. Indeed, in some parts the Old Ways and Purity Laws already rise again."

"Your Grace—" Harric began, but Rudy clapped a hand over his mouth. The lord lifted a great glob with the brush, which he slopped in the hair of Harric's forehead.

The ladies squealed in delight.

"You are marked for judgment," the lord announced, loud enough for the porch to hear. "You will stay here on public display until the mark dries. And this fine man"—he nodded to Rudy—"shall be my deputy until a gentleman of greater than green blood arrives to carry out justice for the crime of"—the lord swirled the brush in the hair, leaving an algae-colored cowlick where Harric could see it—"the crime of lying to a lady."

A pulse of shame struck Harric at the thought Caris might be present. A glance found her easily at the rear of the crowd, head and shoulders above the others. On her face he saw a look of hurt and confusion, as if it were her he'd conned. She turned for the inn too late to hide a grimace of pain on her face. The sight stabbed deep into Harric.

Rudy was stammering, "Won't you give justice yourself, Your Worship?"

"That is for one of higher blood than mine, sirrah. But fear not," he said, raising his voice for the market to hear him. "Before nightfall, I promise you this: a waterwheel shall land with more lords of high color than this cesspit's ever seen. Indeed, you shall find a Phyros-rider among them. One of the Old Ones, I believe?"

A murmur of shock rippled through the market. Several merchants near Harric began packing up their stalls. Emigrants behind the carriage agitated to squeeze past and win clear of the crowded gauntlet, which would be a trap to them if a Phyros should come.

The lord beamed with pleasure. "You will be great sport I'm sure, Sir Bastard. I would stay to see the famous Gallows Ferry gallows in action, but an Old One can be…unpredictable. Caution bids me go." He tore most of the additional charms from Harric's neck, and returned to his carriage, where he showered the stones upon the delighted ladies.

The carriage lurched into motion, trailing ladies' laughter behind.

Rudy released Harric and socked him in the side of the head. White spots dashed across Harric's vision. His knees hit the planking, hard. "I'm keeping you right here, lord-boy," said Rudy. "You heard what His Worship said. An Old One's coming. And I ain't never heard of an Old One that didn't fancy a hanging."

Of all in the Old Ones Sir Grippan was wildest,
And first to be slain in the Cleansing.
Most hated was Bannus, the vilest despoiler,
Who fled to the Isle of Phyrosi.

—From *Oral Histories of the Cleansing*

6

Hexes & Hangings

Willard urged Molly from the beach onto the foot of the Hanging Road. In his left hand he held the ponies' leads, so they would follow near the cliff wall, and so he could leave them in a crisis without untying them first from his saddle. The ambassador rocked in his saddle beneath his blanket, but Willard knew he was alert as a cat, the knots binding him to the saddle set to untie with a single tug in emergency. In his right hand Willard cradled *Belle*, the massive greatsword balanced over the front cantle of his saddle.

"This ought to be fun."

Brolli chuckled. "Remind me to ask what in your language means *fun*."

Iron-shod hooves rang from the stone as they climbed.

They were ants now, insects tickling the ankles of the mighty granite wall, tiny motes on a scratch above the water.

"Sun has set, yes?" Brolli said. "Your night hex is with us."

"Yes. But that is no guarantee it will wake tonight. Can't be sure until it gives a sign."

"A sign?"

"A victim. We won't proceed until we have one."

The ponies strained up the steep-cut incline of the road, pulling against their leads in Willard's hand. Even Molly snorted with exertion. Willard halted them some sixty paces below the Sapphire, and waited. *Ought to be close enough*. He'd seen his hex reach men from twice as far.

The nobleman's company maintained their disciplined stillness, lances standing tall in the holders attached to their stirrups; Willard saw no drawn swords flashing. As he anticipated, the nobleman was not planning to attack. Not here, or now. Not yet, anyway.

Molly tossed her head, impatient.

"Soon, girl. We need a sign."

Like Kogan, Willard had a healthy fear of his hex. It struck out randomly, often at him, or his friends. But unlike Kogan, he also recognized that, in a pinch, it could be a valuable ally, for it was generally as destructive to his enemies as it was to him. *Generally*. That was the problem. It was unpredictable. It might not wake at all, or it might strike *him*, which could scuttle the whole moon-blasted thing.

Roll the dice, old man.

"Ever wonder why this damned hex never strikes you, ambassador?"

"There is no hex curse among my people." Brolli shrugged. "We are not human. Another sign of Kwendi superior, I think."

Willard heard the humor in his voice, and smiled. "As far as hexes are concerned, it'd be damned hard to argue with that."

The Sapphire stirred. He signaled his men with a wave of his hand, turned his horse, and rode away northward, with his men in tow.

"Ah, they leave," said Brolli. "Is the hex not waking?"

Willard said nothing, his gaze still fixed on the place below the gallows where the Sapphire had been. He counted thirty heartbeats, and was on the brink of giving up when a trio of riders appeared again beside the gallows: a knight and squire, both armored, accompanied by a groom.

Willard smiled. "A silver says these men bring me my sign."

"Make it two silvers, and you have a bet."

"Done." Willard dropped the ponies' leads, and urged Molly into a slow walk up the steep shelf. "Wait here. It could be a trap. In any case, things could get messy, so stay alert. And remember what I said about my people's opinion of magic — even so-called good magic — as there may be other witnesses up by the gallows."

"I remember. I use it only if dying."

As Willard neared the waiting trio, the harsh light of silhouette diminished, and he was able to ascertain the knight's armor was enameled in an azure blue, a color signifying one of the highest blood ranks. Though not quite as high as Sapphire, Azure was considered "royal" blood by Westies, blood descended from an ancient prince of that isle. The knight wore an open-faced helm. Deep-set black eyes flashed above a neat black beard and fierce grin.

Willard did not hang back to parley, though the man held up his hand for it. Instead, he brought Molly almost nose to nose with the waiting riders. The trio's horses stepped back and shied sideways in dismay, giving Willard time to glance around the corner to verify the Sapphire had not waited there in ambush; he found the lord already halfway across the mile of Hanging Road to Gallows Ferry. From his position he could see the entire expanse, including the sun-bleached buildings of the outpost, but there was no sign of Kogan's caravan. The priest had made good time and already entered the settlement, so he'd be well past it by the time the Sapphire arrived.

That was good. Kogan would be in position to execute their plan. *Whether or not he has the brains to pull it off is something else entirely.*

"The famous Sir Willard," sneered the Azure, who had finally got his horse under control. "So it is true after all. You're mortal, like the rest of us. I never would have believed it if I hadn't seen it with my eyes. You truly have gone mad."

Willard raised his visor, and spat. "Think you can defeat me, then. Is that it?" He nudged Molly so she danced a step closer, then reined her back in a way that always made her toss her head and roar. She did not disappoint, howling out a challenge that nearly blew the mane back on Sir Azure's stallion. "Of course, Molly's as immortal as ever," Willard said. "But you knew that."

The knight snorted. "Molly won't give a damn when you're gone." He hauled a heavy crossbow from his side and aimed it at Willard's chest, the armor-piercing bodkin glinting dully. "She'll probably eat your sorry carcass."

His squire and groom produced short-stocked spitfires with flint-wheel triggers and flaring mouths like trumpets. The squire wore a leather blast mask in the shape of a hawk's head. The groom wore none, and bore the pockmarks of prior misfires on his cheeks.

"At this range you haven't a chance." The Azure's grin showed the purple teeth of a blood-painter. "One bolt, down you go. Molly walks away, and I take the Queen's wedding ring from your stinking pockets. Or you can hand them over now, and I let you go back to your ferry."

"Ah! So you know of the ring, do you? And you know their power. I took you for a glory hunter, looking to slay the great Sir Willard, but now I see now your aim is much higher. You wish to use the ring to force the Queen to marry you! You wish to be king! I think your Sapphire friend will not like that you came back here to take them for yourself."

"Tut! He is a fool. He will wait for orders. But I, too, am a prince. I, too, of royal lineage."

"Not as high as sapphire."

"High enough! Hand them over."

Willard shrugged. "You're too late. They could cause quite a lot of mischief in the wrong hands, you know. I flung them in the river as we crossed."

The man's eyes faltered. "You lie."

"But why stop with the ring?" Willard continued. "Why not take the ambassador too? That's what your sapphire friend intends, is it not? If he can, he will take the ring, and attempt to force the Queen to marry. But that plan is flawed, if the ring is lost or destroyed. Surely he also plans to capture or slay the Kwendi ambassador in order to provoke the Kwendi into war. A war in the north would drain the Queen's armies from her position in the south, and set the stage for your precious West to rise again and seize the throne."

The Azure's lip curled. He spoke through grinding teeth. "I give you to the count of five to save me the trouble of searching your corpse. If you do not hand them over, I shall kill you both and take the ring. *One...*"

The squire and groom shifted in their saddles, grinning like idiots, their spitfires held steady on Willard. All three of them had the signs of the hex upon them. Rash fearlessness. Wild eyes. Impetuous speech. The hex seemed to take all inhibition from its victims, unleashing their inmost selves in all their purest follies. *Like Tam, Gods leave him.* Squire Tam had charged ten knights, alone, in some hex-addled heroic sortie, before Willard had noticed the signs of hex in his eyes. How many squires, friends, allies had he lost that way? Much better to lose enemies like Sir Azure.

Willard waved the count off at three. "Come, Sir Azure. You will have to slay me. I have no ring, and your counting is tedious. But may I not know the name of my slayer? West Isle knights once had courtesy: they said please and thank you as they raped our dogs and children."

"Enough! Four, and—"

Willard turned Molly so her massive head and neck shielded him from the bow. Without a perceptible signal from Willard, Molly lunged, seizing the man's face in her teeth and shaking him like a dog shakes a rat. His armored legs flailed into the face of the squire, whose horse shied sideways into the groom. The squire launched a sizzling spitfire wad, but his aim was wide, and the wad screamed past Willard's ear, peppering his armor with flaming resin. Sir Azure's scream cut short with a wrenching crack of his neck. The squire turned his horse down the harbor road and spurred it for Brolli, sword in hand, and groom in hot pursuit.

"Brolli, they come!" Willard shouted.

Molly dropped Sir Azure, and leapt in pursuit, too far behind to protect the ambassador, but near enough to lend aid once engaged.

The horsemen galloped down the incline, as if they'd bowl Brolli and the ponies over the precipice. Brolli had dismounted, and Willard glimpsed him loping up the incline in the bizarre knuckle-walking manner of his people. One of his long arms windmilled, launching a globe of witch-silver the size of an apple. The globe struck the stone at the foot of the squire's charging stallion and erupted in fire and smoke. It was as if the apple had set off a boiler explosion, pitching the squire and his horse together into the void.

The groom's mount scrambled to a halt in the smoke, rearing and throwing the groom to the road, where Willard drew Molly to a sparking, skidding stop. The boy's spitfire spun from his fingers and cracked on the stone, where it discharged, spraying its flaming resin on the cliff wall. Molly reared, pawing the air. One hoof bore a spot of blazing resin, and she came down with it on the chest of the scrambling groom with an audible crunch. Dancing sideways, she stamped in a vain attempt to snuff the fire.

"Brolli!" Willard shouted. "Are you all right?"

Brolli emerged from the dissipating smoke, daylids pushed up on his forehead like dark-glassed tooler's goggles. His owlish gold eyes shone. "That felt good." He rested on his knuckles and flashed Willard a wide grin with thick and prominent canines. "My aim is not so fine, though. I must practice."

Willard grunted, relieved. "Admirable aim from my perspective." Swinging a leg over his saddle, Willard dropped from Molly's stirrup, a move that sent nails of pain through his feet and spine.

A quick examination of Molly's chest and legs revealed no other resin burns. The spot on her hoof had burned out, leaving a crater of blackened keratin.

"Blasted spitfires," Willard muttered. "Damned messy."

"Not so clean as my magic, yes?" Brolli flashed the wolfish smile.

Willard peered back up the road to the gallows, where, sure enough, several heads peeked from a makeshift cabin built into the foundations. "Let me remind you that all magic is dirty to my people, Ambassador. Now mount up and get that blanket on, if you please. Probably too late, but it can't hurt." He hauled himself into his saddle with a pained grunt. "By the way, you owe me two silver."

Brolli grinned. "Your hex struck out at these men, yes?"

"Oh, yes." In the harbor below, Willard saw the squire's horse standing on the beach beside the ferry, dripping and trembling, its saddle sideways. The squire would have drowned in his armor. The groom's horse had fled back down the road to the landing; it now trotted out on the beach to join its stablemate.

Brolli cocked his head to one side, brow furrowed. "How did you acquire this hex?"

"You make it sound like I bought it at market. No idea how it came to me, or why. It first appeared some ten years ago, and soon after it ended my career. Queen banished me from court. Had to. You can imagine the havoc it made there."

Brolli nodded. "It is sad. I am sorry."

Willard grunted, and took up the leads of the ponies. When Brolli returned the blanket to his head, Willard led the ponies huffing and blowing up the remainder of the incline. When he reached the gallows and could glimpse the road across the cliff face, he paused to let them rest.

The Sapphire had stopped his company short of Gallows Ferry. Some in his company pointed to Sir Azure's riderless stallion, which trotted up the road behind them. As Willard watched, several grooms and squires rode back to intercept him.

Willard smiled wearily. *Your numbers dwindle, Sir Sapphire. How you must wonder what just happened.*

Willard removed his helmet and thumbed the sweat from his eyes. Though the sun had set, its heat still radiated from the granite all around him as if it were noon.

Something moved at the base of the gallows. A door had opened slightly in the cabin. Inside, panicked whispers.

Willard ignored them and fastened his helmet behind his saddle. Let them look. No sense hiding his mortal skin any longer. If he fell outside Gallows Ferry, at least Anna would hear that his skin had been of ordinary hue, that he had not drunk the Blood.

A grimy man appeared in the door of the cabin, dressed in the coveralls of a tooler.

He ambled out to the edge of the road with a hint of swagger to his stride and not a whiff of the usual cringing due a Phyros-rider.

To Willard's eye, such rash boldness spoke of hex madness, as sure as sunset in the western sky. *Black Moon take it.* He did not relish bystander casualties.

The tooler advanced upon Brolli and stopped several paces away, hands on his hips, eyes prying suspiciously at the blanket. Behind the tooler, an apprentice cowered. The lad clearly hadn't been stricken by the hex, for he trembled like a reed in a windstorm.

"Master tooler," Willard said, in a tone of warning that made the apprentice cringe. "Return to your cabin."

The tooler peered sidelong at Willard, as if noting his lack of immortal features, then turned back to Brolli. "We seen magic just now on the road," he said, in an accusatory frontier drawl. "You bring us a witch to hang, Your Holiness?" Willard couldn't miss the tone of irony in the title.

"That was no magic," Willard said, ignoring the irreverence. "It was an ordinary resin charge, like those your brother toolers used to blast the Hanging Road. It worked rather nicely as a weapon, don't you think?"

The tooler squinted down the road where the spitfire's spray still smoked and smoldered on the rock. "Might be." He returned his scrutiny to Brolli. "But a resin charge big enough to toss a horse will leave a soot patch twenty times that size."

Brolli moved beneath the blanket. The hole through which he peered had been trained upon the tooler. Now it shifted upward to gaze at the massive gallows with its complex of cables and pulleys, and the massive wheel blocks supporting man-sized counterweights.

The tooler sprang back from Brolli, pointing at Brolli's long-fingered foot, which now poked beneath the hem of the blanket. He'd inadvertently raised it when he lifted his head to view the gallows through the hole. Brolli jerked the blanket back over his foot as the tooler cried, "What in the Black Moon *is* you?"

"He is a Kwendi," Willard said, turning Molly toward the tooler. He did not wish to kill the unfortunate man, but he couldn't let him harm Brolli. If the truth might calm his hex-maddened zeal, it was worth a try. The man was too far from the outpost for the knowledge to do any harm. "He is under my protection, Master Tooler, and under the express protection of the Queen. Indeed, she has licensed his magic in cases of self-protection."

Willard held his breath, gripping his sword and readying to prompt Molly to lunge.

But the tooler's face smoothed in wonder. He took a step backward, as if better to imagine the figure under the blanket, and his eyes widened in surprise. "A *Kwendi...*" he breathed. "Well, send me to the Black Moon itself! It's on account of you, Master Kwendi, that these Ibergs is swarming across the water. Every one of these witches want the secret to your magic. They're mad to get their hands on it, and it's on account of you I'm in business. I owes you gratitude."

"This gallows is yours?" Brolli said, peering up through the hole again at the complex of cables and pulleys. "To me, it is all confused ropes and trees. I do not understand it."

"Pity I don't have no witch today to show you how she works," said the tooler. Then his face lit with inspiration. "But we don't need no witch! I can show you myself!" He grabbed the ear of his cowering apprentice, who all this time had seemed near fainting, and dragged him to the control panel at the cabin. "You watch, Master Kwendi," he called, stringing a ready noose around his own neck. "You'll see how she does it!"

The apprentice gaped, petrified. "Show him how we hang 'em," said his master, giving him a smart kick in the shins. "I said show him, you lazy runt!"

The kicks grew fiercer until the apprentice jerked a lever and a massive counterweight plummeted from above. The tooler launched skyward, gripping rope under his chin. His eyes bulged and his legs flailed as he swung over the river like a boy on a rope swing.

"Master!" the apprentice cried. The boy yanked a brake that jerked the tooler's ascent to a halt. The tooler swung back over the road, face red with panic. The boy pulled a lever that dropped another weight and shot another noose upward, before he found the release that dumped his master abruptly to the ground.

The tooler lay stunned and gasping in the dust beside the cabin.

When he was certain the man still breathed, Sir Willard turned Molly and led Brolli away.

"Ah…thank you, Master Tooler," Brolli said from beneath his blanket. "I think I understand now, how it works. Very nice."

Brolli rode up beside Willard, hugging the cliff wall and bouncing in his saddle like an ill-stowed sack of firewood. He twisted around to peer through the hole in his blanket at the tooler, who sat dazed and choking.

"That was most strange." He turned back to Willard, chuckling grimly. "It was your hex, yes?"

Willard nodded, brows pinched in worry. "I've never seen it so active."

"It is a good sign, though, yes? It still does not strike you. Maybe it will not."

"We can hope."

"Or maybe that is all it does today?"

"Oh, no. It'll strike again," Willard said. "Once it's awake, it's awake till dawn. Near as I can tell, it strikes when I am in danger. In battle, say, or hunted, like we are now. Or when I'm with women—don't ask me why," he said, to head off a chuckling response from the ambassador. "I don't understand it, but it's so."

"Women are danger, then!" Brolli rocked with pleasure. "And women is why you are exiled from court, yes?"

Willard peered suspiciously at Brolli. "A woman, yes."

"The Lady Anna, I think?"

"How in the Black Moon do *you* know that, Ambassador? You've been among us for, what, a month?"

"A month in your court was long enough for me to learn of the Sir Willard ballads. 'Sir Willard and the Queen's Maid' was my favorite." Brolli hummed as if seeking a note.

"Do *not* sing it," said Willard.

"It is very catchy—"

"Have I told you how I detest those ballads?" said Willard, trying not to snarl.

Brolli sighed. "I will not sing it."

"You save me much pain. Let's talk about something more pleasant, shall we? Like our present situation. If my hex strikes *me* in Gallows Ferry, there are many who could be in serious danger. Especially you, Ambassador. If I am lost, you must race through the outpost and find Father Kogan on the road. Tell him what has happened and have him block the road after you pass, as we'd planned."

"Race? I can barely sit a horse when you lead me."

"Run on foot, then, if you have to. The next danger is your identity, Ambassador. That blanket must not slip again. If it does, be ready for a lynch mob of Arkendians that will make our treatment of Ibergs look hospitable."

The ambassador grunted. "Worse than my reception in your queen's court?"

"We're on the frontier, Ambassador. They hang Ibergs for sport. And Ibergs are human. No telling what they'd do with you."

The apprentice crept to the tooler's side. "Master?"

The tooler coughed and rubbed his neck as the boy helped him sit. When the man had recovered enough to breathe normally, he stared after the Phyros-rider, lost in wonder. "That was powerful strange," he muttered. "Don't hardly know what I just done…"

The man found himself perspiring, his hands trembling.

The cabin door squeaked as his brother and nephew emerged and moved reverently to the tooler's side. "You was witched," his nephew said, eyes wide and earnest. "You was taken by a god." The boy reached down and held up the tooler's sweating, trembling hands, as if in confirmation. The boy's father nodded sagely.

"Taken by a god, master!" the apprentice yelped. "You're lucky she let you go."

The tooler snatched his hands away and boxed his apprentice's ear. "Superstitious fools! Ain't no such thing. A tooler looks for a better explanation. A *real* explanation." He blinked and tried to still the trembling in his hands. "It was the Phyros made me nervous, is all," he muttered. "People *do* things when they're nervous."

In the War of Creation, Arkus made the Isle of Arkendia as a bastion for himself and his people, free of magic and slavery and worship. Krato, jealous of his creation, hid altars to himself throughout the west of the isle and corrupted its people with magic and slavery. Arkus severed the west like a rotting limb from the island. Thus in shame was the West Isle born.

—From *Arkendian Creation Stories*, collected by Sister Cornelia Barti

7

Bastard Brains

On his hands and knees in the back of his cart, Harric raised his head and locked eyes with the priest across the market. The man's gaze burned into him from forty paces, dark eyes riveted to the curl of green paint on Harric's forehead. The father's beard was as huge as an unstrung bale of wool. He towered above his flock, and his already immense size was magnified by a smothercoat of square carpets through which he poked his head, so he looked like a hairy, walking siege tent. The priest drove his people through the market as hunted by hounds, and scowled the hawkers into silence. Yet his eyes never left Harric for long.

Harric let his hair hide his eyes and risked a glance at Rudy. The stable master stood directly behind him in the cart, railing at the revelers, as several fistfights broke out between them and Rudy's cronies.

The priest stopped abruptly at the cart, and though he stood in the mud below, he still towered above Harric. The wind of his personal odor made Harric's head reel.

The priest waved his flock on by, but a stout peasant man among them paused at his side with a jar in his hands that he opened to reveal a watery resin. The man winked at Harric as the priest sank his fingers deep in the jar and began stirring a greasy unguent from the bottom.

The father squinted at Harric's green cowlick. "That slave paint?"

Harric nodded. His eyes flicked to Rudy, who now traded blows with a reveler across the porch rail.

"We only got each other, and no god will help us," the priest said. It was the opening line of a familiar sermon, and a test, Harric judged, of whether he was faithful to the Three Laws.

"No, Father," Harric answered, in the expected response.

"Do you see gods among us?"

"No, Father."

"That's right, you don't. And why? Because they no longer exist, is why. Leastways, hardly anything left of 'em, and what's left is as mad as a drunk cat and don't merit worship. No, they spent themselves in the act o' creation—passed the best part of their divinity into everything you see, including us." He swept his hand in a circular motion, encompassing all quarters of the world. "All that you see is what's become of them."

"Yes, Father," said Harric. "So we must worship ourselves?"

The father peered from under beetled brows, still stirring the resin with his fingers. "That's the way of a breaker, not a maker, you un-sufferable pup." A sly smile played in his eyes. "What we must do is at all times *create*, as they did, and fight the ones who live only to break and enslave."

"I will, Father. I do."

"I believe you."

Without warning, the priest seized Harric by the scruff of the neck. Lifting him into a headlock, he pinned him against the smothercoat. The woolen rugs stank so potently of body stench it seemed to collapse Harric's head around his nose. Yet the fumes from the unguent were worse. When the priest slapped the stuff on Harric's forehead it burned out his nostrils like he'd inhaled a compound of goat piss and whiskey.

Floods of tears welled from Harric's eyes. "Stop!" he choked. "Enough!"

The giant scoured Harric's scalp with fingers like knobs of granite. "Slave paint don't come off easy," he muttered, drubbing Harric's hair in the smothercoat between scourings. "Just lucky we had some resin left."

He released Harric as suddenly as he'd seized him, but kept hold of his collar while he studied his handiwork. Harric staggered and coughed, blinking tears from his eyes. The father frowned and dragged him to the edge of the cart. He scooped up a handful of muck from the road—which largely *was* goat piss and whiskey, or at least whiskey puke—and rubbed it into Harric's hair. When Harric thought he could take no more, the priest grabbed the hair on either side of his head and scrubbed the painted locks up and down against a part of the coat that wasn't yet green from the paint. There was no point in crying out.

"There," said the priest, releasing him and nodding approval. "See it don't happen again."

Harric blinked and gaped, unable to speak.

A portly peasant woman bustled to the priest. "Do you have to rub out every slave mark you see?" she whispered. "We got enough trouble without calling attention—"

"Ho there!" Rudy called, stumping across the cart and grabbing Harric's collar. "That paint was the rightful mark of—"

The priest's fist was as big as Rudy's head, but faster. The two collided with a sound of ham dropped on stone, and the impact spun Rudy over the cart-rail to fall flat on his back in the muck.

"Trouble, Widow Larkin?" said the priest. "What trouble?" He lumbered on, now at the rear of his flock, the matron hurrying beside.

"Be a maker," he said to Harric as he passed.

Harric prepared to leap from the cart and flee, but stopped short when he saw the saffron liveries of Lyla's ex-master waiting on either side of the market. In their hands they held cruel-looking staves. A quick check of the porch confirmed the location of the two others, short staves over shoulders. He was surrounded. Though the lord's saffron blood rank wasn't high enough to legally execute justice on Harric, they did not appear to be above murder.

A couple of Rudy's cronies helped the stableman to his feet, where he swayed as if he would faint. When Rudy could focus his eyes again, he glared at Harric. "You go anywhere, lord-boy, and I'll kill you myself. I swear it. I been deputized, and I got the right." He stared a general challenge to all the watchers, and with the addition of Lyla's master's bodyguards to his posse, no one contradicted him, which puffed him even further.

He shrugged off his helpers and lurched up the stairs to a bench with a view of the cart. From there he directed his cronies to positions in the market north and south, "to make sure the whoreson bastard don't bolt, and that Old One skins him proper."

Harric ran a hand through his hair. It came away pungent and gritty, but free of paint. The priest had been his first stroke of luck all evening since he'd felt the curse leave him after he'd completed the twentieth con. He'd broken a death curse! Surely he could escape Rudy's grasp.

As if in reply to that hope, a noble Sapphire rode in through the south gate with more than a dozen knights in tow, all in full plate armor. The bottom dropped from Harric's belly. Sapphire was a blood rank more than high enough to execute the judgment against him.

"Don't tell me," he muttered. "He's come from court." But this couldn't be the doom. He'd won. The sun had set.

The market's din fell to murmurs at the sight of the noble, for none of so high a blood rank had ever graced Gallows Ferry; nobles as a rule avoided the shore, preferring the comfort of palatial waterwheels on the river. Many on the porch glanced at Harric as if they too saw his executioner in the Sapphire. Rudy chuckled, but dared not hail the nobleman, for the Sapphire's aspect was grim and his shield emblem covered, suggesting some dark and urgent business of his own.

The Sapphire signaled his men, and the knights stationed themselves through the market like shining metal rocks in the dirty river of peasants. The Sapphire alone proceeded through the market, studying the stalls as he passed, until he halted in the middle at Harric's cart. Hard eyes peered at Harric from a fierce, clean-shaven face.

"You will sell no more grain today," he said, in a marked West Isle accent. "Pack in your cart and go." He did not wait to see Harric's response, but turned to address the market in general. "All of you! You're done for the night! This market is closed. Anyone trades, and they pay with his life."

Merchant heads bobbed up and down the line. Those who hadn't started packing in at the rumor of a Phyros-rider now set to pulling their wares.

"Begging pardon, Your Worship," said Rudy to the Sapphire, "but this bastard's marked for your judgment, and I'm bound to tell you he'll run free if you send him out of the market."

Harric jerked free, but didn't dare leave now. "Your Highness, there's been a mistake—"

"I see a hint of paint in his hair," said the Sapphire. "Why is it so faint?"

"Rubbed off, Your Worship. A peasant priest done it. But the whole market seen this bastard lie to a lady, and seen the lord mark him, too."

Harric flushed as the nobleman's gaze fell to his bastard belt. "Your Highness, I—"

A stinging slap spun Harric to his knees. "Bastard, be silent!" the Sapphire hissed. To Rudy he said, "We shall stay the night here. Hold him until I call for him."

"Yes, Worship!"

"Phyros!" someone screamed from the south gate. "*Phyros!*"

The Sapphire cursed and struggled to turn his horse in the narrow market.

Revelers on the porch pointed down the Hanging Road beyond the south gate. "There!" Murmurs of fear rippled through the market as a rider in black came into view through the gate, climbing the road upon a gigantic wine-black destrier.

Like a sudden wave in a sluggish river, emigrants fled away from the south gate, abandoning carts and belongings. A gust of wind must have brought the Phyros's scent along the cliff and into the outpost, for several oxen shied, bashing into people and toppling a grocer's table. A mule jerked free from its master and galloped for the tiny gap behind the Sapphire's stallion, and ended up crashing into the tinker's wagon across from Harric. Pots and tongs and toasting forks flew through the air and scattered in the mud, like caltrops.

"Back!" the Sapphire called to his men. "Back to the wall! Let him pass!"

Harric saw his chance to flee, and stepped forward to spring, but the Sapphire's stallion jinked sideways into his cart, toppling him hard onto the feed sacks, knocking the wind from his lungs. He struggled to his feet, gasping, but by the time he regained his breath, the immortal horse had entered the gate, bearing directly for Harric's cart.

It halted before him, violet eyes glaring, tusklike blood tooth bared.

Harric froze.

A Phyros in Gallows Ferry.

Impossible. Sir Willard and the Blue Order had slain every Phyros during the Cleansing or else driven them back to Phyrosi. The only Phyros left in Arkendia were those of the Blue Order, but this rider was not one of them. His armor was black, not blue.

But there was no mistaking one of the beasts of the Sir Willard ballads. Its scars were thicker and wilder and more violet-black than the ballads sang them. Centering around the eyes, the scars radiated outward in a mask of forking rays along the paths of veins beneath the skin. Thick as fingers, they clutched at nostrils and lips, probed like roots around the throat, and fell upon the chest like a shower of lightning. This was the work of an immortal rider skilled in the mysteries of blood drafts, and yet the scars were so numerous it was difficult to imagine where a new incision might be made.

Harric raised his eyes to the rider, expecting a blue-skinned giant—a youth-eternal, transformed by the Blood of the Phyros in his veins. What he saw instead was a bull-necked man of some three-score years, with a bald head and gigantic salt-pepper mustachios.

The knight was huge—there was no denying that. Plated arms as thick as cordwood. Chest like a steel barrel. His hawkish gray eyes glinted with the quiet confidence of power. But this was no immortal. Though his skin bore the traces of blue that suggested blood painting at one time or another in his life, it was nowhere near the deep violet of the true immortals described in the Willard ballads.

Purpled from the Mad God's veins.

Blue-black blood, and skin the same.

Moreover, his breastplate had been punched to accommodate a substantial belly, and his armored legs seemed so comparatively scrawny they might have belonged to his tailor.

Harric stared as the old knight swabbed his sunburned pate and fished out a fat roll of ragleaf from a saddlebag.

"Think you could find me a spark around here?" said the knight, in a voice hoarse and weary. "Might as well have a quiet smoke while I can."

Hawkers and emigrants who hadn't fled out the gates or crammed the already crowded porch now peered from crannies between stalls or from rooftops of the sturdier booths. Heads massed in windows above, drawn to the sudden silence in the market. The air became eerily still, as all ears strained for the conversation at the cart.

Before Harric could move to fetch the old knight a flame, Caris emerged from the crowd on the porch, a burning spitfire punk in hand. The rider raised a bristled eyebrow at the sight of her, apparently taken aback by her size or unfeminine clothes. Nevertheless, when she halted at his stirrup without fear or flattery, he leaned down to receive the flame.

The creak of his leather harness pierced the stillness. "Much obliged, girl."

The old knight puffed his ragleaf to life, and sighed. He sat back and regarded the Sapphire and his men where they now stood across the market at the south palisade, blocking his retreat to the ferry. It seemed they expected him to continue north on the Hanging Road, as they did not block the north gate. The Sapphire returned the rider's gaze, unmoving.

Since the old man was not an immortal, Harric reasoned, he must have stolen the Phyros. The Sapphire, in turn, probably intended to steal it from him, or why else would his company travel with identities concealed?

Harric felt a surge of admiration for the old knight. What gall he had to steal a Phyros! It was a deed itself worthy of a ballad. *The ballad of the Jack-Knight and the Sapphire.*

The old thief clamped the ragleaf between square, smoke-stained teeth, and dug a purse from his saddle. He grimaced, sending a web of wrinkles from his eyes. "Looks like the market's closed down for me, but I have a great need, at present, for a pair of feed sacks."

From across the market, the Sapphire locked gaze with Harric. The nobleman moved his head just perceptibly to the side, as if to remind Harric of his order. To Harric it seemed not a nobleman, but his mother, who glared imperiously from the blue enameled armor. *A hanging, Mother?* he asked her memory. *Was my sin so great you doomed your only son to hang?*

The old anger burned, and his lip curled involuntarily.

"Where do you want the sacks?" he said, shifting his eyes to the Phyros thief.

"In the saddle packs, son. On the second pony."

Harric slipped off the cart and hefted a sack of oats to his shoulder, nodding to Caris. She shouldered another sack of oats, and he followed her to the pony. As she passed the Phyros, the rider hauled the beast's head to the other side and held it there, snorting and champing its bit, as if it might otherwise lash out in fury. Caris never flinched. She seemed oblivious to her danger, scanning the beast greedily, perhaps with horse-touched senses Harric could only imagine, eyes wide, nostrils flaring to scoop every particle of information from the legendary creature. For someone more attuned to horses than fellow humans, he guessed it was a dream for her to be so near. She'd probably sensed its approach all the way from the stables, and come running.

Once past the Phyros, they approached the two mortal ponies that followed on tethers. The first was a gangly spare mount draped from nose to crupper in a tournament caparison made from the same faded green as the half-cover draping the hindquarters of the Phyros. The last was a stocky pony with saddle packs and a rider who appeared to be hiding under a blanket. A captive? Drugged and bound to the saddle?

Harric quelled an urge to peek under the blanket, and dumped the oat sack in the saddle pack.

This was his time to flee. Rudy and his men were paralyzed. The Sapphire was still at the south end of the market. The deserted north road beckoned, but he couldn't run; curiosity and ambition held him thrall. What if the old knight would help him? How much better to ride out with a Phyros as escort?

Harric clambered back onto his cart and met the old man's gaze. "I helped you. Now I need your help. Take me with you. Just far enough to get me out of Gallows Ferry. I could ride your spare mount till we gain the next valley."

The old man gave a sad smile. "No one rides her, son. She'd throw anyone who tried. But you'll find your way. You don't look like a marked man to me."

"Funny you should say that—" Harric began, but the old knight cut him off with an impatient wave, and the Phyros started walking.

"There's my thanks, son," he said, tossing a purse to Harric. "Go north one day. And when you do, ask for me, Sir Willard."

A drunk on the porch guffawed at the joke. "Sir Willard! The Champion!"

As the old knight rode north from the market and through the north gate, Harric sprang from the cart to sprint after, but Rudy's cronies had snapped back into position and stood ready for him. He slid to a halt and spun to run south for the servant entrance beside the porch, only to see the Sapphire's squire had spurred his horse from the south gate to meet him.

"Pox!" Harric veered for the crowd on the porch stairs, which began to part for him.

"You let him pass, and you'll *all* hang!" Rudy bellowed from above.

The crowd panicked. Hard hands repelled Harric, who whirled to face the squire as he reined in behind. The squire's horse danced sideways amidst the tinker's ironware, blocking Rudy's cronies from the north side, but also blocking the road for the Sapphire, who left the south gate in pursuit of the Phyros.

To Harric's astonishment, the squire seemed interested not in Harric, but in someone on the stairs—Lyla, it seemed, whom Harric had not noticed among the others on the lower stairs.

"Pursue!" the Sapphire commanded his squire, pointing after the Phyros.

The squire showed no more awareness of his master than of Harric. With a wild look in his eye, he planted his lance in the crotch of his armor and beckoned to Lyla, grinning. When she turned to flee up the stairs, he swept the lance in her wake, caught her skirts from behind, and lifted them high.

At that moment the Sapphire drove his horse into the squire's, making a grab for his reins. The squire maneuvered aside, but the jostling of his horse thrust his lance with more force than he'd probably intended. The spear lifted Lyla's skirts past her ears and over her shoulder, pitching her face-first into the stairs, where the spear bit deep in the planks and pinned her. The squire burst into laughter, even as his master swore. Had the Sapphire simply forced his way past his squire through the cluttered bottleneck, he'd have been well on his way to the north gate, but he clearly hadn't anticipated his squire's rebellious behavior.

Just as astonishing was Caris, who leapt from the top of the stairs to land with both boots on the lance, snapping it with a loud report.

The squire blinked in surprise as she slapped the stub aside and seized his reins.

"Was that noble?" she spat. "Was that knightly? You cob! You runt!"

Harric had never seen her speak so many words in public. But even as he marveled at the change, his own spirits buoyed with a sudden sense of gleeful invulnerability. His heart swelled, muting his thinking and compelling him into motion like a leaf on a stream. He turned and marched up the now emptied stairs to Lyla's side, where he wrenched the broken spear from the planking and freed her dress. The moment she gained her feet, she rushed weeping into the lodge.

Caris stared, eyes unfocused, in a horse-touched trance clearly directed at the squire's horse, which began to kick out at the Sapphire's stallion, forcing him to retreat. When the squire reached to draw his sword, Harric leapt to prevent him. He'd been standing at the same height on the stairs as the squire in his saddle, so his leap brought him near enough to grab the hilts of the weapon with one hand. Holding tight, he crashed against the horse and hung against the stirrup, one foot flailing for balance as the other just skimming the mud.

The horse bucked, nearly unhorsing Harric and the squire together, and drawing a string of curses from what Harric assumed was the Sapphire.

The squire beat at Harric's arm and tried to pry his fingers from the hilt.

All but a tiny corner of Harric's mind rejoiced, lifted by an invading glee. Only that tiny corner was his own, and that corner was horrified. It watched helplessly, unable to affect his will. Then the euphoria abandoned him as quickly as it had come, and the spectating corner snapped back to the fore.

He let go of the squire and stumbled backward into the stairs.

The squire looked just as bewildered as Harric felt. The youth stared about, hands trembling, eyes wide. When his sapphire master finally grabbed the squire's reins and hauled him toward the north gate, the squire stammered apologies. With one hand he groped absently for the spear cup, as if he couldn't recall where he'd put his lance; the other felt for the purse no longer hanging at his side.

A stab of panic hit Harric. *Gods leave me...did I lift his purse?*

Harric passed a hand across the cargo slip in his sleeve, and found the familiar weight of a coin purse against his skin. *In front of all those eyes! How could I do that?* His mother's most basic lessons as a child screamed against such a lift. Even if no one saw the act itself, the squire would surely guess who took it, which would be as good as proof to the lord.

Caris uttered a low cry beside him. He turned in time to see her crash to her knees on the stairs and ball up like someone had slammed her in the gut. Her eyes clamped shut, hands pressed to her ears. He'd seen her react this way before, when something brought her abruptly from the world of horses to the world of people, or when the world of people confused or overwhelmed her. His hand went out to comfort her, but then pulled back, as he recalled a similar occasion when she'd rewarded his attentions with a boot to the shin.

The crowd around them muttered and pointed. Rudy emerged at the top of the stairs, poised to fall upon Harric, but the stableman held off when he saw Caris. Horse-touched as she was, she was bigger and stronger than he, and she wore a very large sword at her side. Rudy bit a lip, unwilling to approach even when she was clearly incapacitated. Harric crouched beside her, his eye on Rudy. When she finally lowered her hands and opened her eyes, she stared at Harric without recognition.

"You all right?" he asked, chancing a gentle hand on her shoulder.

She nodded, just perceptibly. Then she climbed ponderously to her feet, pale as plague, and pushed past Rudy to stagger into the lodge.

Rudy grinned like a dog. Harric bolted.

He leapt over the porch rail and fled south down the market for a servant door in the side of the inn. A horseman blocked his path, and Harric skidded to a halt, nearly slipping beneath its hooves. Three others closed behind him, hard eyes and Sapphire liveries surrounding him. He'd been too panicked to notice the nobleman had left his grooms behind.

Harric darted for a gap between them, but a spear butt jammed his cheek, and he spun to his knees in an explosion of pain.

"Why'd you do it, boy?"

"Forget your bastard colors?"

"I was witched!" Harric choked. "It wasn't me!"

The circle of horses widened and stopped. A half-dozen spear points angled in at him.

When three of the grooms dismounted, Rudy stepped forward to take their reins. "I been waiting nineteen year for this bastard to get what he deserves." He crammed a podgy fist into Harric's gut, doubling Harric to his knees. "No fancy words, lord-boy? What a shame."

The grooms hauled Harric to his feet. Harric felt the eyes of friends and acquaintances on the porch as they pushed and dragged him into the stable yard. Once out of view from the porch, the largest groom slammed him against the side of the inn and stripped his purse from his belt. He opened the purse and peered inside. "Gods leave us! Look at the coin he's got!" He showed the others, who gaped. A sly look entered his eye. "I'll wager there's more where that came from."

A second groom flashed teeth that had gone orange at the roots with little jackets of tartar. He swung a fist at Harric's head, delivering a knuckle punch to his temple. White fire shot through Harric's skull. "Where's your room, Bastard? Where do you keep your things?" The groom started a game of jabbing him in the ribs with pointed knuckles, which the others quickly joined, asking, "Where?" with every jab.

"Up there!" Harric said, gesturing to the garret.

"Tie his hands," said the biggest groom, apparently the leader of the three. The third groom bound Harric's wrists behind his back.

Harric knew what they planned. When they got to his room, they'd rob him blind. But in that indignity he also saw a glimmer of hope, for he knew more than one way in and out of the place. If they were going to imprison him somewhere, there could be no better place.

When the third groom tied Harric's hands, the leader knuckled him in the ribs. "Show us."

Harric limped across the yard toward the back entrance to the south wing. His eye felt like it was full of mud. His head throbbed, and his jaw ached when he clamped his teeth. With his tongue he felt a chipped tooth.

Out of habit, his eyes lit upon his mother's solitary grave cairn where it stood at the edge of the cliff above the river. He'd piled it himself, a tower of stones as tall as he could reach. Now it seemed an accusing finger against the dying orange of the sky. Old anger burned beneath his breastbone, giving him new strength in anger. *Don't celebrate, Mother. I haven't joined you yet.*

They entered the lodge and climbed four flights of narrow stairs to his room. Leader opened the door with the key from Harric's purse and went in. The groom with tartared teeth grinned and shoved Harric after. When they were all inside, the third groom closed the door and leaned against it, arms crossed, as the others ransacked the place. They pushed aside dishes in the cabinets, cracking them to pieces on the floor. They dumped drawers, stripped his weather cloak from its peg, tore sketches from the walls.

Harric kept his eyes on the floor, and studiously away from the corner of his mattress, in which his saddle knife hid, and away from the wainscot behind which the secret closet lay. His mind raced for a way to get them to leave him in there, alone, but his head throbbed, and his ribs ached with every breath.

Tartar knocked Harric on his back and wrestled the riding boots from his feet. He flashed Harric his orange grin. "I don't see why the hangman should get this fine pair of striders."

The third groom stepped away from the door to rifle Harric's desk, which the others had somehow ignored. He threw Harric's drawings on the floor. When he found Harric's quill knife, he glanced at the others to be sure no one noticed, and quickly pocketed it. He picked up the bottle of harts-horn spirits, and lifted the stopper to give it a greedy sniff. The ammoniac stench rebuffed him like a kick in the face.

He staggered back. "Moons!" Spontaneous tears blinded him, so he nearly toppled the bottle when he stoppered it and returned it to the desk.

Harts-horn. That's it, Harric thought. He'd find a way to spill it, and the reek of it would drive them from the room. Getting them to lock him in with the tortuous fumes would be comparatively easy.

Harric took a furtive step toward the unguarded door. As he expected, the third groom's head snapped toward him. Third's eyes narrowed as if contemplating a sadistic kick to Harric's crotch. Harric jerked away from the anticipated blow, making sure to stumble toward the desk.

Third resumed his post at the door, while Leader and Tartar dumped their loot on Harric's bed.

"Fair shares," Third said to his mates, who sat on the bed, sorting loot.

Leader nodded. "Only I get first pick, since this was my idea."

"It was *my* idea!" said Tartar. He knuckle-punched Leader in the thigh as if to better remind him. Leader flushed and delivered a counterstroke to Tartar's shoulder of such disproportionate force that Tartar toppled from the bed and cut his hand on a broken dish. "Moons take you!" Tartar shouted. "It was my idea!"

"My idea," said Leader. "You get second choice."

Tartar glared, rubbing his shoulder with his uninjured hand. Apparently he thought better of escalating the battle. He shifted his glare instead to Harric, who was careful not to meet his gaze or indicate he'd even noticed their transaction. Tartar nevertheless rose and knuckled Harric's shoulder so hard Harric bumped his head against the wall beside the desk.

The other grooms laughed, and their tension evaporated.

"Second choice, then," Tartar conceded. "But I keep the boots on top of it all."

"Wouldn't fit us anyhow," said Leader.

They took great joy then in holding up Harric's possessions one at a time, as if at an auction. A new shirt. A pair of ivory dice he'd won from a hunter that summer. Tartar flipped through the set of painted playing cards he'd willed to Wallop. "What you suppose these are worth?" he asked Harric. "Fifty queens? They're beauties!"

Much less, fool. The Jack of Souls is gone. The best of all. The wild card in the deck.

Harric could still picture the dashing figure on the missing card: a half spirit, half carnal rogue, dressed for courtly revels, his masquer's visage lowered enough to reveal the look of wit and mischief in his eye. Harric had pinned the card to the wall when he was young. He fancied the Jack a sort of hero for his trade. Mysterious, wonderful, wild. But his mother had visions about it, and threw the card away. "You are a courtiste, not a ballad knight," she'd hissed.

Leave it to you, Mother, to take the romance from a thing.

"I'll bet it's worth fifty if it's worth two," Tartar said. "I'm glad we made your acquaintance, Master Bastard."

Trumpets sounded and rebounded off the cliffs outside. It sounded like a royal heralding, so Harric doubted he'd heard it correctly. Perhaps another nobleman?

"Prince Jamus," said Third, a hint of fear in his voice.

Leader looked up. He crossed to the east window with Tartar, where they poked their heads out and peered up the road. "Prince Jamus!" Leader hissed. The trumpets sounded again, louder. From the sound of it, Harric gauged they were yet a half-mile up the Hanging Road. Surprised voices echoed between cliff and lodge from the porch below. Someone shouted for the stable master and the hostess.

Third fidgeted. "Think it's wrong we took the bastard's truck for ourselves?"

A shadow of guilt or fear darkened Leader's face as he hurried back to the bed. "Get over here," he snapped at Tartar. "We have to divide it up before they get here. Choose it or lose it."

They set to sharing with quiet efficiency then, each of them hiding their loot in boots or in shirtsleeves.

Harric backed to the desk while they were distracted. His hands were bound at the wrists, but he easily found and unstoppered the bottle of harts-horn and laid it on its side to drain. By the time the stench of it hit the grooms, Harric had sidled away. He waited for the first twitch of nostrils among the grooms, then shouted, "*Stupid cobs! You spilled the harts-horn!*"

The face-collapsing stench hit him then, and he choked in earnest. He staggered to the door, eyes watering, gasping for fresh air. "Get me out of here!" he demanded. "Open the door!"

Third slugged him in the stomach. "Shut up." Then Third's hand went to his nose, and he recoiled, momentarily unable to inhale. "Moons!" he gasped. "Let's get out of here."

"Let me out, you idiots!" Harric said. "Don't leave me here!"

Leader opened the windows, gulping fresh air and peering out at the steep roof on each side, and the yard four stories below. "A right tower prison, this is." He closed the windows with a laugh, picked up his loot from the bed, and ran for the door. "You're staying here, Bastard."

"No—wait—" Harric choked.

Third and Tartar piled out the door, followed closely by Leader. "We'll be on guard at the bottom of the stair," said Leader, in mock servility. "Do ring if you should need us." He slammed the door and tromped down the stairs, laughing, as Harric coughed and cursed. On the landing below he heard them arguing quietly about how best to conceal their theft, and whether squire Keeter should know, and if so, if he would demand a share.

Harric crossed to the bed, choking and blinded by tears. He fumbled the saddle knife from the mattress and, despite the awkwardness of manipulating it behind him, managed to slash his bonds without cutting himself. Staggering to his feet, he threw open the window and gasped in the fresh air. When he'd caught his breath, and the throb of his headache no longer threatened to knock him out cold, he tore the blankets from his bed and smothered the puddle of harts-horn on his desk. That made it much easier to breathe. With a chair from his desk he barred the door. It wouldn't stop a determined foe for long, but it would grant him the warning he needed to flee out the window.

From the east window came the sounds of hubbub and trumpets as the prince's retinue entered the market and stable yard, but Harric did not waste time looking. He went straight for the wainscot and opened the closet to claim his things so he could leave. Hope swelled his heart at the sight of his mother's travel pack, in which he kept his wallet of savings.

He threw the saddle knife in his pack, along with his mother's fur-lined travel cloak and a pair of breeches and shirt he found strewn in the chamber by the hasty grooms. As he stuffed them in the pack, an ornament on a pack string clapped loudly against the siding. Irritated, he grabbed it to pull it off and toss it on a shelf, but stopped as he remembered how it got there.

When he was ten he'd discovered the ornament in a box in the closet—a spindle of white alabaster about the size of his little finger. He fancied it, and attached it to the pack string, but his mother had snatched it away. "That is the most valuable item in the closet!" she cried. In her madness, however, she said that about everything. When she died, he'd reattached it to spite her, and kept it there even though he found it tacky.

As a token of his victory that day, he let it remain.

From the closet floor he picked up his best boots, a little too stiff and new, but better than nothing, and crammed them on his feet.

Tower prison, indeed, he thought, looking out the window at the Bright Mother setting beyond the scablands. The groom who'd said it clearly hadn't grown up climbing river cliffs or lodge gables. It seemed almost too lucky to be true: the road from Gallows Ferry glittered with possibilities.

Moving as quickly as he could, he removed from his sleeve the purse of coins he'd lifted from the squire, poured it onto the mattress, and stuffed the damning purse in a crack in the wall, where it dropped between the laths and was lost.

The mere sight of the coins made his stomach lurch. How could he have pulled the thing in daylight with a hundred eyes upon him? It broke every rule in his first years of training. The fact that he couldn't even recall deciding to do it was what galled him the most. It was as if someone else had controlled him. He had to have been witched.

He divided the coins in three portions on the mattress, then knotted them in socks he found beneath his bed. The greatest portion would go to Lyla for her torn dress and humiliation; the rest he'd split with Caris. *Share spoils handsomely*, his mother had trained him. *Buy allegiance from strangers, and increase love in allies.* To her, everything was political. She'd have him share his take with Lyla to "increase love in an ally," not because it was the decent thing to do. He hated it. In their last months together he'd argued this point on several occasions, and her lecture always ended the same: *never throw away gold upon sentiment.*

It gave him some pleasure, therefore, to give Lyla the largest share of silver, for he'd probably never see her again. If he could manage it during his escape, he'd leave it with Mother Ganner in the kitchen.

As he slipped the socks into his shirt, he found the purse the Phyros-thief had tossed him, and emptied it in his palm: its only content was an odd nut, like an elongated walnut, only larger. He smiled wryly. Cheap old fart. But the nut held his attention, for he'd never seen its sort before. It was brown and wrinkly, vaguely phallic.

Taken by a sudden inspiration, he crept to his desk and found a near-empty inkwell the grooms had left as worthless. He wet a quill in it and scratched a message to Caris on the nut.

My heart.

- Harric

He blotted it dry, and slipped it into his sleeve with the rest. She always told him his heart was in his pants. With luck, she'd get the joke.

The sounds of a scuffle broke out among the grooms below. One shouted. A tremendous crash followed, suggesting Leader had laid one of his disproportionate wallops on Tartar. Silence followed. Then someone stumped heavily up the stairs. Tartar, Harric guessed: aching from his beating and coming to take out his frustrations on Harric again. His head and jaw throbbed anew with the memory.

"Not this time, thank you," Harric muttered.

He crossed swiftly to the west window above the stable yard, and hoisted a leg over the sill, just as he had that morning to escape the fog. This time, he wouldn't halt on the peak of the gable to await his doom; he would scramble across the spine of the main wing to Lyla's room in the female servant dormers. From there it was but a short hop down the service stairs to the stable yard, and thence to freedom.

As he swung his legs over the sill and onto the lowest rung of the roof ladder, he heard a light rap and a whisper at his door.

"Harric? It's Caris. If you want to live, get over here and let me in. And hurry. There's no time."

Arkendian Fool's Nexus is a soft, pearl-silver metal found in great abundance on the island of Arkendia. Its distinctive aura of magic is detectable by magi of all three moons, yet efforts to reveal its nature are fruitless. It is therefore much celebrated among Arkendians, who mockingly call it "witch-silver," and regard it as a symbol of the weakness of magic.

— From field notes recovered from the Iberg Bright Mother Library in Samis

8

Father Kogan's Outdoor Stage Play

Father Kogan jogged to the head of his caravan as it approached the first trestle on the road. The bridge was a colossal timber affair, spanning eighty or ninety paces over a deep-cleft gorge.

"That's the one," he said, calling the wagons to a halt. "Gather up and listen."

The Widow Larkin pushed to the fore. "Tell me you didn't bargain with that Phyros-rider, Kogan," she said, as if speaking for them all. "Tell me you didn't pledge us in some scheme." His flock clung near, frightened eyes searching his face. Many frowned and avoided his gaze, as they always did when unhappy with his decisions.

"We isn't pledged to mix with no Phyros-lord," a drover ventured. "I won't do it."

"We ain't obliged," another agreed.

Nods and murmurs passed through the flock until the priest stumped the haft of his ax on the road.

"So *that's* how it is," Kogan said. "*Ain't obliged.* Who was it freed you and brought you here? Who was it won you 'cross the river when you was like to be starved out and sold back to lords?" He glared at the drover till the man dropped his eyes, and raked the others with his gaze. "Everything you got you owes to me. And everything *I* got I owes that Phyros-rider, 'cause if it weren't for him I'd be dead and hung this six months gone."

Exclamations of surprise at this new intelligence.

Kogan spat. *"Ain't obliged."* His nose wrinkled above the matted beard. "Time you thought as free men, and stop skulking for handouts. Freedom don't come easy, and it never stays without you have to fight for it."

The Widow Larkin wrung her hands. "They don't mean nothing by it, Father. They're scared, is all. They don't know no fighting."

"Ain't asking you to fight," said Kogan. "I'm asking you to listen and do as I say." He studied their faces in silence for several heartbeats, and found contrition and grudging resolve where there had been opposition. He nodded. "Listen then, and I'll tell you what we'll do. We'll keep our teams still whiles he rides past. Then we'll make like the oxen panicked, and block this bridge with flipped wagons and such, so then that follow can't get past."

Kogan put the drovers in charge, and took ideas from the others. When they set to work, he was gratified to see some who had been loudest in opposition were now most vigorous in support. First, they parked the train of wagons as close as possible against the cliff wall, providing the Phyros-rider a clear channel along the edge of the road. Others emptied wagons on the side of the span, and prepared to flip them there. Boys tickled their noses with spear grass and dribbled the blood on their foreheads to feign injury in the wreck.

When shouts went up that the Phyros-rider approached, they were ready. Mothers held children close. Drovers hurried blankets over the oxen's heads and fed them handfuls of grain to munch in darkness.

The Phyros galloped past in a clatter of hooves and rattle of harness, dragging two miserable-looking ponies behind, and thundered across the trestle.

Uproar—not all of it staged—erupted behind it. An ox nearest the trestle shook free of its drover and plummeted blindly over the edge with its wagon. A pair of mules dashed their cart against the cliff side and broke a wheel. But the priest's flock stayed calm enough to think. The long line of wagons and carts moved out from the cliff face and jammed awkwardly against each other, blocking the path to the bridge for more than a hundred paces. They flipped a wagon at the rear of the jam, to make an obstacle against the knights if they should think to attack or push the peasants off the ledge. Kogan stationed a dozen men with bow staves in hand, unstrung, but visible, enough to discourage such a ploy. On the trestle itself they flipped no less than four wagons, and piled the place with bodies and beasts and baggage in convincing disarray so there was no hope of the flock moving forward.

When the Sapphire's company appeared around a bend, they pulled up at the flipped wagon and blasted their trumpets for passage, but there was nothing to be done. The peasants made a good show of hurrying to restore order, but by jamming so tightly together they'd guaranteed a struggle to clear even a narrow path along the edge for the knights to pass in single file; every ox and mule had to be unhitched and turned or backed along the ledge, and often this resulted in even more tangling of traces and confusion. By the time they managed a path to the trestle and cleared a space across the span, full darkness had fallen, and the Phyros had long disappeared.

The Sapphire sent a party to give a cursory pursuit, but turned the bulk of his party back. In the torchlight Father Kogan glimpsed lips pressed tight with fury inside the sapphire blue helm.

"There is a bastard in Gallows Ferry who shall suffer for this delay," said the Sapphire to his men. "When I am done with him, you may hang what is left."

Though the Bright Mother shower her healing light on the world,
and the Mad Moon send tides of war and fire,
who knows what the Black Moon brings?
Ill luck and fear, I say, and doom to those who view it.

—From "Sermons of Hardan, First Priest of Arkus"

9

Of Hexes & Wedding Rings

Willard rode at an uncomfortable trot so the other horses could keep up at a canter. Molly had never had a smooth trot. Sir Beldan once described it as a runaway cart full of boulders on a badly cobbled hill. Of course, it had never mattered when he was immortal. Then, she could have trotted *over* him, and it wouldn't have much changed his mood. But as a mortal man, it threatened to shake his teeth from their roots and his eyeballs from his skull. Worst of all was the misery it made of his back, where each jolting stride felt like the blow of a fish-bat in the hands of a mischievous imp: *Clop! Clop! Clop! Clop! Clop!*

At least it kept him awake. If he fell asleep now he'd topple from his saddle and fall through twenty fathoms of air before he hit the river.

He looked back to be sure Brolli was still in Idgit's saddle. Happily, she had a smooth, rolling canter, and Brolli had learned to stay seated for it. He was hopeless at a trot, for his legs were simply too short to embrace the animal's sides.

"Glorious!" Brolli called, seeing the knight turn. He gestured with a long arm across to the glittering ribbon of the Bright Mother's moonlight on the river below. His huge night-owl eyes were wide with excitement. "And this road! Cut through the mountains that separate our people for so long."

"Blasted, actually. Our toolers cleared the river in the same way. Used to be logjams as big as islands and older than I am. Now open and clear for waterwheel traffic."

"Magnificent! Your toolers have their own kind of magic, I think."

"Not magic at all. That's the point of toolery. And just wait till you see the cliffs of the Giant's Gorge. That road will make this seem a garden path."

Already they'd come a mile past Gallows Ferry across the sheer cliff face, the river on one side, a mile-high wall of soaring granite on the other, the wild wind in their faces as if they were hawks gliding above the moonlit waters.

Far behind them Willard could see a long stretch of the road, and still no sign of pursuit. Kogan's ruse had worked beautifully. Ahead he could see an eastward bend in the cliff marking the place where a tributary river valley joined the Arkend from the east. As they rounded the bend they gained an expansive view of the eastward valley, dark with forest into which the Hanging Road dipped and disappeared. The road crossed the valley, beneath the trees, to the opposite side, where the cliffs of the Arkend rose again, even higher, and the road rose above the trees once again, etched into the cliff face and continuing north.

The Bright Mother illumined the confluence of the rivers. Willard reined Molly in and strained his eyes upon the water, searching for a waterwheel ship at anchor.

Brolli halted behind him.

"I can't see any ships, Brolli."

Brolli surveyed the new vista. "There are none. I am sorry. That would have been best for your rest." Willard grunted. "But we can hide in there," Brolli said, pointing to the forested valley to the east. "I will find a place."

"Moons, I'm tired of camping and roads."

"Try to think of it as an adventure."

Willard waited for the quip about it being a Sir Willard ballad, but it didn't come. It seemed the ambassador was learning. "We have no maps of this area, Brolli. I doubt if any exist except for the surveys the toolers made originally. We have no idea where to go in that valley."

"We have no choice."

"True enough."

"A strange expression, *True enough*. Do your people see truth as something that can be mixed with untruth, as the teller sees fit?"

Willard waved him off. "I'm too tired for philosophy, Ambassador."

"For a later time, then." Brolli urged Idgit to walk up beside Willard on the cliff side of the road. He extended a hand up to Willard, his thick canines flashing in a grin. "Now that I am awake, it is time for me to take over the lead, and time for you to give up the wedding ring for safe keeping."

Willard grunted. "And good riddance to them." He slipped his hand into the saddle purse on the front cantle, found the purse by touch, and drew it forth. He tossed it to Brolli. "So much trouble over so small a trinket."

Brolli threw the purse back. "This is not my ring, old man."

Willard frowned. He slipped a finger in the purse and found two coins. A stab of cold fear pierced his middle. This was the coin purse he'd meant to give the bastard in Gallows Ferry. He searched the saddle again, this time pushing his whole hand in the pocket, but a moan of despair filled his chest even as he did it, for there were only ever two purses, and one of them he'd given to the bastard.

"What is wrong?" Brolli's voice was sharp. "Sir Willard. What is wrong?"

Willard bowed his head. If he weren't so weary he'd weep. "I told you we would rue it if my curse struck me. Well, it did. In the market, in Gallows Ferry."

"I don't understand. What happened?"

Willard turned to Brolli, his heart full of lead, all hope of rest and quiet flown. "I'll tell you what happened: I gave your cursed magic ring to the bastard."

10

Fingers Over Fist

Harric froze, his legs still straddling the windowsill. He looked back to the door, beyond which he'd heard the voice. "Caris?"

"*Hurry*, Harric. I mean it.

He swung his legs back in and crept to the door. "Are you alone?"

"Yes! Open up."

Harric moved the chair and lifted the latch, but cried out in alarm when he saw the glint of armor beyond, and tried to close it again. Caris cursed, and slammed it inward, staggering him back. Only then did he realize it was she who wore the steel.

"It's me. Calm down."

She shouldered past him in an enameled blue breastplate and matching shin and knee cops on full quilting. The blood color alone would cow any groom to silence or obedience, but a glance down the stairs confirmed she hadn't relied on that. In the dim candlelight from his room he glimpsed all three grooms lying crosswise on the landing. She'd knocked them senseless. He blinked in silence, stunned by her quick justice.

"Wow, Caris."

She shifted impatiently. "They stole your things."

"Hey, I'm not complaining. Don't get me wrong. It makes my escape a lot simpler."

From her shoulder she dumped a heavy bundle of oiled canvas on the rug.

Her hand went to her nose. "Gods leave me. What's that smell?"

"Harts-horn. I needed the room to myself."

"Hart's what?"

"Ammonia," he translated, though she gave no sign of recognizing that name either.

Harric slipped down the stairs to retrieve his purse from Leader, and his boots from Tartar. Leader groaned. The side of his head was swollen and blue.

"Caris," Harric hissed up the stairs. She appeared in the doorway above. "Help me move these guys."

"I need your help arming. Come back up here."

"Arming will take a while. They could wake and raise an alarm while I dress you."

She exhaled loudly through her nose, then stumped down the stairs. With Tartar and Leader suspended by the collar in each fist, she dragged them up the stairs like they were mere woolsacks. Harric struggled up with Third (who, fortunately, was the smallest), and they stashed all three in the narrow storage room off his apartment.

When he'd pegged the storage door shut, she handed him a piece of shoulder armor. "You know how to do this, right?"

He nodded. "Part of my mother's training."

"Then start buckling, squire."

Harric smiled, and buckled according to what he remembered from when his mother bedded a knight for a season in exchange for his training in the deployment of arms.

Caris reflected none of his humor. "There's a Royal in the lodge. A *Westie Royal*, Harric, so he's sure to practice the Old Ways against bastards. He's with the Sapphire. You need to get out of here."

"I'm going. I'm not crazy."

She brushed his hands away from the shoulder piece. "Good enough. I can do the rest of that one." From the canvas she unearthed a pair of clamshell thigh pieces: more steel enameled in cobalt blue. "Start these. Then the skirt."

Harric buckled, admiring the craftsmanship. "I'd guessed you were of gentle blood, like I am. A noble, maybe, but I had no idea you were a Sapphire."

"It's Cobalt."

"Either way, that's high nobility."

"You have blood rank on the brain."

"All bastards do." But it was more than that. She was a noble *runaway*. A staggering secret, really. And no wonder she'd fled her home. A nobleman wanted a daughter for marriage alliances and as few embarrassments as possible, not some giant-sized genius horse handler. Her father might be searching for her just so he could bring her home again and hide her.

"Stop gawking, Harric, and buckle me. If they find me with everything dangling I won't be able to move."

He kept his fingers buckling, but his mind spun with the revelation of her blood. If it weren't for the Royal in the outpost, who outranked her, she could practically walk them both out of the place unmolested. Reflexively he ticked through the Cobalt houses he'd memorized in his youth.

House Ratingale, of western shores,
House Conaddos of highland moors,
House Tilling in its southern post,
House Moss Isle, the northernmost…

Moss Isle, he guessed, by her accent. She hadn't enough drawl to be of the others, which were farther south.

"I don't know what happened to me today," Caris muttered, as she worked a stubborn hasp. "The squire, I mean. I felt…" She scowled, unable to find the words. "That wasn't me."

"Like you were drugged. I know. Me too. The Sapphire's squire seemed just as confused."

Her eyes lit with this confirmation. "We were witched. We had to be. There was an Iberg with the Sapphire in the yard. Did you see him?"

"No."

"He was all dressed in blue, and riding with the Sapphire, so he must be under the Sapphire's protection. It had to be him. He must have witched us."

"If the witch is with the Sapphire, he wouldn't witch the Sapphire's squire."

Her brow pursed with worry. "Oh, right."

Harric draped the armor's skirt around her waist from behind and held it as she fastened it to the quilting in front. The closeness thrilled him. For all her size and uncanny strength she was still very much a woman, her face and figure neither unattractive nor unfeminine. Not for the first time he wondered what it would be like to taste that shy mouth and feel those generous curves against his skin. He wondered too if he could love her with more than just his flesh. Or if his mother had destroyed that part of him in his conditioning.

Caris had turned to watch him, brows bent and serious.

He smiled. "Just admiring how good you look in blue. I'd bed you right now, but we'd have to unbuckle everything."

She frowned and looked away. "Don't joke about that, Harric. I'm…horse-touched." Her eyes flickered as if in an attempt to meet his eyes, but failed and remained steadfastly on the floor. She scowled, gaze distant and inward. "Never mind. Help me pull this up," she said, struggling with the bolster beneath the skirting.

"You're afraid you can't love," he said, trying to make it sound simple and matter-of-fact, to put her at ease. "I've heard that about horse-touched." As he said it he realized it was partly this that made her attractive to him; that there was safety in her emotional detachment. "I like that, Caris. It's pretty much the same with me. I mean, my mother tried to burn the heart right out of me. We'd be a perfect pair."

She threw down a cloth, her face darkening. "That's not funny, Harric."

"I'm not joking."

"And I'm not afraid of anything like that."

"I'm just saying—"

"Just shut up!"

She raised her hands to her ears and clenched her eyes as if to shut him out. It didn't look to him like she was going to fall to the floor in one of her fits, but he stepped back to show he was done, hands raised in surrender.

"Sorry, Caris. Look, I misunderstood. Anyway, forget that. How about you and I leave this place together," he said, trying to change the subject. "I'm heading south, of course, since the Sapphire's going north."

Her hands unclenched. She lifted her gaze with what seemed like great effort. "I'm going north. I'm following that Phyros-rider."

Harric blinked in surprise. "That old fraud? Caris, you noticed the Phyros, but not the rider. His skin isn't blue. He's old as dirt. He stole that Phyros."

"I don't care. In the last month I've asked three knights to mentor me. One laughed. The others attacked me. I have a feeling about this one."

She set her jaw and narrowed her eyes. She didn't meet his gaze, but this was a look he'd seen before when there was no talking her out of something.

A scream drifted through the window on the market side, followed by shouts from the revelers below, and an eerie silence. Harric crossed to the window with Caris at his elbow, and stared in shock at what he saw below. A gigantic knight in wine-black armor entered the market lane through the south gate on a scar-torn Phyros. In the white light of the porch lamps, the rider's extraordinary size was cast into stark relief. Blue skin shone from behind his open visor.

"A Crown of Horns," Harric said, pointing in horror at the ring of spines atop the helm. "Gods leave us, the Old Ones are returning." In a flash he understood this Old One hunted the Phyros-thief who had passed through the market that evening, and why the Sapphire hadn't attacked the old man then; the Sapphire only tracked him until the Old One caught up.

The rider halted his Phyros below the steps of the porch and raised a curled black horn to his lips, blasting a note that rebounded between cliff and inn like the thunder of a rockfall.

A woman at the foot of the stair screamed, and the immortal horse lunged as if taunted. Its massive head struck forward as nimble as a snake's and slashed sideways at her pale throat. Blood showered the stair, and the woman sprawled at its feet.

"Bow before the Phyros!" the Old One roared.

Knees hit planking. Eyes averted, as described in the ballads. Though four floors above, Harric felt his knees grow weak at the boom of the command.

A lord in emerald robes hurried from the lodge with a dozen purple-liveried servants, who kneeled. The emerald lord bowed at the waist. A stiff smile thinned his lips as he placed a fist to his chest in greeting. "Sir Bannus. Your chambers await."

The immortal surveyed the lord and the prostrate people around him. The circlet of horns rotated with the motion, then tilted upward to the faces peering out of the upper windows.

Harric glimpsed cruel eyes and scars like a nest of adders inside the helm, then ducked away, heart pounding in his throat.

Caris turned and stalked from the window to her pile of gear, her face intent as her hands moved quickly through her canvas bag. Harric followed, dazed with horror of what he'd just witnessed, and what it meant for Arkendia. Old Ones had returned. Did the Queen know it? Had Willard and the Blue Order been alerted?

Caris belted on a heavy longsword and donned an open-faced helmet, then started stuffing oilcloths in the canvas.

"Caris. What are you doing?"

She said nothing. She stood, slung the canvas on her shoulder.

"Caris, you have no delusions about…confronting an Old One, do you?"

She met his gaze, face pale and drawn. "I'm not an idiot, Harric."

"I didn't think so."

"I'm getting out of here. And you should, too."

He nodded. "Yeah," he said, adjusting his pack. "So, I guess this is goodbye, then." A pang of regret surprised him, distorted and amplified by the fear still buzzing through his body. "Here…" He produced the bundle of silver he'd prepared for her. "A token to remember me by."

He tossed it, and she caught the bundle in one hand. "What is it?"

"It's your share of the squire's purse. It wouldn't be right for me to keep it all."

Caris froze. Her jaw nearly clanged against her cuirass. "You *stole* this?"

"I didn't mean to," he explained. "I was witched, same as you."

She tossed the sock back as if it were an infectious rag. "You stole that! You're a common jack!"

"Jacks don't share this way. Nor do they serve justice, or the Queen. I'm sharing it out because it wouldn't be right for me to keep it. Sort of a code of honor."

Her eyes flashed. "Honor? You're a jack and a liar. You're trying to tell me there's honor among jacks?"

Harric sighed. "Look, I don't want to part this way. But I wanted to tell you the rest of the truth about me while I can. I know you aspire to be a Queen's Knight, and you follow their code of honor. But try to look at it this way. In card games, the jack is wild—outside the rules—so he's one of the most powerful cards in the deck. He can make a royal hand unbeatable. Like the secret sisterhood of courtistes help her." He hadn't said it outright, but he'd come as close to naming his art as he could.

"More lies." She seethed, fists balled at her sides. "You lied to me, Harric. You said your father was a knight. That your mother trained you to serve in court."

"She did, Caris, but by—"

"Conning lords? Like that lord in the carriage? They say that's what you were doing today. Is that true? Is that what you've been doing all this time I've known you? How dare you say that's serving the Queen."

Harric's heart fell. He had no words she would understand. He stepped forward, instead, and pressed the Phyros-thief's nut in her resisting hand. "The Phyros-rider gave this to me. If you won't take the silver, take this. It'll bring you luck."

After a heartbeat, she balled her fist around it. "This better not be one of your tricks."

"No trick," he said, hoping she wouldn't regard the joke he'd penned as a "trick."

She turned to the door just as hurried footfalls sounded on the stairs.

"Prepare, Bastard!" Rudy cried, his voice strained with excitement and magnified in the narrow stairwell. "Your judgment is upon you!"

Harric crossed to the west window and slung a leg over the sill. "Caris," he whispered, motioning her to follow. "This way."

Caris tied her cloak behind her. "This knight doesn't flee out windows, Harric."

"Oh. Well, this one does."

The door thumped, jumping the latch in its slot. "Open up, lord-boy, or we'll break it down!"

"Leave, Harric." She did not look his direction. "I cannot be seen with a lying jack."

The words stung, but they also struck fire in his heart. "If I live long enough, Caris, I'm going find a way to serve the Queen. I owe her everything, and it's what I was trained for, and I'll do it as well as any knight," he said, slinging his legs out the window. "Better. I'll prove it."

As soon as Harric left, Caris unlatched the door. Rudy and two grooms stumbled in like clowns. She hurled an armored fist into Rudy's vapid mouth, sending him backward over a groom into the stairwell, where he hit the wall so hard he broke three boards and fell partway into the resulting hole.

The grooms gaped, speechless. As she polished the knuckles of her gauntlet for another blow, they broke into stammered apology, retreating.

"Your Eminence! So sorry."

"This knave here told us a—

"—very sorry—"

"—a bastard jack—"

"—you know our master, Lord Ellentane?"

The four bowed and scraped and backed from the room, stepping on each other and on Rudy's unconscious body, nearly tumbling down the stairs in their haste.

When the sounds of their muttered oaths faded, Caris opened the purse and examined the nut Harric gave her. Her nose creased. It was wrinkly and brown, vaguely obscene, with ink scratchings:

My heart.
- *Harric*

She sensed he meant it to be funny. A reference to the size and hardness of his heart? She turned to toss it out the window after him, but it opened and nearly spilled its contents.

It wasn't a nut, after all. It was a very clever container. A tiny hinge held the two halves of the nutshell together on a spring, revealing three delicately crafted circlets of witch-silver inside. Each circlet was about the size of a lady's finger ring, but looped with the others like a three-link segment of chain. The metal wasn't precious, but the craftsmanship was very fine.

Any meaning it would have had from Harric was sullied by his dishonesty. Even thinking of it made her angry, and sad. He'd been the only man beside her brother who didn't think her simple and wasn't put off by her hugeness. Ultimately, however, the circlets of the ring hadn't come from Harric, but the Phyros-rider, and as such they were a symbol of hope, not betrayal.

She studied them in the palm of her glove, where they fell naturally into a common center, as if a single ring. Tugging her glove off with her teeth, she slipped the rings on her smallest finger. Warmth and regret filled her, and she realized she would miss Harric in spite of herself. The realization surprised her, but, unaccountably, it pleased her as well. It also seemed not only possible but probable she would find the Phyros-rider and, against all odds, find a mentor in him.

As she replaced the gauntlet over the trinket, her mind turned toward the stables and escape. Her rank would protect her, if it came to a confrontation, but the Sapphire would almost surely know her father, and she did not want word of her whereabouts to reach her family. If she could saddle her horse unmolested, she was as good as free. With any luck, her armor would in fact be an effective disguise; she did not want trouble or bloodshed to complicate things further.

As she made for the stairwell, her wrist brushed an unfamiliar lump on her belt. Her brow furrowed as she uncovered a sock of coins tucked carefully behind a buckle. After a moment's puzzlement, she recognized it, and muttered a curse that included Harric's name.

It was her share of the squire's coin.

Yet even as Krato knew victory, the mortal horse Imblis stumbled, gravely wounded.
Krato's power was not in healing, nor could he persuade the goddess Selese to aid him.
So the Lord of Dominion opened his veins and joined them with the mare's.
Thus by his Blood was she made immortal and cruel like her master,
and he renamed her Malhourig, mother of the immortal herds.

— From Lore of Ancient Arkendia, by Sir Benfist of Sudlin

11

Of Gods and Monsters

Harric stepped out of the servant stairwell into the darkness of the stable yard. He closed the door silently behind him and leaned against the rough stonework of the inn to let his eyes adjust to the darkness. Above, the stars sparked cold and distant in their high stations. The two light-giving moons straddled the sky, each of them just beyond sight: the Bright Mother had set, and the red eye of the Mad Moon had not yet cleared the high bulwark of the Godswall. Between the setting of the one and the rising of the other was a span of darkness long enough to fit a meal and a song, or a careful escape. *Jacks' Hour:* the time of action for thieves and rogues.

Harric took it as a good omen.

He searched for the Unseen Moon, which had no predictable path through the sky. He found it directly overhead, blotting three stars in the Wanderer. This too he took as a good omen—for what was he now if not a wanderer?—and though his jaw and ribs ached from his recent beatings, a quiet joy lifted him.

When he could see the outline of the stables across the yard, he stood and crept along the base of the inn, where shadows deepened, toward the head of the yard. His first stop would be the kitchens. He'd fill his pack, bid Mother Ganner farewell, and find one of the boys to bring out his horse.

As he crept past an inset guest door, he halted, alerted by the sound of heavy footfalls within, and retreated. The door flung outward, away from

Harric, spraying lamplight across the yard. A giant figure stepped out. Harric glimpsed naked blue flesh swarming with muscles and ropelike scars, and then the door slammed behind and submerged all in darkness.

An immortal. It had to be Sir Bannus. Harric froze against the inn, willing himself invisible.

Sir Bannus grunted somewhere in the darkness before Harric. Waves of heat emanated from him, bringing with them odors of salt and iron. Then came the rustle and stink of urine in the dust, and a throaty sigh from the immortal.

Gods leave me, he's pissing. He's only pissing.

In a bar of indirect candlelight from an upper window, Harric could just make out the giant figure looming before him, an arm's length away. He struggled to silence his panicked breathing, but it felt as if his lungs had shrunk to the size of peach pits, while his heart leapt up in his throat. He dared not move even his eyes, lest they flash and betray him to the immortal.

A tiny sound drew his attention to the giant's side. A small figure with her wrist in Bannus's fist. She sagged in his grip, and with her free arm she hugged her torn dress to herself.

Lyla! A wave of grief and horror hit Harric. Then Bannus hauled her away, striding back through the door.

Before Harric could think, he followed into the lamp-lit hallway. The door slammed behind him as he crouched inside the threshold and watched Sir Bannus reel away. Harric saw now that the immortal was indeed gloriously nude, his gargantuan body a map of scars and impossible clefts of muscle. Bannus filled the hall, set it vibrating with his presence, half humming, half growling something that might be a song. When he stopped before a door at the end of the hall, he lifted Lyla by her hand and dangled her before his mouth to kiss her naked arm. Lyla saw Harric over Bannus's shoulder. Tears streamed down her face. She shook her head vigorously, as if to warn Harric away.

Then Bannus dropped her down to her feet, pushed open the door, and twirled her through as if she were a dancer at a ball. She made no resistance, no sound whatsoever, but the despair in her eyes smote Harric deeply.

When the door slammed behind them, Harric sped to it. He heard muffled sounds from beyond. A whimper. A rumble, as the giant spoke.

Gods leave me, I have to help her!

He laid a hand on the door latch, arguing with himself. Help her *how?* The sad fact of the matter was that there was nothing anyone could do. He should leave while he still could. Anything else would be suicide. *Maybe*

I could distract him, divert him long enough for her to escape. It might be possible. But even if she made it away, Harric probably wouldn't. Bannus would have his head off in a second.

Grief tore a widening gulf in Harric. *I have to do something!*

Before he could lean his weight on the latch, a gloved hand snared his wrist from behind and twisted his arm painfully up between his shoulder blades. Someone had been standing in the shadows around the corner of the corridor, and Harric had been so preoccupied he hadn't even glanced that direction. Harric stifled a cry of pain as his assailant body-pressed him against Sir Bannus's door.

"His Holiness wants no visitors," a rasping voice said at his ear. "Especially no snooping bastards." Something was muffled about the voice, but Harric could not see his captor, even when he turned his head.

"I bring a message for His Holiness," Harric said. "His Majesty, the Sapphire, bids Sir Bannus join him in his chambers. I am to take you both."

A wet, snorting laugh, strangely muffled, as if in a helm. "His Majesty would not send a bastard, unless to his death. Perhaps that was precisely what he had in mind?"

"His Majesty sent me. I am his messenger."

"You are his *offering*." His captor reached another gloved hand around and removed a lamp from its hook beside the door, and illumined Harric's features with it.

Harric's guts froze as the red-stone mask of Bannus's shield bearer appeared at his shoulder. *A Faceless One!* The mask's features were calm and tranquil, but the eyes studying Harric through the graven eyeholes were red and tortured.

His mother had told him of the Faceless Ones. Zealous squires, flayed and kept alive with the blood of the Phyros. But unlike their masters, who drank the Blood, the flayed bodies of the Faceless Ones were only allowed to bathe in it, which healed them incompletely, leaving burning scars. These they endured for years until allowed to take new skin.

"A fair covering," the man whispered, more to the face, it seemed, than to Harric, who wore it. The man's breathing came in clipped little gasps near Harric's ear. A sweetly foul odor issued from behind the mask, causing Harric to gag. "Yes, fair. It matters not that you are a bastard." The lamp rose, and the bloody gaze followed to Harric's hair. "And the hair is fine."

Beyond the door, more whimpering and rumbling. Panic strove with helplessness in Harric. He rose on his toes to gain some advantage in freeing his arm, but the man rose with him and twisted it even worse. He pressed

Harric into the door, and returned the lamp to its hook. With the free hand he probed Harric's skull. He spraddled the thumb and forefinger from the nape of the neck to his crown, and again from ear to ear, as if measuring. The gloved thumb snuffed the lamp. In the darkness the man seemed somehow closer, tighter against him.

"This might do," he breathed in Harric's ear. "I must confirm it with my tools."

He took Harric's free hand in his and guided it to the latch. "I could live with this face, this hair." His voice was strangely faint, remote behind the mask. "I could wear this skin, and you, fair one, could have mine. If the god will have it."

Something warm dripped on Harric's neck, and he struggled to turn away, but the Faceless One twisted his arm, stealing all resistance.

"Stop... wait... please..." Harric said.

With his hand on Harric's, the Faceless One squeezed the latch until it popped and the door sighed inward.

Bannus's chambers were dim and humid, the air heavy with earthy odors. In a far corner, a single candle burned low, as if choked by the close air. Its flame was barely enough to illumine the space, but Harric caught suggestions of wrecked beds and bunks piled against walls. The mattresses and bedding appeared to be mounded in the midst, and it was there Harric expected the immortal already lay.

The Faceless One kicked Harric's knees from behind, forcing him to kneel, then dropped to his knees beside him. "Master," he said, his little gasps near Harric's ear. "I captured a bastard spy." His voice had become supplicant, eager. He didn't whine, but his voice nearly cracked with restrained excitement.

Sir Bannus grunted. The sound was not from the mattresses, but from nearer in the darkness before him. Harric looked up from the bedding to see a dim outline of the giant standing with his back to them, perhaps two paces away. Harric averted his eyes, heart pounding in his ears. He found no sign of Lyla.

"Did I not say to leave us?" Bannus growled. "I care not. Take him. Test him. If he is a match, keep him, or parts of him."

"Oh, Harric!" Lyla cried, from somewhere beyond the giant. Harric's heart caved.

Bannus grunted. "What's this? My little chickie has a nest mate? Was this a rescue?" Laughter boomed in the chamber, loud and harsh as gravel in an iron bucket. "When you are finished with him, Titus, bring him back for her to see." The floorboards groaned as the immortal turned to face them. Harric kept his eyes down, but felt the immortal's gaze like a scouring flame upon his cheeks.

The Faceless One hauled Harric to his feet, and backed him toward the door. "Your Holiness is great and generous."

"Wait." Bannus's voice lowered to a menacing growl. "What is that behind his shoulder?"

The gasping at Harric's ear hitched. "He wears a pack."

"No. Do you not see it? To my eyes it blazes like a signal fire."

Bannus reached for him, and Harric cringed away, but the Faceless One held him steady. He felt a tug and heard a rip as Bannus jerked something from his pack. The immortal's heavy breathing ceased for a moment as he studied something in his hand. Bannus thrust the massive hand before Harric's face, thick fingers flattened to display the white alabaster ornament at the end of one of the strings of his mother's pack. The spindle of stone seemed a bead in the giant's hand.

"What is it, Master?"

"What do you see?"

"I see a white stone bauble."

"It is a blood seed."

An intake of breath behind the mask. "Is it intact?"

Sir Bannus made a sound like the snort of a bull. He closed his fist around the bauble. With his other hand he gathered Harric's shirt and collar and the straps of his pack in a constricting fist, and lifted him into the air.

Harric dared not meet the immortal's gaze. His breath came in tiny gasps as his ribcage contracted in that vise.

"Bastard," said Bannus, "do you know the abomination you carry? The god's blood mocked and stolen?"

Harric knew of blood seeds. He'd never seen one, and his mother never revealed the nature of the ornament on her pack, but he knew now it was not a solid bauble at all, but a vial, cleverly disguised to keep a dram of blood from one of the Phyros slain in the Cleansing. Blood seeds were potent. They had been a kind of relic, or souvenir taken by the victors from the vanquished Phyros, but to an Old One—to the immortals so bitterly destroyed—they were an unholy abomination.

"I didn't know!" Harric gasped, prying in vain at the biting straps of his pack. "My mother's—"

Mother's.

Her laughter echoed in his brain as his lungs squeezed shut, and spots swam before his eyes. She'd won. Even after the sunset. She'd known it all along.

The Faceless One appeared with a cup beside the giant. "Surely it is dust by now, Master?"

"Dust? No. It is the blood of the god, Titus. Like quicksilver. It cannot spoil." Bannus held the bauble above the cup, and snapped it in two between his fingers. Dark fluid drained from the broken halves. Bannus held the cup before him. His breathing grew deep and resonant, as if he were steeling himself for a great task, or aroused by visions of glory. "This is a gift, Titus. The god sends his blessing. When I drink this, Blood will be united with Blood, and I shall dream."

Bannus downed the contents of the cup and sighed, head tilted backward. "Leave me, Titus. Return to your post."

"Yes, Master," said Titus, but he did not leave them. Harric could still hear the man's little gasps, as if he waited for Sir Bannus to return his prize.

"Do you not hear, Titus?"

"Master," said Titus, his voice shaking between gasps. "The bastard's crime is great. He must be punished. But his measurements…they seem to match. If I am right, and if his blood also matches, perhaps I might be allowed—"

"You are not ready, Titus. Return to your post, and this time make certain I am not disturbed."

"Yes, Master."

The Faceless One's gasps faded, and the door opened and closed behind him, leaving Harric hanging in the darkness before the immortal, who had gone still, as if sleeping on his feet. "Gristhi," Bannus murmured. "I see Gristhi. O, beautiful Phyros of old! It was Gristhi's blood in the stone. Visions throng my eyes…" He swayed on his feet, head thrown back in ecstasy, still holding Harric above the floor.

Somewhere in the room, Lyla gasped.

Run, now! Harric wanted to say. *He falls asleep! Go!* But he had almost no breath.

Movement in the darkness at Bannus's side. Lyla! He motioned frantically for her to flee, but when he turned his head to locate her in the gloom, he stopped and gaped in shock at what he saw: standing at the immortal's hip, fingers tracing the scars of his thigh, stood his mother.

"Sir Bannus is remarkably easy to manipulate from the spirit world." She smiled, cocking her head to the side to peer up at the colossus. "He scarcely has a will of his own any longer, just a mass of urges and unfiltered impulses.

So easy to tug at his desires. I pull one string and he notices that little slut who told you about your Proof. Another string, and he has the urge to piss and drag her with him as you pass outside his hall."

Harric choked on fear and rage, and she laughed.

"Did you really think if you broke my hold on you I'd abandon you, Harric? I'd let you go down the path that will destroy our queen?" She stepped up to where Harric dangled. "Sir Bannus will do for me what my curse could not. And if I cannot urge him now to kill you, I'll make him follow till he does. *I* am your curse now, and I am not so easily broken." She stepped back and gazed at him fondly. "I love you, Harric. Soon you'll join me in the spirit world, and we'll have all the time we need to make up. I'll finally be the mother that in life I never could."

New horror filled Harric. He shook his head, tried to scream, "No!"— tried to pry the fingers holding him, but he was a mouse in the talons of a hawk.

She glided back to Bannus and around to his back, and disappeared from sight.

Bannus's head jerked up. The mad eyes found Harric. Bannus's grip tightened until Harric had no breath at all and his head began to ring. White flashes raced before his eyes. His body wrenched. His head whipped to the side and his face grew heavy with blood.

Distantly, he experienced the sensation of flying.

Caris stalked the unfinished servant passage between the inn's largest bunkrooms, armor clanking dully. The passages were narrow, made for smaller maids than she, and certainly not for a big one in armor. She turned sideways to get through some places, and even so bumped the panels of bare wattle, knocking out chunks of rough plaster.

She had found no sign of Harric in these passages, however, and none of the servants had seen him in the public spaces, though they said the place was crawling with squires on the hunt for him. Dreading the worst, she'd finally asked a potboy which room had been taken by Sir Bannus, and ended up here. Bannus was on the other side of the wall to her right. Was Harric?

The immortal spoke on the other side of the wall, a low rumble that raised the hairs on the back of her neck. Another voice followed, but too faint to identify.

Where are you, Harric?

A familiar roar of confusion rose behind her eyes. It had been growing since she left Harric, and now it began to reach a dangerous pitch. Her heart pounded in her chest; her breathing felt choked and crowded.

Not now. Not here...

She sank to her knees and leaned against the left wall of the passage. Squeezing her eyes shut, she slipped her fingers under her helm, into her ears. The sound of her own breath grew loud in her private darkness. She let the rhythmic rush of it calm her, like the crash of waves on the beach below her father's castle, which had hushed her to sleep as a child. *Breathe. Breathe.* The roaring receded. When her heart slowed to a manageable rate, she opened her eyes and dropped her hands. She felt a small twinge of hope at the knowledge she was getting better at stilling the roar this way. *Two months ago, when I first came here, I would have balled up and moaned on the floor.*

She climbed to her feet, careful not to bump the right-hand wall. The immortal's voice rumbled again, laughing this time. It sent more needles up her spine. She ground her teeth in frustration. *Even if Harric was in there, what in the Black Moon would you do about it? Anything?* She snorted. *Why are you even looking for him? You should be on the road by now, on your own, and gone. You should walk out of here right now, mount up, and ride.*

She stalked forward to find the first exit and leave. As she balled her hands into fists, Harric's ring bit into her finger, and her guts flipped with unfamiliar emotions. She stopped in her tracks. The roaring returned behind her eyes.

Gods leave me! Where in the Black Moon is he?

The wall before her exploded, and Harric flew through it in a shower of shattered wood and plaster. He slammed the opposite wall, rebounded, and crumpled at her feet, limp as a dishrag. If she'd been two paces farther along the passage, she'd have been clobbered. Harric too had been lucky, in a way, for if he'd hit one of the posts between panels of wattle, he'd have been crushed by the impact; instead, he'd hit square in the center of a panel that tore free from the posts and flew with him into the passage.

In the darkness beyond the new hole, a shadowy colossus loomed alone.

A chill confusion rose and swallowed her. Part of her knew that as a woman in armor she was an abomination to Sir Bannus and the Old Ways. She knew Bannus was probably mad with bloodlust. She knew he was probably drunk and unpredictable. But all of that was lost in blind panic for Harric. While dust still swirled in the passage, she scooped him in her arms and ran.

Deep laughter followed. "Sir Cobalt! Well met. Take the bastard and hang him. I will sleep and dream."

Then the sound of scuttling as a small figure darted from the gapping hole in the wall and sped past her up the servant's corridor. One of the servant girls had been inside. Lyla?

Caris turned from the scene and blundered away through the passage until she found an exit and burst into the stable yard. She staggered to one side in sudden darkness, caromed off the stone wall of the inn, then stopped and laid Harric in the dust. She tore off her helmet and laid her ear to his chest, terrified at what she might find.

His heart beat loud and strong. Tears of relief welled in her eyes, yet even as she wept she cursed the unfamiliar emotions.

What's wrong with you? Get hold of yourself!

A guest door from the inn opened, not ten paces away. For a terrifying moment Caris feared it was Sir Bannus, but it was only a trio of squires. They swaggered into the yard, wearing silk evening clothes and light swords, and the expressions of eager hunters. When they saw Caris stooped over Harric, they halted, then came to her.

"You found him!" one said.

"If you thtand him up, thir," said another, "and I'll bash him a new thmile." The speaker grinned, displaying toothless gums as he polished a rock the size of an apple on his tunic.

"I have the right to cut his balls off," said the third. This one Caris recognized as the Sapphire's squire, whose lance she'd broken. She stood, and he halted short, confusion on his brow as the torchlight illumined her face. Before he could draw his sword, her mailed fist crashed into the side of his head and he fell like a stone. More blows followed, but Caris barely remembered them.

She woke from a blur of fury to find herself on her knees, straddling a motionless body. She'd been balled over it, rocking back and forth. She had no idea how long she'd been there, only that her arms were tired from blows, and the face of the squire beneath her was so crushed and disfigured it nearly made her vomit. Three others lay senseless beside her. One was Harric.

What in the Black Moon is wrong with me?

Trembling, she stood and surveyed the bodies around her. She had to get Harric to Mother Ganner. He always called her his "true mother." Mother Ganner would hide him and get him on his feet and out the door in the darkness. *The kitchens,* she thought. *It isn't far. I can leave him with Mother Ganner, and depart without any more delay.*

She dragged the squires to the deepest shadows against the inn, then hoisted Harric to her shoulder. He was surprisingly light, even with a pack on, so she bore him quickly along the back of the lodge to the kitchens.

The yard was empty. It seemed there had been no witnesses, and darkness was deepening, which would completely cloak her escape, once she left Harric in good hands.

The door to the kitchen was open. She looked up and down the yard to be sure she wasn't spotted, then mounted the stone step and entered.

Red Moon, White Moon, full in the sky
Red like a witch's evil eye.
Black eats White,
And leaves the Red.
Kratos' Moon, we'll all be dead!

—Children's rhyme describing *"Kratos' Moon,"* a mythical event in which the Unseen
Moon eclipses the Bright Mother, heralding tides of war and plague, as the Mad Moon reigns
unopposed in the sky.

12

Ill Met in Gallows Ferry

Caris laid Harric on a bench in the kitchens. Mother Ganner stood at the bread table with her round, fat back to Caris, working flour into one of many mounds of dough on the boards. Caris removed her helmet, and looked about warily. Even in her present state of excitement, she noticed the uncharacteristic silence in the kitchen. The serving girls stood together in the pantry, as if afraid to be noticed. More ominously, the great room adjacent to the kitchens, which usually roared with revels till midnight, lay hushed as the pale hours before dawn.

"Mother Ganner?" Caris said.

The widow turned her plump face toward Caris, without interrupting her kneading. A baby hung in a sling across her bosom—one of her cooks' daughters—sleeping peacefully to the rhythmic swaying of her work. When Mother Ganner saw Caris, she stopped kneading and curtsied with a muttered "Lordship…"

Her face seemed odd to Caris in the uneven firelight, but what first seemed a trick of the shadows snapped into clarity as Caris stepped closer: the left side of Mother Ganner's face was as swollen and purple as a wine melon.

Caris sucked her breath. "Mother Ganner! What happened?"

For several heartbeats the widow stared at Caris, trying to reconcile the familiar voice and face with the hard and polished armor.

"Caris, girl? What—" Her eyes found Harric and widened. She wiped her hands on her apron and bobbed to his side. "Harric, la! You should be far away by now. What you gone and done?" She brushed his hair from his eyes and examined his battered face. "Don't we make a pretty pair," she muttered.

Caris's breathing eased, but her heart still reeled with fierce emotion. The berserk reaction she experienced when she found Harric in danger upset her deeply.

"He's got to run," said Mother Ganner. "You both best run."

"We are. I mean, he was. I am, too." Caris grimaced, uncertain now why she'd planned to go alone.

Two serving girls crept from the pantry to peer at Harric, but Mother Ganner jabbed a fat finger at them, the flesh on her arm shaking imperiously. "Get back in there. Go on! I don't want you tattling he's here, tempted by their dirty silver. Soon as Missy and Wallop come back from the great room, they'll stay with you too, till I say. But one of you fetch me that kettle with the herbs I meant for Lyla. And bring a bowl of rags."

"I need to go," Caris said abruptly. She dropped the sock of coins Harric had given her onto the bench, then forced herself to take a step toward the door.

Mother Ganner looked at her, brow furrowed, but only nodded. "Gods leave you, girl."

Caris stalked to the stables.

Free.

She'd done the right thing. She could mount and ride from Harric and Gallows Ferry with clear conscience and clean heart.

Harric opened his eyes and stared at the widow for a moment before he recognized her. "Ma?"

"Hush. You're in the kitchens."

He stared about in confusion, then peered closer at her face.

"What happened?" He reached up for her swollen cheek. He tried to sit, but pain lanced his ribs and head. He moaned and fell back.

"Hush, now. It's all right."

"How—"

"Caris brought you. All clammed up in metal, la! I thought she was…" Her jaw quivered, and she pressed her lips together.

"I mean what happened to you? Your face…"

The bowl of steaming herb-water came, and she busied herself soaking the rags. "You hush. I aim to clean you up. Take a drink of the blood, la. It'll help to heal." Mother Ganner held a cup of stallion's blood to Harric's swollen lips, and he forced down a bitter swallow. She wrung out a rag and daubed his brow. Pain stabbed through the cuts on his forehead, but she held him still, her face grim and intent. "No time to be gentle. Hold still, and I'll make it quick. And while I clean you up, you listen, 'cause you have a right to know what happened here."

She lifted her chin as if steeling herself for what she was about to say, but a trembling lip betrayed her grief. She laid the rag across his forehead and lifted another from the bowl. "A second Phyros-rider come through tonight after you left your cart." Her voice grew hoarse and tight. "A real one. One of the Old Ones, gods leave us."

Memories of Bannus and the Faceless One crashed into Harric's mind. His mother, influencing Bannus. Still trying to kill him. He moaned. "Lyla… Bannus. Is she still…?"

"Bannus, la!" Tears streamed from her eyes. "Oh, Harric, he bust into the foyer like a god, all blue-faced and wild. He grabbed our Lyla where she stood sweeping, and roared for drink, and laughed, and smashed things and dragged her to a room. I grabbed his arm to stop him and he swatted me down like a child. I'm lucky he only smashed my fool head and left it on my shoulders."

The widow choked, and her round face wrinkled in a mask of grief. "Oh, Harric, her eyes. I couldn't do a thing for her. Oh, that poor, sweet girl!"

Harric sat up, head pounding. "She's still there."

Mother Ganner's weeping eyes went suddenly hard. "Where the Black Moon you think you're going, you damn fool? You think you'd get her back? That monster'd take your head clean off with a thought. Only reason you're alive now is luck. Only reason *I'm* alive is I'm an old fool of a fat thing, and there ain't no glory in killing a cocklehead as that."

"But—will he let her go?"

She shook her head, swallowing hard. "I don't know, Harric. But I ain't about to lose two of my chickens in one night. Your mother's ghost would never let me rest if any harm come to you."

Harric's swollen lips twisted. "I'm pretty sure she'd be comfortable with it."

"Don't be a fool. Your momma'd want you to live to set this right." She leaned close and thrust an angry thumb at her ruined cheek. "Take a good look at this, Harric, and don't you forget it. This is what it was like before Her Majesty come. No law but the whim of blood rank. No lady learned her letters like your mother, no widow owned her own timber lodge like me, and no bastard lived to manhood with a chance at freedom. Her Majesty is all that's standing between us and the Old Ways. And if the Old Ones are come again, then she's our only chance against 'em."

Harric grimaced. Something was coming clear to him—an old obstruction dissolving in his heart, a new purpose filling his mind and cleansing his conscience. "I'm going to Her Majesty," he said, raising a hand to cup her swollen cheek. "I'm going to tell her what I've seen, and pledge to serve in any way I can."

A cautious hope wrinkled her brow. "You mean that, la? Just like your momma wanted?"

"No. Not for her. Never for her."

Something in his voice made her pause. She regarded him between swipes with the rag. "You wasn't like this before she died."

"Like what?"

"You ain't been nothing but mad since that day. All full of hurt and hate. Always talking how you'll resist her doom and you won't be her puppet."

"And I won't."

Mother Ganner stood abruptly. She towered above him like a mountain, chins trembling with emotion. "I don't want to hear another word about it, Harric. *The Old Ones are returning.* Think of it. I fear the Breaker Moon is coming. It hasn't come since before the Cleansing, but that time it near burned us from the map. That means the Queen's in real trouble. The *world's* in trouble."

"Krato's Moon?"

She nodded gravely. "Call it what you like. I been having dreams on it. Thought they was just dreams till Bannus turned up."

It made sense. Old Ones returning, a new magic in the north, rumors of the Iberg Imperial Concord stirring across the sea, its greedy eyes on Arkendia. It could all point to the coming of the Breaker Moon.

"When the Bright Mother goes dark," she said, "we're gonna need every maker we can get, so we don't have no time for you moping about your mama. Time for you to be a man, and we needs whatever your mama taught you, no matter how bad it hurt you to learn it. You understand? Queen didn't free you to have you shrivel up in bile."

"I will, Ma. I'll make good of it. For you and the Queen, I will."

A look of love and pride spread across her face. In it he saw her old strength return, which did him more good than all her bandages.

He fumbled in his sleeve and pressed the last share of the witched squire's silver into her hand. "This is for Lyla. Make sure Lyla gets it?" The widow hefted the purse for a heartbeat and smiled with the good half of her face. She dropped the bundle in the baby's sling and climbed ponderously to her feet, raising Harric with a sturdy hand.

"I'm so proud of you, Harric, I could near bust myself. Helped raise a right gentleman, I did. Proudest thing I ever done. Now, you get. If you find yourself north and with simple folk what can give you help, you tell 'em you're *my* son. Like enough I done them a kindness when they come through, and they're good folk who'd jump to return a favor."

Harric's eyes teared. He caught her hand and held it to his lips. "Thanks…" was all he could say.

"La, sweet boy! It's me that owes the thanks. Made my life a song all these years. You just come back when you're safe and ready. And don't worry about us. We'll get on."

Then she swept him out the door with a strong and gentle hand.

Harric pressed his back to the lodge and paused to let his eyes adjust to the dark. The Mad Moon still hadn't risen above the Godswall; he guessed there remained no more than a half-hour of darkness before he bathed the cliffs and river in his fiery light. To his left stood the foot of the stable yard, where the Hanging Road entered through the south gate and split off behind the inn through the market place; to his right the yard flared into a wide carriage turnabout, bound on two sides by the inn and on the opposite side by the stable where Jacky slept, unaware of Harric's intention to wake him for a very long ride.

When he could see well enough to make out the outlines of the roofs against the sky, he began skirting the head of the yard, keeping the inn to his right and navigating mostly by memory. He hadn't gone five paces before he stumbled upon something and fell. Throwing out his hands to break his fall, he bit back on a yell, his battered ribs erupting in protest with the impact. What he found on the ground, however, was the unmistakable softness of a body. Groping, he found the face, where he felt no breath, but his hand came away sticky and smelling of blood. He shuddered, and wiped it off on the victim's breeches. Had this been one of the grooms that attacked him? Had Caris slain the man and dragged him here?

A scuff from across the yard made him crouch and freeze. He peered in the direction of the sound, and at first he saw nothing. Then he caught movement along the stable, though it was so dark he couldn't be sure whether he'd actually seen it or merely heard it.

He was in near perfect darkness at the foot of the inn, but some of the windows above allowed a faint and indirect candlelight to tint the darkness farther out in the yard. In one of these pale shafts two figures moved parallel to his course. One was tall and thick, the other short and broad, with the larger making considerably more noise—limping, perhaps?—with an occasional click of metal on metal, as from armor plates. The smaller figure moved with a rolling, loping gait Harric could not make sense of in such low light. Crawling? Hobbling on all fours?

"God's socks, this place stinks," one of them whispered. "Whole place is an open privy."

"Hush you, now," said the other, in an accent Harric had never heard. "We're not alone."

The figures stopped, and Harric froze. He couldn't have been spotted. The darkness beneath the eaves was complete, and he'd made no noise. He scanned the yard for evidence of some third party, but saw nothing, and guessed someone must have appeared in a window above him. The figures changed course directly for Harric, passing through a swath of candlelight in which Harric glimpsed a bald pate and long mustachios.

The Phyros-thief.

"Here is your man in the green belt," said the voice with the accent. "Was he a walking bruise when you left him?"

"No. Where is he?"

"There. Behind the barrels."

"Moons take your eyes, Brolli. I can't see any barrels."

"I'm here," Harric whispered. He stepped out, hope rising in his heart. "Here."

The old man drew near, breathing heavily and smelling strongly of ragleaf and oiled iron. "Moons, I'm glad we found you, son. There's been a mistake—"

"This is not good place to talk," the shorter one whispered. "Come this way."

"Follow Brolli," said the knight.

Brolli led them to the head of the yard, in the deeper shadows against the inn. Harric caught confusing glimpses of him as they crossed swaths of candlelight. His proportions seemed wrong. The legs were too short for his prodigious upper body. He used his arms while walking, like a child playing at horse, but his legs followed his arms in a kind of hop or lope. A dwarf? Once it had been fashionable for knights to keep dwarfed men as squires, but the young Queen Chasia found it distasteful, so it fell from fashion. Could the old man be so backward he kept a dwarfed squire? It might be the reason for his outcast blackened armor.

"Here," Brolli said, pausing in a pool of darkness at the head of the yard, where the stable joined the inn. Harric still couldn't place his accent.

"Sit guard for us, will you, Brolli?"

Brolli said nothing, but by the sound of it he climbed onto one of the water barrels lined up beneath the eaves, then leapt to the side of the stable and scrambled onto the roof.

Harric listened in astonishment, trying in vain to follow with his eyes.

"Born climber," the old man grunted. He groped Harric's shoulders and found his backpack. "Good. You were leaving. Smart boy. I assume you have the purse I gave you. I need it back."

Harric blinked. "The purse?"

"Don't play daft, son." An edge of urgency crept into his voice. "That trinket's very important—it was a mistake that I gave it—"

A door in the lodge at the head of the yard banged open, ten paces to their left, casting a beam of lamp light into the yard. The old man hushed Harric before he could speak. A tall man stepped from the lighted corridor into the yard and closed the door behind him, to be swallowed by the dark. Harric stared at the place where the man had been, and picked him out as a darker patch against the lodge, padding softly in their direction.

Harric glided to the side until he rested his hand against the lodge, and crouched behind one of the water barrels. The man's eyes would not be as well adjusted to the dark as his were, and if the man continued his current course he'd pass right by Harric without knowing it. Harric could pick his pocket or trip him into the old knight, or grab him from behind. But the man crossed half the distance to where they stood, then stopped, his back against the siding.

The scent of spiced perfume reached Harric's nose. *Aconite, also called "witch cloud,"* he thought, as if it were one of his mother's blindfold tests in courtly tinctures. *Aconite is an Iberg favorite: mildly stimulating, anxiety inducing if used in incense, associated with magic.*

As if to confirm the correlation, the man muttered something in the rich, round syllables of the Iberg language as he slipped a hand into his shirt, removing it with something clasped in his fist.

Then he vanished.

One moment the Iberg was there—the next, he simply wasn't.

The old knight cursed.

Harric stared in astonishment at the spot where the man had been. He'd heard tales of witches using the power of their witch-stones to enact incredible feats of stealth, but he'd never dreamed he'd see it. How vain he'd been to think himself invisible by virtue of his stillness and the man's ill-adjusted eyes! Harric felt naked and vulnerable, his own tactic rebounding against him with double the force, but remained motionless in hope he had not been spotted.

"I don't fear your magic, witch," the old knight rumbled, suddenly loud in the darkness. "You won't be the first witch *Belle's* tasted, nor the last." The scrape and chime of steel on steel suggested the drawing of a long and well-tuned sword. A brag, perhaps, but a convincing one: most Arkendian knights would have pissed themselves in the presence of such magic, but the old knight seemed truly unfazed. Harric remained motionless, letting the knight draw the witch's attention until Harric could pinpoint the Iberg's location and…what? If he could grapple him, he might find his witch-stone and take it away. That would make him visible, Harric guessed, since it was a witch's source of magic.

"I see you," said a voice with a thick Iberg accent. The voice sounded hollow and distant, as if passed through a pipe, which confused Harric's sense of its location. "You put us to such troubles today."

"I don't need to see you to kill you," the old man said.

"And who is this? Una tricola bambi! Ha-ha! Do you know she follows you? No? You no see her. She is clever. Aha! She try to protect you! So much now come clear."

Harric had no memory of *tricola bambi* from his Iberg lessons, but he saw no sign of anyone else in the stable yard. He felt his heart thumping harder in his chest. *Keep your eyes on the old man,* he willed the invisible Iberg. *Give me a clue where you are, and I'll have that stone before you even know I'm here.*

Harric's heart stopped for a beat as another thought crashed through his fears. *What if the magic of that witch-stone would keep Mother away?* His heart beat faster. *You have to fight magic with magic…right?*

The door at the side of the lodge flew open again, followed by an enormous knight in orange silks and cloak, and a torchbearer with a half-dozen young knights. All wore swords, but none wore armor. Harric tensed to flee, but the old man made no move, so he forced himself to stay.

"There!" cried the torchbearer, pointing to the old knight in the shadows. "I told you I saw him!"

The orange knight grinned, and flipped a coin to the torch boy, who caught it, beaming, and stood back to watch. Sir Orange drew his sword with a flourish and strolled forward, and his companions followed suit with a chorus of chiming steel.

The old knight limped back to put the stable doors behind him, and took a stand there as his enemies formed a semicircle before him. Harric remained crouched behind the barrels, only paces from the nearest knight. He discarded the idea of running to open the doors behind the old knight so they could escape inside; if the stable boys had done their duty, the doors would have been barred at sunset. Harric himself could slip into the crack between the stable and the inn at the corner of the yard—a narrow rat run that opened on the other side of the stable on a scaffold cantilevered over the river—but the old knight would never squeeze in the gap, even without his armor.

"Stay down, son," the old man muttered. "Brolli, you try to find that witch."

Harric had no idea if he'd been spotted by the witch, and the witch had given him no clue of his location.

The old knight wrapped his cloak around his left forearm as a shield, and raised his sword vertically before him in both hands, hilt at a level with his shoulders. He chanted, his voice flat with ritual:

"Though you wound me I die not.
Yet there will be honor in your passing."

The words sent a shiver down Harric's spine; it was the Salute of the Blue Order, and in the ballads it preceded the death of wicked knights. Several of the younger knights before him seemed also to feel its power, for they paused, eyes darting furtively at their leader.

The orange-clad knight laughed, white teeth flashing in a well-combed beard. "Words to frighten children! Don't let his name fool you. This is no ballad knight or champion. This is an old man who can barely stand without a prop. And, boys, you fight beside Sir Yolan!" He thumped his chest with a fist. "And Sir Yolan never bows."

The old man grunted. "It's as a good a night as any to go to the Black Moon, Sir Yolan." He completed his salute in the old-fashioned hilt-to-forehead manner, but when his opponents failed to return it, he snorted in disgust. "You're no knights. You're cutthroats. You're the reason our queen makes knights of women."

Sir Yolan lunged, and three of his companions joined in a simultaneous attack. Steel clashed, and a blade sparked across the old man's breastplate. One of Yolan's companions fell heavily. As the others fell back, the old man's sword pursued for half a beat longer. A young knight yelped and dropped his sword, a finger severed.

It had happened too quickly to track, yet the old man moved so positively and powerfully that the others seemed like children with wooden training swords. Moreover, what they just witnessed was so clearly at odds with Sir Yolan's boast that his remaining companions stood stricken, staring as blood pooled around the fallen.

An eerie voice irrupted from the air beneath the eaves.

"*Nebecci, Destego!*" Iberg words, unknown to Harric. The moment he heard them, an icy pain seized his heart, and he fell to his knees.

"*Nebecci, Destego, Raghat!*"

The old knight bent as if kicked in the gut.

Harric watched helplessly as his protector stumbled into a barrel, one hand clawing at the armor over his heart. Only Brolli remained unassailed by the magic, hiding somewhere in the darkness above.

"To him!" cried Yolan. Leaping over his fallen companions, Yolan swept his blade over his head and downward in a devastating two-handed blow that the old knight barely parried. Yolan grinned, pressing his advantage, until he retreated and whirled to face a fourth knight, who had emerged from the darkness behind him to haul him away from the old man by the tail of his cloak.

Harric stared in shock. *Caris!*

As Yolan whirled, his blade whirled with him in a hissing head-high sweep. Caris ducked and lunged beneath the cut. With one hand she flipped his cloak up over his blade, while the other guided the tip of her sword to lick beneath his beard. Yolan lurched back, a lock of beard falling to the ground. As he attempted to disengage his cloak from his blade, Caris brought her blade down hard on Yolan's wrist and sent his sword spinning to the dirt. Yolan roared in pain. With surprising speed, he bent and snatched up his sword, but Caris was quicker. Her blade darted again beneath his beard, and this time it loosed a gush of scarlet like she'd broached a wine keg.

The eerie voice echoed nearer to Harric: "*Destego!*" The pain in his heart redoubled. Expecting the invisible Iberg to knife him at any moment, he slung his pack around to his front and donned it backwards as a kind of improvised armor. Unexpectedly, the pain in his chest diminished, as if the pack also shielded him from magic. He took advantage of the temporary reprieve by fumbling it open and drawing out his saddle knife and cloak. With one hand he slashed the knife through the air before him, and with the other he whipped the cloak out in an attempt to reveal the witch's location.

When none of this made contact, he toppled an empty rain barrel to one side, so as to obstruct one direction of approach.

"Destego!"

Again the terrible pain in his breast, this time so severe he convulsed and fell flat on his back in the dirt. Above him the dark sky whirled, half star fields, half torch-lit eaves. Brolli's strange face appeared over the eaves to look down at Harric, round eyes glowing like a cat's.

Harric flung his cloak out one last time, and this time it collided with something at his feet and fell there, rebuffed. Brolli launched himself from the eaves, long arms spread for a flying embrace. His descent halted abruptly in the air, where he sprawled and grappled with an unseen opponent, then the Iberg appeared beneath him, eyes white with surprise, and the icy hand vanished from Harric's heart. In the next moment the witch and Brolli collapsed upon him, and the weight of the two men forced the wind from Harric's lungs. The witch's stubbled cheek squashed against Harric's. In spite of all, Harric had the presence of mind to drop his knife and immobilize the man's arms in a desperate embrace, but just as he secured them, the witch's head dashed sideways with a concussive shock and the man went limp upon him.

Brolli peeked down over the Iberg's shoulder, round golden eyes like coins in a flat, hairless face. He grinned, exposing huge canines. "Good!" he said, then turned and disappeared from Harric's view.

Something leaked on Harric's cheek from the Iberg's head. "Moons!" he gasped, "Get him off me!" But no one came. He struggled under a welter of perfumed cape. The pain of his ribs screamed with the effort. When he finally managed to flop one of the man's arms sideways into the dust, something rolled from the dead fingers and stopped directly before Harric's eyes.

A glassy globe the size of an egg, night black, yet oddly luminescent. *The witch-stone.*

Harric palmed it.

By the time he squirmed free of the dead man's embrace and struggled to his feet, the fight in the yard appeared over. The dead Iberg lay tangled in the blue cape that marked him as "protected" by the Sapphire lord. It had kept anyone from getting the idea to hang him while in Arkendia, but fortunately did nothing to protect against cudgels. The old knight leaned on his sword, breathing raggedly, all his opponents motionless and prone, but for the whimpering torch boy and a squire who knelt before Brolli.

"Stop crying," Brolli said, as he bound their hands and gagged them. "Be glad. You live to tell the ballad of Sir Willard and the Foolish Yolan."

"What the Black Moon took you so long, Brolli?" the old knight growled.

Brolli gave another wolfish grin. "I see in night light, but I cannot see into the Unseen. And I only use ma—" He seemed to catch himself. "—my people's weapons if we are dying, remember? You are not yet dying."

"Fair enough."

Caris stared down at the inert forms of Sir Yolan and a young knight at her feet, her armor spattered with blood.

"First kill, son?" the old man croaked, mistaking her sex in the armor. "It gets easier. But that's the trouble with it, mostly. To whom do I owe my thanks?" No reply from Caris. "Well, you were most welcome here. Damned witch had me falling over with a heart stroke."

Caris moaned, and dropped her sword in the dust. Hands on her ears, she fell to her knees and rocked back and forth.

Harric rubbed his chest, where his fingers inadvertently found a pendant lump of witch-silver the green lord had left behind, and which the Iberg had reached right past to seize his heart. He managed a brief smile at that irony, but it stung his split lip like the jab of a pin.

Brolli left the captives behind the barrels and loped to the old man's side. In the light of the single torch, it became quite clear to Harric that the dwarf-man was not even human. No dwarfed human had such long or powerful arms, such eyes, or such teeth. But if not human, what? A thrill of wonder managed to rise above the fog of his pain. A *Kwendi*?

"You bleed." Brolli pointed with a long arm at the old knight's side.

"It can wait. I'm more concerned about our young knight here. Son?"

Caris stopped rocking, and slid her hands from her ears.

The dwarf-man loped to the burning torch and flipped it into a rain barrel. It hissed briefly, and darkness engulfed them again.

"Snap out of it, son. No reason to be ashamed. Shows you're not an animal. I'd rather have one man like you at my side than ten beasts like Yolan. Are you hurt?"

After a heartbeat, Caris murmured something. Then again, louder, but hoarsely: "I'm alive."

"Good man. And where is our unfortunate grain monger, Brolli? He's still with us?"

Brolli chuckled. "He is looking worse than when we find him," he said, in his strange accent. "But he not looking good then, either. Over by the barrels. No, other way. Four pacings."

"Harric?" Caris said, reviving. "He's all right? Harric?"

"I'm all right. Sort of."

She groped her way to him and held him by the shoulders. "I tried to leave," she whispered, "but—I worried—" Her voice hitched, and Harric cocked his head to hear her better, for it almost seemed she was...what? Choking up over him? "I thought we should travel together," she continued, with an awkwardness somehow magnified by his inability to see her. "Leave together. For safety."

"You know each other," the old man observed. "Pairing's a wise idea, considering your situation. Now, there's no time to explain, but I gave you the wrong purse today, son. My mistake. I need that trinket I gave you, and I have another purse to make up for your trouble. I think you'll find it a more than fair trade."

"Make up for my trouble?" Harric chuckled. "You can't afford the trouble I've had."

"I'm sorry about that. But I'm not stingy, and I know you're an honorable lad." He located Harric's arm and pressed a purse tight with coins into Harric's hand. "Take this. More than that ring is worth."

"What ring? It was a nut—"

"We want to go with you," Caris interrupted.

The old man snorted. "Ridiculous. You have no idea what you're saying."

"We all need to get out of here," Harric said, taking up Caris's cause. "We know the area and can help you escape."

"I know someone who can hide us," Caris said. "There's a stream we can follow west in the next valley—"

"No time for this, son—"

"Show us this stream," Brolli said, in a tone of decision unlike any servant. "We travel together."

"Wh—" The old knight choked. "Brolli, we've brought them enough trouble."

"We can't keep running, old man. You have wounds. And they know of safe places."

The side door banged, followed by the murmur of hushed voices. At the edge of the porch, two housegirls appeared—neither with customers, which was unprecedented that summer. Harric guessed Bannus's arrival had cast a pall over any merriment in the place. The women bent their heads in worried conference, close enough for Harric to smell their rose perfume, but the two were too self-absorbed and unadjusted to the dark to notice others near.

When the women slipped back into the lodge, the old man spoke. "Very well. You two fetch your horses from the stable and meet us on the road. We'll be sure the north gate's open for you. But I want that ring now."

"So you can leave us again?" Harric said. "No deal. Once we're safe and clear, we'll settle up." To Caris he said, "Stay here at the doors, and I'll unlock them."

Before the old knight could protest, Harric slipped his pack to his hand, felt his way along the stable to the corner of the yard, and slid sideways into the rat run too narrow for the others to follow.

It's a horrible mess that I have to confess,
I haven't a hope of redressing.
My might is with swords, not with ladies and words,
Yet I beg you continue undressing.

—From "Sir Willard and the Mistaken Lady"

13

Unholy Heximony

Harric's head pounded in pain, but his spirits rose in spite of it: he lived. And it now seemed he would make it out of Gallows Ferry. For Caris's sake too he rejoiced, for she had just aided in a fight for the life of the very man she sought as mentor. As long as the old knight didn't guess in Harric's absence that it was she who had the ring, he might leave with Caris and the old knight together.

The rat run was a tight fit. For the last few years he'd had to exhale and sidestep his way to the other side, scraping his chest and back on the rough-sawn planking, whereas in boyhood he'd fairly galloped through for pranks and missions. As he sidled through, the witch-stone he'd stashed in his shirt pressed against his chest, right beside the useless nugget of witch-silver. Without the magic of his nineteenth birthday to keep his mother at bay, he was helpless. Surely the stone was as potent as the Proof…or would he have to know how to use it for it to do any good? The thought chilled him. No one in Arkendia could teach him how to use it. All he could do is hope that merely having the stone in his pocket was enough.

A gust of cool air greeted him as he emerged onto the west side of the stable and looked down to the black waters far below. The stable itself cantilevered over the void, as space was at a premium in Gallows Ferry, so there was no room to walk on the rim of the cliff. Instead, a narrow maintenance plank rimmed the exterior, and with nimble fingers and feet one might negotiate its length without trouble.

Gritting his teeth against the pain in his ribs, he stepped out onto the plank and stood with his back to the windy void. When the pain subsided, he clung as close to the wood as he could, lest a gust of river wind pry him away, and sidled his way down the length, keeping his eyes steadfastly on the plank before his feet. Midway, he found what he looked for: a floor-level dung trap left open for ventilation.

Gripping the top of the hatch, he kneeled on the narrow scaffold and stooped to peer inside. He hadn't gotten his head around for a proper view before a gust of wind bulled along the scaffold and nearly knocked him flying. Cursing, he held himself in place as it drove its wedge between him and the siding. Had he still been standing when it came, it would have swept him into the void. As soon as it let off, he peered through the trap into the stable. As he'd hoped, the stall beyond was empty. The sweet smell of hay and horses greeted him, the air warm and humid. The place was in near darkness, lit only by Rudy's lantern by the front doors, some half-dozen stalls away. Somewhere near the front Rudy cursed and threw something metal against a wall.

Harric pushed his pack through and inchwormed after, ribs screaming and limiting him to tiny agonizing movements.

When he finally succeeded, his shirt was soaked with sweat, and his injuries throbbed. He lay for long moments, listening to the sounds of the stable. Rudy, it seemed, was in a fouler mood than usual, cursing the stable boys and thrashing about by the south doors. By the time Harric crept across the empty stall to the right down the main aisle, the stable master had scared the boys out of sight and stood alone in the south doorway, muttering. Rudy fished a roll of ragleaf from his belt purse and lit it in the lantern, then stepped into the yard to smoke.

The horse in the stall to the left of Harric's snorted loudly and snuffed at him through the rails. Farfit, one of Mother Ganner's blood stallions; he had a bandage at the top of his neck where Caris had bled him to make travelers' tonics.

As he let the beast snuff his hand, the three stable boys skulked by with brushes and hoof picks. Wallop and Gander were both nearly twelve, but Honald was only eight, and lived in terror of Rudy.

Harric hissed their names, and they started and squinted about until they saw him beckoning from the shadows. They lit up at the sight of him and gathered in his stall, glowing with admiration.

"Harric, you give Rudy that fat lip?" Wallop said. "He's mad as a dragon."

"Fat lip?" Harric grinned, guessing it had been Caris. "No. That was—a knight. A friend. But listen: something's going to happen here now, and I don't want you to get in trouble for it. Do you think you can find a reason to leave the stables, all three of you?"

They nodded. "We could fetch Rudy's vittles," Gander said. "He always wants vittles 'bout now, but Ma Ganner won't abide him near the kitchens with a stink-roll lit up."

"Good. Go fetch his vittles, but take your time. Be standing by the kitchen door when you hear him holler, and I promise you'll see something to keep you laughing a fortnight."

The boys nodded eagerly.

"You leaving, Harric?" Honald asked.

"Have to, little man."

"We're gonna miss you," said Gander. "You're the only thing keeps Rudy in his place. If you go, there won't be nothing holding him back."

"And nobody to give us silver pennies," said Honald.

Harric felt a pang of helpless loss. The three were the nearest thing he had to younger brothers, and he took it as an unspoken duty to protect them—especially Honald—from the worst of Rudy's depredations. "I'll be back some day. And if Rudy isn't in his place when I do, I'll put him there for good."

"You promise?" Honald asked, eyes large and worried.

"I promise."

Harric gave each an affectionate pat with one hand while his other moved unnoticed and dropped pennies in their pockets. "Now get his vittles, only make it look like it was his idea. And don't look too eager…wipe that smile off your face, Honald. Look all tired and ornery. That's it."

The boys shuffled away, and Harric listened to their words with Rudy. After a few grunts from the stable master, the boys' murmurs faded, and Harric guessed they'd gone to the kitchen. He crept from the stall to the back doors, where the light of the lantern was weak, and opened them for Caris.

"The boys are gone," he said as she slipped in. "Rudy's drunk and smoking."

Her eyes were already glazed in the comfort of the horse world. At the sound of his voice she blinked, and frowned, until her eyes lit upon him and focused. "Open the stalls," she said, eyes distant. "All stalls. Bring them out. We'll run them up the road. They can't pursue without horses."

Harric grinned, and winced at the split in his lip. "If it wouldn't hurt so much, I'd kiss you."

Too late he realized that simple flirtation was too fraught with human emotions for her to process in her horse-tied state. She covered her ears, sealed her eyes, and lurched away from him. He feared she'd howl as she had on similar occasions, but to his relief she remained silent. He gave her as much space as he could, and after long moments she breathed normally. She gave him a warning glare, to which he raised his hands in silent apology. Then she turned away, submerging herself, he imagined, in the world of horses.

Harric slipped away and set to work opening the stalls of the mares and geldings first, and leading them out to stand together in the central passage. Their stillness under Caris's influence was eerie. Though many of the beasts were unfamiliar to Harric and to each other, in Caris's presence they became as a unified herd, their mood following hers. Even the stallions, when walked out to the floor, hardly seemed to notice each other. Jacky, who was wont to nicker in greeting whenever he saw Harric, stood still while Harric saddled him and slipped the bit between his lips.

Rudy smoked outside the doors to keep his spark away from the straw, so Harric's work was swift and easy. But the last horse he released stood nearest the front doors. It was a pampered-looking Iberg stallion—the witch's horse, judging by the odd-styled saddle on the peg. Ibergs horses were generally high-strung and irritable, but even that beast stayed calm at his touch.

A voice of alarm sounded in the yard. Someone spoke with Rudy, and Harric heard the words "murder" and "bodies."

Harric turned toward Caris to signal trouble, but a movement above him caught his attention. In the rafters he saw a shadowy animal figure—*a moon cat!*—no bigger than a rabbit, that crouched and leapt and landed on the back of the stallion. The stallion paid it no mind, but the cat craned its long neck toward Harric and eagerly nosed at the stone in Harric's shirt.

How? A whiff of aconite from its fur. *Oh…the witch's cat.*

The south doors flew open no more than five strides from Harric, and Rudy stood between them, jaw agape at the sight of all his horses standing calmly in the aisle. "What in the Black Moon…?" His eyes fell on Harric. "You!"

Caris let loose with a bizarre shouting whinny, and the horses lunged as one for Rudy and the doors.

Harric grabbed the Iberg's mane and hauled himself astride as it lunged through the doors and shouldered Rudy into a straw rick. The moon cat clawed its way from the horse up Harric's sleeve and his shoulder, where it clung like a burr, its long neck craning about, blank white eyes wide and bright. From its fur, a whiff of Iberg perfume.

Through the yard they raced with the thunder of twenty horses behind them. Three stable boys cheered as they cornered the yard and dove into the road behind the inn, galloping for the gate. Caris passed him on her own mare, Rag, which she must have saddled while Harric emptied the stalls. From that moment Harric made no effort to steer, for he knew the stallion followed Caris, and it was just as well, for its jarring stride sent stabs of pain through his ribs, and it required his full attention to minimize the jolts without stirrups.

With every stride the witch-stone in the cargo slip of his tunic also swung against his ribs like the clapper of a bell, but he dared not remove a hand from the mane to detain it. He managed to hunch his shoulders and cave his chest in such a way that the tunic cradled it far from his skin, but the jolts still tortured his sides, and there was nothing he could do to keep the claws of the moon cat from needling at his collar.

The gates stood open, as the old knight had promised. They dashed through and onto the Hanging Road carved from cliff above the river, now bloodied by the light of the Mad Moon glaring over the Godswall. Four-score iron-shod hooves sparked and rang up the hard rock grade, then thundered across the trestles over canyons. To their left, the vast black gulf of air above the river; to their right, vast curtains of echoing stone.

A bubble of triumph rose from Harric's lungs and escaped in a shout of joy.

Free! He'd done it, and he was free!

He lifted a hand to the cat, which had clambered to a more comfortable station in the crook of his neck and shoulder. "And you, my little beast, are free to stay on!"

After a mile, the road rounded a bluff and dropped toward a wooded valley intersecting the main river from the east. As they curved down toward the forest, Harric gazed across the valley to the far side where the road rose up again, resuming its course across the cliff face and burning in the light of the Mad Moon like a path of fire.

When the road dove beneath the canopy of trees, the herd slowed, hoofbeats abruptly muted on earthen road. Splashes of red moonlight illumined the path, and soon the camps of emigrants sprouted along the landward side. Men and women stood at fires, faces reflecting firelight and curiosity as they peered to the road. At one, he glimpsed the unmistakable figure of the peasant priest in his tentlike smothercoat, squinting out with worried brow.

The camps dwindled, and they rode through stump lands where wood had been cleared to fuel waterwheels. On the water side they passed a tooler's yard with docks and the makeshift structures of its tiny wharf.

As soon as they crossed the rocky ridge near the middle of the valley, the caravan camps ceased altogether, and Caris finally slowed the herd to a walk. She stopped them in a shallow stream that crossed the road, where they stood blowing and snorting like tooler's bellows. The Iberg's stallion's neck steamed with sweat. Harric's ribs blazed with pain from the jarring, and his legs ached from clasping without stirrups. He groaned in general misery.

Behind them, the distinctive cadence of the Phyros grew louder beyond the crest of the ridge. The herd began to shy. Caris maneuvered Rag beside Harric and motioned for him to climb over to sit behind her saddle. He guessed that calming the whole herd would be too difficult near a Phyros.

"What about Jack?" He indicated his horse, still wearing its saddle.

She shook her head, expression strained. "Can't."

He sensed her urgency, so in spite of the pain it caused his ribs, he wrapped his fist in her cloak, placed one foot in the stirrup she offered, and hauled himself across.

The Phyros exploded over the crest of the hill, and Caris gasped as if in pain. The herd shuddered, then shied. Almost as one, they bolted away up the road. Caris sagged, letting out a long sigh of relief. Rag still breathed in great gusts, but otherwise seemed unfrightened as the Phyros slowed to a walk behind them.

"Bye, Jack," Harric muttered, as his horse disappeared with his saddle.

He arranged himself on the blanket behind Caris's bulky saddle and laid his hands on her waist, where the curves of metal felt hard and strange beneath his palms. The moon cat sniffed at her hair from his shoulder, and peered into Harric's face. Its eyes looked blind—milk white, without pupils— but it seemed to gaze about like any other cat. It had probably been asleep near the witch's saddle when Harric moved the stallion and disturbed it. The cat sniffed his nose, and Harric stared back, amused. "I name you Spook," he murmured. "You're my pet now."

Caris jerked her head. "Mm?"

The towering shadow of the Phyros approached, with Brolli's pony clattering down the ridge behind it, Brolli bouncing awkwardly in the saddle. When he stopped beside them he seemed dazed by the ride, hunched and panting as if it had been as hard on him as on Harric.

"Bravely done, lads," the old man said, emerging in a patch of ruddy moonlight. His bald head shone faintly. "Now that ring. Let's have it." He extended an armored hand from the intimidating height of the Phyros.

Caris was so horse-tied she showed no evidence of hearing.

Harric frowned. He cleared his throat. "What ring?"

"Don't play daft," the knight growled. "I've been more than patient with your foolery. I mean the ring in the nut box."

"There was a ring in the nut?" Harric indicated Caris with a nod. "Then she's got it."

"*She?*" The old knight scanned her armor, and another qualm of disgust crossed his face. "*She*, is it!"

"Yes. She."

"Well, girl? Where is it?"

Caris returned his gaze abstractedly, like a ragleaf smoker who'd had more than strictly necessary.

"She's concentrating on keeping her horse calm," Harric said, not wanting to interrupt her trance. "She's probably got it in her pack, unless she figured out it was a box and opened it." That struck Harric as mildly funny. He'd left her the nut as a joke, but had actually given her a valuable ring. "Maybe she's wearing it. I'll see if I can get her glove off."

As Harric moved to find Caris's hand, the old man's jaw dropped, and his ragleaf tumbled from his lips into the stream, where it snuffed with a tiny sigh. A qualm of doubt rippled through Harric. What if Caris had rejected the trinket as she did the squire's silver? She might have thrown them out the window and into the river, or simply left them on the floor of his chambers.

Harric teased her left hand from the reins. Then he coaxed the gauntlet off. On her smallest finger, three interlaced rings of witch-silver glowed as if red hot in the light of the Mad Moon. Harric smiled in relief. "There. See?"

The old man released a string of blistering oaths.

Brolli's laugh barked in the darkness. "She isn't your sister, is she?"

"No. Why? What's wrong?"

Caris put her warm hand on Harric's and drew it tighter around her waist, then lower, below her belt. It was a gesture that came from her horse-tied self: an animal urge, unconscious, and so without the charged meaning it would otherwise have. Even so, it sent a buzz of excitement through Harric, and he wondered if she would remember it when she was back in the human world.

"It's not a problem, sir," he said, retracting his hand to return her gauntlet. "When she's ready she'll take them off and return them."

"Bolts and shackles!" the old man spat. "You *can't* take them off!"

"Why not?"

The old man's gust of cursing prevented further response.

"The ring is a love charm of my people," Brolli said. "A wedding ring. It is stuck on her finger, and she is stuck on who gave them to her. *You*, yes?"

Harric blinked, and Caris's mouth hung mute, as if she'd heard what Brolli said but was too horse-tied to respond.

"Look, you two, I'm sorry," said the old man. "We've rather made a mess of things today—"

"*We?*" said Brolli. "You give a love charm to a bachelor, but *we* make a mess?"

Caris frowned, eyes still distant. "I've felt so…different. This is why?"

"Now, girl, don't panic—this magic is *good* magic," the knight said, misreading her expression as Arkendian panic over magic. "Kwendi magic isn't like Iberg magic at all—"

"You're saying you gave me a love charm without telling me?" Harric said.

"It was a mistake, son. I was tired—grabbed the wrong purse, you see, and…" The old knight rubbed his eyes and sighed.

Caris twisted around in her saddle to meet Harric's eyes. Her gaze was distant, as if still deep in concentration on the horses, but seemed to focus on him. "You gave me a love charm?"

"Caris, I'm so sorry. I had no idea."

Her brow furrowed as the meaning reached her.

"More than a love charm," said Brolli. "It is for make a marriage."

"A *marriage?*" Harric said.

Pointed canines flashed in Brolli's grin. "*Force* a marriage, yes. The magic makes sure it can't be removed."

Rag shied as Caris came fully into focus on Harric, and slugged him in the thigh. "*It won't come off?*"

"Ow! Caris, I didn't know—"

"I killed for you tonight!"

Rag sidestepped the Phyros, and Caris struggled against the reins, seething.

"That was your choice," Harric said. His pains made him petty. "You want to see what it's like to love? Here's your chance. But don't blame this on me. Talk to these two about it."

She clenched her teeth, eyes brimming. "I didn't ask for this, Harric."

"And I did?"

The Phyros shouldered against them, stumbling Rag sideways, and forcing Caris to concentrate on her mount. "Get a hold of yourselves," said the knight. "We're not out of danger. Is this the stream you had in mind? Girl! Is this the stream we follow to find your friend?"

"Yes. This is it."

"Right. Brolli, you lead. Both of you follow. Now! And not a word till I say we're clear."

"Come on, you two." Brolli grinned. "You can court later."

…The Blood of the Phyros made men immortal, but it also made them wild. Many immortals slew friends or lovers in rages, later to take their own lives in grief. Others embraced the rage, and when all friends fled or perished, lived only for battle and rapine. It was the excesses of these last that led ultimately to the Cleansing…

—From *Arkendia's Iron Age,* by Timus of Prand

14

The High Prince & the Hostess

Mother Ganner followed two purple-liveried servants through the north wing of her lodge for an audience with the newly arrived prince. Krato's Moon must've come early for a prince to stay in Gallows Ferry. He'd taken over the north wing with his army of servants. Yet his people were civil, paying twice the fee for his rooms and twice again to the lodgers he expelled. In the few hours since his arrival, his servants had transformed the place under a multitude of carpets and tapestries and scented candelabra so that she hardly recognized it. Even the door at which she waited to be announced had been nailed over with cloth of gold, as if no surface should meet his royal gaze unless it be a comfort to the eye.

Two stolid guards waited on her in the dimness of the foyer. Her chins quivered with fear, which made her curse herself for a fool. She hadn't forgotten the pain of Bannus's blow, and the likelihood he'd kill her if he saw her again. But it was her own house, wasn't it? No matter if a prince waited beyond that door, *she* was queen here.

"His Highness will see you," a guard said.

The words stole her breath like a plunge in cold water. She followed the guard into a bunkhouse transformed with gold candelabra, fine furniture, and wine-purple rugs and tapestries. The air seemed heavy with sweet, soothing scents. Lightheadedness came and went, and things around her took on a strangely sparkling clarity. She feared for a moment she might be fainting.

Another guard led her through a wall of hangings to a brightly lit alcove, where she found the prince upon a carven audience chair. A candelabrum stood on a gold-leaf table behind him, beside a glittering crystal liquor service.

At first he seemed no man at all, but a god—some separate race as far above men as mountains above mounds—for he wore naught but gold and violet, and his skin seemed flushed with lavender, as though his blood were truly the purple of the gods. Yet his stature was not great. She surely outweighed him. Nor was he tall or physically powerful; rather he was thin, almost waiflike in face and body, with fragile features and exceedingly fine white hair that fell straight to his shoulders.

The power of his presence came instead from a sense of calm that suffused the space around him like a perfume in a pleasant room. The calm violet eyes especially drew her. They did not judge her, nor prejudge anything, it seemed, but rather beheld each thing anew, seeing past the temporary to the eternal. He seemed to her somehow outside of time as she knew it, and things moved more slowly, and calmly, where he was. It calmed her nerves simply being near him—so much, she noticed, that her trembling ceased altogether.

She bowed low. "Your Majesty, I'm sorry to bother you, but it ain't for me I come."

"Yet it seems you have some cause, for your cheek is injured," he replied, his voice as calm as his eyes.

She stared at the golden carpet at his feet, unable to look up. Words tumbled from her lips as if he'd uncorked her heart with those eyes. "There's a girl here works for me, Highness. She disappeared since you arrived, and I'm powerful worried for her. I don't ask for much, but if Your Majesty could see to sending her back to me I'd be obliged and your humble servant."

"Send her back? Good lady, do you believe I or my servants have delayed her?"

She glanced up, uncertain whether he took offense at her assumptions. She wrung her big hands before her, then hid them behind her back, for they seemed suddenly ugly and profane in his presence. "I know you arrived before Sir Bannus did, but I guess he must be with you, Majesty, and—he…"

The prince stood. "Sir Bannus. He abducted your girl?"

"I tried to fetch her back, but I daren't try again." She indicated her cheek with a thumb, and the prince's cheeks flushed.

"Good lady, it grieves me to hear it whispered I am his master. Indeed, I think he no longer has a master. But he may yet respect a prince, so I shall attempt what I can for your girl."

Mother Ganner fell to her knees weeping in gratitude, her love rising near worship. "Gods leave Your Majesty!"

When the guards ushered the hostess from his presence, Prince Jamus turned to the brandy set and poured a crystal of the amber liquor.

"Come out now, Carlon, and tell me what you saw." A hanging behind his chair stirred and his nephew emerged, ten years old, eyes sparking with interest.

"You lied to her, Uncle Jamus," Carlon said. Accusation shaded his tone.

"Yes. But why?" Jamus could see the boy knew the answer. He saw just as clearly that his pride kept him silent. Jamus smiled. "Because now I own her trust."

"My father says a prince should never fear to speak the truth."

"And your father is a wise man, Carlon. Wise enough to send you here with me, to learn what he cannot teach you. Remember this: *nothing that serves the greater truth is a lie.* Are we not right? Do we not have the god's seal and canon?"

"Yes."

"Then if all we say is in service of his cause, our lies are not lies at all, but holy things."

"Will you save this girl?"

"I won't need to. Sir Bannus will release her when he's done. What better way to remind these people of the Old Ways than to leave a sacrificial survivor? But I will surely tell the hostess it was I who saved her, and further win her trust."

"But why should you want it, Uncle? She's a stupid, smelly cow."

"Hence the incense prior to her coming."

The boy smiled in spite of himself. "It *is* smoky in here."

The prince sat, and waved Carlon to a chair beside him. The boy slipped onto it, pulling his legs up to his chest on the seat. He was very much like Jamus in appearance: slender, fair almost to albinism, small for his age. He'd never be a warrior, like his father. But also like Jamus, he was uncommonly clever, well suited for statecraft.

"There's more to the incense than my dislike of smelly cows, and there's more to her dullness than mere stupidity: there is *sacrium* in the incense. You're used to the drug, but for her it dampened her wits and amplified good feelings. But to answer your question, I want her trust because trust is often more powerful than fear. And she knows this area and all in it, so her goodwill is a useful thing." Carlon squirmed a little in his chair. "What else did you see, Carl?"

"It happened just like you said it would with Bannus. He attracted bad attention to us."

"Yes?"

"But now she'll say we aren't allied to him."

Jamus nodded. "Ironically, tonight I must approach Sir Bannus and win him to our family."

"Tonight, Uncle?"

"To delay would show I fear him, which is worse than confronting him in his rage. Do you remember your great grandsire when he'd taken the Blood?"

Carlon nodded, eyes widening. "He scared me."

"He scared us all. But you never saw me show it. Once you master yourself in the presence of an immortal, few things in life will trouble you. It's a shame we can no longer learn that from him."

Jamus stood, signaling the end of his lesson. He glanced at the tiny gold clock on the table, and frowned. "Before you retire, find Prince Ellentane and send him to me. He is late."

Carlon nodded, but hesitated, frowning. "Why do you call Ellentane a prince if his blood rank is only Sapphire?"

The rigid views on Blood Purity—so sacred to the boy's father—now echoed through the son, and they caused Jamus's shoulders to stiffen. "Prince Ellentane has married my sister, your aunt, and *she* is as royal as Krato himself. The title is a courtesy, Carlon, that you will use at all times. Is that clear?"

"Yes, Uncle."

A commotion sounded in the hall beyond the tapestries. A moment later the guards announced a young knight, who entered in haste and dropped to his knee.

"Your Majesty...six men," he panted, as if he'd been running. "Slain. It was Sir Willard, Your Highness. Here in the stable yard."

The prince closed his eyes briefly as a spike of anger passed. He put his brandy aside. "Who saw it?"

"Prince Ellentane survived it, Your Majesty. He saw it all."

"*Ellentane?* What in the name of the Black Moon was he doing in a fray?"

"I don't know, Your Majesty. He was unconscious when they found him, but sitting when I left. He said himself they were hexed, and he bid me find you."

Jamus found his brother-in-law sprawled against the back of the lodge with a burly squire at either shoulder. His sapphire silks bunched in dusty disarray, and a nasty red lump swelled above his right temple, with a slight break in the skin. He held his head motionless, eyes barely open, as if he strove to placate a titanic headache.

"Ellentane," Jamus whispered. "As the last of your line, you ought to be more careful."

Ellentane smiled weakly. His voice was faint, as if speaking might aggravate his pain. "Lovely skirmish. Pity you missed it."

Jamus dismissed the squires and produced a small leather box, which he set in Ellentane's lap. From it he removed a dark vial of Phyros blood. Ellentane sighed in relief as Jamus prepared it.

"What were you thinking?" Jamus muttered. "You were supposed to meet with me, not follow a brawl."

"Willard was here. Couldn't find the ambassador." He gingerly indicated his swollen temple with a gloved finger. "He found me."

"If you had come to me instead of attacking, we'd have captured them. Sir Bannus is *here*, Ellentane. Here. Why did you abandon our plans?"

Ellentane groaned. "Hexed. I'd swear it. Doesn't make sense…" His hand trembled as he wiped the perspiration from his brow.

Jamus sighed. "Willard seems to have that effect on people these days," he murmured. "First your squire breaks rank and delays your pursuit, now you go after Willard in your dinner silks. The Mad Moon appears to have affected your wits tonight. Here." He held the vial to Ellentane's lips. "Drink this." Jamus tipped the vial to Ellentane's lips, and he swallowed.

"Willard had help. A Cobalt, or a Sapphire."

"Surely you would know the difference."

Ellentane frowned. "I was too occupied at the time to compare my sleeve with his."

"Either way, it was undoubtedly the same knight my grooms found in the bastard's apartment. The stable master claims this Sapphire is but a horse-touched half-wit in blue armor."

"The big girl? The one that broke Keeter's lance?"

Jamus nodded. "There is only one Cobalt house that might have such a one. I suspect she could be Moss Isle's oddling daughter."

Ellentane chuckled. "The First Sword's sister? Oh, that's rich."

"It would be rather awkward for the family, I should think, were it known."

Jamus studied the lump on Ellentane's head, which the Phyros blood had shrunk substantially, turning it from red to faint purple. "Feeling well enough to stand?"

"I think so."

Jamus helped him to his feet, and signaled to a young knight sorting the bodies. The youth joined him, face grim from his work, and slick with perspiration. He bowed. "Your Majesty?"

"Did you find the witch's stone?"

The young man stiffened, looking for a moment like he would make the sign of the heart as a ward against the Black Witch's spirit, but stopped himself as if to hide his discomfort from his prince. "I…searched him, Your Majesty. I didn't find it. And the squires scoured every cranny with torchlight, but still nothing."

"Hardly surprising," Ellentane said. "It probably goes back to its moon when the witch dies, wouldn't you think?"

This time the young knight made the sign of the heart without hesitation. "I should hope so, Your Majesty."

"Have Dilbury search the witch again, and I want you to personally search the yard again with torches. Look in barrels; dismantle woodpiles. He may have hid it before he died, and we can't have it rolling about causing more trouble for us here. If we find it, contain it, and bring it to me so I may fling it in the river and be done with it."

The youth nodded and left, just as one of Ellentane's grooms brought the flustered stable master before them. The groom forced the stableman to his knees before Jamus.

"I was beaten!" the stableman pleaded. "Robbed! I couldn't do nothing, I swears."

"You stink of ale vomit and ragleaf," Jamus said. "You were easy prey."

"Your Maj—"

The groom boxed the stableman's ear, cutting his protest short, and the prince continued as if uninterrupted.

"Gentlemen perished here. Our horses taken. For this, someone must pay. Either you, for your negligence…or another. Do you understand?"

The stableman stared, eyes like peeled eggs. He nodded.

"Listen carefully, then, while I tell you what you saw here tonight. There is a peasant priest camped with his flock of masterless slaves to the north. Tonight he and his slaves murdered several gentlemen here in the yard and stole all the horses from the stables."

The stableman nodded vigorously. "I seen him, Majesty."

Jamus rose, and signaled the squires to aid Ellentane in standing. Without looking at the stableman, he said, "Then you know what you must do."

The groom holding the stableman jerked him to his feet and released him as a crowd of inn lodgers swarmed from the south side of the lodge, shouting and following torchbearers to the stables.

The stable master lumbered to intercept them, bellowing, "Robbery! Murder! Lords is dead and the stables empty! It was the peasant priest done it! He and his lordless slaves!"

Jamus and Ellentane watched from the far side of the yard as the stableman stoked the crowd to a mob with what seemed a practiced hand. In the time it would have taken them to pour a cup of brandy and raise it in salute to Ellentane's health, the mob hit the road with torches and swords and ropes held high.

"You've always been a gifted motivator," said Ellentane.

Jamus scarcely heard him. Now that the crisis was over, he let his anger have rein in his blood. "Had Sir Bannus been alert tonight and not gorging like a boar at a trough, our business here would be finished, our future secure, and tomorrow we'd board my brother's waterwheel for a comfortable cruise down the river."

Ellentane winced. "I'm sorry. I should have told you we had Willard—"

"I do not hold you accountable, Ellentane. I believe the ambassador's magic witched you, just as it witched your squire today in the market. Sir Bannus is a different matter. He is wild, and requires a master. I must bring him to heel as my grandsire did before me."

Ellentane raised his brow in surprise. "Bannus. To heel."

"Come. Shall we see if I'm as gifted at motivating immortals?"

"Er. Tonight? Wouldn't tomorrow be best?"

Jamus studied the wounds on two of the corpses Willard left in the dirt— efficient cuts, just deep enough in just the right spots. He frowned. "There is no best time for dealing with immortals."

Two knights waited by the bodies in the stable yard as their squires inquired after carpenters to construct coffins.

One rested against a water barrel, gnawing a fingernail. The other squatted beside the glassy-eyed corpse of Sir Yolan, whose face seemed stuck in vain astonishment. The squatting knight tried to shut Yolan's eyes with his hand.

"His eyes won't close."

"Leave him, poor chap. A decent fellow, was Yolan. Ate like a Phyros-rider. That Willard seems as stout as ever, what?"

"Shouldn't have tried to take him. I don't care how big you are, you can't take a Phyros-rider. And they were fools to try without armor. What do you think came over them?"

The standing knight crossed to peer down at the body of the Iberg, and shuddered. "Glad to be rid of that witch, though. I don't know why His Majesty brought him, but he gave me the cold shivers. He and that horrid moon cat."

"Haven't seen it, have you?" said the other, still fussing with Yolan's eyes.

"Not a glimpse, and I don't care if I ever do. Even dead I wouldn't touch it."

"Pah. It's just an animal."

"I beg to differ. I've seen it *do* things."

"Like?"

"Where do you think the witch's stone went?" He raised an eyebrow and waited out a meaningful pause.

"You think a cat took it."

"I most certainly do. That cat isn't natural, I tell you. I've heard a witch keeps *spirits* in his moon cat. Dead ghosts from the unhallowed moon that he feeds with the souls of his victims."

"You're afraid of a cat."

"I'm afraid of witches, and so you should be. When you look in the eyes of that cat, it's the witch's spirits you see looking back out. *Unnatural* is the word. And with no one to feed them now, there's no telling what trouble may come of it."

The color violet represents Arkendian royal blood in the blood-arch.
Only families married among royals for five or more generations may claim it.
Each generation of royal-to-royal marriage is signified in the coat of arms
with a gold "bar," or ray, radiating from the central device.
Shields of the oldest royals have so many bars their emblems a
ppear as sunbursts of rays, hence the moniker "Suns of Arkendia."

— From A Study of Arkendian Heraldry, by Chani of Losif Major

15

On Treating with Gods

Jamus and Ellentane entered the south wing of the lodge, where six of their knights stood watch over the hall in which Bannus chambered.

Sir Grennit, a stocky knight in green armor, stepped forward officiously. "It has been a quiet watch, Your Majesty."

"Sir Bannus remains within?"

"He does, Your Majesty."

"He took a girl from among the staff."

Ellentane raised an eyebrow. "Same Bannus, I see."

"The girl is gone now." Grennit nodded toward an adjacent servant passage. "Seems to have slipped out of a hole His Holiness created in a wall."

"Send word to the hostess that I secured the girl's release."

Grennit signaled a squire, who left with the message. "Sir Bannus's shield bearer is on watch," he said, as he ushered the princes to Bannus's door. "It's said that he…" The knight seemed to search for appropriate words. "That he's become a…" Grennit frowned.

"You refer to Titus," said Jamus. "Indeed, a sad story. A bastard of my father's making."

Grennit bowed, signaling his gratitude to be so deep in the prince's confidence. He opened the door to a dark passage, giving Jamus a candlestick.

Jamus met Ellentane's eyes only briefly, to assure himself his brother-in-law was prepared, then led him into the paneled hall. Grennit closed the door softly behind.

In the light of Jamus's candle, Sir Bannus's shield bearer cut a lean, straight figure upon a stool outside his master's door. He sat erect as a pillar, wrapped in clothes and capes of deep royal violet, his gloved hands folded in his lap. Before the princes' arrival he'd sat in complete darkness. He did not stir when they approached, nor did he turn to meet them, but remained in profile, as motionless as the carving of a man.

The yellow light reflected from his partly hooded face in little glimmers, as though his cheeks were made of glass. When they halted beside him, they saw he wore a glassy red-stone mask concealing his features.

"Gods leave us," Ellentane whispered.

Jamus fought back his own revulsion. Titus had become a Faceless One. Bannus had resurrected the vilest cult of the worst days before the Cleansing, and imposed it upon his squire.

"Welcome back to the Isle of Heroes, Titus, Bastard of Pellion," Jamus murmured.

The figure remained motionless, but the candlelight now illumined him fully, allowing Jamus to study him. The mask was carved of wine-red alabaster, the traditional material, for the coolness of the stone was said to soothe the heat of the scars. The mask's expression was mild and serene, its features of idealized male beauty—cleft chin, cut jaw, delicately sculpted lips and nose—and with an air of dreamy, almost sleepy repose.

"You see my devotion to His Holiness," Titus gasped through the mask. He convulsed slightly with the effort of speech.

Jamus's nostrils flared. "Is that what your master calls it? Devotion?"

"All is discipline. All is will. The body nothing. Pain unreal."

Jamus regarded him for several heartbeats in silence. He exchanged a grim glance with Ellentane. Then, as if his bastard brother were no longer present, he turned crisply, and seized the handles to Bannus's chambers.

One of Titus' gloved hands flashed to Jamus's wrist. His breath came in strangely hissing rasps. "His Eminence does not wish to be disturbed."

The prince did not look at the Faceless One, nor did he remove his hand from the door. "Is he sleeping?"

"Resting."

"Is he with company?"

"Alone."

"Will he...punish you, if I enter?"

"He"—there was a strange, dry-throated swallowing behind the mask—"left orders. None enter."

Jamus quirked a tiny smile on one side of his mouth. "He makes you immortal with the Phyros blood? Heals you with it?" Titus said nothing, but his breathing was harsh and gurgling. He released Jamus's wrist, and stumbled from the stool to face the prince on one knee. Red-rimmed eyes pleaded mutely within the mask. Jamus snorted in disgust. "So refreshing to see the—what did you call it? Devotion?—to the Old Ways, Titus." Then, sadly, "You could have stayed with us, you know. Our father didn't offer immortality, but his sort of devotion paid well in other ways. You would have found it so."

Titus stood. He straightened his cloak around him and sat back on his stool, still and erect. Once again a carving of a man. "All is discipline. All is will..." he chanted, as if the princes had left him.

Jamus met Ellentane's gaze. Beneath his brother-in-law's stern aspect, Jamus sensed horror. "Ellentane," Jamus said, softly but firmly. "Worse than this lies beyond these doors."

Ellentane nodded curtly.

"Under no circumstance must Sir Bannus sense your fear, or it will send his wildness past recovery. Remember this: an Old One is half god, half rabid beast, but he respects one thing above all else—royalty. Which we must appear to be, or he will tear us and our titles to pieces."

Jamus laid his hands on the doors in preparation for heaving them inward. "I should probably tell you, too, that he is also likely quite insane. The most ancient of the Old Ones usually are, which is why they're so unpredictable."

This time Ellentane's face remained an undisturbed shell of indifference. "Ah, well," he said lightly, "who isn't a bit mad these days?"

"Steel yourself," Jamus warned, and heaved the doors inward.

Twelve men had been evicted from the room Sir Bannus commandeered, and all dozen beds lay stacked against the walls. Their mattresses had been heaped in the middle of the room like a hedge boar's midden, at the foot of which lay a clutter of grease-streaked platters, stripped ox bones, and discarded mugs of blood drafts.

The immortal Sir Bannus sprawled across the summit of this mountain like a drunken god, as gloriously nude as a court painting of some West Isle scene in the days before the Cleansing. His body was a shocking topography of popping veins, impossible muscle, and quantities of ropy purple scars: the wounds of twenty lifetimes in battle, all healed with the Blood of the Phyros. It was a scene few in Arkendia had witnessed since the Cleansing, but one quite common before it—a glutted god, his blood rage cooled with flesh and drafts, sated, half fallen, half reclining, like a sleeping lion.

Pieces of outlandish Diurn armor adorned the edges of the room, and against one wall stood the monstrous Phyros sword, *Basilisk*. A lacy bit of white cloth concealed Sir Bannus's face, draped there, perhaps, as a scented souvenir of the innkeeper's girl.

A faint suck of breath from Ellentane. He closed the doors quietly behind, and remained in Jamus's shadow as if he'd disappear there.

"Welcome back to Arkendia, Sir Bannus," the prince murmured. "It has been…eighty years, has it not? Before my father's birth."

The immortal remained, lolling magnificently, horribly, arms thrown wide, face turned to the rafters. After what seemed like an eternity, the graveled basso finally welled from the massive chest like a cataract of grief. "Liar. You lie. This is not Arkendia. This is some other land. Ruled by women, peopled by dogs. I do not know this land."

"It has indeed changed in your absence."

"This is not Arkendia. In Arkendia, my order is revered. Our will is law. We are worshipped with fear."

"Gone now. All has changed."

The immortal clutched his head with both scar-knotted hands, as if trying to hold his mind together, or keep out an unwanted truth. "Are there none left now?" he cried in anguish. "None of my order? Is it possible? All slain? All hiding? And do the peasant priests strut openly, unchecked like wild dogs? Arkendia! O, father of gods, where have you gone?"

"Arkendia is not gone, Sir Bannus, only weakened, as with a disease. But the source of the disease—their queen—is weak also, which gives us hope, and opportunity."

The Phyros-rider lifted the lace from his face and peered from one eye at the grandson of Jormus Mont Pellion, his one-time liege lord. Jamus recognized immediately the signs of madness. The visage was a wreckage of scars. Not the scars of battle—even the battles of twenty lifetimes would not account for this, if one bothered with a helmet—this was gratuitous scarification. Self-mutilation.

Jamus had seen it in his grandfather, the last immortal of his family. In ten years he'd fallen from incisive intellect and sound, reliable judgment to morbid meditations and self-dismemberment. At banquets, he removed fingers and displayed them on forks. "Am I not still I, without this?" he would ask. Ears came next, and his nose, and, most horribly, his eyes and left hand, discarded in odd places around the palace, and left for others to find, like the leavings of a molting serpent. "If I remove my face, am I not still I? Is there any meaning in this vessel at all? This world?"

Yet his grandfather had enough sanity left to sense his own end, and prepared to offer himself in sacrifice. He constructed a blood throne of complicated troughs and runnels, according to an inner knowledge. On it he opened his veins, and from the paths the Blood chose in the runnels he made a powerful augury.

Sir Bannus's face suggested that he, too, had progressed well into similar madness. He had no ears, and now that he knew to look for it, Jamus noted pruned fingertips, amputated toes, and ritual scars meandering heel to crown. Such madness did not bode well for Jamus's hopes of winning the immortal's loyalty back to his family, but it was not wholly unexpected.

"Do the true immortals hide?" Bannus rumbled. "Are all lost? Is there only the Abominator, whom I track?"

"Helsig and Gravens remain in the West Isles."

"Two. Send for them. Tell them I have returned."

"I have already done so, Sir Bannus. As you may remember, it was I who called you back for a purpose."

"You?" Bannus's eyes narrowed. A strangled laugh clattered from his throat. "I see a rouge of dried Phyros blood in your cheeks," he sneered. "You take it in your wine, to paint your blood as if you were an immortal. Behold! A Sun of Arkendia paints his blood like a woman paints her face. You do not drink the Blood from your family's Phyros, as your grandfather did. You are weak in the Old Ways. Unfit for the Brotherhood."

"Of what use is this Blood to the Brotherhood if it cannot be controlled? Tonight we lost six good men to Sir Willard. Yes, he was here while you lay feeding your bloodlust in bed. Outside these very walls. And unmounted. Such disorder is the reason Willard and his Blue Order triumphed in the Cleansing."

Bannus did not rise to this barb. He stared at the prince, still mocking. "Pretty painted prince. You are the image of your great-grandfather at your age. Which son are you? Second? Third? They would not send the eldest to me."

Jamus closed his eyes and performed a hint of a nod. "I am the third son of the first son of your lord, my grandsire."

"As I thought. Disposable." Sir Bannus sat and met Jamus's gaze. His scar-ripped nostrils flared. "Then let us come to the point, painted one—

to the only matter between us: it was your grandsire who betrayed me, who abandoned Arkendia to the weak-blooded Abominator, Sir Willard. The same, traitorous blood flows in your veins. Give me a reason I shouldn't spill it here, in vengeance."

"It was Sir Willard and the Blue Order that killed your order—"

Bannus roared, veins popping from his face and eyes. "*It was Pellion, your grandsire. Pellion who betrayed me to die. Pellion who ran me from the land.*"

Jamus kept his face impassive, though a cold fire of fear burned steadily behind it. Of all men in Arkendia, Jamus knew what it meant to treat with an immortal, and how to survive the encounter. He had been raised with his immortal grandsire, who used several techniques to test, overawe, and intimidate, which Jamus now saw in Bannus. There was only one valid response to any of these techniques: calm, patience, and mild superiority.

And even that could fail.

Jamus closed his eyes and allowed himself a tiny sigh. "I see the Blood is still wild within you, and you have lost the power to reason. I haven't the time to return, so I'll speak slowly in hope you hear some of it. The reason you will not kill me is that you need me."

"I need only to slay the Abominator, and I don't need you for that."

"True. I can't help you kill Willard. But you need my family to return your order to power."

"There are other Suns of Arkendia, Pellion. They can serve that turn as well as you."

"There you are mistaken, Sir Bannus, or misled. Only House Pellion survived the Cleansing intact, and only because of my grandsire's wisdom, which you call betrayal."

The immortal howled, his rage shuddering the windows. "Wisdom! Witness, Arkendia. See how dishonor is become wisdom, treachery become faith."

Bannus rose slowly from his bed, towering over Jamus like a blue-skinned colossus. "I served your family for centuries, and your lord grandfather honored me and my order with *betrayal*. He hunted us like dogs with Sir Willard. And now a poor three of us left. Three! He sided with the Abominator—O vile allegiance!—and lent him strength and men." Sir Bannus foamed at the corners of his mouth, panting, wild-eyed, the blood rage returning. He threw back his head and howled again, a deep, unearthly furor that curdled the skin on the spine.

Ellentane stirred, and the baleful eyes snapped to him, a mad wolf scenting fear.

"Sir Bannus," said Ellentane, his voice faint but unwavering. "My family salutes you."

A blur of motion from the giant, and something flew across the room to crash against the door beside Ellentane.

A beef bone.

Jamus raised an unimpressed eyebrow at the missile, but didn't dare turn enough to see Ellentane, lest Ellentane mistake him for leaving and lose his resolve. To his relief, he could see Ellentane peripherally, standing unflinching.

"Thank you, my lord," said Ellentane. "But I have dined."

The Phyros-rider glared as if his gaze might set fire to Ellentane's skin. Abruptly, he laughed. He threw back his head and sank back on his mattresses. Jamus breathed a private sigh of relief.

"Your *family* salutes me," Bannus sneered. "Your family is dead. First of the Suns to fall to the Abominator, and all heirs lost but a *girl*." The torn lips twisted into what might have been a sneer. "You married a Pellion, didn't you." It wasn't a question. The immortal could see it as clearly as the clenching of Ellentane's jaw and the flush of blue in his cheeks. Bannus's laughter was hoarse and broken. "To salvage your beggared blood, House Ellentane married Pellion. You're a slave now, Ellentane. You and a hundred generations of your get. The Purity Laws require you marry your *own* sister, not his."

He flicked another bone to rattle at Ellentane's feet. "There is only one true Sun left in Arkendia, and that is House Dremousi. I have spoken with them," he said, measuring the lord's reaction with his eyes. "Yes. Even since I returned. They too, have plans."

"Oh? You are sworn to them?" Jamus allowed himself a wry smile. "Let me attempt to guess their plans. Could they be planning yet another assassination attempt of the Queen? What original device will it be this time? A poisoned hairpin?"

"The Old Ways still work, Pellion, though you have forgotten them. The Dremousi remember. They tell me you are no better than the Abominator himself. That you soften the Old Ways, so the Brotherhood grows weak. That you love peasant priests and compromise to win favor with the Bitch Queen. They say you walk with her, share counsel with her, that she trusts you."

Jamus let his scorn show openly. "Shall I be openly against her, like the Dremousi brothers? Shall I earn exile from the court, as they have? In exile they remain ignorant of her schemes, and she forbids trade with them, so their coffers are hollow. I, on the other hand, am in her counsels, and my coffers are full. More importantly, my blood is pure for one hundred royal generations, while the Dremousi are broken and fallen to a pair of exiled bastards, raised on the milk of foreign lands." Jamus snorted softly. "House Dremousi is an incompetent ally. And if they sit the throne, they make mockery of Blood Purity in Arkendia."

"You need me, Prince, but I don't need you. Your house played me false once, and now you try it again. I ride for the Old Ways. I ride for Dremousi."

Bannus made a show of examining an ox bone for a bit of stray meat. But whatever he had once been, this Old One was no longer a closed book. His soul seeped through the cracks in his sanity, where Jamus saw clearly the immensity of his grief at the perceived betrayal by his immortal liege, Jamus's grandsire.

Jamus shifted his tone to signal an end of argument and beginning of parley. "My grandsire did not betray you. When he appeared to join the Abominator in seeking you, he put them on false trails and exulted when he learned you escaped to the Immortal Isle. He loved you. He longed to recall you, his greatest ally. But it was not time, nor did the time come while he lived. He watched for generations, for a time when Arkendia would grow soft and forget, and that time is now. I said I called you back, but truly it was he that called you. And you must know that, or you wouldn't have answered the call."

"I answered no *call*. You merely woke me from a dream, and I came for revenge. For the Abominator. To pay him for his treachery. And to see…" Bannus halted, mid-snarl, hesitating.

"And to see my grandsire," Jamus finished.

Bannus's scarred jaw twitched, and Jamus knew he had the giant's attention.

"Unfortunately, no one can grant you that wish, Sir Bannus. Not even my grandsire. Lord Jormus of Pellion joined our god this winter when he chose the blood throne, and augured Krato's will from his own mortal wounds."

Sir Bannus's eyes widened, and naked hope peered from behind them. Battered allegiance, aching for explanation. "The blood throne?" His voice was a ragged whisper. "He took the blood throne? He died in augury?"

"It was from his dying words that I took the instructions to call you. He left prophecies to raise the blood of every Sun and immortal in Arkendia."

The immortal clambered to his knees, violet eyes wild with new hope. Before he could doubt again, Jamus drew forth a folded, blood-addled parchment, sealed with the mark of Jormus Pellion, and held it for Bannus to see.

"Here you will read for the words he left for you alone, scribed himself in his dying blood upon the bleeding throne. In his canon to my eldest brother he instructed us join in marriage to Ellentane; therefore we are bound to trust the union. In his canon to you he surely repeats that Willard must be slain and the Blue Order destroyed. He hints as much in the canons to his grandsons."

Jamus laid the stained seal gently in Bannus's hand, like a butterfly lighting on a talon. "This should suffice to convince you I am not a shadow of the former world, but an agent of the former world itself, and that Pellion is as close in Krato's will as any have ever been."

The giant's body grew still and taut, bunched and focused on the fragile parchment. His knotted fingers broke the seal, and he read the contents greedily.

Jamus concealed his disappointment that Bannus could read, but watched the immortal carefully, and counted the lines of text from the motion of his eyes. It soon became clear that the prophecy and instruction given to Sir Bannus was substantial indeed, easily as long as his own, which, until that moment, he had thought the only lengthy canon.

Doubt sprouted in Jamus's mind. Until then it had appeared his grandsire trusted Jamus with the greatest burden of the prophecy. Even his elder brother, the object of their ambitions for the throne, had but a few uncomplicated lines, and Jamus had seen them all. Jamus's canon was detailed and dynamic, with contingencies and layers—like a master plan—for he was the smart one, the clever one, the subtle one, the patient one.

This canon to Bannus threw all into question. Had his grandsire told the immortal anything he had not told Jamus? Would he play them off each other for some purpose of his own? Terrifying as it was, it seemed clear now Jamus was not the highest pinnacle of his grandsire's designs.

Bannus lowered the parchment, and met Jamus's gaze with something like peace in his violet eyes. In that moment it seemed the cracks in his sanity drew up and sealed tight, and he peered now from a cunning, secret mind. He folded the canon. "It seems by this that the Brotherhood of Krato yet lives. Your grandsire sends me to slay the Abominator, as you say. And he gives me the title of Lord High Executioner, first held by Gristhi, and after him Marlank at the time of the Cleansing. And I am to name the Justicar…"

Banus halted, eyes flashing to Jamus. He raised a finger in the air between them, mocking Jamus's façade of indifference. "There are other things, my painted prince, but they concern true immortals. Helsig and Gravens shall have titles. And orders."

Sir Bannus tossed his head backward, and threw his arms wide to the sky. "O wisdom. O wisdom of the god!" His eyes flamed with purpose, and it seemed to Jamus that the broken god upon the midden had risen, reborn, the fire of divinity in his veins. Bannus pressed his tangled lips to the fragile parchment, eyes closed as if in bliss. "I shall bind this canon into *Basilisk*, under the wires of his handle, and it shall give him such authority that the Abominator will tremble, and he will know that the god himself seeks him, to reclaim his stolen Blood."

"You should know, Sir Bannus, that Sir Willard is no longer immortal. He stopped taking the Blood and grows old."

Bannus reacted as if slapped; his brows contracted in confusion. "*Stopped?*" He laughed harshly, doubting, but saw no mirth in Jamus's face. "What do you mean? No Blood? What is he, then?"

"He's a man. Old and soft. Dying, like any other."

Something like panic—or anger—flickered in the immortal's eyes. "It can't be. You lie."

"He is yet formidable, as he demonstrated this night."

"Pah! He keeps his wounds?"

"You wouldn't know him if you saw him. But you will know Molly. And the Blue Order still live in Peridot Rock. They are twelve, and Willard sits at their table."

Bannus's grin returned. "Yes. The *bread eaters*. They will still have some fight to them, though they've shrunk to the size of little girls. I'll send to Phyrosi for the brothers who returned there with me. Fichris, Tygus, Grippan, Stiggard. They yet live, and their names bring fear."

Jamus nodded as if approving a vassal's suggestion, but instantly felt the hollowness of his authority in light of Bannus's secret canon. "We shall lead our own Counter-Cleansing, in time," he said, reasserting his stamp on the discussion. "But first you must capture Willard. He must be alive, and able to stand, and speak, and stand trial. I know this much from my own canon. Do you understand? He must not be slain."

Bannus snorted. "Willard is already dead. He has slain himself. But I need understand nothing from you, painted one. Dance your little dance with the Queen. I take my orders from the god himself."

Sir Bannus reclined again on the summit of his mountain and held the canon above him at arm's length to behold it. "Leave me, now. And let Arkendia know I've returned. Sir Bannus, Lord High Executioner of Krato, has returned, to save Arkendia from disgrace."

Jamus stood at the dining table in his chambers, palms flat on its surface, leaning his weight upon them so his shoulder blades jutted from his back like bony wing stumps beneath the silks. He hung his head wearily.

In the audience chamber behind him, Ellentane rattled the brandy decanter on the crystal service, pouring two crystals full, by the sound of it, then stealthily knocking one back and refilling. His boots thumped across the rugs drawing nearer until he stopped at Jamus's side, and a pale hand set a tumbler precisely between his hands.

Ellentane stepped back. He inhaled as if he would speak, then let the breath out slowly. He said nothing.

"Sir Bannus did not swear himself to House Pellion," Jamus murmured. "He serves the words in his canon, which he does not show to us." He stood and faced his brother-in-law. Ellentane tried to meet him with a wry smile, but the attempt looked more like the grimace that comes of a bad memory.

"To your first encounter with an immortal," said Jamus. They raised glasses, and some of the usual triumph returned to Ellentane's eyes. "It was not all bad, for we live, and Sir Bannus is not outwardly against us. To small victories."

Ellentane drained his tumbler. Jamus drank only half. "I must replace my lost witch. I believe there is one on my brother's ship, is there not?"

Ellentane nodded. "A fire caller of the Mad Moon, as I think."

Jamus nodded. "Just so. Immortals do not like fire, Ellentane. Do you know my grandsire forbade fire witches to enter Pellion lands at all? He dealt only with the Unseen or Bright Mother."

"I have heard fire does not heal for them the way a blade wound does."

"It heals, but remains a torment. They respect fire like nothing else." Jamus smiled, and drained the rest of his glass. "I will send for this witch. A fire caller at my side will be as great a comfort to me as it give Bannus pause."

...Of all the Blue Order, Sir Willard retained most of his humanity, despite the extreme discipline of the Rule of Anatos. For this reason — and for his leadership in the Cleansing — Sir Willard appealed to the popular imagination. Some scholars contest that this appeal came not from his victories, but from a talent for bungling in matters of love and politics...most agree now this was invented by balladeers for dramatic affect.

— From *Legends and Lies*, by Tulos of Burry

16

A Triumph of Trickery

Harric and Caris rode together wordlessly on Rag. They followed Brolli, splashing up the stream through a broad wooded valley. The dwarf-man perched awkwardly upon his pony's saddle, as if crouching, for his legs and rump were too small for proper riding, and his long arms bent akimbo to clutch its mane. The Phyros-thief brought up the rear, leading his "unridable" spare on a tether.

Even if there were no fear of pursuit and no reason to keep silent, Caris would have been unable to speak, for she devoted her entire concentration on calming Rag near the Phyros. Partly, too, Harric suspected she welcomed that immersion just then, fleeing into it from the baffling revelation of the wedding ring on her finger. That was just as well, for Harric himself was in shock on a number of fronts. He had no idea what to make of the wedding ring, but even worse — if that were possible — was the revelation his mother could influence one of the immortal Old Ones — the mad Sir Bannus, no less! — to hunt and slay him.

Frustration and despair tore at him. He wanted to rage and weep and break things. Even the excitement of their escape from Gallows Ferry was short-lived — bludgeoned from him over the mile of jarring road until he wanted nothing more than to crawl his beaten body beneath a log and expire.

Brolli never paused long enough for Harric to indulge that fantasy. They sloshed through sandy shallows, stumbled through stony rapids, maneuvered around fallen trees, putting miles between themselves and the road. Occasionally the stream crossed rough forest roads or through pastures cut from the woods by sleeping farmsteads. Most of the farms were low, dark buildings with smoldering beast-pots outside their doors, to keep the yoab and mountain cats away.

Shepherd fires winked on hillsides above them where dogs barked, low notes lonely in the distance.

On one occasion they passed within bowshot of a barn full of light and laughter and fiddle music. Brolli led them up the opposite bank in a wide arc through pastures, returning to the stream when well past danger of a sighting. Once past, they halted again among the willows along the stream and waited while he dismounted and retraced their steps to erase or conceal the evidence of their passing.

During the longest of these halts, Caris removed her armor and packed it in the oil cloths and canvas she kept in her packs. Harric made no apology for lumping his own pack there as well, and letting her sort the armor herself while he soaked his battered face in the cold stream. One eye was swollen shut. One lip was fat and the other split. Funny how he hadn't even noticed during the escape. He found several crab apples beneath the scalp, which explained why his skull felt as if it were shrinking around his brain. The ribs on his left side, though surely only bruised or he would not have been able to stand, nevertheless felt like broken crockery in his chest.

Cupping the cold water to his face, he held it against his bruises until it drained, then cupped it again, and again.

Voices dogged the edge of his consciousness. It wasn't Willard's voice, nor Brolli's or Caris's. He wasn't sure how long they'd been there. All night? Faint whispers at the edge of his awareness. He stood, disoriented and dizzy as they murmured, warped and unintelligible, as through a pipe or bottle.

From the bank the moon cat watched through egg-white eyes.

"Bannus knocked my brain loose, Spook," he muttered. Spook stared. Harric splashed water in the cat's direction, but it only retreated a few paces and went back to staring.

"Boy?" said the knight. "You all right?"

"No," Harric said. "I'm not. But I'll live." He stooped again, cupping water to his eye. The voices had ceased.

"This friend you're leading us to, boy. She's a fire-cone warden?"

Harric paused, water dripping from his cheeks and chin. "*Caris* is leading us."

"She…helped me this winter," Caris said, speaking in the strained, halting tone she took when trying to attend to people and horses at once. Rag fidgeted, backing and pulling against her tether, as if part of Caris's attention was not enough to calm her near the Phyros. "I stayed with her," Caris managed. "She'd…welcome us."

The old knight only glanced at Caris, and spoke again to Harric. "This fire-cone warden. It's got to be a few days' travel to a fire-cone grove, doesn't it?"

Harric cupped more water to his face. He'd only seen a fire-cone tower once as a boy, on an adventure with Chacks and Remo. They'd plotted to the famous trees to steal bushels of the resin-rich cones and make their fortunes (or at least enough to make a walloping resin charge). They had grand times hiking and camping and dreaming how they'd spend their shares, but like all boys, they found their stomachs less willing than their spirits once they ran out of food the second night. As they had turned back, sunrise mocked them with a clear view of the tower on a distant ridge.

"Farther than it seems," he answered. "At least a couple days."

Caris nodded. "It's two days from the road to a high pass. After we cross the pass, it's not even a full day's ride to the fire-cone grove and the tower. It's a very good place to disappear…I wouldn't have found it on my own. I was lost. Abellia found *me*."

The old knight grunted. "Just what we need, boy. Horses need rest. I should tend to these wounds. Been running too long."

Harric watched through the water in his lashes, looking for clues that might explain the old knight's strangeness toward Caris. Surely he couldn't blame Caris for his blunder with the ring…

Spook arched his back and hissed, scattering Harric's thoughts.

"Spook, what—"

The cat stared into the darkness of the wooded bank, where a pair of shining red eyes flashed in a glint of moonlight. Before Harric could raise the alarm, a voice greeted them from the darkness.

"It is me," Brolli said. "Sorry to surprise." He loped from the darkness into a larger patch of moonlight, and halted before Harric. Harric stared at the foreign features, trying to make sense of what he saw.

"Now that you can see me," said Brolli, "you must tell me: what am I? One of your Arkendian gods? A very big chimpey?"

Harric blinked. Chimpey was closer to his impression: long arms and short legs said as much. But "very big" didn't say the half of it. Brolli's trunk and arms were as powerful as any blacksmith's, and his hands were as wide and flat as baker's paddles. As Harric stared, the details he'd glimpsed earlier that night fell in place, and he began to understand just how *other* Brolli was. His face was flat and smooth and broad like an owl's, with an undersized nose and oversized eyes with enormous pupils.

When Brolli grinned, he bared thick, feral-looking canines. "Not a dwarfed man?" he said, as if reading Harric's thoughts.

Harric smiled with the half of his face that wasn't a swollen pad. "You're a Kwendi. I'll bet you're the ambassador that disappeared from court. Everyone's looking for you."

The owl eyes widened with pleasure. "Yes, you have it, young Arkendian. First Ambassador Brolli, at your service."

Harric bowed reflexively. "Harric Dimoore, at yours."

"Cut the chatter," said the old knight from where he stood with the horses. "Tell me how our trail looks."

Brolli winked at Harric, and loped on all fours to the others. "We make a good escape. I see no hunters behind, and I erase our tracks well."

The old man grunted. "Health bless your Kwendi eyes. They ought to find their horses well past us up the main road, and the hoof marks of the other horses will make it difficult if not impossible to decipher where we've gone. With any luck they'll conclude we boarded a raft or a waterwheel."

Caris nodded. "It'll take hours to fetch their horses."

"They didn't lose them all," said the knight. "Molly sensed another Phyros nearby. It was probably tied back at the gallows to keep the stables calm. I must assume its rider is an enemy."

"It's Bannus," Harric said. "I wanted to tell you. He was in Gallows Ferry tonight."

"Sir Bannus?" The old knight muttered a curse. "Then he's here for me. Gods leave us, that's grim news. But if he follows, Molly will sense his mount, Gygon, well before he could surprise us. That's something."

Harric made a wry face. "*Molly*. As in Sir Willard's Molly."

"Just so."

"Come on," Harric said. "We aren't total bumpkins, so you can leave the absurd fake names. Or at least make up something plausible, like, Sir Fumble-Ring or something."

The old man let out a cloud of ragleaf, his eyes flashing.

"You might have something there." Brolli chuckled. "'Sir Willard and the Fumbled Ring'? Perhaps I'll make one of these ballads myself."

"Do, and they'll never find your body," said the knight.

The Kwendi laughed.

"It's her, Harric," Caris said. She stood aloof, eyes distant, face strained. "It's Molly."

Harric blinked, dumbfounded. There was only one Phyros mare in Arkendia—Willard's Molly. The rest were stallions. He'd assumed the old knight's Phyros was male, because the tournament caparison draped across her haunches had concealed her sex, and because the old man *couldn't* have been the immortal Sir Willard. But there was no questioning Caris's horse sense.

The old man's eyes sparkled with amusement as he watched Harric's jaw wag soundlessly. "Not what you'd expect from Sir Willard, eh boy?"

"But…you're not immortal," said Harric feebly.

"Stopped taking the Blood some years ago, son. Best thing I ever did. Seven generations is a long time to live, and a man isn't made for it. It's a hard life, with the Blood. Changes a man."

"It didn't change you," Harric protested, as if his knowledge of the ballads were greater authority than the man himself. "In the ballads—"

"Damn the ballads," Willard growled. He snorted smoke through his nose, which made his mustachios smolder like tinder. "The truth wouldn't make a nice ballad. It isn't a good life." A shadow clouded his eyes, only to be lost behind a puff of ragleaf. "Past time to claim my mortality. Grow old with people I love, if they still live. Is that so strange?"

"Do not let him fool you with that speech," said Brolli wryly. "He tell me the same one, but I don't believe it."

Harric's head throbbed. He closed his eyes tightly and tried to put it all in order. His childhood hero, Sir Willard—Queen's Champion, Chief Architect of the Cleansing, greatest of the immortals and Blue Order—was right there before him, and dying. He climbed to his knees, bowing his head.

Old and dying, yes. But it was Sir Willard. *The* Willard, and *the* Molly. It made sense now that the old knight barely flinched when the witch vanished before his eyes. The ballads told of dozens slain by Willard and *Belle*.

"See that, Brolli?" said Willard. "That's the kind of respect I ought to get. None of this ballad nonsense."

"That is good. But why is he laughing?"

Harric couldn't help it. The whole procession of ludicrous events with Caris and the love charm that day suddenly made a kind of sense to him, for disasters and bungles involving love or politics were the trademark of a Sir Willard ballad. In them the great knight always ultimately triumphed, but not without creating some preposterous bungle on the side. "Caris, we're in a Willard ballad," he said, his giddiness growing. "We're the bungle. Don't you see? It started with that squire in the market, and our flight from home, and now that ring."

Caris smiled distantly. The Kwendi cast a confused look at Willard, who scowled.

"But if we're the bungle," said Harric, gaining control of his mirth to direct his words to Willard, "then what's the burden of this ballad? What's the main heroic theme?"

"What's the what?" said Willard. "I don't follow."

"I mean, what are you doing here? A magic love charm—a pack of murderous knights—Sir Bannus. What's it all about?"

The knight puffed silently on the ragleaf, the tip of the roll pulsing in the darkness. Sir Willard appeared to study Harric as if calculating what to reveal.

The Kwendi shrugged. "They with us now, for good or ill. Shall I tell it? We owe it."

Willard frowned. He nodded.

"It's simple," said Brolli. "When your people invent blasting resin and blast a road through the Godswall mountains, they see for the first time the big land beyond. They see only wild animals there, so your queen opens them to settlement and calls them Free Lands. Of course, she is wrong about no one lives there." Brolli bowed ironically. "For *we* live there."

"Yes, I know that," said Harric, "but what I don't know is why you and Willard are here with this ring, in the middle of nowhere."

Brolli flashed his feral grin. "I am sent to your queen's court as ambassador, to negotiate a peace treaty."

"And he couldn't stand the place." Willard laughed softly. "Said it was full of liars and deceivers, each worse than the next. Which it is."

"No treaty is coming from that visit," Brolli said. "I am ready to leave and recommend war to my people, when Willard comes to court and seems to me the one honest Arkendian. This gives me hope there might be others. Maybe the liars are only in court."

"I was there for the Day of Pardons, as I am every year," said Willard. He shrugged his ironclad shoulders. "She never pardons me, but I go anyway. To see...old friends."

"And when Willard leaves, unpardoned, I follow."

Willard chuckled. "Noticed I was followed by a drunk who could barely keep his saddle. Turned out it was Brolli, and he'd never ridden a horse in his life. When he told me who he was, I tried to take him back to court, but he refused. Said if there were any chance of a treaty, it would come of seeing Arkendia *outside* the court—"

"I tell him to escort me through his land on the way back to mine," Brolli interjected.

Willard raised his eyes and hands as if in surrender. "What could I do? So I pledged my support, and here we are. Would have been an easy ride north, but those West Isle knights went out looking for him and got lucky. Hence the gang of curs at our heels."

Harric stared at the ambassador, his temples pounding in pain as he struggled to put the story together. Something about it didn't ring true to him. The enormous danger Brolli put himself in by leaving the court. Even escorted by Sir Willard, it seemed less than reasonable to risk the peace of two nations on anything less than a full military escort. The fact that Willard embraced it led him to think there must be more Brolli that hadn't shared.

"I am meaning to ask you," Brolli said to Willard. "Your curse is still active tonight?"

Willard cast a hard look at Brolli, then glanced meaningfully at Harric.

"They're with us now," Brolli said, a slight apology to his tone. "They must know. Your last squire…he is dead of it, yes? There is some danger."

"You had a squire?" Harric said.

A look of pain or regret settled in Willard's face. He closed his eyes, and sighed in resignation. "Tam. A good lad." He sucked the ragleaf again, the red eye glaring. "I am plagued with a…*condition*, son. A curse, I call it. When I'm threatened, or…possibly, around women…something happens to people around me. All judgment leaves them. They do things they wouldn't normally do, and afterwards have no memory of it."

"Like I did in Gallows Ferry," Harric said. "Caris too. We thought we were witched."

A scowl wrapped around the ragleaf clamped in Willard's teeth. "Witched is a strong word, boy."

"And that's what happened to Tam? He did something foolish?"

Willard nodded. "As did I when I gave that ring away. Didn't remember a thing of it. Had to reason it out after the fact."

Harric stared, understanding gradually dawning on him, and a laugh welling up from his lungs. He suppressed it, but it leaked out in lines around his eyes and the corners of his mouth.

"Something funny, boy?"

"Well, no, but it does explain a lot about the origin of the comic bungle in your ballads. These things actually happen to you. It isn't made up."

"They aren't *my* ballads, boy, and in my experience this curse isn't comic, so you can wipe that foolish smile from your face. People get hurt. Dreams shatter. Lives end." The old knight glared through gouts of ragleaf.

"Sorry," Harric muttered, dropping his gaze. "That was stupid of me."

Willard sighed, and chuckled ruefully. "Hardly your fault, boy. Fact is, it's the very reason for my banishment from court. I'm a bloody lodestone of catastrophes." He stared off for a moment at something only he could see, then his attention snapped back to Brolli. "That clear me of my obligations to this boy, Ambassador?"

The ambassador bowed ambiguously.

Willard turned to Harric. "Well, boy? What do you say? Are we even?"

Harric glanced at Caris, whom Willard seemed to pointedly ignore.

Willard frowned. "It seems not," he said, mistaking Harric's hesitation for discontent. He dismounted the towering Phyros with a grunt, lowering himself from the saddle with powerful arms.

As Willard stepped toward Harric, Molly aimed a vicious bite at the old knight's neck, as if she'd grab him and shake him like a rag. Willard crammed a mailed fist blindly in her teeth, halting her attack and barely interrupting his limping path to Harric. Molly snorted. She shook blood from her lips, evidently decided against another lunge, and went back to sharpening the long blood tooth in the left side of her jaw against a stone.

"Willard assures me that's completely normal for a Phyros," said Brolli.

"It is," Willard grunted. "So keep your distance."

Willard loomed above Harric, his bulk broad and dark, lined face illumined by a spray of scarlet moonlight. "Son, I owe you an apology for the events today. Things didn't work out as planned, but I intend to make it up to you." His tone altered subtly toward the formal. "I've come to a decision. I wish to make you my manservant. My valet-squire, if you will. You're too old for training as a proper squire, but as a valet you'll have to know how to handle a blade, and if you show promise in arms we can talk about other possibilities."

Harric gaped. Rag whinnied and tossed as if Caris had lost concentration.

"Moons, girl!" Willard hissed. "You want the whole valley to hear us?"

Caris blinked as if stunned. Her hands covered her ears and she bent double as if to block out the words. Rag calmed, but continued to toss her head in agitation.

"You're—serious?" Harric said to Willard.

The knight stepped back, evidently pleased with Harric's awe. "Lost my squire on the road, as you know. You'll take his place. Do you accept?"

"Of—course I do."

"In that case, let me inform you that if anything should happen to me it becomes your duty to escort Ambassador Brolli and his wedding ring safely to his people in the north."

Harric bowed deeply.

"The ring is valuable and dangerous," said Brolli. "Those who want them will torture and murder to get them. With them they can force your queen to marry. Instant king, you see? And once she takes a king, her power is lost."

Why did you bring them in the first place? Harric wondered. He wanted to ask it, but his focus diverted to Caris, who stared resolutely at the earth between her feet as if her gaze could bore a hole to swallow her up. It must have become clear to her the old hero did not recognize women in his trade. She'd approached several knights of his kind since she came to Gallows Ferry, soliciting them as mentors, only to be scorned and rebuffed. He could see she had no intention of shaming herself and Willard both by asking it of him.

"Very good," said Willard. "Now, I gather that moon cat's your pet…"

"Actually, I've never seen him before tonight. He just hitched a ride."

"Name him yet?"

"Spook."

"Then you'll have to keep him." Willard smiled at his own joke. "Peasant folk think them associated with the moons and magic. If we get out on the open road and it brings trouble, the cat goes."

"Among my people, this does not matter," said Brolli. "We have fond tales of Moon Cat, the hero trickster. Be careful, or he will steal your eyes and ears," he added, chuckling.

"Good," Willard grunted. "Then I believe I can safely say my debt is paid."

The seed of an idea sprouted in Harric's mind. "Ah…your debt?" Harric echoed, setting the bait.

Sir Willard frowned. "Son? What is it? Out with it."

The seed grew rapidly in the fertile soil of his mother's training: *Seek your opponent's blind spots, and in them lay your traps.* "Sir Willard," he said, calculating the formality of his tone and manner carefully, "I do have a boon to ask."

The old man responded instantly to the heightened tone. "I see my debt is not fully paid." He drew himself up. "Name what boon you will, and I will grant it."

Caris's head snapped up as if she'd been stuck with a pin.

Anyone who knew the ballads would recognize what had happened; there was even a ballad titled "Sir Willard and the Rash Boon."

Harric bowed again, formally. "Then I ask that you take Caris as your apprentice. It's what she wants, though she's too proud to ask it. And it's what she deserves, even without your debt to her."

The old knight blinked as if to clear his vision. Caris's mouth parted in blank wonder as she turned to Willard, who gaped, then startled as if she'd appeared there from thin air.

"Ha. Her? A girl?" He nearly inhaled the dwindling stub of ragleaf. "Well, throw me down. Is *that* your way, boy?" He raised his steeled arms and dropped them to his sides in a gesture of dismay. "That's the way of our queen, but you too? First her father learns 'em letters, and now it's women fighting wars. Maids in court have books and tutors till book learning is common as knitting! Bust my girths, it isn't right! Next she'll ask the men to have the babies!"

"It's what she deserves, sir," said Harric.

"What she deserves!" Willard's eyes bolted from his head. "And she as late as you in life? Impossible! And it isn't *natural*, I tell you. It's out of the question."

"I've trained before now," Caris said, voice and head lowered reverently. "And there are other woman knights. This year Her Majesty knighted two and started the Star Company—Sir Miyda and Sir Kethla. I've even heard it said that—"

"Yes, *yes*. You heard it, girl. All the world has heard it. And she nearly lost her crown in the outrage that followed. I guess you didn't hear *that*, did you? Our queen moves too fast, and she has enemies, blast them all. And blast these bugs too, while you're at it." He swatted his neck and sucked fiercely on the ragleaf, which was so small he had to pinch it between thick fingers.

"I have training," Caris repeated quietly. "I've got the family and blood as well. Cobalt," she said, though the knight seemed deaf to it.

"Training?" Willard drew the greatsword from its sheath with a musical chime. *Belle.* The fabled weapon of Willard's days as Champion. "What's this?" he asked, holding the weapon before him at an odd angle.

"Widow's ward," said Caris softly.

"Bah." He snapped the blade to another position above his head.

"The Plowman."

He grunted again and held it behind his head, the tip angling back and into the earth.

Caris smiled. "Queen's Ward, or Sir Gregan's Lie. Often followed by a Reaper."

The knight stared in consternation. "*Gregan's* Lie?" He let forth a furious cloud of ragleaf. "*I* invented that one. Gregan only popularized it." He snapped the greatsword into its sheath, and dug another rag-roll from his saddle.

"It might bring favor with the Queen," Harric suggested.

Willard squinted at Harric as he lit the ragleaf by puffing it against the end of the tiny fragment between his lips. A corner of his mustachio burned, shriveling whiskers like retreating antennae on a snail.

"Who said I need favor?"

"Well, your armor—"

"Enough quibbling." The knight fixed his gaze on Harric, as if seeing him, too, for the very first time. "I promised. It's done." He spat a bit of ragleaf. "For good or ill, it's done."

Caris fell to her knees and kissed the old man's armored gauntlet, which he retracted as if from a snake.

"You can keep the theatrics, girl."

"You won't regret it," she whispered. "You'll never regret it."

"I already regret it. But no matter. You won't last a week."

Caris blinked as if slapped. She dropped her gaze and clenched her jaw. "You'll see I can take it as well as Harric can. Maybe better."

"You'll have to do better than that, girl. You'll have to be better than *everyone*. And not just a little better, either—ten times better! Twenty!—because they'll all be after you and itching to prove you the weak, foolish thing they know you are. You'll fail, girl. Fancy blue armor doesn't make a knight. You'll quit of your own right."

Tears of anger filled her eyes, but she would not blink and send them down her cheeks. "I'll be the best student you ever had," she said fiercely. "I'm better than all of them."

Willard returned her glare, but something in her words or her face seemed to reach behind his bluster, and his eyes softened. He sighed. "It isn't you, girl. It's your sex. Look at that arm." He tugged her elbow from her side and held it out to expose the profile. "You're strong—horse-touched strong—I'll give you that. But the best knight's arm is bigger, and burly like a root. The kind of strength you'll never have."

"I don't fight with strength."

"Is that so?" Willard's eyes sparkled over his smoking moustache. "So tell me what you'll do when a knight with shoulders like a bull is raining blows that could fell an oak?"

"Like Sir Yolan?"

"You won't always have him by the cloak."

"Then I'll use his strength against him. Like you do."

"You're flattering me, girl."

"I don't flatter. I saw you fight."

A complicated expression flickered briefly in the old man's face, impossible to read. Curiosity? Scorn? He studied her face intently for a moment, as if he might read her fate in her eyes. Then the mask of bemusement returned, and he sighed gruffly. "Did you see that, Brolli? A woman prentice. What would

Gregan say?"

"What do the balladeers say?" said Brolli.

"Cork it, Ambassador."

Brolli laughed. "But what you say is true. There is no respect for women among your people, so your women wish to be men."

Caris's jaw clenched briefly. "I don't want to be a man. I want to be a knight."

"But as Sir Willard says, the warrior's way is a mystery of manhood; you can understand some, but you cannot know all, just as he cannot know mystery of birth."

"*Queen's* Knight," Willard muttered. "I give her a week, at most."

"We shall wager on that?" the Kwendi asked.

"Of course. What stake?"

"A favor to be asked at a later time."

"Done." Willard turned from Brolli to Harric, and nodded with an air of instruction. "First lesson as my valet, boy: ambassadors' favors are valuable things. Remember that. And if you ever snare me again with a boon like that one I'll denounce you as a jack and trickster and leave you hanging at the nearest gallows. "

Humor sparked in the old man's eyes, but his words had an edge to them. Caris's dark eyes searched Harric's face, strong emotions moving behind her gaze.

"I'll remember that, Sir Willard," Harric said. "But with regard to trickery, I'm afraid I don't know what you mean."

...As your nexus stone channels the Life-giving power of the Bright Mother moon, so do the nexi of the Fell Moons channel to the Fell Magi. And as your nexus stone is white and pure in accordance with the Bright Mother's purpose, so is the nexus of the Mad Moon as red as blood and fire, in accordance with His opposite cause. Therefore too is the nexus of the Unseen black and impenetrable as the secrets of that moon and its servants.

—From *The Tutelage Manual of Bright Mother* neocolytes

17

Whispers & Wounds

They stopped several hours before dawn to bed down in a shepherd's camp beneath a wide-spreading weeping willow overhanging the stream. Sheep pies and insects abounded, but the encircling curtain of branches hung thick enough to screen a camp of twenty from errant eyes in the valley. The Mad Moon, now setting in the western sky, scattered shards of orange light on the stream. Stripes of red light slashed across the campsite, through the branches.

To Harric's relief, the campsite was wide enough that when Caris picketed Rag at one end, he was able to bed down at the other, while she would have to stay near Rag. He was in no condition for wrangling about any aspect of their new condition together. He quickly chose a reasonably soft spot along the opposite perimeter of branches, and laid his bedding out before she laid hers, so it wouldn't be so obvious he avoided her.

Willard grimaced in pain as he dismounted, though he'd smoked enough ragleaf to numb a lance wound. Brolli insisted he remove his armor to examine his wounds, but Willard refused.

"I've had wounds before, Ambassador."

"You are immortal then."

"These wounds are nothing."

"Is that why you leak blood like the rain pipes?"

Willard followed Brolli's gaze to the knight's right hip, where the strain of his dismount had conjured bright new red stripes on the black iron skirt.

"We must stop that. I must clean or it grows foul."

"And if I'm ambushed in my bedclothes this whole ballad turns foul."

The two argued so long Harric did not wait for an outcome.

He rubbed down Brolli's pony—Idgit was his name—fed him a ration of grain, and cleaned his shoes as best he could in the low light. When he tried to do the same for the gangly "unridable" filly in the faded caparison, Willard shooed him away.

"Holly's mine, boy. You can leave her to me."

Harric nodded. "Holly. Like Molly. Cute."

By then, Willard had reached a compromise with Brolli to clean and wrap the worst of his injuries at the joint between breastplate and hip. With Brolli watching, Caris helped Harric unbuckle the breastplate and lift some of the quilting. He expected Caris to ignore him in her semi-horse-tied state, but she continually glanced at him across that emotional gulf. Her expression, if distant, seemed open, but clouded with doubt or worry. Such a babe she was in the ways of courtship, Harric realized. Her horse-touched nature left her without even the most basic of skills to mask her feelings, nor perhaps any inkling of why she should.

Strangely, he found that appealed to him deeply. There would be no games with Caris. No hidden agendas. No tests. With her there would never be guessing. No bluffing, no calculating, no manipulating. His mother would despise her. He laughed inwardly. By that measure alone, she was the best girl in Arkendia. If only she'd accept him as he was, what more could he ask? And if only she wasn't magically forced to love him, he might hearken more to the stirring he felt every time she was near.

Too many "if onlies."

When the armor had been removed, Brolli moved in, waving Harric aside. "Go rest now. I do the bandage."

Harric happily bowed out, leaving the others to tend the dressing. As he limped to the edge of camp, seeking a private place to relieve his bladder, Spook trotted up to him, meowing.

"Hey, catty," he said. He was too stiff to bend and pick him up, so he let the moon cat follow, and pushed his way through the drape of willow branches on the uphill side. Following a well-trodden path—and the smell—he found the shepherds' latrine a little way beyond a ferny hummock. As he laced up his pants after relieving himself, Spook hissed at something behind Harric, back arched and bristling, then whirled and bolted into the ferns.

Harric spun to find his mother in the path before him, white makeup flashing in the moonlight like a ghoulish mummer's mask. She held herself like an empress in her threadbare gown, and regarded him from heavy-lidded eyes.

"Oh, this is precious," she drawled. "Ring-bound to the horse girl, and valet to the Queen's fool, Willard. How mighty you are grown without me."

"Get out of here, Mother," Harric hissed, trying to keep his voice down so the others wouldn't hear. "Go back to your pet Bannus."

"I've been watching the horse girl over there," she said, as if she hadn't heard him. "She's off in horse-land now, rocking back and forth like a bear in a pen." She snorted her distaste. "Kill her, Harric. She endangers the Queen."

"What?" Rage choked his words.

"I see it in the Web," she said ominously. "This girl endangers the Queen. If you will learn of me, kill her, Harric, and save your queen much trouble."

He stumbled backward and turned to stalk back to the camp before she started shouting.

"Stay, Harric, and hear! You endanger more than the Queen's safety—indeed, you endanger your very soul—with that vile stone in your pocket."

Harric halted. He turned and glared. His heart was sinking, his hand reaching unconsciously for the stone beneath his shirt. It hadn't kept her away.

"Of course I know of that cursed stone," she snapped. "I came here tonight to warn you: if you have not cast that wretched stone away before Bannus sends you to the spirit world, even I will be unable to help you. Kill the foul cat that follows it, then cast the stone away. Even now the spirit of the stone inhabits the cat—"

"Kill my friend? Kill my cat?" Harric barely kept his voice in check. "You're mad! You're still mad!"

"I speak of your soul, Harric. Please…" She fell on her knees, her hands clasped in the air between them, beseeching. "This life is temporary—it matters not—but the soul is eternal! Cast it away, before it is too late! Do you understand? Answer me!"

He stepped back from her. He felt his heart leap with hope. He removed the stone from his shirt, and she recoiled as if he'd produced a rotting head. He smiled. "I think I finally do understand."

"Keep that thing away from me!" Clambering to her feet, she backed away from the stone.

Harric walked toward her, stone extended before him, and she retreated. "You don't like Caris because she's different. And you don't like this stone because…why? It must be because it threatens you somehow, just as my Proof threatened you."

She began a sneering reply, but he advanced, thrusting the stone in her face, and she cried out, falling over herself in retreat.

"Idiot boy! Sir Bannus comes! Do not think I value your soul above the Queen's survival! I will kill you to save her! You have been warned."

"Leave!" he said, pursuing. "Leave me and *never come again!*" He ran at her with the stone, but before he reached her she vanished, leaving him panting among the ferns.

Below him on the hillside, the willow branches jerked. Harric could see the old knight struggling to part the curtain of branches. "Boy! What in the Black Moon are you playing at?"

"Sorry," Harric whispered. "I just… Sorry. I'm okay. Just talking to the cat." He tucked the witch-stone back in his shirt, and made a show of limping back toward the willow camp, hoping the old knight would be satisfied to leave him alone.

Willard's scowling head emerged from the willow curtain. He studied Harric briefly, muttered something under his breath, and withdrew to the other side.

Harric let his breath out, and paused halfway to the willow to collect himself. The sight of Willard had added a layer of guilt to the complex stew of emotions boiling in his chest. If his mother led Bannus to Harric, then Harric endangered Willard and Brolli and everyone else. But how could he tell them? They'd think he was mad as she was. His heart beat high and loud in his ears. He closed his eyes tightly, fighting down an expanding bubble of despair.

At least I have this, he thought, bringing the witch-stone out in his fist. *She's afraid of this.* In the light of the Bright Mother, the stone was a glossy egg of blackness. *A witch's link to the Unseen Moon — forbidden — death if I'm caught with it. And my only hope to keep my mother away.* If she returned, he'd take it out, and she'd flee. That was all that really mattered. Maybe it could somehow keep Bannus away, too. That was an idea. Maybe it was the stone that made Bannus less…what had she said? *Less tractable* than she'd thought? *Slower to rouse?* Another good reason to keep it.

The bubble of despair shrank a little. It was the very reason he'd grabbed the stone to begin with. If she'd been so afraid of the magic of his Proof, how much more would she fear a witch's stone? Even if he never learned how to use it properly, the stone was worth its weight in gold if it kept his mother away. Would it keep Bannus away? That might be another story.

Spook meowed, rubbing against his leg.

"Where did you come from, scaredy?" This time Harric stooped and picked him up to hold him before his face and gaze at the strange white eyes.

Spook peered back and meowed, showing tiny sharp teeth and a pink tongue.

"What the Black Moon does she have against you?" Too tired to ponder it, he parted the curtain of willow branches and reentered the camp. Sir Willard cast him a complicated look from a fire they'd built to boil up his ragleaf sleeping tea. Harric shrugged another apology, trudged to his blanket, and laid himself gingerly down. Tomorrow, if he had a moment of privacy, he'd study the witch-stone. Tonight, he'd sleep.

There was no comfortable position. No matter how he lay, some part of him objected, and the witch-stone seemed to lie against his flesh like a hammer, but he dared not lay it aside lest his mother return, or someone among their camp accidentally find it. Ultimately, he simply lay on his back, hands folded on his belly like a corpse in a coffin.

Spook climbed onto his chest and settled there, sphinx-like. The tiny nose leaned so close to Harric that the breath of his purr tickled Harric's chin. Exhaustion pinned Harric's eyelids and sat upon them so he could barely open them enough to meet the gaze of those milk-white eyes. Spook planted a soft paw on his forehead, between his eyes, and left it there as if Harric were a mouse it had pinned to the ground. Harric closed his eyes. "Catch some other mouse, Spook," he murmured. "I'm too big for you."

Voices whispered again at the edge of his awareness, dreams calling across the border of sleep and waking life.

And he sank into darkness.

Harric woke to Spook yowling and spitting and clawing at his chest. His hand went to swipe the cat away, only to find a set of cold hands there already, grabbing at his shirt and grasping at the cat. Red moonlight illumined a cloaking fog and glimpses of pale bodies striving around him.

"Fog!" he cried out, beating the hands back, but they persisted with fiendish strength. The cat staged a yowling frenzy in his arms. Caris cried out, her voice uncannily loud and near in the fog, and the body groping him suddenly crashed sideways and tumbled over him, its bony knees sending daggers of pain through his ribs.

Caris was cursing like a raftsman. Her sword flashed, deadly silent, and the body beside him vanished into mist. Another jolted, her blade transfixing its middle, and vanished before it hit the ground. Harric rolled to his side, the cat still tangled in his shirt, and scanned about, ready to run.

They were alone.

Caris stood over him, sword glinting dully. In the red light of the Mad

Moon he caught a glimpse of rage and terror on her face. All around them, the fog sank into the earth with uncanny speed. In the space of a half-dozen breaths, it vanished.

"Hurric?" Willard's voice slurred from Brolli's sleeping concoction. "Whad in the Black Moon're you playin' at?"

The old knight tottered in a patch of red light, gigantic whiskers askew, sword in his hand, still in its sheath. He'd somehow waked and clambered to his feet, despite the sleeping draft Brolli had given him. The act had called forth new blood from his hip, which already filled the bandage.

Harric saw no sign of Brolli; apparently the Kwendi watched their trail for pursuers.

"Just the cat, sir," Harric said. "Must have rolled over on him. Won't happen again."

Willard stared, face slack and groggy. "The cat. Gods leave us. Sounded like the Battle of Arkam."

Caris turned so her body partly concealed the sword in her hand.

"Sorry, sir," said Harric, trying to keep the knight's attention from her. "You can go back to sleep. No problem."

Willard stared at Caris. "Awfully big sword for a cat," he said. "You two aren't fighting, are you?" A wry smile twisted his mouth beneath the crooked mustachios. "If he tried to kiss you, girl, a good slap would do the trick. In your case, it might knock him out. No need for a sword."

Caris didn't seem able to meet his eyes. Her brow furrowed, and Harric sensed she was about to curl up in crisis.

"You're bleeding pretty bad, sir," Harric said, trying to divert Willard's attention.

"Eh? Damned bandages." Willard scowled at the mess of linen.

"We'll have to change those wads out before you go back to sleep," Harric said.

Caris had begun to crouch, hands to ears, but these comments drew her out. She looked up, and Harric followed her gaze to the ruined bandages. The panic drained from her expression, replaced with outward determination rivaling her intensity during combat. Her hands dropped; she stood erect and strode to Willard.

"Lie down, sir," she said, "I'll fix your bandage."

Willard scowled. "What, you haven't kept me awake long enough?" He limped back to his bed as Caris went for the linen. "Here's a hint, boy," he said, crouching into his bed. "Don't go feeling her up when a sword's near at hand."

"You think I'd need to steal a feel when she's got that ring on?"

Willard grunted as he sank heavily into a seating position. "Probably not. Here's your only warning, then: if that cat wakes me again, I'll boil it for breakfast."

Harric watched as Caris moved through the camp, all signs of panic gone, hands moving rapidly through her saddle pack for linens. External crisis, it seemed, focused her and held her together; when it left she might clap her hands to her ears and curl up in a ball, but until then she was as cool as any field captain—maybe more so. He recalled the first night his mother's spirits had attacked, how she'd fought and triumphed with him, then after the fight fled to the stables.

Caris changed Willard's linens as best she could. The old knight slept before she'd finished. Without a word, she fetched her blankets from her sleeping spot near Rag, and dropped them beside Harric. She sat and faced him, seething with emotion. "I'm sleeping here."

He nodded, a queer mixture of guilt and dread and anger brewing in his chest. "I'm sorry, Caris. I thought it was over. I thought we'd beaten her."

"She attacked *me*, Harric. Why'd she send her—creatures?—after *me*?"

"You?" he said, stunned. "I thought they grabbed *Spook*."

She displayed a bandage she'd wrapped around her arm, slightly red with blood. "The only reason I survived is because you had woken me with your moaning."

"I was moaning?"

"You were having a nightmare, I guess, weeping and talking so loud it woke me up all the way across the camp. Only the ragleaf tea kept Willard from waking. And when I woke I saw the fog, and it made me worried, so I came to sit with you." She glanced away, blushing, as if caught in a confession, but kept talking to hide it. "There were three of those fog men, and only *one* went for the cat. The other two came at me. *Me*, Harric. Not you. If I hadn't heard them coming, they would have got me."

A cold pit opened under Harric's stomach. He clenched his teeth. His hand found the stone beneath his shirt, and he balled his fist around it so hard his knuckles ached. "I've got to end this."

"*We've* got to end this."

"This is my problem—"

"Not anymore it's not," she snarled. "Now it's personal, and if I ever get a chance, I'll cut that bitch in two."

Harric grinned, surprised at her vehemence. "Best girl in Arkendia," he muttered to himself. She gave him a quizzical look, but he shrugged the question off. "Thanks. You're my guardian spirit. Maybe that's why she doesn't like you."

Caris snorted. She relaxed a little, and he could see she was pleased, but her brow remained furrowed. "First thing we have to do is tell Willard. I'm going to tell him."

"Whoa! Wait." He laid a hand on her arm as she made to get up. "That's not a good idea…" His mind whirled to address this unexpected turn. "He needs his sleep, Caris. The fog's gone; we're not in danger now."

Her eyes narrowed. "I'm not going to lie to him, Harric."

"Of course not. I'm not asking you to lie to him. But we don't have to tell him, either. Think about it," he said, climbing painfully into a sitting position so he could meet her eyes. "Willard has enough to worry about, keeping Brolli safe and getting us through this wilderness, and honestly, Caris, we're fine. She hasn't hurt us yet. Just given us a good scare."

"She's tried to murder us both!"

"And we handled it both times, thanks to you." He laid a gentle hand on her arm, and in spite of herself, she gave a small smile. "The fact is," he said, lowering his voice and glancing at Willard, "If we tell Willard, I'm afraid he might think we endanger his mission and reconsider our apprenticeships."

Caris's eyes widened in alarm. She opened her mouth as if to ask a question, then closed it, her brow furrowed in distress. "Do you think he would?"

"He might. But it really doesn't involve him, and it would only worry him unnecessarily. He really doesn't need to know." And *she* didn't need to know about his mother's influence on Bannus. Not yet. Not until Harric knew if his mother was bluffing, or if the witch-stone somehow protected them.

She stared at Willard, chewing her lip. "I suppose you're right. For now."

Harric nodded. He sighed inwardly, feeling like he'd dodged a disaster. "Good. Right."

He lay back on his blanket, wincing as his ribs shot daggers through his flesh. "Think we can get any sleep tonight?" In spite of everything, the moment he closed his eyelids, he struggled to lift them again.

A look of concern passed behind Caris's eyes. "From now until we get to the fire-cone tower, we sleep together." She drew her sword from her scabbard and laid it naked between them. "We'll take turns keeping watch for the fog. If it comes back, we'll both be awake together."

*When the Phyros-rider Sir Anatos wearied of his blood rage, he sought freedom from
its grip... Though unable to wean himself from the Blood of the god in his Phyros, he
succeeded in controlling the rage through a discipline of fasting, physical austerity,
and near constant meditation and training. When others joined him, they learned
from him the Rule of Anatos, and formed The Peaceable Order of The Blue, commonly
known as the Blue Order, whose number is twelve.*

—From *Divine Blood, Cracked Vessels*, by Tulos of Bury

18

Father Kogan & the Mob

Father Kogan hunched above the glowing remains of his campfire,
one burly arm about the plump waist of the Widow Larkin. For the
first time since they left their homes, a full month before, the night
camps of caravans along the road lay silent. No blazing bonfires, no
bawdy songs with rousing choruses, no ballads recited by squires and
grooms. News of Sir Bannus's return had spread like a plague wind up
the road.

The priest's camp bristled with nervous glances and whispers. There
had never been a greater foe to the free peasants of Arkendia and their
priests than the immortal Sir Bannus. They set their camp far from the
road, well behind the other camps, which had cursed them bitterly
and pulled stakes to move farther upriver, afraid to be near them. A
wide berth surrounded them. A killing field, Kogan thought grimly. He
instructed his folk to keep the fires small and close. Boys stood watch
in the darkness beyond, and along the road. Those in camp kept their
backs to the fires, baggage at hand, ready to flee to the forest. Already
there'd been strange things moving on the road that night. Herds of
horses. A Phyros, sure, judging by the action of the oxen when it passed.

None in the camp slept.

"Finally got acrosst the river," the widow muttered, "and you throw it all away. What're you gonna do if Bannus come for you?"

"What we always done. Run and hide." The priest sighed. "Trouble always follows Will."

"Oh, *fie* on Will! And fie on all his troubles, you great ox!"

She stabbed the coals with a stick, sending swarms of sparks in the air. "Never thought of the others around you. Had to pay some fool debt from your fool years as a brother."

The priest grew abruptly gruff. "You know I done right. I done right and I stand by it."

She turned to him, defiant, but said nothing, only searched his face as if for a courage she lacked.

His tone gentled. "Be brave, sweet. It ain't always safest to do what's right, but we do it."

"Even if this gets us killed? What's so right about it then?"

"Well, then it ain't about us at all. It's about Will."

The widow struggled to fight back tears. "It's always the plain folk what pay for them in wars, and in peace, too. Why can't he pay his own way and leave us be?"

"Will's troubles are our troubles. If he falls, we fall."

"I just wish it were different, Kogan. We've come so far, and now we stand to lose it."

A low cheer drifted through the trees from the south road. Kogan frowned, and eased the widow to the ground. He'd heard such noise too many times to mistake it for carousing. He stood to his full height above the fire, the smothercoat unfolding stiffly before and behind. Another cheer, this time closer. A shimmer of torches appeared through the trees where the road emerged from the south slope of the valley. Fifty, maybe one hundred hands, he estimated.

"It's a mob, sweet."

She stood, eyes hard, hands balled in fists. "Oh, Kogan. What'll we do?"

He glanced around their caravan—two-score tents, two hundreds of men, women, and children—and saw there was no need to warn a soul; every one of them sat ready at their fires. With one hand he threw fresh wood on the fire.

"No, you fool!" the widow hissed, kicking the wood out again. "You call attention to us. We have light enough if it comes to that."

Kogan cursed and hefted the ancient Phyros ax.

"Father Kogan! Father Kogan!" A small voice rang from the darkness, followed by a young boy with nose bloodied and eyes as wide and white as hen's eggs. "Father, they're coming. Twenty swords and spitfires and rope. They want to *burn* you! They say you burned the stables. You have to run." He sobbed. "They hung Rich and Bailer."

"Hung?" the priest roared. "Where's the justice o' the peace? The constable—damn them!"

"There ain't none this side the river."

The widow scrambled to the priest's side. "Run and save yerself, Kogan. Head 'em away from camp, and find us later when it cools off."

"By the laws, I won't. Stay here, and I'll meet 'em myself, I will." He strode toward the road, seething. The widow clung to his arm, dragging her feet ineffectually in the dust.

"Think what you're doing, you big ox! What'll you do? Pound 'em all like nails, one two three? If you do, every boy in the camp'll join with you, and they'll have a *real* reason to hang 'em. Listen to me. You run and lead the mob away—that's the only way to save the rest of us. Run. And tell them boys to stay low and give the mob no reasons. Say you will."

The priest hesitated, grinding his teeth and panting like a chained bull.

The widow laid a soft hand on the fist clutching the ax. Her voice became tender. "Save your fire for a better time, Kogan." She lifted her chin, but it quivered a little in spite of her. "I'll see you again right soon. Sure I will. Listen to me now. I got more in my head than you got in yours, and you knows it. It's the only way."

Tears welled in his eyes. "They won't let us be," he growled. "And what o' the caravan? I can't leave it now. Who'll lead?"

"*I* will, ye great ox! Ain't I been a help so far? And ain't I got more sense than you? I'll do it, and you find us when the trouble's past."

"You have my store o' coin?" The widow nodded. "So be it. But don't you wait for me. I'll find you." He kissed her on the forehead, and grinned. "You're one fine woman, Widow Larkin."

"And you're a great bull of a father," she said, beaming. "One who best stay quick if he knows what's best for him."

"Untie Geraldine," Kogan said to the boy with the bloodied nose.

"Lead her to the forest where I can find her, and be quick. Go on!"

The boy untied the huge white cow, whose udders were heavy with milk, and whipped her toward the wood.

"All of you stay here," Kogan said to his worried flock. "Widow Larkin is your leader now till I come back."

"Father, they come apace!" someone cried. "The torches!"

A murmuring gang of shadows and firelight filled the road, a long bowshot away. Father Kogan trotted into the darkness to meet them.

When the mob saw him, it roared and surged forward.

The priest held his giant ax aloft, like a god, and roared back. "You goat-headed fools! I ain't done nothing wrong! Go choke yourselfs!"

Spitfires popped. A pair of white-hot charges sizzled past in wavering arcs to skip harmlessly on the road beyond. Another splattered on the smothercoat and burned there ineffectually.

The mob rushed, and Kogan fled barefoot toward the forest.

19

Flushed & Hunted

Harric woke from a dream-tortured sleep. The moon cat crouched on his chest, purring, watching him through green-slitted eyes. *Green.* They'd been milk the night before. Some trick of the moonlight, perhaps, had made them so. When he was young his mother had allowed him to keep a moon cat kitten with green eyes. She'd let him keep it long enough to love it, then made him drown it to prove he was beyond sentiment, as a courtiste must be. He'd refused, but she withheld his food for five days, and finally he succumbed. The memory made him sick to his stomach. And it was just such memories that tortured his dreams. It seemed the worst of them had been dragged out of their tombs to terrorize his soul. And unlike ordinary dreams, these had been vivid and true in every forgotten detail.

…Harric, role-playing seductions with his mother.

…Harric, on "missions" to seduce other boys and girls.

All done unquestioningly, with the eagerness of a doting only son.

Shame scoured him anew. *It wasn't my fault. I was just a kid.*

He turned and retched. Nothing came up, but the action provoked lancing pains through his injured ribs, and his headache pounced with a vengeance. Mercilessly, the dry heaves persisted as his body sought to expel a pollution in his soul.

When it finally stopped, he wiped the perspiration from his brow and lay back again. Above him, the willow branches arched protectively. Clouds moved high and bright beyond gaps in the upper branches, lit by the rising sun, though it had yet to climb high enough over the eastern ridges to warm the valley. The scent of porridge and wood smoke drew his attention to a cook fire, where an orange-haired figure with the arms and chest of a giant and the legs of a dwarf tended a steaming pot.

Brolli, he recalled, as if it were a memory from another life.

The Kwendi turned to look at him with huge, bulging black eyes, and flashed his feral grin. Caris joined Brolli at the fire, brow furrowed in curiosity.

The Kwendi grinned. "You no recognize? It is the eyes."

"And your hair," she said. "It's orange."

"Ah. You are blind for colors at night. I forget." Brolli gathered the mane of orange hair and tied it in a tail behind his head. The same bronze hair fuzzed his long arms and stubbled his face. "I am just as blind in day without these," he said, tapping the black coverings over his eyes. It was clear now the bulging "eyes" were cup-shaped lenses held in place with a strap behind his head.

Harric rolled gingerly to his stomach, careful not to alarm his injured body. He crawled to his knees, then climbed to his feet and limped out of camp to relieve himself. Spook followed, mewing hungrily. When Harric returned to the fire, Brolli had removed the black eye covers and held them up against the light so they could see it shine through like the glass of a bottle.

"We wear them to make day less bright," said Brolli, returning them to his eyes. "The lenses are like your brewer glass, but much stronger, and lighter."

"Stronger than glass?" The tooler in every Arkendian awoke in Harric. "Are they a gemstone of some kind?"

The ambassador grinned. "Can you believe they are dragon eyes?"

"*Dragon* eyes?"

"Well, not *eyes* so much as the *lid* of the eyes of a *terroc*—what you call spear dragons."

"Spear dragons!" Caris said. "So they really exist."

"Do you have to slay a spear dragon to make those…eyes?" Harric said.

Brolli grinned as if this were a very good joke. "That would be very difficult. Lucky for us, they drop eye covers every year like the deer drop antlers. If you find one from young male, it is too scratched from fighting. We collect lids from yearling females and dye them dark, so we can wear them when we stay up late."

Harric raised an eyebrow. "So, this is late?"

"It is dinnertime." Brolli lifted the lid off the pot, and peered in with a curl of displeasure to his lip. "This is oats, for Willard, when he finally rise. I eat real food already." He illustrated by producing a charred stick from beside him on which an impaled and roasted eel glared up with dulled eyes. "You call it 'smoking eel,' I think. Would you like?"

Harric swallowed. "I'm not hungry."

"Wake up, slumber-guts," said Brolli. "You can eat oats while I report of my scouting."

"No need to wake me, you great chimpey," said Willard, behind Harric.

The Kwendi barked his peculiar laugh.

Willard had sat up in his blankets. "Used to eat whatever the Black Moon I wanted. Now it's oats, or look out." The old knight climbed from his blankets to his feet, grunting and grimacing. When he finally gained them, his face was gray and perspiring.

"I see you recover from your wounds quite nice," Brolli said ominously.

"I see your mouth's still wagging." Willard limped to the fire. He studied Harric with something like concern in his sleep-bleared eyes. "You look worse than I feel, boy." He held a fat roll of ragleaf to Harric. "Get this going for me. You need it as much as I."

Harric received it gratefully, and lowered himself gingerly to the fire, where he puffed it alight against a brand.

Brolli looked at Willard's blood-crusted armor. "Let's have a look, then." He motioned for Willard to let him unbuckle the breastplate.

Willard scowled, but held his arms to the sides as the Kwendi attempted the buckles under one arm. Caris unfastened the others. Brolli's eyes grew no less grim when he pulled away the armor and quilting. Blood had soaked through the bandage and thoroughly blackened the wrap.

"What did you see in your scouting?" Willard asked.

Brolli paused as if considering whether he'd allow the old knight to change the subject so easily. Then he sighed. "You want good news first, or bad?"

"Bad."

Brolli unwound the wrapping around Willard's waist, while Caris held aside the blood-stiff quilting. Harric watched, inhaling as much ragleaf as he could before the knight demanded it back.

"Bad news is that knights ride and waking up homesteads in this valley," said Brolli, not looking up from his work. "Good news is that they do not have our trail. Not once do they follow our stream."

"Gods leave us if they pick up our trail. Boy, is that roll ready?"

Harric handed the ragleaf to Willard, who sucked it so hungrily its crackling coal seemed loud beneath the willow.

Brolli set aside the wrap and teased the clotted linen from the wound, exposing a swollen, red-smeared wound like a harlot's mouth, complete with yellow teeth in the form of fat beneath the skin.

Harric's stomach rose in his throat.

Brolli lifted his eyes to Willard. "It is hot and weeping. And you still lose blood. You need big rest and healing."

Willard snorted smoke. "If Bannus finds us, it won't matter how I'm rested."

"I am not skilled in my people's healing magic."

"I wouldn't take it if you were."

Brolli made a harsh sound that was surely a curse in the Kwendi language. "*Then take the Blood of your Phyros,*" he said fiercely. "Your oath must wait! Your life is in danger. Everything is in danger."

Willard sucked the ragleaf calmly. "That is not an option, Ambassador. Do your best with the bandage."

"In one day you are unconscious."

"Then tie me to my saddle. I will not take the Blood."

"In two days you are dead."

Willard dropped his eyes.

Brolli stood. "Take the Blood."

Willard's eyes flashed. "I swore an oath to a lady, Ambassador. That may seem trivial to you, but to me —"

"Your lady would prefer you die than break this oath?"

"I might as well die if I do!" Willard snapped. The suddenness of his anger made Harric jump. The Kwendi didn't flinch. Willard sagged again, and sighed. "If I thought I could take the Blood only this once, to save my life, I might find forgiveness in her eyes. Of course. But I fear once I take it I will not stop. I don't even dare a plaster, as I did yesterday. That plaster alone nearly broke my will, Brolli, made me forget everything. You have no idea how strong the Blood of a god is in your veins. I would sooner accept your magic healing."

"Sir, there is healing at the fire-cone tower," Caris said.

Willard grunted. "What? Your friend's an herb-wife?"

"She's Iberg," said Caris. "A sister of the Bright Mother."

Willard choked smoke out his nose. "A witch? You've been leading us to a witch's tor?"

"No, sir…" Caris stammered, face flushing. "One of the Queen's fire-cone towers. She licensed Abellia to live there."

Willard sorted his rag-roll to the other side of his mouth. "The Queen, you say. I've heard about that." To Brolli he explained, "White witches use the Life power of the Bright Mother moon, Brolli. Healing, calming magic. They can use it to snuff out fire to keep the fire-cones safe." He shot a cutting glance at Caris. "And I guess *you* weren't afraid of her magic, being from the West

Country. Probably an ordinary thing to you."

"It would be hard to be afraid of Sister Abellia," Caris said. "Once you meet her you'll see."

"You accept her healing there, old man," said Brolli. "That is good compromise."

"Blast it, Brolli, I've lived five lives and never let the moons touch me. Not starting now."

"Stubborn old man! You once take Phyros blood! How is that different?"

"Phyros blood is the Blood of a god, Ambassador. It is not of the moons."

"The moons come from the gods."

"*Blast* your logic, Brolli! Arkus gave us Three Laws, and they distinguish Arkendians from all of our neighbors, including you. The first law states that we worship no gods, including Arkus himself; the second forbids slavery; the third states that we use no magic. Ever. Only Three Laws, Brolli, but they're what keep Arkendians strong and independent, and I don't question them."

Brolli glowered. Then a grim smile lifted one side of his broad mouth. "None of this matters. You will be unconscious from your wounds by time we arrive at white witch, and unconscious is agreement to heal."

Willard laughed in spite of himself. "You crafty little impit. You mean if I pass out you'll have me healed whether I want it or not? If you were an Arkendian officer I'd have you court-martialed."

Brolli bowed. "This quest is not about your conscience. It is about our futures, about the treaty I must propose to my people. And since I cannot survive without you, it is about your healing."

Sir Willard's eyes smiled, but his voice retained an edge. "I'm Arkendian, Ambassador. Refusal of gods and magic has made me strong. I won't pass out."

Brolli snorted. He handed the clotted bandage to Harric. "Rinse in stream, best you can."

Harric kept the gory rags at arm's length as he hurried to the stream. Under the influence of the ragleaf, his pains diminished. The herb also made his ears ring, however, and his head seem rather heavier than usual.

By the time Brolli and Caris had packed the wound with new rags and bound it with a tight wrap about Willard's waist, Harric had scrubbed the gore from the rags.

Willard looked gray-faced as he fished in a belt purse for a fresh roll of ragleaf.

A horn sounded in the valley.

Harric's head snapped instinctively toward it. It sounded again. No farther than a mile behind them in the west, he judged.

Brolli muttered another Kwendi curse. "Get up, old man." He and Caris helped Willard to his feet as Willard lit a new rag-roll from the stub of the old.

The horn sounded again, this time in four musical notes. A higher horn echoed the tune, farther south.

Harric smiled and relaxed. "That's not a hunting horn. That's 'Heave-Ho, Father,' a peasant work tune about a priest hauling a wagon."

"Peasants don't sound horns, boy." Willard snorted. "It's a *priest-hunting* song from the West Country. Same tune, but the Brotherhood changed it to 'Hang High, Father.'"

Brolli's brow creased above his daylids. "Why they hang priests?"

"For the crime of freeing peasants."

"That is bad. They must hunt the priest who blocks the bridge for us yesterday?"

"Most likely."

"We cannot let them!" Brolli confronted Willard. "We must help him as he helped us."

A flicker of irritation crossed Willard's eyes. "Ambassador, I've saved that man from hunters more times than he can count. And I say it *may* be Father Kogan they hunt. Just as likely there isn't a priest at all and they're using the song to lure me out for some asinine rescue."

"What is ass-nine?"

A third horn, higher than the others, sounded to the northwest.

"They're all over the valley," Harric muttered, as he stuffed his pack on Rag's back.

Brolli scrambled up the side of the willow as quick as a squirrel, grappling foot and hand to the highest crook that would take his weight. The southern horn sounded its merry notes again, and Brolli pointed in the direction of the sound. "Down this stream. Maybe a mile away."

"Can you see them?" Willard asked.

Brolli moved another branch. "No. We're too low."

"Doesn't matter. Saddle up."

Brolli descended in a controlled fall. Harric and Caris hurried to saddle the horses.

"Boy, be sure we leave no sign of being here. Heeled boot prints and hoof prints have to go. Must seem nothing but shepherds camp here. Girl, lift Molly's saddle for me."

As they flew about the camp, the horns sang to each other across the valley. Then a throaty blast answered from the far west.

Willard froze. He bit off a curse. "That's Bannus's horn. Gods take him, I haven't heard that for a long and blessed time."

A pulse of guilt hit Harric. Had his mother put the immortal on their trail?

"Girl. How far before we leave this stream and climb out of this valley?"

Caris stared. Her gaze wandered from Rag to Willard, unfocused.

"Girl! Keep an ear for the rest of us! How far till we leave the stream?"

Her eyes found Willard. "Soon. I'll know the path when I see it."

"Mount up and lead. Brolli! Dust any tracks the boy missed."

Let none of you worship or pray gods for favors,
Nor bow down to high lords among you.
Neither rely you on magic,
And you shall be strong.

— The Three Laws of Arkus

20

Father Kogan's Hidey-Hole

Kogan saw the farmer from across a field of oats, and set out for him at a trot down a well-trod path between the furrows, clutching the Phyros ax beneath its massive head. The man saw him and stopped outside the front door of a small log farmhouse, tilting his leather hat back to watch the priest's approach.

"I need a place to hide, brother," Kogan said when he reached him, panting. "Crossing your fields. I seen the collar on your scarecrow, and knowed you was friendly to the cause o' freedom." Kogan pulled aside his hedge of beard to expose the forged iron collar of his calling. "Father Kogan's the name."

The farmer doffed his hat and nodded his respect. "Name's Miles. We owes everything to Father Oren. He run us out three year gone, and helped dig our first cellar, too. Be a right shame if I didn't help ye now. What's chasing ye?"

"Westie knights." Kogan spat.

"Don't surprise me none. Heard horns all morning. They seen ye?"

"Not as I think."

"They got scent-dogs?"

"None as I heard."

The farmer gave a sly grin. "Not that they'd need 'em. Father Oren weren't much for bathing neither." Before Kogan could regain enough breath to object, Miles turned into the house. "Step inside, Father. We'll hide you in the old root cellar."

Kogan followed, ducking low beneath the doorframe, and once inside stood tall amidst log rafters and the scent of new-baked bread. His stomach growled so loud it startled the farmer. "Mighty obliged, brother. But a cellar's the first place they'll look."

"We got two cellars. Old one went sour last spring, so we dug a new. We'll let 'em search the fresh one and they'll never guess we got another."

Kogan glanced back through the door and across the hay field, where the lance pennons of his pursuers bobbed beyond a distant rise. "Let's see it."

"Help me move this table, Father. It's right under."

Together they moved a massive log table across the plank floor. The farmer swept aside the rag rug that hid a trap door sealed with tar.

"Puttied her with tar to keep the stink in."

Kogan frowned. "Can a man breathe in that hole?"

"I reckon *you* could, Father." The yeoman grinned.

"Now, hold on there! Just cause a man don't bathe don't mean he like the smell o' shit." Kogan frowned as he dug the hand ring from its recess in the door, and yanked. "Unless it's his own shit, a'course. But everyone likes that."

The door swung up, stretching and tearing the tar seal at the edges. A smell like soured cream and compost wafted out. Below, the hole was deep and wide, and every visible surface—including the underside of the door—hung in thick sheets of downy white fungus.

Kogan peered in doubtfully. "You don't got a third cellar?"

"No, Father. But get in quick. I can hear the hoofs now."

A horn sounded brightly in the fields. The tune was "Hang High, Father," which gave Kogan visions of ramming trumpets up the arses of the squires who played it.

"Quick, Father, so I can get the table back!"

"I'll be found out if my belly growls like that again. Best you give me a loaf or two to quiet her."

The yeoman scrambled and fetched a loaf and tossed it down the hatch. "There!"

"That weren't but a crumb for a man my size!"

"Blast it, Father, if ye get us found out—"

"Just toss another," Kogan said, dropping his ax into the hole and placing a bare foot on the first step. The step folded like paper beneath his weight, and he fell like a stone through the rest of the treads to the bottom.

"Sit tight now, Father," Miles said, an edge of panic in his voice. "Quit your cursing or they'll hear ye sure."

Fear in the man's voice made Kogan bite his tongue. The trap door slammed, engulfing him in darkness. He wrestled free of the wooden wreckage, and located the loaf flattened beneath him, now slippery with sour-smelling fungus.

"Coulda done with another loaf!" he shouted.

Hunting horns sounded again. Bannus's throaty basso drew steadily closer, to join the others.

"Help me to my saddle," Willard growled. "No sense busting all your fancy bandages before we've even started."

With the help of all three of them, he swung his good leg across Molly's rump. When he finally sat at up in his saddle, his face was the color of bone. "Just stiff," he said. "I'll limber up."

"You bleed," said Brolli. "Any movement and the rags are already full."

A line of bright blood scored the black skirt and dripped upon his spurs. "It'll stop." Willard urged Molly up the stream, puffing hungrily on the ragleaf.

Brolli boarded Idgit, his face dark with frustration. As he bound himself to the saddle, Spook clambered onto the warm saddle pack in which he'd stowed the porridge pot, still full of steaming oatmeal, and settled in for the ride.

"Harric," Brolli said. He'd pushed his daylids up, revealing the worry in his golden owl eyes. "Watch Willard while I sleep. If he get worse, wake me."

In less than a mile, Caris led them east out of the stream, up a trail that climbed the head of the valley. Once they struck the trail, Rag seemed to recognize it; she snorted, her tail twitching eagerly, and picked up the pace as if for a particularly cozy stable at the end of the road.

After cresting the stony spine of the ridge, the trail plunged down the other side into a wooded valley untamed by farmstead or mill. Another stony ridge bounded the far side of the valley, and beyond that still more ridges running north-south across their path, like rows of jagged teeth.

"Halt!" Willard said, before they descended the track into the valley. He squinted into the far distance. "Can we see our tower on one of those ridges, girl?"

Caris shook her head. "Too far away, sir. Two days' ride."

Willard spat a fragment of ragleaf. "We'll never make it. Not if they find our trail. Brolli! You awake?"

Brolli had already removed his blanket. "Hard to sleep with the horns." He grinned. "You wish I go back to cover any tracks on the trail?"

Willard nodded. He seemed to have paused to catch his breath, as if talking taxed him.

Harric exchanged glances with Caris and Brolli.

Willard intercepted their looks, and scowled. "I also worry that once we cross this ridge, we won't hear their horns, so we won't know how close they are. While you're smoothing our tracks, take a good listen. Before you come back, see if you can gauge whether they follow."

In all his battles, all his fields,
Sir Willard proved the best.
He loved the Queen,
But then her maid,
And never more was blessed.

— From "Black Armor Becomes Him"

21

Attacked

Harric dismounted, and laid himself out on a rock shelf warmed by the sun. By the time Brolli returned, Harric had managed a ragleaf-induced — and thankfully dreamless — sleep. He woke to a tirade of cursing from the old knight. Brolli's news was not good. The horns seemed to be converging, and growing louder.

"Saddle up, Brolli. It's a race now. Nothing for it but to put our heads down and ride and hope we make the tower before they catch us."

Harric led Idgit and Brolli, following Caris as the trail descended steeply into an ancient torchwood forest. Massive trunks soared skyward like columns in a giant's palace, some as thick as windmills. High above, a canopy of coin-shaped leaves winked green and gold in the sunlight, while underfoot a carpet of deep moss swallowed sound and beckoned Harric to lie down and forget everything in a deep, hushed sleep. Yet as he breathed in the scent of ancient life, the immensity of the silence soothed him.

How long had it been since he visited the hollows of these ridges? Since his mother died? In the years before her death, when her madness made her vicious, he'd escaped to such places often, to camp alone in the blessed stillness. Why'd he stop?

Harric glanced back to check on Willard. The knight remained upright in his saddle, smoking steadily. He'd closed the visor on his helm to rebreathe the smoke inside the helmet, so smoke poured from eye and ear slots like the helm of some demon knight in a ballad. Surely the pain of age had driven Willard to the leaf. Could the aches of five lifetimes of wounds have returned now that he was mortal? That would turn anyone addict.

By mid-morning the herb's effects on Harric faded. His pain returned with interest, until even the peace of the ancient forest was lost upon him. His brain seemed to swell again as his skull shrank around it. His swollen lip began to throb worse than before, irritated by a newly chipped tooth. Each step sent a stab of fire through his bruised ribs.

When Willard called for a halt in a mossy grotto, Harric wanted only to eat in silence on a cushion of moss. Careful not to wake Brolli, he retrieved bread and cheese from one of Idgit's saddle packs and found a spot to eat that was close enough to the others that his isolation wouldn't look intentional, but far enough away that he wouldn't have to talk. As he lowered himself onto a hummock of springy red cork-moss, Spook scampered to him and sniffed the cheese hungrily. Harric chewed stale bread slowly, jaw aching, and fed Spook hunks of cheese.

Caris staked Rag far from the Phyros, and joined Harric. Without the burden of concentrating on Rag, she seemed worried, distracted, and itching to talk. He knew she would sense his mood, and that his sullenness would confuse or anger her, but he found it very hard to feign cheer.

He acknowledged her with a grunt.

To fill the silence and take his mind off his pains, he laid his mother's saddle knife upon the back of his left hand and made it walk from knuckle to knuckle, back and forth across the hand. After a few revolutions he flipped it to stand on its pommel on the back of the hand—almost dropped it—then let it fall sideways to the back of his other hand, where he walked it across the knuckles the same way. It was a hand-limbering exercise his mother taught him, and it helped clear his head when he needed. It was also a form of showing off that might take the place of talking for a while. With it went an Oliitian mantra his mother had chanted until he giggled.

> *All he catches, Mad Moon strangles*
> *All she hatches, Mother keeps*
> *All unknown the Black Moon tangles*
> *All in dreams of death and sleep*
> *Ever one and other warring*
> *Ever Darkness wedding War*

Ever mated, never pairing
Every mother, Nature's whore.

Caris and Spook both watched as if hypnotized for two or three revolutions, then Caris swatted the knife to the ground, and Spook startled and sped away into the ferns.

"What in the Black Moon are you doing?" Harric snapped.

"*Don't be a fool,*" Caris hissed. She cast a furtive glance at Willard, and her cheeks flushed with anger, or shame.

"What do I care if he sees it?" Harric said.

"Think what you're doing, Harric! He's made you his *valet*. You've got a chance to become something honorable. If you had any sense you'd never do another jack trick as long as you live."

Harric's face burned. With an effort, he restrained his fury. *Anger is master, never slave*, his mother whispered in his mind. Very deliberately he bent and retrieved the knife. "Then go somewhere else. I'm not lifting anything. I'm meditating."

"*Meditating.* It's a jack's trick, and any fool can see it. You'll throw this chance away if Willard learns you're a trickster. He isn't bound to train a jack."

A jack? Was that what she thought of him? He was an *artist*, to borrow his mother's words, and though he hated his mother for his mad childhood, he had a kind of pride in what he'd made of it. He clenched his jaw and cradled his head in his hands. "I can't talk about this right now. All right?"

Caris seemed at a loss. She wrapped her arms around her middle, hugging herself, something he'd seen her do when she was upset enough to curl in a ball with her hands on her ears. She rocked forward and back a little, but her hands did not rise to her head.

Her words came with effort. "Can you listen?" she asked.

He nodded. He could see it took everything she had to resist balling up and retreating from whatever she had to say. Her voice quaked, and she spoke quickly, without meeting his eyes. "I talked to Brolli last night about the wedding ring. He agreed it hasn't taken my wits. He said I'll be the same person. And I have my *will*, too." She looked up to meet his eyes, something she rarely did in tense conversations, and he knew it required immense effort from her. "I could leave you if I had to, Harric. Did you know that?"

"No."

"Well, I could. If you did something I couldn't accept, like—like…" She halted, her nostrils flaring as they did when she was angry. "Like the squire's purse."

Harric chuckled. "The purse. You found it."

"Harric, I swear if you ever—"

"You know that Iberg witched us, Caris. You can't hold that against me."

She clamped her jaw, eyes hard. "Just the fact that you could do it. And that you planted it in my belt without my knowing, like—"

"Caris, we were witched—"

"Let me *say* it, Harric! I have to say it."

"All right. Say it."

"There is nothing more important to me than being a knight. This wedding ring doesn't change that. And I swear if you play another purse, or deception, or any other jack trick, I will leave you. I don't care how much it hurts me, I will."

Tears welled in her eyes, but her face was hard as flint.

Harric's heart ached, even as it burned with anger. "It was my 'tricks' that won your mentorship in the first place. Have you forgotten that? I know I seem a kind of useless fop to you, and probably to Willard. Manservant material. But my training is as deep as yours. In my way. I plan to serve the Queen as well as you or any knight."

Caris's hands went to her ears. She stood, then staggered away to Rag, where she buried her face in her mane.

The old knight eyed her with distaste. "What in the Black Moon's she doing?"

Harric laid his head on his knees, unsure he'd accomplished anything— unable, in his pain, to care if he had.

Harric volunteered to lead Idgit while Brolli slept, thereby escaping an awkward ride with Caris. If it bothered her that he'd abandoned her company in that way, she never showed it; as he trudged behind in a haze of absorbing pain, she never once looked back to see if she moved too fast for him. At about the point at which he became vaguely aware of the low angle of the sunlight slanting gold beneath the canopy, Rag stopped and Harric nearly plodded into her hindquarters. He had to raise a hand to Idgit's bridle and stumble sideways to keep her from pinning him under Rag's swishing tail.

The Phyros drew up behind Idgit. "What is it?" Willard asked.

"I don't know." Caris's voice was distant, horse-tied.

Willard rode around for a look, trailing Holly behind.

Harric followed, leading Idgit.

They'd halted at the edge of a wide clearing where two giant torchwoods had toppled in a storm, creating a giant hole in the canopy. The clearing glowed with golden sunlight, and buzzed with a ruckus of sparrows and jays feeding like flocks in the fields at threshing time. But the strangest thing—and that which attracted the birds—was the bareness of the forest floor. Where there should have been an explosion of fresh young undergrowth in the newly sunlit space, there were no plants at all, only a tumult of rich black soil. It looked as though it had been cleared and turned and trampled by the work of a madman's plow.

"What is it?" said Caris, scanning the new scene.

"A yoab site." Willard glanced around the riven landscape, brow furrowed. "Don't see a yoab, though." He raised a water skin to his lips and drank greedily. Once he'd sucked it dry, he tossed it to Harric. "Give me your skin, boy. I'm burning up." The old knight's cheeks shone rosy with fever, but no new blood scored his armor, so Harric let the Kwendi sleep. Harric swapped skins with Willard, who guzzled more, and dribbled some down his back, under the quilting.

"I've heard about yoab up here," said Caris, "but I've never seen one."

Willard grunted. "Imagine a garl bear, only bigger—the size of a twenty-man field tent, say—with a head like a bull toad. Now take away the fur and give it a blanket of moss and grass and such. And instead of clawing up grubs from rotten logs, imagine it chewing down the whole log and the dirt and everything else like a sea whale drinks the sea."

Caris wrinkled her nose. "It eats the soil?"

"You have it." Willard nodded. "Giant pests to farmers. A big one'll eat an acre of wheat and all the topsoil with it in a day. One that's got whiff of a horse will let out a roar to be heard miles away, and then trample horse and rider or swallow them whole. They love horses."

"Farmers use resin charges to scare them off," said Harric. "You don't have any, do you?"

"Aren't you listening, boy? We can't have that thing waking and bellowing out a challenge. Bannus could hear it miles away, and who else would have horses in this wood besides him or us? No. If we see it, we hope it's sleeping, and give it a wide berth. It's not here, so we can cross this patch. Lead away, girl, only keep a sharp eye."

Rag picked her way across the turned soil, and after some exploring located the mule track on the other side. She'd gone no more than a bowshot when fresh bird noise erupted ahead in the forest. Soon, brown and white birds with bills like woodpeckers darted between the trees around them, scolding at their intrusion. Caris plodded by, peering with curiosity at their behavior. The birds concentrated in greatest profusion around a mound of moss and lichens no more than a stone's throw to one side of the trail. When Willard drew near, the scolding increased, as if it were a nesting colony and Willard had come for eggs. They flew at Molly, and at Holly, who still trailed on her tether, then reeled about their mound. Some flew into holes on the mound as if to guard nests.

Molly snorted and snapped ineffectually at the agile birds. Rag danced sideways. Idgit backed, eyes rolling, until Harric grabbed her bridle.

A muffled curse from Brolli. The Kwendi threw off his blanket, shouting, "Yoab!" before he'd even taken in the scene. "Back away!"

The mound of moss and lichens lurched, scattering birds. Legs like muddy tree trunks levered the hillock to its feet. The beast would not have fit into a *fifty*-man tent. Before Caris could turn Rag or ride past, a fissure at the near end of the mound became a cave, and released an air-riving roar of fury.

22

Steel & Magic

The horses screamed. Holly reared, pulling her lead line free of Willard's saddle. Molly snarled, and Willard's sword chimed from its scabbard. Caris kept her saddle, but Idgit bit at Harric, and when he dropped her bridle she spun and bolted back the way they'd come, followed by Holly. Brolli toppled from Idgit's saddle like an ill-tied sack of meal.

"Girl! Get those horses!" Willard bellowed. "Don't let them run!"

Caris whirled Rag and galloped past Harric.

The mossy hillock shuddered and rose on stumplike limbs. Twigs and detritus cascaded from its peaked back in miniature avalanches. The yoab's head rose, a mossy boulder, weaving drunkenly, then dropped with a sound like a falling tree. It lifted again. Nostrils the size of badger holes snapped open and closed, gusting and sucking the air.

"Back off, Willard," Brolli said.

"I'm trying." Willard cursed. "Molly won't have it." He jerked the reins to turn her, but she growled in fury at the notion of retreat.

"Its belly is too full to move," Brolli said. "Belly dragging. We turn and leave it if it doesn't"—the monster convulsed, and a wave of blackness surged from its gullet to bury the moss—"vomit. Now it moves."

Harric backed to Brolli's side, unable to tear his gaze from the Phyros and her rider, who shrank in comparison to the walking hillside before them.

Brolli drew a pearly globe the size of an apple from his satchel. "Cover your ears!" he shouted. With a straight-armed overhand motion, like a catapult, he flung the globe at the yoab's head. The globe arched over Willard and Molly and thumped before the yoab, then vanished in a flash and deafening concussion.

Dirt and rocks rained beneath the canopy. Birds scattered.

The yoab charged. It moved with more speed than Harric would have dreamed possible for anything so huge. Molly surged to meet it, but before the yoab could muster its full momentum, she swerved along its left flank and Willard's sword rang musically off its skull. The yoab roared and spun, clawing a wall of debris that hailed upon Harric and Brolli. Its jaws clashed together with the force of logs in a whitewater whorl. Harric saw no teeth, only bony ridges like continuous molars in a ferocious underbite, and heavy folds of skin like the throat of a pelican. Harric could see no eyes on the creature, only nostrils and jaw.

Molly swerved again and again, and Willard aimed jabs at patches of gray skin amidst the carpet of flora. Willard seemed anything but injured. It seemed as if all the years of Phyros blood in his veins somehow welled up in him in this moment of need.

The knight and Phyros moved as one, with a sureness and power Harric had never witnessed in anything. Willard held no reins, but communicated with his knees and whatever unknowable bond he shared with Molly, wielding the Phyros sword in both hands. In spite of his age—or rather, because of it, because of five lifetimes of battle—Willard moved with grace and precision almost hypnotic to behold. From his thigh, however, bright blood ran in stripes down his armor.

The Kwendi scooped globes blindly from the satchel and lobbed them at the yoab. "Throw!" he said to Harric, spilling some at their feet. Brolli's second globe bounced from the yoab's side and burst in a cloud of yellow sparkles. A third split in half and erupted in music like out-of-tune bagpipes. Harric snatched another and hurled. His ribs screamed in pain, truncating the effort, and the globe fell well short, but took a lucky bounce into the yoab's knee, where it stuck like a wart without further effect.

"Will you stop throwing toys?" Willard shouted. "Do something!"

The Kwendi muttered something then sprinted, foot and knuckle, as if he would run up the yoab's fern-crested back. Unwilling to remain behind, Harric limped after.

Willard's sword rang from some bony structure on one of the monster's forelimbs, then he turned Molly and sped up the mule track away from the others, shouting, "This way, you great worm!"

The yoab ignored the ruse—possibly unaware of where Willard had gone—

and instead charged the opposite direction, straight for Brolli and Harric, who almost ran into its mouth. Brolli dodged aside, lobbing a red globe into the bellowing maw before the monster's passage cast him sidelong into a hump of ferns. Harric plastered himself to a torchwood bole as the beast tore past, flattening smaller trees and shuddering the ground with its passage.

Crimson smoke spouted from its mouth and nostrils and from holes that might have been ears atop its skull. Its roar grew to a deafening squeal as it coughed like a firesaw and redoubled its speed. Blind and raging, it charged down the slope in the direction Caris had gone after Idgit.

With every roar of the yoab behind them, it took almost all of Caris's concentration to hold Rag's fragile nerves together enough to keep on Idgit's trail. But she'd never had such difficulty calming a single horse, and this bothered her. Even more worrying, the equine fear was so potent it began to penetrate her own mind. She'd felt a similar difficulty the night before, when the effort to keep Rag calm around Molly had been almost too much for her. If it hadn't been for the upsetting matter of Harric and the wedding ring, she'd almost have looked forward to each time they stopped to rest, so she could hobble Rag far from Molly, and re-enter the world of humans.

In all her life she'd never craved the world of humans over her usual escape into horses. Was she changing? And if so, was this a good thing?

The yoab's noise grew suddenly louder, and then it appeared on the slope above them, flattening saplings like grass, blasting crimson fire from mouth and nostrils.

Idgit veered to one side, and Rag followed. Rag's fear entered Caris now, and she let it have rein. When she finally regained her senses, she realized the yoab had not veered with them, and was far away. Slowly, she pushed the horses' fear from her mind, and reestablished calm in Rag. She rode Idgit down and took her bridle, stopped both horses, and dismounted. Nuzzling them both, she comforted them silently for many heartbeats in a quiet copse of dapple-nuts and fern. Gradually their blowing calmed and their eyes ceased rolling.

Safe. Safe, she told them. She stroked their velvet cheeks, pressing forehead to muzzles, until they all breathed normally together.

Another horse snorted nearby, and Caris looked up to see Willard's spare horse. Holly? Dolly? The animal gazed at her from across the copse. The tournament hood Willard had kept on her now hung by a mere string, torn from her face in the frantic flight. Caris stared for long moments. When she realized with the certainty of the horse-touched that she was looking at a Phyros foal, she sucked her breath in surprise.

No one had ever seen a Phyros foal in Arkendia. Only grown Phyros were brought to Arkendia from the Sacred Isle, and all those were stallions, with the single exception of Molly.

Caris hobbled Rag and Idgit, and walked, entranced, toward Molly's miraculous offspring.

Holly tossed her head and trotted across the ferns to her side, peering at Caris intently with pale gray eyes.

How strange that her eyes were not violet. That must be an adult feature, Caris mused, like how an infant human's eyes are generally black or blue before they settle on an adult color.

Holly snuffed her fingers and let Caris stroke her cheeks. Caris extended her horse-touched senses toward her, probing.

She sensed nothing in Holly like the fierce maelstrom of Molly's aura. Holly bore some of the inexplicably deep nature of the Phyros that set them apart from mortal horses, but the horrible violence and domination that defined her mother was absent. In fact, the signature presence of Phyros was so soft in Holly that Caris hadn't sensed it before, or perhaps the distraction of calming Rag—and the overpowering aura of Molly—had prevented it. But now it was palpable.

It was just as palpable that Willard had more priceless cargo to protect on this journey than just the ring on her finger.

She was deep in the world of Holly's emotions when Rag suddenly reared in her hobbles, terrified. Caris gasped in surprise, stepping back from Holly and shifting her attention to Rag.

Willard arrived in a tempest of pounding hooves. "Gods leave us, you're safe." His face shone with sweat and a mottle of ash and fever spots. When he saw Holly's hood, and Caris's distant focus, he choked on anger. "Get away from her!"

Caris startled. "I—she—"

Willard rode to Holly with obvious pain, and leaned down to fit the torn hood across her face. "Didn't I tell you to leave her be? What were you doing with her?"

Caris's mouth moved mutely as she struggled to access the world of language. "Rag—" she managed. Roaring began in her ears, and she raised her hands to shut it out.

Willard shoved her shoulder with his boot, and she let some of her connection to Rag slip away, to keep herself from collapsing with the strain of both worlds. She staggered against Willard's stirrup and stared up as he searched her face.

"Do not fraternize with her," he panted, eyes glassy and wild. "Do you understand me?"

Caris followed Willard's gaze to Holly, as he affixed her lead to Molly's saddle. "Holly…" She looked quizzically into his face. "She's Molly's…but Phyros can't breed on this island—"

"Moons *blast* your woman's tongue! *Never* repeat that. Do you hear? Have you any idea what you've said? Do you know what would happen if it were known?"

Caris blinked, uncertain.

"Tell me you understand, girl. Never repeat that. You understand?"

"I…I won't tell Harric."

"You won't tell *anyone*. Not Brolli. Not your white witch friend. Not ever. This is a more dangerous secret than that wedding ring, girl. No one knows it but you and I."

Caris stared at the filly, her attentions divided perilously between worlds. She released more hold on Rag, and pointed at Holly. "But she's a—"

"Phyros. Yes," he hissed, barely a whisper. "Moons *take* your horse-touched eyes!"

"But they only breed on the Sacred Isle." She thought about the Chaos Moon eclipse that Mother Ganner predicted, and wondered if this miracle were another sign of its approach.

Willard's eyes closed as if he were suddenly too weary to keep them open. Only then did she notice his pale skin and the blood caking his leg below the wound.

"Tell me you understand, girl. Are you here, or are you in your horse there?"

"I understand. The Brotherhood. They'd try to start herds in the West Isles."

"Yes."

"But she's different than Molly. Her eyes…"

"Hasn't been blooded yet, or any fool could see it in her. Molly will blood her in time, gods leave us."

He closed his eyes and swayed forward in his saddle. The encounter with the yoab had taxed his reserves. "Mount your horse and draw up beside me."

She complied quickly, worried for his fever, and wanting to be near if he should fall from his saddle. When she stopped Rag beside Molly, however, it took almost all her concentration to keep Rag calm. Vaguely, she sensed Willard removing a gauntlet. Then he thrust his hand before her face, red blood welling from a slice across its back. She looked up in surprise.

His eyes shone, glassy and intense. "Kiss the blood and swear you'll never reveal this. Swear on your apprenticeship."

She kissed the blood. "I swear," she murmured, and he smeared the blood across her lips as if sealing a letter with wax.

He nodded, then spurred Molly back up the slope the way he'd come.

Holly followed on spindly filly's legs, casting curious glances back at Caris.

Harric heard Molly's hoofbeats drumming the moss before he saw her. When she appeared on the trail with Willard on her back, the old knight rode slumped over the front cantle of his saddle, a sheet of red blood down his leg. Caris followed close upon Rag, as if she expected him to topple at any moment. When Molly approached, Harric stepped away, unsure Willard had full control of her.

"Water," Willard croaked, as he reined Molly in.

Harric lifted a newly filled skin, and Willard sucked at it greedily. Brolli and Caris gathered bandages from the packs and hurried them to Willard's side. Willard glanced down, water streaming from his mustachios. He snorted. "If you think to coax me down off this saddle so you can patch me up, you'd better have a crane to put me up again."

Brolli frowned. "We stand on a tree, then." He pointed to one of the fallen torchwoods. "You ride up beside."

Willard positioned Molly beside the fallen tree as the others scrambled onto its mossy side. With Harric holding supplies beside them on the tree, Brolli and Caris set to work.

"How in the Black Moon did you make the beast run off?" Willard said, as Brolli attempted a blood-crusted buckle.

Brolli smiled grimly. "I get lucky. That hurler was a smoke charge. For decoration only, but I get it right in the mouth, which ruin its smeller for a time. Probably scare it, mostly."

Willard grunted. "Well done."

"I must apologize for the—what you called them—party favor?" Brolli said. "When Idgit run, I try to grab my weapons, but I only got these." He drew an apple-sized globe from his satchel, and held it out for their view. It appeared to be a solid globe of pure witch-silver.

"Why do you have party favors?" Harric said.

"For the Queen's parties." Brolli grimaced. "Has not been much to celebrate. Here," he said, laying the globe in Harric's hand. "You threw well today. Toss and see what it do."

"Don't you toss it, boy!" Willard stared at Harric, eyes bright with fever.

"I wasn't going to toss it—"

"The moons you weren't. Brolli says you tossed one already. That true?"

"But the yoab was charging you—"

"Are you an Arkendian, or an Iberg?"

"I did not mean to tempt him." Brolli retrieved the hurler from Harric's hand.

Willard panted, the red mouth of his wound lolling grotesquely. "It seems I must remind you, Ambassador, that Arkendians are bound by the Third Law to use no magic. Nor do we trust it in any way." Though Willard addressed the Kwendi, his gaze bored into Harric. "Magic consumes and maddens the user. You need only look to what is left of the creator gods to know that."

"What if you're already mad to begin with?" Harric said. "Would it cure you?"

"Shut your trap, boy!" Willard grimaced, as if the effort of shouting caused him pain. "*Ibergs* use magic," he continued, his voice lower, but hoarse with strain. "*Kwendi* use magic. West Isle lords employ it. But no true Arkendian. And no man of mine. That clear?"

Harric nodded. He wished he'd kept his mouth shut, but he also wished the old knight had become more worldly in five lifetimes of travel. Harric's mother had encountered numerous cultures when serving the Queen abroad, each with different ideas about the moons and their magic, and she'd always preached openness to magic, if it served the Queen's safety.

"Take no offense, please, Brolli," said Willard, "but to Arkendians, magic brings weakness. Harric, like any other Arkendian, relies upon himself. I don't like how comfortable he is with that globe in his hand."

23

Of Herbs & Hauntings

Harric tried to stand, but his body had grown so stiff and sore from his recent exertion that he failed miserably, doubling back over in pain. Willard plucked his ragleaf from his mouth and extended it to him.

"Here. You've been roughed up pretty good."

Harric smoked till his mouth stung, and it quelled enough pain to get him back on his feet. When he glanced at Caris he saw softness in her eyes, but when he met her eyes she clenched her jaw and turned away.

Willard said, "How far to the mountain pass you spoke of, girl?"

"It's at the head of this valley."

Willard grunted. "We could reach it tonight, if we pushed."

"There's a fortification and gate in the pass," Caris said.

Harric found that funny. Even if he and Chacks or Remo had packed enough food for their expedition to their grove, they may well have faced a fort wall, too. He must have made an unseemly giggle, because the next thing he knew Willard plucked the ragleaf from his mouth and replaced it between his own teeth.

"You didn't mention a guarded fort, girl," said Willard. "How'd you get past when you came through?"

"It was unmanned in winter, but I suppose it's occupied in summer, to protect the harvest."

Willard frowned. "We might find the guards sympathetic to our cause, and we might not. Is there no other pass?"

"I don't think so. The mountains are awfully rough up there."

"Maybe we worry for nothing," said Brolli. "Night comes, and you camp near the pass while I scout it. Who know? Perhaps the gate is abandon and we worry for nothing."

"Unlikely," Willard said. "The fire-cone represents a lot of revenue for the Queen."

The Kwendi grinned his feral grin. "Then I have a way we slip by." The mischievous twinkle in his eye was unmistakable. Harric guessed he planned to use magic to do it, and delivered the proposal like dropping a gauntlet before Willard.

Willard grunted and looked away, but Harric believed the old man knew exactly what the Kwendi implied, and tacitly—hypocritically—approved. *So, magic is okay if it benefits Willard, and he doesn't have to acknowledge it.* Harric kept that thought to himself, but it might have leaked out in his look, for Willard avoided his glance.

"Very well," Willard said. "Stop us a mile from the place, girl."

Harric fell into a rhythmic trudge behind Idgit, staring at the trail and seeing only the next spot he'd place his feet. As the sun sank behind them, and his shadow lengthened before him, Harric slowly emerged from his trance, aware of a strange sound around him. At first he thought Caris might be humming or singing. Or perhaps Brolli spoke in some pet voice to Spook beneath his blanket. It didn't seem to have a direction, or it seemed to come from near him, accompanied by a hollow kind of echo.

It was a voice. Female. Hysterical. It seemed beside him, a presence at his ear. He flinched, looking about, but saw nothing.

Little fool! You'll ruin everything!

He startled. The court accent and intonation were unmistakable. It was Mother. Warped and strange, but Mother.

Your destiny is nigh! The familiar, horrible wail that accompanied her worst visions seemed to erupt from the air beside him, setting him staggering to one side, eyes bolting from his head.

"Stop it…" he gasped. "Leave me alone…"

Another sound, a hissing and snarling, and she cried, *Get away from me! I am last kin! It is my right! I have right of last kin!*

Harric clapped his hands to his ears, but the sound merely erupted into a gabble of voices like crows. It ceased abruptly, leaving him panting, standing in the middle of the trail as if to face an enemy. Around him a soft breeze sighed through the branches, a distant fall of water chattered over stones, and the horses' hooves plodded heavily on the drum of the packed earth.

Was this what it had felt like for his mother, when her madness started…a gabble of voices in her head? The Sight had come to her at around this age. Had it begun as a trickle, like this, and grown to a mind-consuming torrent she couldn't control—visions of futures and possible futures slamming into her brain unbidden and torturing her nights?

Perhaps Sir Bannus had knocked something loose in his head and set the dike to leaking.

The trail climbed out of the forest up switchbacks along rock faces that stood like teeth along the jawbone of the ridge. From the edge of one switchback they glimpsed the low walls of a gatehouse in a gap between teeth. Caris found a grotto among boulders in which they made their camp. Harric found a nook between rocks that gave him some privacy from the others, and there he rolled up in his bedding and lay with his back to the camp.

Spook curled in the crook between his neck and shoulder, studying Harric's face with white, glassy eyes. White eyes. Truly white, it seemed, opaque as porcelain, not merely seeming so in moonlight. Could it be the trait of an Iberg breed he'd never seen? He jabbed his fist in the air before Spook, who flinched as if it saw him clear as day.

"Sorry, Spook," he murmured, scratching the cat's ear with one hand. "Just trying to figure out those pearly eyes of yours." He couldn't decide if they were pretty or ugly. Ugly, mostly.

He teased the witch-stone from his shirt, and held it close to keep it hidden from anyone who peered over the rocks at his back. Spook purred, watching intently.

The stone had depths that belied its dimensions. Light bent in unexpected ways within it, yet no reflection appeared across its surface. Rather it seemed the dim moonlight directly illumined the vague depths beneath its surface. It was easy to imagine the stone in his hand was not a stone at all, but a hole through which he peered into a misty, starless night. Shapes materialized and faded. His imagination could make them into anything, like shapes in clouds, but they also seemed slightly warped, as if viewed through a bottle.

Faintly at first, the voices returned. The merest hint of speech, fading in and out. No words discernible. Fear pulsed in his chest, but hope rose with it—hope that it might well be the witch-stone, not the madness in his blood, that brought the voices. But if it wasn't madness, had he heard spirits? Ghosts of the dead? Did the stone draw them somehow? Could they hurt him?

He shuddered, and closed his hand around the stone to hide it from his eyes. Though the whispering had stopped, it was only the knowledge that his mother seemed to fear it that kept him from hurling it into the ravine below their trail.

Spook yawned, baring tiny, sharp teeth.

A wave of exhaustion took Harric, and he slept.

He dreamed he and Caris ran off to be married and become knights in the forest, but everywhere they went, mosquitoes and Sapphire grooms plagued them. Then he was alone with only Spook at his side, and the grooms found him and surrounded him. He heard Lyla whimpering, and Mother Ganner crying, "Run!"

Then a ring of dark-robed witches appeared between him and the grooms, black witch-stones in their hands. Together they chanted secret words and faded from sight: *Nebecci, Bellana, Tryst.* He didn't recognize the words, but in the dream, he knew the witch who tried to kill him in Gallows Ferry had spoken the very same syllables to become invisible.

Speak it! Speak it! the fading witches urged. *Nebecci, Bellana, Tryst!*

When the last witch vanished, Harric was alone again, and the leering grooms drew closer. They never reached him, but the dream repeated. Only Spook seemed slightly different in each dream—sitting in one, lying in the next—watching him intently with his plain milky eyes.

The peasant priest's god is Arkus, who has only three commandments: Worship no god,
Bow to no lord, and Use no magic. Therefore it is the chief virtue of a peasant priest to
deny his god and preach others do the same. A peasant priest is immune to the irony of
this. His second virtue is to persecute magic, and the third is to free men from slavery.
Scholars disagree on which of these is most hateful to Westies.

—From *Bloody Insanity*, by Sir Millifred Doorge

24

Father Kogan the White

Kogan tore a hunk of bread off and chewed experimentally as he found a comfortable spot against a snowy wall. If he imagined it were a ripe old cheese, the mold didn't taste half bad.

Above him the table ground against the floor, accompanied by urgent whispers between the yeoman and some family member who'd come in from outside or been hiding in the house.

It was then he realized he could see. Something glowed before him, like mist in moonlight.

A ghost. In a fit of anger he realized the yeoman had tricked him into hopping into a grave still occupied by its previous owner. "Just you stay in your corner, ghost, and I'll stay in mine. I don't aim to be here long. Then you can have it back."

The glow didn't move, and it didn't speak, so if it *was* a ghost, it was a right feeble one. Kogan chewed another hunk of bread off with his teeth.

As his eyes adjusted further, he realized the glow didn't hang in the air before him, rather that it was the *floor* of the place that glowed.

"I'll be hung and dyed," he muttered. "It's that glow fungus." He'd heard of such a thing. Gods leave him if they didn't say it soaked up sun in daylight and shone like the blazes all night. In fact, the only part that glowed was the patch below the hatch where the indirect daylight had fallen while the hatch was open.

He considered a moment longer how this might affect his plans to limit his travel to the hours of dark after sunset: he was covered with the stuff. At nighttime he'd shine like a man afire.

The knights entered the house with a rumble of shouts and hard-heeled boots on the planks above. The voice of the yeoman and his family punctuated the din with pleas of innocence and offers of humble hospitality, and pledges to hunt for the stinking priest day and night and report him the moment they saw him. He heard the sound of a second trap door opening. Muffled shouts followed.

Kogan swallowed the last of the bread, settled back comfortably in his smothercoat amidst the drifts of fungus and rotten stair treads, and slept.

He woke to a fresh breeze and voices newly loud and clear in his close earthen hole. He'd been aware of muffled thumping and voices from above during his sleep. But these voices were no more muffled than the sound of his own breath.

"Father? You alive?" a voice called from above. It was the yeoman's voice.

"Course he's alive, Miles," said a woman's voice. "Just sleeping."

"Should we let him sleep?" Miles asked.

A child laughed. "Wake him, Pa! I never seen a priest before. Are they all white and powdered like dumplin's?"

"Be a hairy bunch of dumplin if they was."

They laughed.

Kogan smiled and opened his eyes. Above him a rectangle of candlelight had appeared in the ceiling of his grave. Three honest, curious faces rimmed the gap: the yeoman Miles, and what Kogan guessed was his goodwife and boy-child.

"Reckon you sent those lords a-packing?" Kogan flashed his crack-toothed grin.

The boy squealed with delight.

Miles said, "Didn't you hear them stumping around and hollering to beat the wolves? "

"Might be I did, though I don't much recall it."

Miles gave a sly smile. "Don't nothing much bother you, do it, Father?" He slid a notched log down the hole, and Kogan climbed out. Outside, night had fallen. No light came through the window skins, but fire burned in the stone hearth, and bread and butter in quantity awaited on the table.

The yeoman's wife stood between him and the table, one hand extended imperiously toward the door. "Out! You look like you slept in an ash pit. Hang up them rugs in the barn and wash the rest o' you in the trough."

Kogan chuckled. "You got a good woman, Miles."

"Name's Marta," she said, hand still extended toward the door. "You know anything about a Phyros-rider come through the north?"

Kogan's attention perked. "Sir Willard come through a day past. What'd you hear of it?"

"These knights asked if we seen one."

Kogan grinned. "Old Will gave 'em the slip after all. We done it."

Miles and Marta exchanged uncertain looks. "And they named another," Miles said. "An Old One. Only no one says his name in this house."

Kogan shook his head. "Them knights was trying to scare you."

"Them knights was scared as we was, Father. Hardly wanted to say his name themselfs." Miles studied his hands until his wife made a tiny sound of impatience. "We was glad to help you, Father. But now as you're clear of your trouble, you best be moving on. This valley's a dead-end trap, so you best get out the way you came."

"Or else maybe climb up to that fire-cone pass," said Marta. "Don't nobody go there, but there's a road."

Kogan opened his snowy arms to display the carpets of his smothercoat, white as linen in sun. "Expect me to hide out when I'm painted like a snowman?" He batted the carpets on his chest, and a few flakes fell to the floor, but most clung like greasepaint.

Miles stepped closer with the candle, squinting at the stuff and frowning. "That all shining too?"

"Glow fungus," Kogan said.

Miles and his wife exchanged guilty glances. "Gods leave us, Marta. We can't let him go out like that. He'd be a lit up like a signal fire saying, 'Here I is, come and get me!' We has to keep him till we can wash that out."

"Glow fungus don't come out overnight, fool," Marta muttered. "Gonna have to scrub him up with boiling water more days than we got before that Phyros-rider come sniffing round."

"I don't mind no glow fungus," Kogan said, puffing his chest. "I'll be on my way and bring no more danger to this house."

Marta snorted. "You ain't going nowhere. No priest leaves my house looking like a sheet ghost. Get to the barn and scrub yourself with straw and water till it don't come off no more. Then come back for some bread, and we'll talk about you earning room and board while you're here. First thing you can do for us is to dig the fungus out of that cellar. I reckon you'll be hiding down in that hole again before too long, and we can't have you coming out looking like a puff cake again. Soon as we get you cleaned up, you'll leave us. I aim to be rid of you in less than a seven-night."

The existence of the blood-arch is traditionally attributed to moon sprites, woodwives, gods, and witchcraft, but it is the task of a tooler to quash such superstition. As our Master Toolers show us, the colors of the blood-arch have nothing to do with such hokum, and are easily created with light through a simple prism of glass…

— From First Tooler's Prentice Manual, Vol. I, Master Erkan of Wend

25

Locks & Magic

Harric woke, and peered groggily around him. Spook lay panting beside him, green eyes glazed and twitching in the firelight. His pink tongue licked foam from his whiskers.

"Shut up that cat, boy!" Willard growled from his blankets.

Brolli beckoned Harric to the tiny fire, where he boiled water in a kettle. "I have tea."

Harric shook his aching head in apology. He felt as though he hadn't slept all night.

"Ragleaf," Brolli whispered. He indicated the kettle. "Drink. Before I rouse Willard."

Harric almost groaned with gratitude. "Gods leave you." He rolled to his knees and gingerly clambered to his feet.

"I have selfish reasons," Brolli said, handing Harric a mug. "I want your help tonight."

Harric drank, expecting explanation to follow, but Brolli said nothing more. As soon as he'd drained the cup, he felt his body relaxing and warming, the bands of pain that held him fast loosened and fell away. Brolli filled the mug again for Willard, and delivered it as he roused the others. When all gathered at the fire, he told them what he'd found at the pass.

"The gate is shut and the guardhouse occupied," he reported. "It's not a huge building, but its wall spans the pass. I think the gate is run by a machine inside the walls."

Willard twisted the end of one mustachio between thumb and forefinger. He looked groggy and weak, but his fever seemed to have broken. "You're sure the pass is the only way? There's no other way across these ridges?"

Brolli shook his head. "Caris is right. The toolers took the easiest way when they blast their road through the pass. But I have a plan to cross without notice."

Willard raised one grizzled eyebrow. "Something in your bag of tricks?"

Brolli nodded. "Unless you have another idea."

"Go on."

"In some ways it is better the pass is watched," said Brolli. "Then they tell our hunters the pass is secure. No one has come through. One thing only I need for this, and that is assistant; I wish Harric goes with me."

Willard frowned. "Remember what we said about magic and this boy's values."

"He does not touch a bit of magic. That I promise."

"He can't see a lick in the dark, Brolli."

"He does not need to. We set out when the Mad Moon is high, so he sees enough to follow to the gatehouse. Once we get to the wall, all will be lit by the Mad Moon."

"All right. When do we follow?"

"I come back for you when all is ready. In one hour, saddle the horses and pack. Snuff the fire. I come back for you when all is ready."

Harric followed Brolli out of camp as Caris scrambled to saddle the horses and Willard stared into the fire, the dull eye of his ragleaf pulsing red.

The trail traversed the ridge, rising steadily on a ledge blasted across its rugged face. Much of the pathway was lit by the Mad Moon, but in dark patches Harric followed Brolli by holding to a lead line they'd borrowed from Idgit's bridle. Brolli steered the line around the worst obstacles, and warned him with a whispered "rock" or "root" when needed. As the Mad Moon climbed the sky, more and more of its crimson light illumined the contours of the rock. In one particularly long stretch of illumined path, Brolli slowed to walk near him, and flashed his toothy grin. "This is a hard few days for you," he said ambiguously. "I am glad you come with me."

Harric gave a non-committal nod.

When he offered nothing else, Brolli spoke again. "This Caris, she sleeps so far from you. Why is it so? She wears the love ring, yes? You give it to her, yes?"

"Yes."

"Then I must ask why you sleep so far apart. Is it custom with your people? Perhaps you wait until Willard sleeps and I am away for secret tryst?"

Harric tried to read the alien features of the Kwendi's face, but found it difficult. He judged from his tone, however, it was a serious question, not mocking. "Well, the first reason is simple," Harric said. "She's angry with me."

"Ah!" The Kwendi laughed. "She cannot stay angry long."

"I wouldn't be so sure of that. I've seen her when she sets her mind on something. She's not like ordinary people that way."

"She is different. I see that."

"The second reason is that even if she wanted me, it's only because she's got that ring on. One day they'll come off, right? She might think I've been taking advantage of her then, and kill me."

The Kwendi's brow furrowed in earnest perplexity. "Because of the rings? Why?"

"Because she's being *forced* by that ring," Harric said, more vigorously than he intended, "or altered, or whatever you want to call it. It'd be like taking advantage of her when she was drunk for the first time. It isn't right."

The Kwendi stopped and faced Harric in a patch of red moonlight. A mountain breeze sighed across the rock face around them; far below, tumbling water rushed through the darkness. "I thought I watch carefully your mating customs in your queen's court, but I never notice this 'right' you speak of. You have to win a 'right' before you mate? Or is it before you marry? Or is marriage itself this 'right'?" Brolli fetched a traveler's journal and stylus from his shirt, and jotted some notes.

Harric stared for several heartbeats. When the Kwendi put the book away, Harric laughed. "Are you serious?"

Brolli looked at him. "There is no marriage among my people, so I do not understand why you hesitate to mate."

"Marriage isn't about mating, Brolli. It's bigger than that. It's for life."

Brolli's brows pinched. "Marriage is *not* about mating?"

"Well, no. It's more." Harric smiled, bemused. It occurred to him that since he'd never had a father, and since the two women who raised him were unmarried or widowed before he was born, he didn't know the first thing about permanent male-female partnership. His entire understanding of marriage therefore consisted of nothing more than the vague longing of all bastards for something sacred and unattainable.

"More than mating," Brolli repeated. He plucked the journal again from his pocket, and scribbled a note. "Yet her looks at you are about mating. Even

I see that. Such complicated mating rituals!"

Harric laughed. "Hold on. Are you telling me you have no idea what marriage is, but you decided to make a magical *wedding ring* for our queen?"

The Kwendi's face crumpled in something resembling embarrassment. He put the journal away and started walking again. "The ring was meant as a gift," he explained. "She has no husband, yes? We thought, since your people mate for life, that she, all alone and without a mate…well, think she maybe was not so…how you say…*attracting*? With the ring we think she could capture a mate."

Harric laughed heartily. It hurt his ribs and head, but the ragleaf muted the pain. "I'm sorry. But I can't believe you survived that gift. A wedding ring for the Lone Queen of Arkendia? Ambassador, our queen is famous in ten kingdoms for shunning marriage and abusing courting princes. She built a career on it. She built modern Arkendia on it."

Brolli sighed. "Yes. She almost throw us out window. Bad beginning to our talks."

"My own troubles with that ring seem suddenly small. How did you calm the Queen?"

"I give her instead another ring of my own, just as strong."

"So, if your people don't marry, Brolli, may I ask what you do?"

The Kwendi flashed his feral grin across his shoulder. "We mate."

Harric waited for more. None came. He asked, "And then what?"

Brolli glanced back as if for clarification in Harric's face. "We mate again? Perhaps I do not see your question."

"I mean, do you stay with your mate then, for the baby?"

"Ah! No. She raise the baby with her family."

"You just leave her?"

Brolli apparently sensed something in his voice, for he paused and turned to examine Harric closely. "This is the way of *all* my people. When my sisters and cousin have babies, I help raise them with my family."

Harric felt a concealing veil lift from his mind to reveal an aspect of life he'd never sensed possible. "You're a nation of bastards! You have no idea who your fathers are."

"Why should that matter? The woman determines the family. It is easy to know who is the mother. Hard to know for sure the father."

"That's the best thing I've heard all year. You know they used to enslave us bastards in Arkendia? Still do in the West Isle."

"I have heard it. Now hush." Brolli laid a finger across his lips. "We draw near."

As they neared the head of the valley, its sides grew steeper and rockier and closer together, until it became a high mountain canyon with steep ridges on either side. The road wound in and out of the outcrops and promontories, sometimes bridging gulfs with crude timber trestles. In the red light of the Mad Moon, the crags of the opposite side of the valley seemed an impassable wilderness of rockfalls and timber. As their road neared the head of the valley, the rush of the river rose louder from the narrow channel below. Harric heard the roar of a sizable waterfall beyond the nearest bend. Its mist rose in the distance, a bloody veil wafting in the moonlight.

When they reached the last outcrop of rock in the bend, Brolli stopped. He jerked his head in the direction of the falls. "From here you see the pass at the end of the valley. Make a long look at the gatehouse."

Harric peered around the outcrop. A half-mile hence, the valley ended in a V-shaped pass between mountains. A stone fort squatted in the notch of the pass. From the base of its wall, a white waterfall emerged from a frowning water gate, like the tongue from the mouth of a hanged man. Through the gap of the pass beyond, Harric saw open sky, suggesting a wide valley.

The road ended in a wide roundabout before the walls of the fort, on the brink of its boulder-filled moat. The only way across the moat was over a now-closed drawbridge flanked by cone-topped archer towers.

"Ten to one that waterfall is called Horsetail or Maidenhair Falls," Harric whispered. "Half the falls in the north have that name. Timbermen have no imagination."

"How many guards do you guess in that rock?"

Harric frowned. "A fortification that strong wouldn't require many. But half the Queen's income comes from resin sales, so she's pretty careful with the fire-cone ranges." Harric studied the walls and drawbridge. He could see another roofline behind the wall that might belong to a living quarters or a stable. "I'd expect about ten men there. Looks like they keep black pigeons in that cote above the tower. See the roosts? If there's trouble, they'll release a pigeon and lock themselves in."

"Ten, then?"

Harric nodded.

"What is this *pigeon* you say? A bird you eat, yes?"

"Not blackhearts. Blackhearts deliver messages over long distances."

"Messages? You train them to speak?" Brolli dug out his journal.

"No, no. They're dumb as plugs. But they carry tiny written messages, and they always return to their nest." Brolli's wide golden eyes fixed quizzically on Harric. "You raise the birds in one nest," Harric explained. "Then you take them to some other nest far away. When you want to send a message back to their original home, you tie a note on their leg and release them. They fly home, and someone who takes care of the other nest retrieves the message."

Brolli smiled. "Your people so brilliant. No magic, and look what they make." He scribbled in his diary, and Harric glimpsed the characters, which were unlike any he'd seen. "You think these guards fly messages straight to your queen?"

The implications dawned on Harric. "Yes! Or to one of her ministers. If we sent a distress message to her from this gatehouse, she'd send pigeons to a northern earl, who'd dispatch a company to investigate. We have to do it!"

Brolli's thick canines flashed in the bloody light. "*You* have to do it. I take care of guards. You send pigeons."

"What do you plan to do to the guards?"

Brolli's gold eyes sparkled with mischief. "I do not hurt them. They must not know we passed. So I make them sleep deep. I already make the watchman sleep."

"You mean you're going to use magic. I know Sir Willard doesn't want you to tell me, but it's pretty clear."

Brolli continued to smile, but offered no more information. The Kwendi tore part of a blank page from his book, and handed it to Harric with his stylus. "What do you write for the bird note?"

"It has to be short, so the note can be small and light." He tore the page down to a tiny square. "I think we need the Blue Order."

"The order of knights Willard belonged to," Brolli said, as if proud of his knowledge of Arkendian history. "Immortals, yes? That is good. I will like to see them."

Harric knelt and placed the paper against the back of Brolli's book. He scratched nine words with the stylus. *Willard, Brolli in danger. Sir Bannus. Send Blue Order.*

He tore another square and paused, thinking and sucking at his split lip. Ideally he'd send two pigeons, in case one became falcon lunch, but sending too many might tip off the pigeon's caretaker that someone had been fiddling with his birds. On impulse, he prepared a second identical note; if the guards sent regular dispatches of "all's well," he could slip a second note in one of their empty message tubes so that backup message might be sent out with their next dispatch.

"Here is my plan," said Brolli, when Harric finished and returned him his journal. "We cross to a place where I have a tall log beside the track. You and I carry the log to the wall, and you steady it as I scale the wall and slip into the gatehouse from the other side. When I am up, you retreat and wait for me. Stay clear of the gatehouse then, until you see me open the door beside the big gate. You see it there? The little door? Good. It is important you stay clear until you see me. At least a stone's throw away—wait, on second thinking, no. I've seen you throw. Make that ten stone-throws." Brolli flashed his feral grin.

"When I'm healthy I throw much farther."

"After I let you in the gatehouse, you prepare that message, and I fetch Willard."

"What if they discover me while you're gone?"

"They won't." Brolli grinned. "They will sleep like drugged." Harric opened his mouth to ask how, but Brolli cut him off with a wave. "I must not discuss."

"By order of Sir Hypocrite?"

"Hypo-crite? What is that word?"

"It means someone who speaks one thing but does another."

Brolli chuckled. "Hypocrite. You are right. My people call that *sty-du*, twisted mouth. But truly, Sir Willard has lived long and seen much. He is more comfortable with magic than any other Arkendian I have met. Or was, until I met you." The Kwendi's head tilted sideways, his wide eyes shining in the moonlight. "Why are you so unafraid of the moons?"

Harric shrugged. "My mother traveled as a diplomat overseas. She saw a lot, too, and taught me the moons are natural. Arkendians are the only people who fear them."

Brolli chuckled. "Perhaps you and Sir Hypo-crite are more alike than he admits."

Carrying the log strained Harric's aching body, even with Brolli at the heavier end. But stalking to the edge of the curtain wall was easy because of the roar of the falls. Nothing stirred in the gatehouse. No smoke from the chimney. No candle behind shutters.

"For carrying the log, you drank the ragleaf tea," said Brolli.

"I'm going to need a lot more when we carry it back."

They planted the log at the juncture of the wall and the rock of the mountain, and lodged it upright for Brolli to climb. Harric had seen him climb twice before, but it was just as fascinating a third time. It almost looked like he walked up the trunk, his feet pressing against the front of the pole while his long arms reached around and pulled it toward him, keeping pressure on his feet. Hand over hand, step by step, he went up until he reached the top. Once there, he hoisted himself up to stand on the end, from which he transitioned to a much slower rate of climb up the juncture of the cliff and the wall. His strong fingers seemed to find niches and crannies on the cliff face, while his flat feet braced in cracks or against the wall.

Once he reached the top, he swung onto the crenellations and motioned for Harric to retreat. He pantomimed throwing a stone, reminding Harric of the appropriate distance, then disappeared behind the parapet.

Curiosity tempted Harric to stay near to see what would happen, but he decided to retreat and wait it out. He'd barely caught his breath before the small door beside the main gate opened, and the distinctive figure of the Kwendi emerged, trotting in that peculiar knuckle-lope toward Harric.

"The log," Brolli said when he reached him. They returned to the log and lugged it back to where they'd found it, Harric's ribs grumbling.

"Now I get Willard, and you send bird." Brolli waved and loped back down the road until he disappeared behind the bend. As Harric watched the Kwendi recede in the distance, he felt a powerful sense of gratitude that Brolli had entrusted him with this service. After Caris's scathing rebuke that day, it felt a bit like redemption.

Hiking back up the narrow track to the gatehouse, he studied the wall and the turnabout more closely. The builders had left only enough room for a wagon between the foot of the wall and the edge of the cliff above the falls; for fifty paces on either side of the gate, any attackers would be exposed to defenders above and the long fall below. A dry moat had been carved from the rock at the foot of the wall and filled with jagged boulders, and the postern could be approached only by a narrow ledge above the falls, so there could be no space for a ram.

The familiar thrill of entering a forbidden place shivered Harric's senses as he clambered across the dry moat and sidled across the ledge to the open door. A candle would have been nice, he reflected as he peered into the darkness within, but the Kwendi wouldn't have thought of it. He groped along a straight, plastered wall, and found a corner and a stairway, where he barked his shins on the bottom stairs.

Beyond the opening to the stairwell, the wall continued toward a doorway outlined by a very low light as from the embers of a fire. Crossing to stand in the doorway, he heard snoring within what he discovered to be a small kitchen. A big, worn table stood in its midst, with a kettle and pot beside the fire, and bunches of herb hanging from the ceiling. Three cots lay with their feet to the fire, each with a sleeping man as old as Willard. Another ten slept in the room adjacent.

What the Black Moon did Brolli do to them? Nothing, apparently. They looked unscathed.

He rummaged around the hearth and found a tallow candle, which he lit in the fire. Then he left the kitchen and made a quick ascent of the stairs, which took him to a door at the level of the parapet. Above that he found the pigeon cote, its door unlocked. He slipped inside to the familiar scent of pigeons, and the low cooing of one that seemed wide awake and hungry, as if newly arrived. As he'd expected, they were blackhearts. Big, sleek long-distance flyers.

The circular room was divided in three-by-two walls of wattle reaching from the floor to the peaked ceiling high above. It was the same basic design they used in Gallows Ferry, though on a larger scale, to separate the birds into three groups: outgoing birds that could be released to deliver a message, incoming birds that needed to be transported back to their original nests to be useful again, and newly arrived birds whose messages hadn't yet been read. The door from the stairwell opened into the side for newly arrived birds. Only one bird occupied the room, and when it saw Harric, it flapped to the seed jars and pecked at the lids. Harric took a handful from one and held it for the bird while he removed its message with the other hand.

The note read: *Next supply with harvest team at full moons.*

Harric put it in the pocket with his witch-stone and slipped his own note into the empty tube. As the new arrival perched on his thumb and devoured seed in his palm, Harric opened the wattle door to the outgoing birds, and put the new arrival inside, closing the wattle behind him. He poured the seed on a ledge for the hungry pigeon, who abandoned his hand for the seed. This newcomer would take the place of the one he would release, so the caretaker would count the same number as before, and assume the incoming pigeon with the message about harvest had fallen to a falcon en route.

Harric gathered up a sleeping pigeon in a low nest before it could wake and fly to a higher perch. With soft noises and strokes, he calmed it until he could coax one leg out and attach his message. He watered and fed it as much as it would eat, remembering that a hungry bird was more likely to be taken by a predator when it stopped to forage. When it showed impatience with the food, he carried it out through the tower door onto the parapet above the falls, and released it.

The bird gave two powerful flaps with the signature snap of a blackheart, made one wide arc around the towers, and slanted away south along the ridges.

Harric closed the door to the parapet and returned to the cote. So far so good. The place was meticulously maintained, however, so he would have to take care not to upset anything, or the caretaker would notice something amiss. The straw in the cote was fresh and neat. The seed jars were covered and ordered on the shelves. Three pre-written messages hung on the first three hooks in a line of six.

Of the three pre-written messages, Harric selected the third, assuming the meticulous caretaker had been drawing the messages from the right end of the hooks. He took the message out and read it: *Horsetail Twr. Qtr. Moons. All Quiet.* By that he deduced the next pigeon was scheduled to go out at the next quarter moon, a day hence. Perfect luck. If they'd come a day later the second message wouldn't go out for a week.

He slipped his own message in the tube and restored it to its hook. The pilfered note he deposited in his pocket with the witch-stone, where he let his hand linger on the globe's glassy surface.

He drew the stone out and held it beside the candle to illumine its depths. Smoky wisps seemed to move in it, but the candlelight banished them like a gust of wind. A nervous thrill rose in his belly as he recalled the words in his dream that made the witches turn invisible. If the dream were true, he could simply speak them and vanish like the wisps in the stone. But then how would he become visible again? The witch only became visible when Brolli grabbed him. If worse came to worst, he could always ask Brolli to jump him the way he'd jumped the Iberg...

Or maybe if he set down the stone, the spell would cease.

Nebecci, Bellana, Tryst.

He itched to say it, and learn.

Harric moved the candle away, and the wisps swirled in from the sides. In the glassy surface he glimpsed the reflection of a face peering over his shoulder, and gasped in surprise. Whirling, he found no one, but he'd been certain of a presence—as if the air had moved beside him, or he'd heard a soft breath near his ear.

Urgent whispers sounded in the air around him, so faint he couldn't be sure of them at all. *Fly! Fly!* Then the distinct sound of horns and hooves, as through a tunnel, and it seemed he saw the hooves among the wisps in the stone, charging through a campfire.

"Harric!" Willard called from outside.

Harric's lungs nearly leapt from his mouth. He stuffed the stone in the cargo slip of his shirt, and cracked the shutter overlooking the road below. The old knight slumped with his head on one arm across the front of his saddle. Getting into the saddle had taken another toll on him.

"Horns," Brolli called up. He dismounted Idgit, and loped over to the postern. "We must open the gate and hurry through."

"I'm coming," Harric called. His heart raced, spurred by the shock that his vision of Bannus was real, and the conviction that the voices that plagued him came not from madness, but the stone, and that they'd tried to warn him of danger.

All the more reason to trust it.

Harric ran down the stairs and into the winch room above the portcullis, where enormous chains and pulleys ran out of holes in the floor and onto massive windlasses. There he encountered a worried-looking Brolli, and Caris, who hunched over one of the windlasses with a candle to examine the gears.

"We have a problem," Brolli said.

"Is it broken?"

"It is locked. Caris, show him the key."

Caris stood and displayed an iron key as long as a dagger. Harric squinted at it and picked it up from her hand. "It's a half-key," he said, feeling its hemi-cylindrical shaft against his palm. "Where did you find it?"

"One of the men downstairs wear it round his neck. It is half the key?"

"Yes. Someone else has the other half. So no one man can open it without the other."

Brolli frowned. "These men here?"

"Not likely. The other half is probably with the men who come to harvest in the fall. That way neither man could poach the Queen's resin from the grove without the cooperation of the other."

Harric knelt with his candle beside the iron keyhole box bolted to the windlass. He slipped the key in, and felt its action in the lock. Without the other half of the key, its action was sloppy. "It probably lifts half the pins, but not the other half."

Judging by the sounds and action of the key, it was a relatively simple lock. Straight pins to move a bolt. If the bolt was rusty, it could be hard to move with only half the key, but the mechanism looked fairly clean. He removed the key and counted tabs. Three. Probably another three tabs on the other half.

"How do you know so much about locks?" said Caris, glaring.

Harric ignored the bait.

"I say we just break the lock off," she said to Brolli. "It wouldn't be hard."

"Not hard," said Brolli. "But then it is clear someone pass through."

Harric stood. "There's no way to open this without the other half of that key," he said, letting his worry show. "Maybe one of the men here does have the other half. We'd better look. Then, if there's no key, we break it."

He paused, as if uncertain what to do. He laid his hand on Brolli's arm, where Caris couldn't see it. Brolli glanced up, but Harric merely squeezed gently without meeting his eyes. Brolli took the hint and said no more. Impatient, Caris snatched up her candle and stalked from the room down the stairs.

"I hoped she'd do that." Harric winked at Brolli, and unslung his pack. Crouching beside the lock box, he felt around in the pack for the tools he'd need.

Brolli smiled. "There is no other half."

"Not likely. But that should keep her busy."

Harric found his cloth of tools and laid it open on his pack, while Brolli took the candle and held it up for him. He selected two of the larger hooks, which he held in his mouth, and then his favorite bronze-tipped long pick. With the half-key in the lock, he slid the pick along its length; after a few exploratory probings to confirm his suspicions of the location and number of pins, it was a simple matter of lifting two pins with hooks, and the third with his pick.

He turned the half-key gently, but the bolt wouldn't budge. He double-checked all the pins and tried again. Still stuck. He put as much force on it as he dared, then tried brief pulses of pressure. The bolt moved on the third pulse.

Harric turned to Brolli without moving his hands. "Would you like to do the honors?"

Brolli grinned, the teeth somehow more feral when so close in yellow light. "So we tell her I open it?"

"Precisely."

Brolli let out a small bark of a laugh and laid his huge, long-fingered hand over Harric's to turn the key. The bolt scraped in its channel, releasing the windlass.

Harric returned his tools to the cloth, and stashed them in his pack. He passed Caris in the stairway as he returned his candle to the kitchen.

"Nothing." She glared, then avoided his eyes. "I'm breaking it."

He let her pass, and returned his candle to the kitchen. Brolli could tell her.

Outside, Harric found Willard where he'd left him. The other horses stood with him, with Rag picketed some fifty paces hence. All of their hooves had been tied up with muffles to mute the sound, though for what reason, Harric wasn't sure. As long as the guardsmen slept, what did it matter? Perhaps Willard insisted on regular non-magic tactics in spite of their redundancy.

From farther down the valley came a high-pitched hunting horn.

Willard didn't move.

The winch groaned, chains grumbled as the thick-timbered drawbridge lowered and lay flat, revealing an iron-barred portcullis still blocking the way. Molly tossed her head impatiently, and Willard finally raised his. The ropes of the portcullis groaned, tightening against the winch as Brolli and Caris worked the windlass above. The gate rose a hand's breadth, then stopped, and as it did, something clanked against the stonework to one side.

"Wait!" Harric called up. "Let it back down!"

He ran to the portcullis, unslinging his pack as he went. Brolli and Caris lowered the portcullis, and Harric saw the source of the problem: as he'd suspected, a heavy chain had been threaded through the ironwork and padlocked to an iron ring in the foundation. "Moons, could they be more paranoid?"

He plunged his hand in the pack and grabbed his pick from the cloth.

"What is it?" Willard said, looming behind him.

"A lock. But I think I have the key."

"Key?"

"Found inside," Harric mumbled. With luck the old knight wouldn't remember any of this tomorrow.

Without a candle he had to do it blind, but his mother had hooded him many times in his training. Back then it was always in the comfort of a warm room, with no Old One bearing down, but she'd also taught him to slow his breathing and clear his mind for such things. He groped the surface with his hands, searched for the keyhole, and found in its place a waxen seal.

Moons! If he broke the seal, it would be obvious someone had used the lock. And there was no time for him to repair it, for it had been applied while hot. Nothing to do but break it. They had to get through. Probing, he found he could lift the edges with a fingernail, and when he applied a little more force, half the seal popped off in his hand. That was good luck. A few seconds later, and another chunk came off, opening a hole large enough for his pick.

He placed the wax chips between his lips to warm them, and probed the lock with the pick.

It was big and clumsy, and simple. Fortunately, it was also supple, heavily oiled, and had been spared the ferocious mist-rust on the outside of the lock by the protective wax. A quick tick of two tumblers, and a shake to help gravity move the other, and the lock pulled open.

"Go!" Harric called.

The winch groaned, and the portcullis began to rise again as Brolli and Caris labored in the gatehouse above.

Harric let the chain fall, and retreated with the lock into the kitchen as the gate rose behind him. The thump of muffled hooves on wood confirmed Willard riding through with the horses.

In the kitchen, Harric relit his candle and used it to warm the chips of wax from the seal. In a few moments they were soft enough to reattach over the keyhole. Close inspection would reveal the subterfuge, but from a distance they'd seem intact.

Caris ran down the stairs and out the postern. He soon heard the sound of Rag's hooves on the wood of the drawbridge.

"Harric! I need you!" Caris called.

He snuffed his candle and groped his way out with the lock, then trotted after her through the gate. Willard had stopped right inside the gate, but Caris ran Rag fifty paces past him into the canyon that rose up and over the pass behind the fortification. When Harric caught up to her, she pushed the reins in his hands.

"Move her up the road," she said between gasps for breath. "A bowshot from Molly." Without waiting for his response, she turned and pounded back to help Brolli raise the gates.

"Wait—" Harric began, but he bit off the rest as Rag began to fret the instant Caris turned. Lock still in hand, he jogged Rag up the road, tethered her to a scrubby bush, and sprinted back to the gatehouse.

A red eye of ragleaf watched him from the darkness of the gateway. "Boy, didn't you hear that horn?"

"Lock!" was all Harric gasped.

When he arrived at the open gateway, he glanced down the mountainside, half expecting to see their pursuers rounding the bend, but the road remained empty. The ropes to the portcullis groaned, and the gate descended.

"Slowly!" he shouted upward.

Too late, the massive portcullis clanged on the stone like a hammer on a bell, echoing in the valley. He stepped forward and found the chain by touch, looped it in the bars, as he thought he remembered it had been before, then fastened it with the padlock. A gentle touch of his thumb on the wax confirmed the seal remained in place.

As Brolli and Caris resumed winding the windlass in the gatehouse above, the chains jerked and the timber bridge began its ponderous ascent. Harric sprinted around the back of the gatehouse and in the back door, where he groped his way up the stairs to help. He found Brolli and Caris hard at work, one at each windlass, straining and sweating against the levers. He attempted to help, throwing his weight against the spokes where Caris toiled, but the act brought stabbing pain to his ribs, so he ran the window instead, and peered at the road—still empty—below.

"How much farther?" Caris gasped.

"It's halfway up," Harric replied. "Keep going!"

When it was nearly shut, it got much easier, and the two spun the windlasses more rapidly, but when it thudded in place and they'd returned the locking blocks to the gears, both Caris and Brolli were panting and soaking with sweat.

The words "well done" had hardly escaped Brolli's mouth before a horn blasted from the nearest bend in the mule track. Harric looked out the window to see riders rounding the bend.

"Quickly!" Brolli motioned to the door. "Out!"

Caris and Harric flew down the stairs and out the back door, but Brolli did not follow them out. Harric paused, letting Caris lumber up the hill for her horse, and peered back through the door in time to see the Kwendi slip into the kitchen.

"Brolli!" he called.

The Kwendi's head reappeared in the dim light from the kitchen. "Must not still sleeping," he said, then vanished.

Willard rode Molly and the two other horses up the road into the canyon, muffled hoofbeats thrumming from the walls.

Harric left through the back door and followed, only to meet the pungent stink of Phyros dung on the air. He cursed. A dark pile lay in the midst of the road like a "Willard Went This Way" sign.

He gritted his teeth and scooped the steaming clods in both hands, and tossed them into the hungry river running beside the road.

Brolli loped up with a chuckle. "They say Phyros shit give special power."

"Yeah. Makes your crap immortal."

Hoofbeats clattered beyond the wall. A dozen riders, perhaps. A harsh, deep-throated horn blasted and reverberated from the rocks.

"Bannus," said Harric. "That's the sound of Krato's Moon."

He ran with Brolli to a vantage on the road above the fortress. Together they climbed a boulder to peer back. Their vantage was about even in elevation with the tops of the gatehouse wall, which was high enough to see some of the turnabout, but not high enough to see Bannus on Gygon before the gate. The sound of the falls was a faint grumble at this distance, but moon-pinked mist still rose beyond the parapets.

Movement on the walls. The parapet door opened and a handful of men appeared, hiding behind crenellations and peeking out at the commotion below. At least one, Harric guessed, was on his way to the pigeon cote to pen an urgent message.

Bannus's gravel voice sounded beyond the wall. "Open these gates! Open in the name of Prince Jamus, Royal Sun of Arkendia, House Pellion, last of the True Kings in this broken land."

Pellion, Harric thought. *So Pellion is Bannus's master again.* His mother's mnemonics sprung to mind.

> *House Pellion Lingers*
> *Last Sun to Shine*
> *Turned Coats in the Cleansing*
> *Preserving Their Line.*
> *Immortal Lord Jormus*
> *Grandsire of That Stock,*
> *Sir Bannus's Master*
> *In Pellion Rock.*
> *Jormon His Son*
> *Fathered Three Princely Lords*
> *Joff, Jothry, and Jamus,*
> *One daughter called Jordes.*

It was the third grandson, then—Jamus—holding Bannus's leash. Jamus would be the prince that came to Gallows Ferry the night he fled, and the one Mother Ganner told him of.

"Greeting, Great One," a guard called down to Bannus. "What service can we render ye?"

"You can open your bloody gates, you dog. We seek a peasant priest, and a Phyros-rider, to face the justice of their peers."

"I wish you fortune in it, great sir. But we haven't seen another man pass here since spring. And I wish I could open the gate, but it's sealed and locked and we ain't trusted with the key. That comes with the harvesters next time the Bright Mother's full, so anybody'd have to build a winch to get a horse across, unless you come back then. That's how chary the Queen is of her resin, sir: she don't want none of us selling access to the crop."

Harric appreciated the guardsman's savvy. A quaver in his voice showed he was sincerely pissing himself with fear, but he also kept his head enough to maintain a difficult balance of deference and innocence so as to appear cooperative, which might mean he'd survive the ordeal.

"Open this postern, then," Bannus croaked.

"I wants to, sirs. On my life I do. But my queen's a harsh mistress. That iron door is locked as fast as the gate, I tell you. Living here's like living in a prison: all locked and nowhere to go."

"You dog of a man. I will tear your guts from your belly and feed Gygon your liver."

"I hope not, great sir. But if you're hungry, might be we could send some vittles across the wall. Not what you'd call fine fare, a'course, but you say the word and I will, only I can't open no doors."

Silence then, but for the roar of the falls beyond. Then the men on the wall ducked, and the familiar pop of spitfires sounded. A pair of fiery tails streaked above and arced into the rocks across the canyon, where resin wads made torches of bushes.

Harsh laughter from beyond as more spitfires popped and fire sprayed across the roof tiles of the cote and in several pigeon loops. The slate was impervious, but the timbers within caught fire, and soon the flames blazed in the loops like the fires of a furnace.

A man cried out inside. A blackheart flew from a lower loop. Spitfires sent streaks of fire across the bird's zigzagging path. More of the fiery comets sprayed along the parapets, sending the two men ducking and crawling.

Bannus's laughter rang above the noise. "There is no priest here, only dogs. But I shall return with men enough to scale your puny walls. And then we shall see about keys. Talbus! Make camp here on the road. Make certain no one leaves."

A knight in orange armor responded by saluting, fist to chest, then shouted orders to make camp at the foot of a massive pillar of rock at the far end of the turnabout.

On the cliff above the turnabout, Harric saw movement.

Brolli pointed to the spot before Harric could indicate it. "You see it, yes? It is a guardsman. He creeps along a ledge above Bannus's position."

Harric shielded his eyes from the growing glare of the fires and attempted to scrutinize the dark face of the cliff. After a moment, he picked out a small figure creeping across the sheer face above Bannus's position. A guard from the fort. The ledge he traversed originated somewhere behind the wall and slanted up across the cliff high above the roundabout. The man crouched a dozen fathoms above his enemies—if he dropped a pebble it might *plink* off Bannus's helmet—but the ledge on which he stood spanned no wider than a stout man's shoulders, so he was completely exposed if anyone chanced to look up.

As Harric watched, the guard halted midway across the cliff and stood frozen against the cliff. Harric soon realized why: though the darkness had kept him invisible to that point, the tower conflagration now illumined his position with increasing brightness. His shadow had begun to darken and dance across the cliff before him; he froze lest his movement betray him and his enemies feather him with arrows.

The fires also illumined the man's destination above the far end of the roundabout. There the ledge disappeared into a vertical crack in the cliff that had formed when a massive tower of rock split away from the rest to lean drunkenly over the roundabout. The tower was as big as the fort itself, but leaned so severely it seemed a finger's nudge could topple it.

"Is that another trail around the mountain?" Brolli whispered. "Another path we have missed? Maybe he thinks to escape on it."

Harric shook his head. "I think they cut that path to get behind that pillar of rock. See how the ledge disappears into the crack behind it? I'll bet they've packed that gap with blasting resin as a failsafe against attack. If that guard can reach it, Bannus is in for quite a surprise."

The Kwendi's eyes widened. "That is good!"

"It will be, if he can get there without being noticed. I bet he wishes he and his comrades had thought to build a cover wall along the ledge."

Brolli grunted. "They start one, I think." He pointed to the first ten paces or so of the ledge where it emerged above the fort wall. In the growing light, even Harric could see a stub wall of stacked rocks providing cover to that portion of the path. Brolli made a critical *tsk*. "They not finish it. But look! He tries."

The man had begun to slide along the cliff with one hand against the cliff. As the flames of the tower grew taller, his shadow rippled across the cliff face, and Brolli made a little sigh of dismay. "He should lie and wait for the fire to die."

As if on cue, a cry rang out among Bannus's men.

The guardsman sprinted for the cover of the crack.

"Shoot him!" Bannus roared.

Crossbows thrummed. Bolts cracked against the stone around the running guardsman. One caught him in the leg, and he fell to his hands and knees. Before he could rise, another caught him in the ribs and buried itself to the feathers. He fell from the ledge, out of view.

Murmurs of dismay from the men on the parapets.

"Reload!" a knight cried. "Watch that ledge! Spitfires, get some light up there!"

A spitfire popped, then another, sending brilliant resin streaks across the night to splash white fire on the ledge.

"They never reach it now," Brolli said. "That is shame."

Harric and Brolli crept back along the cliff road, hugging the shadows when possible. When out of view of the burning tower, they jogged until they found Willard and Caris with the horses.

"What news?" Willard asked.

Brolli related the incident. When he finished, Willard seemed already unconscious, slumped forward against the front cantle of his saddle. "You know this Jamus?" Brolli asked. "He is the same that come to Gallows Ferry with Bannus?"

Willard opened one weary eye. "His grandsire joined me…in the Cleansing. Switched sides and saved his hide. Too shrewd by half. Jamus too. The Queen trusts him."

"It seems our ruse at the gate succeeds, old man," said Brolli. "Bannus turns about."

Willard closed his eyes and sighed. "Gods leave that guardsman for his boldness. He's likely trembling now, with no recollection of it at all."

The Kwendi's eyes glimmered in the moonlight. "I thought of it too. Your curse."

Willard grunted. "This time it favors us well."

"And Harric does nothing with magic there," Brolli added. "In fact, he is good Arkendian. Sends pigeons from the cote and finds keys."

Caris looked back over her shoulder at Harric, and then the Kwendi, as if she were uncertain whether Brolli were deceived or deceiving.

"Sent birds?" Willard's eyes opened. "That's it, boy. That's what makes us strong."

Harric followed on foot, now last in line behind Willard. The old knight's hypocrisy galled him. On the one hand Willard reviled the use of magic, citing the Third Law. On the other he turned a blind eye if he benefited.

The case of the yoab was a clear emergency, as worthy of that blind eye as the situation at the pass had been. And yet Willard barely batted an eye at Brolli's reliance on spellcraft. If they'd put their minds to it, could they not have found an *Arkendian* way past the gatehouse? Harric himself could have devised a sleeping drug from some of the roots in the region. Wouldn't that have resulted in the desired outcome of making them stronger? And didn't this reliance on magic therefore make them softer and weaker?

He studied the old knight as if he could read an answer in his posture. Willard slumped forward, and Harric realized with a shock that he looked as bad as any wounded man he'd ever seen in saddle. He might topple at any moment.

Harric called for a halt, and limped up beside Molly. Brolli joined him, and found Willard unresponsive. They coaxed the old man to drink some water, then Caris bound him between the fore and aft cantles with a spare lead line.

"That won't hold him, but it might slow his fall." Her strong hands put finishing touches on the knots.

When they started moving again, Harric's anger at him passed, replaced by worry. The old knight was farther gone than he'd let on.

And perhaps it wasn't hypocrisy but necessity. In cases of great import—such as when the Queen's safety was at stake—perhaps survival trumped the Third Law.

Now there was a thought. He laid a hand on the witch-stone thumping his chest with each stride. If that were true, wouldn't the knight's reasoning justify the magic of invisibility in emergency service of the Queen? And didn't the Queen live in a *constant* state of emergency?

Harric smiled. Possibilities glittered in his imagination. To serve the Queen as a courtier spy with the power of invisibility in his pocket. It had been such a thrill to slip into that dovecote on a true quest for the Queen; how much more so to slip past alert guards with true invisibility…like the Jack of Souls, the wild card, who tips a strong hand to certain victory. Even Willard would have to admit that magic was a potent tool for the Queen.

Voices whispered at the edge of consciousness—the witch-stone, Harric imagined, calling to him. The sound no longer frightened him, as it had when he thought it came from madness. Back in the dovecote, the stone had tried to help him, to warn him of danger. How then, could that be evil?

Nebecci. Bellana. Tryst.

He'd take it out that night, as soon as he could get away from the others, and speak the words to the spell. After that, even Brolli wouldn't see him.

26

The Witch

By the time the Mad Moon set, the soft gray light of dawn was enough to reveal the path along the river's course. The walls of the canyon became less sheer, and the roads that had been cut into its walls gave way to a dirt path along the water's edge. The trail led them along a wooded lake into a bowl of rocky peaks. In the middle of the lake was a bare grave island, with crude monuments erected by timbermen or trappers. At the foot of the lake stood a tall, crooked stone like an old man's thumb. They stopped there for a brief rest, during which Brolli dubbed the aged stone "Willard's Finger."

"See what yours looks like after seven lives of battle," Willard growled.

"The lake I name Willard's Tub. May you live to make a soak in it."

Beyond the lake, the mule track climbed a saddle of granite between peaks to descend into the adjoining watershed. A young forest of spoke-limb and ash trees greeted them on the other side, crowding the path with exuberant growth and limiting visibility to sixty paces. Ancient blackened stumps stood like rotten teeth amidst the riot of green, testament of fire in years past.

Caris stopped at the foot of a log bridge where a painted sign stood pegged to a post.

Royal Fire-Cone Range
Open Flame Forbidden Beyond This Point!
NO SPITFIRES

NO ADMITTANCE WITHOUT
ROYAL WARRANT

Turn Back
ON PAIN OF DEATH
By Order of
Her Majesty's Fire-Cone Prelate
Sir Tilate Patche

"Let's see how well you read, boy," Willard mumbled. "What's it say?" When Harric finished reading it aloud, Willard nodded. "We're getting close, then."

Caris pointed to the green-mantled ridge toward which they climbed. "When we reach the crest of that ridge, we'll get our first view of the fire-cones."

Similar signs dotted the mule track all the way to the ridge, each freshly painted and free of obstructing foliage, as if maintained by industrious sprites.

Though green from a distance, the ridge was bare and rocky, which allowed a brief but expansive view east over another forested valley to a yet higher ridge beyond, on whose loftiest spur stood a kingly stand of fire-cones. The golden spires soared into the sky like a many-towered castle in a ballad, and from their midst rose the black spike of the thunder-rod, half again as tall.

"That's the lightning-stealer I told you about, Brolli," Caris said. "Abellia's tower is below it."

Though the trunks of the fire-cones obscured much of the tower, the thunder-rod appeared to rise from its top like the mast of the ship, its giddy height made fast with a multitude of stays slanting down to the forest. To Harric the stays looked like the ribbons of a gigantic maypole, but he knew they were cables of steel.

"And that shine," said Willard, pointing vaguely. "That shine in the top branches, that's the resin cones. Her Majesty's most valuable crop."

"Magnificent," said Brolli, peering through his daylids. "Fire-cone do not grow on our side of the Godswall. Your toolers are clever indeed, to steal the lightning and take the cones."

Willard gazed dully across the valley, face haggard.

"We'll get you there by sunset, sir," said Caris.

Willard swallowed. "I admit, that tower sounds mighty welcome."

"Drink," Brolli said, handing him a limp water skin.

"I should warn you about Mudruffle, Abellia's servant," Caris said as

Willard drank.

Willard paused to breathe, as if raising the skin sapped his strength. He looked at Caris. "Who?"

Caris hesitated. "Well, Abellia is a little eccentric, of course...but Mudruffle. He's actually *strange*." She watched Willard as if the news might overtax him. "He's made of clay, I think," she added. "Abellia made him."

Harric's interest piqued. Willard stared, uncomprehending.

"You mean a magical creature?" said the Kwendi. "Like a shadow or trysting servant?"

"No, no, no—I mean, yes, but... You see, I was afraid of him at first, but he's very sweet and kind, and he would never do magic on you if you didn't want it. He is very respectful. Abellia made him, I think, out of sticks and clay." Caris halted and watched their reactions.

Sir Willard raised an eyebrow. Harric expected the old knight to explode, but he merely nodded. "Seen such...in the Iberg capital. Harmless. Servants for cooking." Willard closed his eyes again and rocked forward in the saddle as if he might faint. Brolli retrieved the water skin before Willard dropped it.

One gray eye opened and found Brolli. "This witch...Abellia. Your...first Iberg?"

"I see some on gallows. We kill one in Gallows Ferry, yes?"

Willard grunted. "Never so many here. Come for your...magic."

Brolli nodded. "They are a magic-using people, yes?"

"But you...you bottle it. In witch-silver...yes?" Willard's eyelids closed. He breathed heavily through a slack mouth, as if the effort of speaking might cause him to faint.

Brolli gave Harric a look of concern.

"I can explain," Harric said. "The Ibergs never figured out how to use witch-silver. They've been seeking it for ages, with no luck. So they want to learn it from you."

Brolli smiled. "I hear so. And she may to ask me for it; is that your meaning, old man?" Willard nodded. "It is not to trouble," said Brolli. "I never to know how we make it. I only use it. So I cannot to tell her."

Upon reaching the far side of the valley, the mule track climbed the escarpment beneath the fire-cones, and the trees blazed orange in late evening light. Within a couple bowshots of the trees, the mountainside leveled to form a peaceful meadow with a chattering brook. The trail took them along the brook and above the meadow into a terraced garden.

Harric stopped his horse and stared. Many of the plants around him, which seemed merely healthy from a distance, turned out to be astoundingly huge and lush. Bean stocks grew like trees, grappling each other toward the sky; cabbages squatted like rockfalls of green and purple boulders. And the entire place had been manicured in a kind of weedless precision.

Caris saw the look on his face and laughed.

"Mudruffle has a bit of a green thumb," Caris said.

"Green thumb?" Willard snorted. "Whole arm must be green."

Harric glanced at the old knight. Willard seemed to find a second wind as they neared the promised destination—much like the horses, who responded to Rag's eager whinnies by increasing their paces.

The track wound up the rocky spine of ridge in a series of switchbacks amid the fire-cone trunks and the sweet smell of resin. Like the garden below, the grove was meticulously kept: lower branches had been pruned to reduce fire danger, the tinder-like needles that collected beneath had been swept up to expose rock-grappling roots, and not a cone lay uncollected.

Once they gained the top, Harric spied the warden's tower, and a pulse of excitement thrilled through him. This near, he could pick out the lanky rod of iron running up the timber mast; he could also see how the timbers of the mast itself had been lashed together with bands and bolts as thick as his wrist. Nearby, several cable stays swooped down to find anchor in the bedrock.

Caris halted their approach when only a bowshot from the tower. "We should leave the horses here."

Brolli stirred from his blankets. He lifted the daylids to his forehead, and gazed about with sleepy golden eyes. "Ah." He yawned. "We're here. Scat, cat."

Spook hopped from his lap onto the fire-cone roots, eyes narrowed in annoyance. He sneezed once, sniffed about, then padded ahead toward the tower. Harric now noticed a pair of barns beside the tower, and a grassy yard and garden surrounding.

"That is the lightning-stealer, yes?" said Brolli, pointing.

Willard grunted. "No magic required."

"Your hex strike here, old man? You say women make it come, too. This Abellia, she to make it come?"

Willard's cheeks flushed an unhealthy red, but he seemed imbued now with a desperate, brittle spark. "She's a woman. But old. So she won't wake it. Otherwise it strikes when I'm in danger; if Caris is right, this Abellia will offer help."

"Caris is woman. Why does she not to make the hex come?"

Willard studied Caris. "She's…different. Horse-touched. I don't know the logic of the thing, Brolli, but maybe that's why." Willard was beginning to sweat and pant again with the effort of speaking, but this time Brolli seemed to want the old man to pass out, and kept talking.

"And Caris wears a wedding ring," said Brolli. "That might to be the difference."

Willard nodded, as if in acknowledgement of some previous conversation on the topic. "That's so. No *romantic* threat."

"Still, we should warn this Abellia."

"I'll tell her in private."

Without explanation, Willard positioned Molly beside a boulder that reached to the Phyros's belly. "Help an old man down?"

Even from paces away, Harric could smell the rot on Willard. His breath stank like pond scum, and his quilting reeked of sweat and blood on ripe flesh. Harric was relieved, therefore, to picket the other horses while Caris and Brolli scrambled up the rock to help the old knight down. It was a messy process, but by the time Harric tethered Idgit and Rag, they got Willard free of the saddle without dropping him or jarring him too hard.

Willard grimaced as he clambered down from the boulder. New stripes of blood leached into the bandage on his hip.

Caris and Brolli each took a shoulder and steered the old man across the swept yard to halt before a fan of ten stone steps at the foot of the tower.

Willard studied the tower with a military eye. "Standard drum. Bottom floor can take a half-dozen horses and hay for a fortnight." He frowned at the upper floors. "Not near enough arrow loops, and the windows are too big. Still, if we stock the place with hay and water and a few sacks of beans, we might hold against Bannus long enough for the Blue Order to catch us up."

He peered into Caris's face beside him. "You think this Abellia would shy from a bit of a siege?"

She tried to hide her alarm. "I—I'll ask her, sir."

"Good."

When they stood before the ironbound door, Caris lifted a knocker shaped like a female hand clasping an agate the size of an egg, and clapped it three times on the strike plate.

Willard peered at an engraved plaque beneath the knocker. "Read it, boy."

Harric glanced at Willard. The old man wasn't even trying to pretend it was a test. Was it possible Willard *couldn't* read? The notion surprised Harric. Many knights lacked letters, but he'd always assumed it was because of their full-time martial training that kept them from it. Willard had no such excuse, as he'd had seven lives in which to learn them.

Harric read aloud:

Here abides Mistress Abellia Pergrossi
by express proclamation of Her Royal Majesty, Chasia,
in the 27th year of her reign:
licensed fire-cone warden
with all powers appertaining.

A second plaque, just below, was much more ornate, and of obvious Iberg style. It featured fat farm animals and children, encircled by rivers and grain fields; outside this was another ring decorated with crescents and half-circles and circles, the phases of the Bright Mother. "The words along the top are Iberg. This one says, *Poverty*. Then *Chastity* and *Service*."

A faint smile ghosted over Willard's mouth. "You're too clever by half, boy. Where'd you learn Iberg?"

"My mother. She worked abroad for the Queen."

Willard snorted. "Explains your looseness toward magic."

The door opened a crack, then swung outward, and the pale ghost of a drowned girl peered up at them from within. A thrill of fear swept Harric before he realized it was not a girl or a ghost, but a tiny old woman in cloud-white robes, a figure so frail she seemed nothing more than crisp papers in danger of blowing away.

Yet there was kindness in the lines of the ancient face, and her eyes, like wet black pebbles, shone clear and alive, as if the spirit behind them were indeed a child's, and an observant one.

"*Mama*," Caris murmured, lowering her eyes and touching one knee to the stone.

The watery eyes squinted at the blue-armored knight, who was Caris, in confusion. Then her wrinkled mouth made an O of surprise, and her attention flitted from Harric to Willard and back to Caris with astonishment. Brolli, Harric noticed, had donned a hood and kept his head down.

"My Caris!" Abellia cried, in a voice thin to cracking and an accent as thick as any Harric had heard. "My Caris! *Mio doso!*"

Caris laughed and carefully embraced the tiny woman as if her steel limbs might crack her to pieces. The sunken eyes went wide, and she drew away, staring in surprise. "You wearing the hard britches! All is well? These steel panty not so comforting, no? Haha! You have the mentor! Yes? O! You must to tell! You must to eat. All your friends. We having plenty spaces. Plenty foods. You must coming in!"

"Mama, my mentor, Sir Willard, is hurt."

The old woman blinked nearsightedly at Willard, laying her hands on Caris's arm for balance. She scanned his face and bloodied armor with gentle eyes.

"You are dying, sir."

Willard bowed with his head. "My lady. I fear we bring trouble and danger on our heels."

She dismissed the notion with a wave. "You are this Willard they sing of?" Her black eyes glistened with pleasure. "I am always knowing Caris is mentored by a great man. You and your dangers are most welcome, sir."

From her robes she produced a glossy egg of pearly stone, which she cradled in both hands. Her witch-stone, Harric realized, as white as his was black. A thrill of excitement pulsed through him as she closed her eyes and the stone lit up her hand like a lantern.

Willard's face fell. "Beg pardon, lady." His eyes flashed to Brolli, whose face remained muffled in the hood. "I am well enough."

Abellia's eyes widened in surprise. The white light retreated, leaving only a distant glow.

"Willard, you promised," said Brolli.

"I acknowledged that in the case of unconsciousness I could not stop you from healing me," Willard said. "Unless I'm dreaming, I'm still conscious. And as long as I'm conscious I claim the Third Law."

"The idea is to keep you alive."

"I *am* alive. What I need is a bath and a rest. You see I am alert."

"I see you happy-sick with promise of rest," said Brolli. "You spending all your strength."

"I'm Arkendian, Brolli. Tougher than I look. Bathe me and rest me and prop me by a window with a rag-roll and a pot of ale, and I'll mend without any god-cursed magic."

Harric glimpsed thick canines grinding beneath the cover of the hood. "I think you want to die."

"I want to live *right*."

Abellia watched the exchange with questioning eyes. The light went from her witch-stone, and she returned it to her robes. "We have nice bathing tub. I have bath filled warm, and you must to bathing right away." Abellia turned her gaze upon Harric. She raised a withered claw of a hand to his swollen cheek and eye. "But what is here?"

"This is Harric," said Caris. "Willard's *manservant*, from Gallows Ferry."

"Ouch," Harric said, but he smiled and bowed his head.

"Such handsome one," said Abellia. "You are hurting, too. And you will have no heal like your master?"

"I'm an Arkendian too," Harric said, wishing he weren't. "I will heal myself."

"But if Sir Bannus returns," Brolli said, unwilling to let it go, "you both must reconsider."

Willard nodded. "We'll cross that bridge when we come to it."

Abellia squinted at Brolli. She smiled hospitably, but with obvious curiosity, trying not to stare. Brolli's stature was much concealed by his position of support under Willard's arm, but his stunted legs were clear enough, and very likely she could not place his accent at all. Unable to politely remain covered any longer, Brolli removed the hood and gave a small bow.

Caris gestured to him with an air of clumsy theatricality, as if she'd saved him for last. "And this, Mama, is Brolli. A Kwendi. He is ambassador from his people to our queen, and we are escorting him back to his land."

Abellia blinked in surprise. Her hands groped down Caris's arm, eyes never leaving Brolli, until she gripped Caris's hand in hers. "You knew," she whispered, turning her deep black eyes on Caris. "You knew…you bringing him to me. O bless you, girl!"

Caris blushed. "No, Mama…" she stammered, glancing at Brolli. "We needed your help, and Brolli is our charge…"

Abellia tottered forward and extended a hand to Brolli as if she feared he might vanish like a mirage. Brolli took her tiny, frail hand in his huge, strange one, and nodded solemnly.

Harric glimpsed a flash of strong emotion in the old woman's eyes. Hope? Hunger? Fear?

"You are being the first of your people I meet," she whispered. "You are most to be welcome."

"It is my honor," said Brolli, "for I never met an Iberg."

For many heartbeats she gazed into his alien features. When it became awkward, Brolli bowed again, and she recovered. "*Mio doso.* I am sorry. Please to come inside. We must to draw bath for the sir. We must to eat and lay rest!" As she turned up the stairs, Willard raised an eyebrow at Brolli, as if to say, *Just as I foretold—she's lulu about your magic…*

Brolli did not smile in return. "Bathe, and when you pass out, I use it on you."

"I don't know which of you is more stubborn," Harric muttered.

As the Kwendi crossed the threshold, his shirt shouted in a strange tongue, and he sprang back, nearly dragging Willard with him.

"What the Black Moon was that?" Willard said.

Abellia appeared in the doorway, confusion in her eyes.

"I apologize," said Brolli sheepishly. "You keep alarms here, Mistress Abellia? I set them all off when I enter: I have a bit of magic on me."

A bit *of magic?* Harric thought. *His very shirt is enchanted.*

Abellia stared, uncomprehending for a moment, and then Harric glimpsed a flash of fear in her eyes. "You are having magicks of the Mad Moon, Ambassador?"

Brolli bowed another apology. "We use all three moons."

Abellia's eyes grew wide. She took a half-step back.

"However, if the Mad Moon's powers be offensive to your people," said Brolli, "then I use none it here. Or, if you like, I show you."

Revulsion in the old woman's eyes gave way to curiosity, and possibly something stronger. "O, yes, please. I am all these years in Arkendia searching the workings of witch-silver. I am most to be wishing to see it. I halt the wards." Her hand dipped into and out of her robe. "All safe now to follow. *Mio doso!* A wonderful day."

"Harric," Caris said over her shoulder. "Put the horses in the barn while Brolli and I help Willard up the stairs. You'll find water and hay in the barn, unless things have changed."

"I'm not your servant," he muttered under his breath. They left him standing at the door with the bad feeling this was now the way Caris would treat him until he forswore his so-called "tricks"—like a noblewoman treats a slave. He had no fear of her betraying the nature of his training to the others— that seemed to be against her code of honor for friends—but it appeared she intended to slight him at every opportunity.

Fabulous. Maybe I can shine her armor, too.

It made him angry because it hurt, he realized. He liked her, but she was slighting him. The knot of bitterness in his throat made him wish she'd left him, as she'd intended to, in Gallows Ferry—that the ring had never involved her—and that he was free and on his own.

His interest in her wasn't inspired by magic, but it might as well be for all the control he had of it. His only consolation was that if the ring made her love him, it was also hard on her.

Love, like rain, does not choose on whom it falls.

—Arkendian proverb

27

Risk & Revenge

Harric led Idgit and Rag into the larger of the two barns, where he brushed their coats and cleaned their hooves as they munched the last of the oats he'd so fatefully sold Willard in Gallows Ferry. The memory drew a wry snort from him. How much simpler things would be if he'd kept the ring Willard gave him that day, instead of leaving it to Caris. Then, in exchange for returning the ring, he could have bargained for two apprenticeships and won Caris's regard without revealing a shred of the "trickery" she loathed.

As he piled hay for Molly onto a barrow and wheeled it from the barn into the dying light, he sighed. It was a false dream, of course. The only reason Caris had stayed in Gallows Ferry long enough to rejoin with Harric at all was because the ring had changed her feelings for him. And if she hadn't stayed she wouldn't have been there to drag his unconscious self from the wreckage of Bannus's parlor wall.

Plus, he doubted whether tricking Caris by hiding his true nature as a trickster would work out very well in the long run. Such deception was how his mother taught him to seduce and manipulate, so it felt natural to him, but anything she taught him was clearly suspect. He doubted whether normal people lied to each other when courting, and in any case seduction was a short-term game and the ring did not appear to be coming off soon.

Better I show my true nature. It doesn't feel natural, but that's because of my mother's poison in my life. I'll win her regard on my terms, so the day we get the ring off she'll find she loves me all the same.

Love! He laughed at himself. What did *he* know about actual love? Lust, gain, seduction, manipulation, all came as naturally as walking and breathing, trained and drilled until they became unconscious habits. But what in the Black Moon was *love?*

And then it dawned on him he was just as much a babe in the wilderness when it came to human love as Caris.

He stopped in the middle of the trail, staring into nothing, astonished he hadn't seen it before. *We're misfits, the two of us. She by nature, I by indoctrination, and neither knows if we can overcome it.*

But you do feel something, another part of him countered. Yes, he did. But what? Lust? Desire? Protectiveness? Hope? Loneliness? Need? Were any of those love? Were some of them? How did anyone know?

The thought depressed him. Could they be a more hopeless cause? And the moon-blasted ring forced them together.

He looked up into the sky, half expecting to see the constellation of Fate's Web laughing down at him, but the canopy of blue was yet too bright for stars.

Molly's snort snapped him out of his reverie. He saw her ahead through the stately columns of the fire-cones, and resumed pushing the barrow to her. It wasn't until he'd dumped the hay before her that he realized Holly was nowhere to be seen; she'd pulled her picket and wandered off.

Shit. The ground had been too rocky and root-bound to sink the stake in deep enough, and the filly had pulled it loose. Willard would have a seizure if he knew.

It wasn't hard to guess where she'd gone. Back down to the garden and meadow to graze.

So much for rest. He'd have to walk back down the mountain to find her, and assuming he did find her, he couldn't ride her back up because Willard had forbidden it.

"Moons take you, Holly," he muttered. Everything conspired against him getting back to the tower, where he could see how Abellia used her witch-stone.

As he trudged back toward the switchbacks above the garden, he put his hand on the lump of witch-stone in his shirt, and frowned. This was one thing he could not yet share with Caris. But magic was the only thing his mother feared. His only hope of truly banishing her from his life. How ironic that she should teach him not to fear magic, then fear it in his hands!

But it wasn't enough to possess the witch-stone; he needed to learn how to use it. But how? Brolli couldn't tell him, as Brolli didn't seem to know anything more than how to use the bottled magic his people made. Abellia feared everything but her own moon's powers, so that was out. But still, he might discover something from Abellia that would give him a clue about his own.

He stopped at the first switchback over the garden and paused to scan the valley below, and saw Holly grazing at the far end of the meadow, by the brook. He let out a growling sigh of frustration and set to descending the trail, each downhill step jarring his injured ribs.

In any case, he could probably count on his mother leaving him alone as long as he remained with Abellia. In the meantime, he must learn how to use his stone—if not from Brolli and Abellia, then on his own. That night, while the others slept, he'd slip away and experiment. He had to access its powers before he left Abellia's protection. He had to be ready.

Caris descended the tower and searched for Harric in the yard and smaller barn, but could not find him. In the large barn she found only the horses, munching contentedly.

"Harric? What's taking you so long?" she called into the glowing gloom.

She stopped by Rag, and fed her a carrot she'd filched from Abellia's larder. Harric had done as asked, watering and brushing the animals. She checked Rag's hooves and found them cleaned, too.

She sighed, not sure why she was irritated, which made her all the more so. Harric had probably wandered off to get some time alone, but even a horse-touched wench like her knew he ought to spend some time with their host before sleep. More importantly, she'd advised Abellia to wait until Harric was present before she introduced Mudruffle to the others. She feared Willard might react badly to Mudruffle's obvious magical nature, and reasoned that since Harric seemed as unintimidated by magic as he was by the old knight's bluster, his presence might soften Willard's reaction.

And yet just yesterday, said a little voice in her conscience, *you loudly criticized Harric for that same lack of regard for Willard's opinion.*

There it was. She was a hypocrite, and that was irritating. Or maybe she was learning something new about those "gray areas" Harric navigated so smoothly—which was even more aggravating.

She growled, and grabbed a brush to work on Rag's mane.

"Fleeing the oh-so-difficult world of humans?" said a smooth female voice behind her.

Caris whirled, startled to find a middle-aged lady of the court confronting her from the straw. Tall, proud, the lady glittered with ornaments accenting a gown of green silk. Amber hair piled upon her head in a mass of ringlets and braids in a style Caris had seen in portraits of her mother's courtier days. Her face glowed with ashen paste, and perfect circles of rouge rode high on each

cheek. At first glance she'd seemed beautiful—once had been, surely—but now only a husk remained; starved eyes, protruding collarbones, and where the neckline of her gown might once have once draped over a swelling of smooth breasts, it now revealed a prow of jutting sternum on a carapace of bone.

"So, you are Harric's latest toy," said the lady, in a voice soft as honey. She pursed her lips, eyes roaming Caris's body. The survey halted on the sword at Caris's hip, whereupon the lady let out a prim little laugh and clapped her hands in delight. "Half-witted, half brute, and mannish to boot. How he baits me! Could he have chosen a more ridiculous boor to vex me with?" Eyes shining, her laughter tinkled beneath the rafters.

Caris barely heard the words. Hairs rose on her neck as her mind flew in circles trying to explain away the obvious. Rag fidgeted, stomping and eyes showing white at the sight of the apparition that was there but not there in the straw. Caris reached into the panicked mare to calm her pounding heart, and, by focusing elsewhere, calm her own.

"Who are you?" Caris said.

"I am the Lady Dimoore," said Harric's mother. Bright, birdlike eyes— Harric's eyes—scrutinized Caris's face. "You're only half here, aren't you. The other half is in that horse." Lady Dimoore's nose wrinkled, sending a fan of tiny cracks through her makeup. "Stupid brutes, horses. They imagine snakes in shadows, lions in puddles. But they can be managed, with training, can't they? Just like you."

"What do you want?" Caris said. "Harric doesn't want you in his life anymore." Her voice sounded thick to her own ears, her words clumsy compared to the lady's clever speech; nevertheless, they struck a nerve in the Lady Dimoore, for her eyes flashed.

"Oh? And you think he wants *you?*" she snapped. "Let me tell you something, my little brute girl. Only one lady will ever have Harric's heart, and she took it out long ago."

Caris clamped her teeth, wishing she could also clamp her ears. She was no good with words and glances, the sort of weapons ladies used so deftly, always piercing her useless defenses and drawing blood. *Another lady*, had she said? The words ate at her. Did she mean Lyla? Harric had gone to such lengths to win her in poker and free her, and then again to save her from Bannus. Did he love her? How stupid she'd been not to see it! On the other hand, Lyla was no more a *lady* than Caris; surely the Lady Dimoore would be just as dismissive of a commoner like Lyla. But if not Lyla, who?

Lady Dimoore's blue-painted lips pressed in a tight, haughty smile.

Caris blinked in surprise. "You mean *you?*"

Her reaction did not please. "Who else, simpleton? Do you know anything about the hearts of men? Do you know anything about your own dull heart?"

The lady stepped nearer, voice lowered, eyes bright with cruelty. "Let me tell you a story, horse girl. Long before your mother foaled you, a certain Lady Dionis gave birth to a brute like you. Against my clear advice, she kept the creature and set out to raise her as a lady for the court. I told her the child would cause irreparable harm to the cause of women there, which the Queen had labored hard to establish. I told her that by keeping the girl in court she would make us all look like the very half-wits the Brotherhood claimed we were—a living reminder that women must be kept and managed by their men. But Lady Dionis didn't listen. She dressed the little beast in gowns, taught her to dance and speak, and indeed the creature danced well enough, and may have liked it for aught I know.

"But when she came of age, she became strange. She fled company. When the Queen held her masques and balls or banquets, the girl would slip away, and none could find her. Of course, *I* knew where she was. Like any horse in crisis, she fled to her stable."

Recognition hit Caris like a pole in the gut. "Mona..." she breathed.

The lady's eyes flashed with pleasure. "Yes, Mona. Of course you know of her. She was a pretty thing, on the outside. The boys found her exterior quite appealing in her low-cut silken dresses. But like you, she was half-hearted, half-witted within."

"Shut up. I know what happened." Caris knew the tale by heart, a cautionary tale to horse-touched and their mothers. The image of Mona and her fate had haunted her imagination since she was small—eating at her ambitions, cutting her hopes off at the knees—until Mona became a sort of long-lost sister never known and always grieved.

"You know what happened, but do you know *why* it happened? You see, her mother ignored my advice. That was quite unacceptable. So, with a little encouragement from me, the stable lads began to woo the girl."

"*You?*" Caris's breath choked off in her throat.

The lady smiled. "Predictably, she gave her half-heart to the first who feigned his love. And one night, while the others danced the masque, he tied her in a stall, fitted her head with training bit and bridle, and he and his friends rode her until I brought the dancers down to see her as she truly was, her false dress stripped away."

Caris sobbed. She knew the end. The suicide hangings from the tower. First daughter, then mother. Grief and rage choked her. Memories of the insufferable gowns her own mother forced upon her—of lady lessons and the mocks of would-be wooer—jumbled in her mind with newer struggles of the wedding ring and Harric and feelings she didn't understand.

Her hands rose to her ears, and she fled into Rag. Dimly, she sensed the lady laughing, leaning close.

"Can you imagine the extent of Mona's ruin?" the lady whispered. "You cannot. For you can only half know anything. But that is how I shall ruin you, if you do not forswear my Harric. I shall ruin you. Cruelly. Publicly. And utterly."

Caris couldn't block out the words. They seemed to enter her mind without recourse to her ears. To her surprise, however, they did not send her over the edge into the blackness she experienced when words overwhelmed her. Though she heard every one, she did not curl into a ball. Indeed, she realized with surprise that she was still standing. That her head was not roaring with confusion. That something had changed in her, and though she had no idea what it was, she was not incapacitated.

Instead, she felt anger. And with anger, she could *act*.

She flung herself from the wall, sword flashing from her side and whistling beneath the lady's startled eyes.

The lady drew back, startled. "I warned you!" she hissed, and faded to air.

Caris replied by thrusting a yard of steel through the space where the eyes had been. "Coward!" she spat. "Stay and face me!" She stalked the barn, muttering curses until she was certain the ghost was gone. Finally, she stopped beside Rag, panting. Rag let out a triumphant whinny, but Caris barely noticed. Staring inward, she marveled at her own stability in the face of torment that would normally have left her rolled up in the straw, and at the revelation about the fabled Mona.

"She killed you," she whispered. "That evil bitch raped you and killed you."

Abruptly, she dropped to her knees, and laid her sword before her. "I found your name," she whispered to the blade. From the dirt she pried an old shoeing nail, and with it etched *MONA* in the steel.

Rising, she held the blade before her. A power and freedom moved through her that she'd never felt before, as if the spirit of Mona entered the blade to give it wings, and she knew it was right, and it was purpose, and that she herself was Mona reforged in tempered steel.

"You warn *me*, lady?" Caris angled the blade so its new name glinted in the dying light. "*I warn you.* Mona is back. And she knows her killer's name."

28

The Witch's Creature

It was more than an hour before Harric brought Holly to a stall in the barn beside Rag. Since she'd gorged in the meadow, he left her only water and a handful of hay, before plodding up the stairs and into the tower.

The base of the tower formed a single, spacious circular room, with stalls for animals and barrels below and heavy timber beams above, and a central pillar of stone that Harric deduced encased the base of the thunder-rod. Stairs curved up the circumference to the right. He climbed toward the sounds of conversation above, and wondered how Abellia managed such stairs when he could barely lift his feet to make it.

He emerged onto a landing with a single doorway, through which came smells and sounds of pleasant cooking and conversation, and he stepped through into a high-timbered hall with windows as big as doors. Lush Iberg rugs blanketed the wooden floor, and two high-backed stuffed chairs faced each other before the hearth. The window shutters were flung wide to admit the western breeze and the last evening light. Brolli, Willard, and Caris lounged upon pillowed benches with their host in a cozy alcove before the western window, watching an orange sunset over the ridges. They'd washed and combed and each enjoyed a pint of something frothy that Harric imagined must be cool and refreshing.

Beside them he felt sweaty, and dirty, and mightily abused.

No one noticed him standing in the doorway. Abellia seemed to be in the middle of a story of Caris's first visit to the tower.

"It gave a horrid wet storming in the sky that day, so she must stay. *Mio doso!* She looking like the poor wet cat!" The old woman cackled, and beamed at

Caris. Caris put on a smile, but Harric could see she was distracted, worried, or upset—probably with him for being so late.

When he shut the door behind him, Caris's eyes snapped to him. He expected her to scowl, but found instead all the signs of urgent worry in her face. Not surprisingly, though she seemed anxious to speak to him, she had no words to gracefully excuse herself from the table.

Willard noted the intensity of her gaze, and followed it to Harric. "Boy! By Bannus's stinking socks, where have you been? Get cleaned up. I can smell you from here." He pointed to a door on the opposite side of the hearth and said, "Bathing room."

The old knight's armor had been removed and replaced with a worn brown doublet and hose. He'd girded the doublet with a clean bandage, over which his considerable guts hung obscenely. It embarrassed Harric to see him out of armor. He felt like he'd walked in on the old man naked—arms and chest strong as fire-cone roots, but the belly grotesque, and the old legs spindly and weak, like a hermit crab plucked from its shell. More bandages wrapped his ribs beneath both arms, and another embraced his left wrist, but all were clean, without seepage.

"Good to see you in repair, sir," Harric said, but in truth the medical attentions appeared to have taken their toll; the old knight's face seemed sunken, and the already pale cheeks had lost all trace of color. The sight made Harric ashamed of his self-pity.

"Molly swallowed Idgit, sir," Harric replied, with his best manservant imitation. "I had a bit of a time making her cough her back up, and when she did, I had a worse time calming Idgit."

The table laughed, and the joke had the desired effect of diverting attention from Caris's obvious need to speak with him in private. *She is useless keeping secrets,* Harric noted, amused. *An open book for all to read. Even Willard.*

He started for the bathing room, but stopped when he noticed a shadow shifting by the side of the hearth. A figure moved there. A child? Whatever it was stood no taller than half the height of a man. It stepped from the shadows and walked with a jerky sort of stride to Willard's discarded armor, where it swept needles and twigs from the blackened steel into a little dustbin. Not a child. Not even human, Harric realized. From a distance it looked like a walking hat rack.

Conversation stopped at the table as Caris rose and crossed to it. She stooped to embrace the strange figure in an awkward hug, and said, "Mudruffle, I'm glad you could join us!" Mudruffle returned the embrace with two long arms, and Harric began to see the creature was roughly man-shaped, but made of staves and dark clay.

"Mudruffle, this is Harric, Sir Willard's manservant." Her tone was practiced and formal, and she stood in such a way that her mentor could get a view of the creature from a distance. "Harric, this is Mudruffle, Abellia's companion."

Harric watched in fascination as the creature jerked around to look at him, and then lurched toward him like a very ill-handled marionette. Mudruffle's arms and legs were too long for the truncated body, and crudely formed, with knob-jointed quality. His clothing appeared to be etched into the clay composing his limbs, with little flourishes like cuffs and collars and coattails extruding. He wore a suit in the fashion of an Arkendian steward's livery, complete with waistcoat, ruffled shirt, and a jacket with tails too short for his spidery legs.

Willard swayed to his feet, belly jarring the table and sloshing the drinks. He stared, chewing at his mustache before he whispered to Brolli, "*What the Black Moon is wrong with his head?*"

"Wrong?" said Brolli. "I see no wrong."

But Harric had wondered the same thing. The problem seemed to be that Mudruffle *had* no head. Or what served as a head was in fact a *hat*—a squat, short-brimmed butler's hat, resting directly on the shoulders. If a head lurked inside, it would have to be a very small one, and it could have no neck to speak of. Harric decided that since the hat was made of the same material as the rest of the creature, the hat *was* the head, but that the face on the head had been scrunched down low beneath the brim amidst the collars as if in an effort at hiding it. Since the creature maintained its bow, he could see only the top of the hat and part of the collars.

"Master Mudruffle, my greeting," said Harric.

"I'm honored, young master," the hat honked. Mudruffle bowed, a spidery hand laid to his lapels. "You are welcome here."

Caris pinched Harric's arm. He'd been staring.

"Ah! The—honor's mine," Harric said, feigning a cough. "Caris speaks very fondly of you, Mudruffle." He bowed then, rather lower than he needed, and stole a glance upward at the steward's face. He saw a small, serious mouth, like a slot, and two buttonlike eyes of what might be polished stone. Then the hat dipped to hide it.

"My appearance must be strange to you," said Mudruffle, honking through the tiny mouth. "I hope it causes no alarm."

"No! Ha—of course not. It's just that I haven't seen anyone like you before."

The creature bowed again, then stalked back to the hearth and disappeared through an opening beside it, which Harric guessed must be a door to the kitchen or pantry.

Sir Willard stared after him, then sat and downed his remaining drink. Abellia watched. Caris bit her lip. It had been a staged introduction, Harric realized. Caris rightly guessed Harric would be less upset by the creature than Willard, so she'd staged a meeting where the old knight could watch Mudruffle without having to interact himself.

Fortunately, Willard appeared to be taking it like a soldier—by pouring another pint.

Mistress Abellia beckoned Harric to the table. He joined them and stood beside the table, for there was only room for four, and if he squeezed in before his bath it would be uncomfortable for all present. She poured him a jar of something she called "honey wine," which proved fizzy and sweet but strong as any ale. Refilling Brolli's jar, she chirped about Caris's first terrified view of Mudruffle—more staged information—and Willard managed a gruff interest. Then Mudruffle appeared behind her, and made a little sound like the clearing of his throat. Abellia performed a very poor impression of surprise.

"Oh! Here he is!" she said, as if it was the first anyone at the table had seen him. Brolli appeared to understand the theatrics, because he watched the whole show with evident amusement, though Willard seemed oblivious. "Sir Willard, Ambassador Brolli, you must be meeting my tryst servant. This is Mudruffle. I think he is having something to show."

Mudruffle cradled a large, rolled parchment in his arms, large enough to cover most of the table. He lurched up to the end of the table across which Abellia and Willard faced each other, and bowed, then laid the roll on the table. Harric noted his knees didn't bend much, which accounted for his jerking strides.

"My mistress tells me you are in need of a forest route northward," honked Mudruffle. He spread the parchment with flat spider hands. Black lines and colored drawings covered the parchment in complex profusion, accompanied by minute scrawls in Iberg. A map. The blue snaking bar along the top had to be the Arkend River. Once Harric identified that, he could make out the hatch-marks signifying Gallows Ferry, and by extrapolation, the fire-cone tower, and some of the other landmarks they had passed. Indeed, it was a map of the region as far north as the Giant's Gorge, and in tremendous detail.

"I make a hobby of maintaining this map, and find the practice very stimulating," Mudruffle honked. "You will recognize the river and the main road." He indicated the blue and black lines. "To this I've added settlements, and signs of yoab I encounter in my expeditions. I have also developed a system of paths and trails for my own use, leading northward; I cannot use the main road, for there is a high probability I would be seen, and a high probability my appearance would cause alarm among the natives. Since it seems you also have need of avoiding being seen, I thought my system might be of use to you."

Willard stared, hypnotized by the toneless falsetto.

Caris cleared her throat, nodding encouragement to Willard.

"Ah. Your routes would be of use, ah…Mud…fellow," Willard said. "A great help."

Mudruffle nodded. "As you can see, it is indecipherable to anyone but me, as I never imagined its utility to anyone else. However, I cheerfully offer my service with the map. It would be very stimulating for me to accompany you as far as the Giant's Gorge."

The knight blinked. "It—would?"

"Indeed, it would give me great pleasure to be of use."

Harric felt a pang of pity for the bizarre creature. *So bored he maps game trails for a hobby.* Looking around the overly tidy tower, he imagined there wasn't much to do with only the old lady as companion. It would also explain the swept dirt around the tower. But he sensed more to the eagerness than that; this was as close as any Iberg had ever been to a Kwendi, and both Mudruffle and Abellia appeared determined to milk the opportunity for every drop of advantage they could get.

"I am an excellent woodsman," Mudruffle was saying. "You may not think so by the festive attire I have donned for this occasion, but I assure you I am as well fitted for an outdoor expedition. Perhaps you would like to view my outdoor gear."

Before Willard could object, Mudruffle's surface altered.

They watched in varying degrees of fascination or horror as his well-tailored ensemble became a dashing jerkin and hose with a broad belt and a buckle the size of a horse shoe. His squat bowler became a spirited tricorn with pointed brim and feather, and his little steward slippers a pair of high woodsman's boots with tops turned down above the knees.

Willard seemed stricken between hilarity and alarm.

Harric pressed his lips together.

"As you can see," honked Mudruffle, "I am amply suited for the task."

Abellia beamed. "Oh, Mudruffle is always able for making other clothes. I make this suiting a long time past. *Mio doso!* Here is the Iberg forest hat!"

Willard stammered something about this being "*Arkendian* forest—more dangerous—"

Brolli interrupted, "I am to believe our generous friend is the excellent guide. We can't take risk of the main road, and we can't risk time lost finding passes on our own. We accept your offer, and are to be grateful."

Willard's mouth worked mutely. He closed it. He lifted his jar and gulped his drink.

Brolli clearly enjoyed the knight's discomfiture.

"Sir, I am a proficient woodsman."

"And he never needs sleeping," added Abellia, "making best for night watchman."

"Excellent!" said Brolli. "I will have a nighttime companion. In fact, as Willard and I discussed, I must to return to the guardhouse in the pass below your valley, to watch for pursuit. I wish to watch the bridge for at least three nights, and would to enjoy a companion who can watch in the day."

Mudruffle stiffened, as if coming to attention. "I would find that very stimulating."

"Then it's decided."

Abellia's eyes shone with some of that hunger Harric had seen when first she saw the Kwendi. "I am too old for explorings. And I will have my Caris near me some days, and that is all I am wanting. It will be good for Mudruffle!"

And good for her too, Harric mused. *She wants Mudruffle to have a chance to pump Brolli about Kwendi magic as much as I want to pump her about witch-stones.*

Willard made the best of being cornered by raising his glass to Mudruffle. "Very well, Mudwallow. You accompany Brolli to watch the pass for a few days, and when we leave, you and your map come with us. We only plan to stay a week here, at most, mind. That ought to be time enough to prepare, heh? Of course, my manservant and apprentice are at your disposal during that time."

Willard toasted his jar to the man at his right, who was Harric, and Harric raised his to Mudruffle, and so on around the table, in the manner of an Arkendian toast. Caris caught Harric's eye across the table, once again full of mysterious urgency. He gave a small nod in acknowledgement, which seemed to relieve her.

"To Abellia," Willard said. "And to an excellent Iberg brew!"

"GODS LEAVE THEM!"

"And to Mudruffle," said Brolli, "for a map through the mountains!"

"GODS LEAVE HIM!"

"And to Caris for bring us together!" said Abellia.

"GODS LEAVE HER!"

Mudruffle served bowls of hot brown soup from the kitchen, along with plates of crusty bread and a hard sheep's cheese. Harric ate his in one of the high-backed stuffed chairs before the hearth, since there was no room at the table for him. And though Caris had attempted to rise from the table before the food came, Abellia demanded the story of how she landed Willard as her mentor, so she could only cast him another glance of frustrated urgency.

Something must have happened with Willard, Harric thought, and whatever that was could probably wait. She took the old knight's gruffness too seriously. Under the spiny shell was a soft heart and a good man. They didn't sing ballads about him for nothing.

Harric had almost finished his meal before he realized a lady occupied the stuffed chair opposite his. Since the chair was silhouetted against the western window behind it, she'd been framed in darkness without him noticing.

"Beg pardon, lady," he said, standing. "I—didn't see you enter." He bowed, a little flustered, as she had clearly been there all along. Peering into the gloom, he suddenly recognized the slippers and the hem of the faded gown, and caught his breath in shock.

"Good evening to you, my dear son."

"Mother—!" He bit the words off, too late. Willard and the others had heard, and gone silent. They stared from the table at the window.

"What's the matter, boy?" Willard said.

"Nothing, sorry," Harric said. "Just a stone in my boot. I beg your pardon."

"I also speak to stones in my boots that way," said Brolli.

Willard snorted, and the joke dispelled the tension, but Caris's look was full of worry. She quirked her head in query from across the room, but he forced a smile and shook his head to show nothing was wrong. When he sat out of view behind the screen of his mother's chair opposite, however, he had to set his bowl aside to keep his trembling from spilling the soup.

His mother simpered. "They can't see me, so you don't dare talk to me. They'll think you mad. And you most surely won't bring out that evil stone while you are here where your friends might see it."

Harric's mind scrambled. How could she enter a tower so full of magic? "Leave me alone," he hissed, barely audibly.

She leaned forward, eyes aflame. "Cast the stone away, Harric. Its spirit corrupts your mind. Soon it will be too late."

"Hah. What's the trouble? Have I finally found a weapon you fear?"

"Fool! That stone poisons you. Its spirit worms into your dreams. Have you not noticed?"

"You yourself taught me the Unseen Moon is part of Nature, like the other moons. It is neither good nor evil, except as it is used by good or evil people. Why the change of story?"

"I was wrong! In the afterworld I see the Unseen as it is, and it is corrupt! As a spirit I know so much more! I must protect you."

He barely contained his fury in a whisper. "Now I *know* you're lying." He slipped his hand in his shirt toward the stone, and she recoiled like a wolf before fire. "You are afraid."

"I fear for you!"

Harric peered over the top of her chair at the table where the others had lowered their voices. Willard sent a worried glanced in his direction.

Harric ducked back and lowered his whisper. "No. I think I am beginning to understand, Mother. This stone, this fragment of the Unseen Moon, is somehow dangerous to you. Something potent in the spirit world."

She snorted, tried to recover her composure with a haughty sneer. "Fool. The spirit in that stone has blinded you to reason."

"I think you're jealous," Harric whispered. "You can't stand the idea that I'll be better than you—that with the trick of invisibility I'll one day exceed your name as a courtiste. In fact, I think that might be how I *truly* banish you—by besting you in your own profession."

He drew the stone from its sleeve with a feeling of control and power he'd never felt over her, and it intoxicated as much as the terror blooming on her face confirmed all his hopes.

She cried out in grief and rage. "I give you this last warning! Cast it away, or I shall do it for you!"

Before he could advance upon her, she'd vanished.

Caris's heavy steps approached from the table. Harric thrust the stone into his shirt just as she rounded the back of the chair before him.

She stopped beside it, face flushed. But instead of anger at his odd behavior, her expression was grim. In her hand she clutched a sharp cheese knife.

"Sorry. I tried to keep it down," he murmured. "It was my mother. She's gone now."

Caris's jaw muscles bulged as she ground her teeth in anger.

"Yeah, that was my reaction, too," he said, as she dropped into the other chair to face him. He forced himself to smile. "Willard heard me?"

At her nod, he leaned out from his chair and waved to the others in the eating alcove. "Sorry!" he called. "Just reciting a ballad." He sat back and winked at Caris.

To his relief, she laughed in spite of herself. *"Reciting a ballad?"* She socked him in the arm. "I told you to stop doing that."

"Doing what?"

"Tricking people. Lying."

He sat back. "Caris, we're *in* a ballad. Everything we do is essentially like reciting a ballad. So how was that lying?"

"She came to me, too," she said abruptly. Her gaze fell to the floor between them. "In the barn." She glanced up, but had a hard time meeting his gaze.

It took him a moment to understand what she was saying. When he did, his eyes widened in fury. "My mother? When?"

"Before supper. I went to find you. That's when she found me. She was looking for me again, not you. No fog or anything. But she…said things." Caris swallowed. She dropped her head so her hair fell forward and concealed her face. She shrugged and gave a badly feigned laugh. "Scared her off, though. Named my sword."

Ignoring the clumsy diversion, he leaned forward on the edge of his chair and laid a hand on her knee. "What did she say?" When she failed to respond, he muttered a curse. "Don't tell me. She said I don't love you. She said I'm playing with you. That you could never be with me."

Caris shrugged again, confirming his guess and broaching a swell of anger and emotion that spilled from him in unplanned words. "Listen to me. She never, ever speaks the truth, Caris. Ever. *I love you,*" he said, before he could think. "And I don't give a flaming shit what she thinks of it."

He lifted her face with both hands, found her dark eyes filled with tears and confusion, and kissed her full and long on the lips.

She returned the kiss willingly, gently at first, then passionately, one hand raised to his cheek. A salt tear seeped to their lips.

It felt right. It felt like fire and vengeance. Was that what regular people felt?

"Boy?" Willard called from the table. Sounds of scraping benches and scooting chairs announced the end of supper. "Hate to interrupt your ballad recital, but I need you to saddle up Idgit. Brolli's heading back to the pass to watch our trail."

Caris pulled back, blushing, glowing with conspiratorial humor.

"Best girl in Arkendia," Harric murmured. Then to Willard, he said, "Coming!"

With a wink at Caris, he rose and limped for the door.

Brolli loped out before him. "I'll join you." The Kwendi chuckled as he preceded Harric down the stairs. Harric was sure he'd seen the kiss, and had some choice comments to make, but Brolli simply noted the food here was better than anything Willard ever cooked in camp.

Harric managed a dazed smile.

"You are well, yes?" Brolli said, looking over with concern. "You were talking to the chair."

Harric had to swallow a desire to laugh. "I'm just tired."

"Yes. Get rest, and I see you in a few days when I am returning from my watch."

Harric saddled Idgit and filled her saddle packs with enough grain for at least four days. Mudruffle brought a sack of provisions for Brolli.

"I do not require sustenance as you do," Mudruffle honked, "so there is no need to provision me. However, I am unable to bend or splay my legs as one must to sit on a saddle, so it is necessary to fasten me to the side of your saddle with a device I have prepared for this purpose."

Mudruffle held up a knotted jumble of ropes that he looped to the horn of Idgit's saddle and around the rear cantle. He held up a loop for their inspection. "This is for my feet. If you would be so kind as to lift me high enough for my foot to intersect with this loop, Master Harric, it will significantly speed the process."

Harric obliged, surprised at the warmth of the clay beneath his hands. His surface was malleable, yet firm, and not wet, though he was also lighter than Harric anticipated, like dry clay would be. Once he'd hoisted Mudruffle to the appropriate height, Harric guided the flat clay foot into the loop. Mudruffle twined his arms into the remaining knots and loops until he seemed irretrievably bound to Idgit's side, his feet angling forward under Brolli's stirrup, his body angling back, with the tricorn forester's hat tilted forward against an imaginary wind.

"To the untrained eye this method may seem haphazard," Mudruffle honked. "But I assure you it is the product of careful design and testing. I expect it will prove satisfactory for me and will cause your horse no discomfort."

Harric raised an eyebrow. Idgit was already peering back in what looked like alarm at the honking bundle at her side.

"Very good," said Brolli, climbing aboard. He gave Idgit a gentle pat, and Idgit seemed to accept his presence as proof that all was well. As they left, Harric had to laugh to himself. He'd never seen anyone less suited to horseback riding than Brolli, who now hunched over the saddle, great arms akimbo, but Mudruffle would jounce like a piece of ill-packed furniture.

"If we should encounter anyone on the road, I shall assume a rigid pose," said Mudruffle, "and you can act as though I am a work of statuary."

The Kwendi laughed and pointed to the north. "Look there! The Black Moon watches our departure. A good omen for our journey!"

Mudruffle jerked as if slapped. "You must not joke of such things. The Unseen is wicked and full of deceits. That would be an ill beginning indeed."

Harric waved as they entered the switchback trail beneath the fire-cones, chuckling to himself. He would miss the Kwendi's humor for the next three days.

When they disappeared, and he could no longer hear their murmuring voices, he laid his hand on the stone in his shirt and stalked in the opposite direction, past the white tower into darkness.

"Time to see what else this thing can do."

What is Seen is temporary, but what is Unseen is eternal.

—Credited to Lupistano Uscelana, Black Moon apologist

29

Father Kogan's Sacrifice

The trap door opened, and Miles's worried face, illumined by candle light, peered down through the hatch.

"The knights is gone, Father. Getting harder to please, though. They're gonna get mean next time."

Father Kogan climbed from the trap and closed it behind him. "Still asking for me, then? Thought they'd forget me by now."

Kogan extended an arm and examined it. The white had dwindled, but stubbornly persisted in places.

"They say they know you're hid up somewheres in the valley, Father, and that someone must know where, so they're fixing to make 'em talk."

Father Kogan frowned. "I don't reckon they mean you."

"No. Seems they got their sights set on some others. But I hate to bring misfortune down on anybody else."

"Time I led 'em away from this valley, then, Miles. I reckon I don't glow so much no more."

"Might be a good night for it, Father," Miles said, a note of eager encouragement in his voice. "I reckon the rest of that glow we can cover with mud and grease, too, so it won't shine so. I'll have Marta pack a sack with cheese and sausage."

"You're good folk, Miles. Luck smile on you." Kogan laid a grateful hand on the man's shoulder, then ducked through the door into the yard.

The night air smelled of new-mown hay, and the stars shone down in perfect clarity. The constellation of Arkus—creator of Arkendia, rebuke of the west, author of the Three Laws—shone down on him. He piously spat at it and muttered, "I'll help myself, thankee." Turning his back, he made his way to the barn to give his arms and braids a final scrub, and black them over with charcoal, just to be sure.

From the northeast came the pop of distant spitfires. His hunters, perhaps, camped in someone's fields for the night. Luck be thanked they didn't camp at Miles's or he'd have starved in that cellar.

When he'd finished his charcoal scrub, he felt sure he was just as black as he'd once been white, and chuckled at what he anticipated Marta would say if he tried to enter her house as a walking smudge. He charcoaled the carpets of his smothercoat for good measure, then slipped his head through the slits and strolled into the yard.

A sound like the bark of a dog in the distance greeted him from the northeast. He halted, stomach going cold, and strained his ears in silence. He heard it again, coming from the little wagon track that led to the place from the northeast. It wasn't a dog. Something else. He pried through darkness with his eyes until he picked out the track. On it moved a tiny dark spot against the lighter dust of the track.

The figure sobbed. That was the sound he'd heard. A boy or girl, he guessed, of some ten years. The child gasped, weaving as if it had run a long way.

Kogan retreated to the dark beside the barn, and watched. Caution taught him that those who ran in the night were often pursued, and he did not wish to be spotted if the pursuers were his own lordly enemies.

The boy threw himself against Miles's door, and pushed into the house as if he knew the place. Crying and sobbing began in earnest. Murmurs of consolation from Miles and Marta.

Kogan watched the road, waiting and listening. Snatches of the boy's cries came to him, and he pieced together what had happened at a neighboring farm. Knights had come. They killed the family pig. They made his family serve them. They hurt his sister. Hurt his granny. Not just bad hurt. Horrible hurt.

Sounds of consolation from Miles. The sobbing dimmed as they took the boy inside.

Marta scurried from the house and made a beeline for the barn.

"I'm here," Kogan murmured from the side. She startled, and rushed to him.

"O, Father...it's horrible..."

"I heard it. Breaks my heart."

"You ain't heard the worst, Father. That Phyros-rider is come at Flaxon's home. *Sir Bannus* is there—" she choked, and her hand shot to her mouth as if to hold her insides back.

"That ain't possible…" Kogan rumbled. But something cold and black and true as iron crept into his heart when she said it.

"Flaxon's boy Dovy's come just now and told us, and he ain't no fool, neither. He'd never make that up. But can it be true, Father? Can he really be back?"

"The boy can't be right. Lemme talk to him."

"Wait, Father, listen," she said, holding his wrist. "It's Sir Bannus and some horror of a squire, and they tortures Dovy's family. My boy let slip to Dovy that you is here, Father, and now little Dovy's wild that you should rescue them—"

The boy flew from the doorway and ran against Kogan's knees. Kogan scooped him up in his blackened arms and held him tight while the boy wept, tiny body convulsing.

"Will you save them, Father?" Dovy said when he could speak. "Take your ax and chop off their heads?"

Kogan looked sadly into the boy's tear-blasted eyes. "Only a one of the Blue Order can do that, Dovy. I'm just a regular man."

"But you're a peasant priest. You have to help them! They're hurting the bastard boy, Yort, and Granny! You don't know—I saw it—if you saw, you'd help, I know you would."

"Dovy, there ain't nothing we can do but hope, and wait till they're gone."

"No! I won't! They—they said it's you they want. They said if we tell 'em where you is they'll let my gran and the bastard go. Let go of me!"

Kogan held him fast in strong, gentle arms. "They'd only hurt you too, Dovy. Come on inside." Kogan carried the boy kicking and screaming into the house, and sat by the fire with the frantic boy on his lap.

"You mean they'd hurt *you*!" Dovy shrieked. "They'd hurt *you* and let Granny go!" His face contorted with silent weeping, but his eyes screamed innocent accusation.

Kogan felt the red rage swelling in his skull, roaring in his ears, and he clenched his jaw against it, recalling the Widow Larkin's wisdom on the night he fled his flock, against suicidal stands against injustice. He held her voice and face in his mind until the red subsided. Tears of frustrated rage welled up in its place. Dovy ceased his struggling and wept, exhausted, despairing.

"Let me tell you a story of Sir Willard and the Blue Order," Kogan murmured. He felt as dark and empty as the cellar in which he'd slept. If he could do a bit of good for his gran he'd give his life for her. But it would be worse than futile. They'd merely catch Dovy too, and foist their horrors on him. Or make him watch his sister's.

"I'll tell you, Dovy, how Willard and the Blue Order, in the Cleansing, how they drove the Old Ones from the land."

Dovy whimpered. "You don't know anything. *Bannus* is a blue man. Blue as sky. I've seen him."

"All immortals is blue, Dovy. I mean Sir Willard's order; they calls themselves the Blue Order. They're the good immortals. Only a member of the Blue Order can face up to an Old One. They did it, too, in the Cleansing, and killed them or drove them from the land."

"Where is the Blue Order now?"

"I don't know, Dovy. In their castle, I expect. But they'll bring justice. You can be sure of it. You'll see. They'll kill the rest of the Old Ones for good."

Marta sat beside them, her own son on her lap. She frowned at the cloud of charcoal surrounding Kogan, but let it go. "Miles is watching the road. If anything stirs, he'll warn us, and we'll all run to the forest."

Kogan told stories to soothe Dovy's misery, and to stave off his own futile rage. It seemed to still Dovy. Marta's boy fell asleep on the rug at the hearth, and eventually Dovy dropped into a twitching, whimpering sleep. Kogan laid Dovy gently in Marta's arms. "Best you keep the boy till Bannus abandons his homestead."

She nodded. "It ain't your fault, Father. You know that. You didn't wish this on nobody."

Kogan nodded, fists and jaw clenched.

"I set a pack of vittles by the door, Father. You aim to leave?"

He did not miss the implicit plea in her eyes; he nodded, and was sure he saw relief there.

"What'll you do, Father? Where'll you go?"

Kogan growled in his beard, something between a sigh and a grunt. "I'll head east into the mountains. I aim to find that fire-cone tower you told me on. Said there's an old Iberg there what the Queen lets do her magic?" He spat. "I'll bring that Iberg the word of Arkus, I will. Let her know magic don't belong here. And she's like to have pigeons, too: someone's gotta tell the Blue Order there's Old Ones about. But I don't mean to run oft and leave you with them monsters, mind. After I'm gone a day, you let on to Dovy that I've run up that pass, and let him inform on me. They'll reward him, that way. Least I can do."

Marta nodded. "I will. It's a day on a fresh horse to that fire-cone tower, mind. Take two day afoot, maybe three."

"I run good. An' once they're in the pass there won't be nobody to torture but me and an Iberg what deserves it."

Night Moon, Soul Moon, Spirit Moon, Fate Moon,
Cursed Moon, Dark Moon, Dead Moon.

—Names for the Unseen Moon

30

Foul Friends & Good Fortune

As Harric crossed the yard beneath the windows of the fire-cone tower, he heard Spook's familiar mew behind him. He turned to see the cat padding after him, purring and pleading with wide white eyes.

Harric picked him up to hush him, and carried him past the barns and up a dirt path amidst the long legs of the trees. The path took him over a rocky hump, beyond which he could no longer see the tower behind him, and down the broken spine of the ridge, where fire-cones mingled with massive roots among the rocks. Spook meowed again, but when Harric offered a piece of sheep cheese, the cat ignored it, peering up at him with blank white eyes.

The night air was cool, and a fresh breeze ran up from the valleys on either side. The stand looked eerily disjointed, cross-lit with the bi-color lights of the Mad Moon and the Bright Mother. As the Mother set in the west, fat and tumid near the horizon, she sent shafts of silver light slanting between the giant trunks. The Mad Moon, on the other hand, had gained on her in their monthly race across the sky. This night he straddled the opposite horizon—a bleary necrotic eye—peering aslant the limbs to stain her silver and slash the trees with strokes of bloody light. On the east side of the ridge, where the Mother could not reach, all was dark and lurid red.

Harric wandered down the ridge on a path beneath the fire-cones. It was longer than he expected—perhaps several bowshots from the tower in the center to the edge, where the ridge fell off steeply in a rocky cliff. He stopped before the edge to look out upon an expansive view of the wooded valleys on either side. The western valleys stood out in bi-lunar color, lit from the west by the Mother's silver light, and by the Mad Moon from above, so their shadows and the entire eastern side of the ridge seemed bloody, and the west a silvered pink.

Harric's heart quickened as he felt inside his tunic and drew forth the witch-stone to examine its glassy surface.

It looked different than he remembered it. Slick as water. Murky within. Shadows like clouds seemed to move there as he held it in the light of the Mother and Mad Moon. Shadows within shadows. A black fog, swirling in a double dome of nighted sky. It also seemed heavier now that it lay in his hand.

A link to the Unseen Moon. Was it a part of the moon itself, fallen to earth and collected by some vigilant magus? He had no idea. His mother's instruction in the natural history of the Black Moon extended no further than common Arkendian knowledge that its path was unpredictable, its period the hours of night, and that, unlike the other moons, it had no effect on the tides.

Harric located it easily, a vacant hole in the broad band of the constellation of the Cup.

Nebecci, Bellana, Tryst. The words came unbidden to his mind.

Visions of achievement paraded before his mind. He saw himself using the trick of invisibility in a dozen different scenarios: invisible, lifting another jack's loot; invisible, spying on Her Majesty's enemies; invisible, visiting Her Majesty's treasury…and personally depositing his taxes with a note. He'd keep his identity secret, but he'd be famous, his services sought by the greatest lords, by the Queen herself, and only the greatest could afford him. He wouldn't do it for the money, for he'd have plenty of that: he'd do it for the simple joy of it. The pure, unadulterated joy of supremacy, and the Westies would fear him. They'd call him the Jack of Souls, or the Ghost, or the Lynx, and they'd write ballads about him.

He laughed at himself, and hefted the stone in his palm.

Nebecci, Bellana, Tryst. There was only one way to find out.

He retreated beneath the protective shadow of the stand until a conjunction of limbs blocked both the Bright Mother and Mad Moon. To the north, the Black Moon still lurked near the horizon, a spy hole in the stars. Harric peered about, making sure no one was near. When satisfied he was alone, he lifted the witch-stone to the cat, as if toasting with a cup of wine. "To trickery!"

Then he fixed his eyes upon the empty moon, and spoke the words from the dream. "Nebecci, Bellana, Tryst."

The air before him opened as if he'd been leaning against a gate in the walls of reality and it suddenly gave way. He pitched headlong into a silent, eerie landscape of spirit and ghostly light, and an indefinable weight fell upon his mind, as if his will alone held the gates ajar. The burden of it was crushing.

He gasped. Yet he was also aware of a thousand details around him. The landscape was familiar—the massive trees, the broken ridgeline, the forest below—he was still in the same site on the ridge, but it was altered. Beautifully and gloriously altered.

From everything there came a faint, internal blue radiance—from rocks and soil, and wood and plants—but it shone brightest in living things. The trees, the grasses, moss and lichens on the rocks; these glowed like ghostly beacons in the pseudo-darkness of the night. Strangest of all was the air itself, which was filled with translucent strands of ghostly light, which rose from the ground like ribbons of blue smoke. The strands floated upward from everything—many as fine as hairs—undulating softly and streaming upward into the sky.

Collectively, these strands limited visibility to sixty paces. They also seemed to dampen sound. Together these qualities imparted an aura of quiet and tranquility.

Harric held his arms out before him and gasped in awe at what he saw. He was on fire with the brilliant strands. Swarms of them burgeoned from his hands—brilliant silken threads unimaginably fine and beautiful and multifarious; bright spider webs cast skyward in a breeze. He followed them with his gaze as they rose from the fire of his soul along some invisible current and mingled with the thousand-thousand filaments of everything around him.

But the sky! The night sky terrified him. Overwhelmed him. To behold it threatened madness, for there it seemed he saw the Web of Fate. The Tapestry of the Gods. And he knew with a certainty that came from part of him too deep to be reckoned, that this was a scene no mortal was intended to behold—pattern of life and rebirth endlessly cycling and complex and sublime.

Fear ballooned behind his ribs till it filled his chest and he could no longer breathe, but he could not look away.

The web moved, shifted, glimmered and undulated in a thousand ways too subtle to express.

Most terrible was the Unseen Moon itself, a noiseless, brooding spider in the center of its web. It was the eye of the spiritual storm around him, drawing all upward to the fringes of the loom, where they vanished in the patterns, or rose onward to its all-consuming well.

All of this he compassed in a single, eternal moment.

Then, from the black heart of the moon, eons distant, something acknowledged him. A pulse of spirit slid down the web, swift as a glimmer of light across water to the place where he stood on the earth below.

Harric recoiled, and something in him collapsed, unable to support the staggering weight of the gate to that world, which once again slammed shut before him.

He fell hard on his back in the loam beneath the fire-cones, and the silence of the Seen grew suddenly loud around him. Above him the web, the moon, had gone, replaced with the familiar shadows of trees against bright pricks of stars. Breath came and went in gasps from his lungs, as if he'd run a mile at top speed, and each labored breath brought aches to his ribs but he was helpless to stop it. His tunic clung to his skin, soaked with sweat.

In his hand, the witch-stone lay cool and silent. He stared at it in horror, and swallowed a knot that had come to his throat. *Gods leave me...what went wrong?*

That was no simple invisibility. He had entered the Unseen. He had breached the veil between worlds and glimpsed the machinations of eternity, a sight reserved for the dead. How he knew this, he couldn't say. He simply *knew*, as he knew gravity, or pain. The knowledge was part of him now, prematurely known, like a return from death itself in one of the ballads.

He wept. The enormity of reality—the gap between what he'd known before and what he now knew both humbled and terrified him. And yet, even as the tears streamed from his eyes, his memory of the eternal moon slipped away, too large for the canvas of his mind, until its vividness faded to mere impression, and the more he grasped after shreds of it the less he could recall.

His heartbeat slowed. His mind reassembled the ordinary reality that only moments before had seemed lost forever, and then he wept for joy. The image of the Black Moon fled. Like ice from a deep cave brought up to sunlight— not meant for this world—it melted to oblivion, leaving only the vaguest impression, the memory of memory.

He sat up, cradling his face in his hands.

If that's the price of invisibility...forget it.

And yet, if he could avoid looking at the moon... Perhaps that had been his mistake. And for all he knew the spell might have *worked*. He might *be* invisible even as he sat there. He climbed to his knees and examined his limbs. They appeared normal. The spell had not worked. Or at any rate, the spell did not cause him to appear invisible to *himself*. The moon cat lay twitching on its side. Its head lolled. Its lips foamed. It seemed the spell had affected the cat as well, and shocked it worse than Harric.

"Spook. Come here, Spook. Can you see me?"

The cat turned its glassy green eyes in his direction. Harric passed his hand in front of the animal's face, and Spook turned away in irritation, tried to gain its feet to flee, but fell over, panting weakly.

Harric sighed, disappointed. "You see me."

A raspy, nasal chuckle startled him from behind. "Look who's the genius."

Harric pocketed the stone and whirled to face the speaker. "Brolli? That you?"

Pointed teeth gleamed from a low shape hunched among the fire-cone roots. "Nebecci, Bellana, Tryst…" it answered, in the same scratchy nasal. With those words, the dim outline of the figure faded and disappeared. "Say it again." The voice returned from the same direction, but strangely altered, as if spoken through a culvert or pipe from very far away.

Harric's eyes widened. His voice came out in a hiss: "*Who are you?*"

"I'm your tryst. You called me, bright boy. Say it."

"My…? Well, I didn't mean to! It was an accident."

An eerie chuckle. "There are no accidents. *Say* it."

Harric gripped the witch-stone in his fist. He couldn't run. Who would he run to? They'd all know he'd been stupid enough to *summon* something with a witch-stone.

There was a rustle of dust as the invisible figure moved toward him.

Harric flung his hand before him to ward the creature off. "Wait!" He braced himself. Faintly, without hope, he pronounced the words, "Nebecci. Bellana. *Tryst.*"

This time the Seen disgorged him fully into the spirit world—it left no doorstep of the Seen from which to safely gaze—and the unspeakable weight of the Unseen fell again upon his mind. Above him the web exploded into clarity—the black hole in its center sucking and spitting the ghostlike threads up and away in its cycles of spiritual tide. He groaned, and forced his eyes down to the shadowless version of landscape around him.

The source of the mysterious voice hunkered there in crystal clarity, only paces away. "First time?" it rasped. "Not bad."

Harric choked and stumbled backward, but his eyes did not leave the figure. Black membranous wings folded untidily behind a horned, hairless black head and a long, bulbous nose. The very image of a trickster sprite from an Arkendian impit tale. Naked legs akimbo, it squatted in the dirt, taloned black hands folded before it, a whiplike tail nestled around its feet. Wide, white, pupilless eyes greeted Harric with a look of cunning and twisted humor above a mouth filled with hundreds of needlelike teeth.

"Go on, you can tell me: you've done this before, right? It runs in your family?"

"Wha—no! Who are you?" Harric's face perspired with effort of supporting the weight upon his mind. By concentration he could hold himself in the

Unseen, but only with tremendous effort. He was already gasping for breath as if he'd been holding up a tree.

"Finkoklocos Marn, at your service," said the creature. It scampered to its taloned feet and stood before him, eyes level with Harric's navel, and performed a mocking bow. What Harric had taken to be the creature's smile mutated into a horrible grin. "My friends call me Fink. You and me? We're gonna be friends, so you call me Fink too."

Harric groaned and collapsed to his knees. The gate collapsed around him, and the familiar world of the Seen embraced him. Sweat poured from him. Fragments of the brief vision of the Unseen crushed in upon his soul again; echoes of the revelation of the afterworld that he strove to consign to oblivion as soon as they came. His breath came in painful heaves. He wanted unbearably much to seek forgetfulness in sleep, but didn't dare close his eyes near the monster he'd summoned.

Spook mewed somewhere near him.

In the air before him, the crouching figure of Finkoklocos Marn snapped into leathery clarity. The imp scampered up to Harric. In his exhaustion Harric could only raise his head to watch as it licked the tip of a taloned finger with a long black tongue, and laid it carefully to Harric's forehead between his eyes. The contact seared like fire, and penetrated inward like a red-hot nail through wax. Harric moaned, but lacked the strength to draw away. He closed his eyes, and in the darkness saw the imp's talon withdraw from a teardrop-shaped aperture near the top of his consciousness. Through it he saw the world of the Unseen moving silently beyond, as through a high attic window in his mind. Yet his hand felt no such gouge through his skin.

He opened his eyes in dazed surprise. The imp popped into the Seen before him. Its hideous grin widened in satisfaction.

Roaring rose in Harric's ears. Darkness crowded his vision, threatening to overwhelm him. Somewhere, his mother screamed in rage. Then all went black.

The air beside Fink tore open with a roar of protest as his sisters manifested in the Seen. The three of them loomed above him in the dark beneath the trees, pillars of brooding shadow.

"Sisters!" Fink said, feigning surprise and delight. "How nice of you to visit. How are things in the Web?"

The largest of them, Siq, stirred. She glided forward until she looked down on Harric's prone body. Fink hid his irritation behind a grin. She wouldn't dare touch Harric, but he could see by the vagueness of her form that it had been long since she feasted. The same appeared true for Missy and Sere. When Siq spoke, her voice was a faded whisper. *"Will he trust you?"*

Fink shrugged. "Too soon to tell." Taunting her, he scooped a few of the cat's soul-strands, and slurped them through his teeth like noodles. "But this little catty gives me a good shell to hide and watch his dreams, learn about him. He's an odd bird. I think he'll trust."

The cat rolled to its feet and rubbed against his leg. He reached down to scratch it behind the ear, but on seeing the talon of his forefinger, thought better of it.

"We question your choice of form."

"You don't like it?" Fink extended all five talons of the hand, admiring his handiwork. "I'm an impit, from his fairy tales, see? They talk this way and everything."

"We are not pleased."

"Yeah? Well, it pleases me," he said, emphasizing the vulgarity of speech he'd found in Harric's memories of impit tales. "And anyway, that's why I go in the cat. But this kid's sharp. If I show up like a feathered angel he'll smell the lie."

A low murmur from Missy. "You take to the impit form naturally. Almost, it seems, it is your true form."

Fink displayed the forest of needles in his jaws. "Maybe I *am* an Impit, Missy. Now unless you have a token from Mother, expressing her doubts, buzz off. I need some space."

The three brooded above him, silent and menacing, then vanished, the air sucking upon itself with a vicious clap.

Fink scampered to Harric's side, enjoying the nimbleness of the form, but tipped over when he stopped, as he'd neglected to fold his left wing in. He studied Harric, his bald head cocked to one side, scowling. He'd spent long hours in Harric's dreams and memories. Siq could question all she wanted. He'd chosen the right form.

"Harric?"

Fink's head snapped in the direction of the woman's voice. He arranged Harric's arms to look as though the man slept, and vanished with a pop into the Unseen.

"Harric!" The big girl strode into the clearing, a lantern in one hand, a huge iron sword on her hip. She stood over Harric, a look of perplexity on her face, then knelt at his shoulder and shook him. "Harric, what are you doing? Wake up."

He did not awake.

The cat padded over to her, mewing. The girl's brow furrowed.

Curious, Fink manipulated a few of Harric's strands so he would not wake even if she burned him with her lantern. When he did not respond to a more vigorous shaking, she let out a broken cry of pain, and half fell upon, half embraced him.

"Harric!" She laid her cheek to his lips and froze there, feeling for breath, Fink guessed. Panic growing, she shifted her ear to his chest, and froze again. At last, she sighed, tears welling in her eyes, and embraced him, weeping quietly.

When she recovered, she raised her face to his. "Moons take you, Harric. What are you doing here?" She glanced around the clearing for clues.

She frowned, and stared at his inert face for so long Fink considered leaving. Then, without warning, she kissed him hard and full on the lips, like a horse sucking water at a stream. When she came up for air she gave a guilty look around, blushing (Blushing! For *that!*), then laid another on him that might have been twice as long as the first.

The cat directed a bored look at Fink in the Unseen, and began licking itself.

Bored, Fink moved to tweak Harric's strands to see if he could wake him, but she came up for air first, and he decided to see what she'd do next? *Climb on top?* He grinned.

"That's what you get for giving me this cursed ring."

She wiped her lips on a sleeve, studied him as if she might lay another, even longer, then she shook herself and stood. Muttering a curse, she lifted him in arms twice the size of his and carried him back toward their tower.

The Unseen Moon is neither unseen, nor a moon. Any fool can find it if he isn't scared to look, and since it pulls no tides and takes no predictable path through the stars, it cannot be a moon like the others. At least not of physical dimensions.

— From Heretical Maunderings, Master Tooler Jobbs

31

A New World

Harric woke to something nudging his shoulder. His hand drifted over to push Spook away, but found instead a boot. He opened his eyes to see Willard standing over him beneath the timber ceiling of the tower.

"Get up, son. You've got work to do."

Harric sat up and looked around. He found himself on a fat woolen mattress before the hearth. Outside the window, dawn still slumbered, a mere lightening of the eastern sky.

He had no memory of how he got there. The last thing he remembered from the night before was the forest in the bicolor light of the moons, and…

A lance of fear smote him as images of the creature he'd summoned flooded back to him. He closed his eyes, terrified of what he might find in the dark of his skull, only to have his fears confirmed by the sight of the tear-drop aperture the imp had poked through the veil of his mind; beyond it he saw the ghostly world of the Unseen, with its floating strands and eerie glow.

Gods leave me, what have I done?

Harric opened his eyes and watched Willard toss sticks on the fire. He imagined telling the old knight of it, but shame and pride killed the impulse. Brolli might understand; perhaps he could confide in the Kwendi when he returned from the pass. But not Willard. Not Caris. And surely not Abellia.

Until Brolli returned, he was alone in this.

Caris rose from an identical mattress nearby, and pulled a heavy tunic over her shirt. She squinted at Willard, who crouched by the hearth with no apparent pain.

"You're well?" she asked, voice rough with sleep.

Willard turned from the fire. "Surprised?" The old knight's eyes blazed as if with suppressed fury. His cheeks looked pink and healthy, his gaze clear and bright, and no bandage wound about his waist. "Hardly a mark where that wound was, today." He slapped his hip to illustrate. "Seems it closed on its own last night. I'd give the credit to good old Arkendian avoidance of magic, but I'm no fool. Our hostess healed me." His gaze drilled into Caris, who dropped her eyes and busied herself with her boots.

Willard grunted, as if confirmed in his suspicions she'd been involved.

"Guess sleeping's considered unconscious," Harric observed.

"So it seems," said Willard. "They get you too?"

Harric ran a hand over his own injured ribs, expecting tenderness, but found no pain at all. The lumps on his head were absent, and the swelling below his eye. *Healed!* Had Abellia found him in the forest and brought him back? And if so, had she learned his secret? *Ridiculous,* he realized. *She can barely walk alone, much less carry me out of the forest.* He must've returned under his own power before she came down to tend their wounds.

"Darn," Harric said. "I was really looking forward to a month of healing the Arkendian way."

Willard lit a rag-roll with a burning stick from the hearth. His eyes flashed to Harric, unamused. When the roll burned hotly, he climbed to his feet and made his way to the door, a simple crutch under one arm. He still limped, Harric realized. The old witch apparently hadn't healed everything; something still nagged him—perhaps an old wound, or he was finally feeling the effects of his long-delayed age.

"We'll be staying long enough to rest the horses," Willard said. "If Bannus follows us, we'll hole up in this tower, so we need it ready for the horses. Enough hay for at least a week. Fill the troughs with water. Bring over the saddles and tack. Is there much to clear out, girl?"

Caris stood. "No, sir. A small armory only."

"Show me."

Caris threw on her boots and trotted out the door, followed by Willard.

Harric climbed to his knees and cradled his head in his hands. The breach in the top of his consciousness shone bright in his mind, and larger than he remembered it. Was it widening? Would he eventually see nothing but the spirit world when he closed his eyes, like the second sight his mother could never control? The thought breathed new life into his old fears of madness. Heart pounding, he peered through the aperture, searching for clues and catching the tail ends of the brilliant blue spirit strands rising up from Caris and Willard. The flames in the hearth, on the other hand, appeared as greedy black tongues casting no light at all. He tried closing the aperture by concentrating on it, but if anything it grew wider the more attention he paid it. Ignoring it was impossible, for it flashed before him with every blink.

Dazed, he stumbled from the room and down the curving stairs, afraid to be alone. Outside, he found Caris and Willard talking in the yard. Caris had removed a pile of gear from the armory, which she now held before her in both arms: quilting, practice swords, and pot helms so old they might have been fashioned when Willard was a boy. On her face she wore an expression of determination and controlled excitement that gave Harric a twinge of panic.

"A little sparring?" Willard asked Harric, amusement in his eyes. "Your paramour here wants a lesson in bladework. Put on that quilting. You can help."

The look of determination Harric had glimpsed in Caris's face now bloomed into exultation. She tossed him a musty quilt.

Harric held it out before him. "She's not the one who's going to need help."

Caris donned her quilting and examined the practice sword she drew from its sheath. Though its edge had been blunted, its polish was immaculate. Indeed, all the gear, though old, was spotless. Mudruffle's work, he guessed.

Harric donned the quilting and pot helm and stood across from Caris with a shield on one arm and a practice sword in the other, determined to at least hold his own.

Willard leaned heavily on the crutch beneath one arm, and studied them, clouds of ragleaf gusting from his lips. "The most important thing you must learn about swordsmanship is not so much the *how to*, as the *why to*. We aren't mercenaries, we're knights. Queen's Knights. A mercenary draws his sword whenever he's paid to, but a Queen's Knight draws only under the Code of Protection, which means in three situations: in the defense of your queen, in the defense of her people, and in self-defense. That's it. A few of the popular orders these days forget this code, thinking it weak, and go out seeking honor and renown with the Order of the Dragon, or the Order of the Bear, or the Order of the Flame. Troublemakers. And if you want to learn to blast a spitfire, you'll have to go elsewhere for it. I'm going to teach you my way," he said, fingering his earring. "The Order of the Flea. I built my reputation on it. You don't hear ballads about spitfire knights.

"Now, normally in an apprenticeship you'd spend a couple of years polishing my armor and tending my horses before I let you pick up a sword. But considering our circumstances, girl, I'd prefer to know what you can do if we run into trouble. We'll keep with regular fitness training and practice each day while we're here, and whenever we can manage on travel days. That goes for you too, Harric."

Willard raised a practice sword and beckoned to Caris.

"Let me see your standard attacks, girl—say, Claxon or Ear Whistle; I'll parry with the Fiddler or Salute. Watch closely, Harric."

Harric watched as Caris leveled a series of crisp attacks on Willard, and the knight parried. After several repetitions, Willard called a halt. "Now it's your turn, boy. Same attacks, only against the girl."

Harric faced Caris, and met her eyes for the first time since she'd promised to leave him if he didn't give up trickery. Her gaze was steel. All business, true to her promise, even if it hurt her. Yet he could also see in the sleepless rings under her eyes that the struggle against her heart was taking a toll.

He performed the Claxon with as much vigor as he could summon, and Caris parried with Fiddler.

Willard frowned.

"You're putting all your weight into it, boy. In a real fight the Claxon's bound to lodge in someone's shield, and that's bad. Even if you wedge it in her head, you can't parry the next man when your sword's stuck in the first. Understand? Control is the thing. Give it just enough power to get the job done. Forget the glory blow. A quick cut kills as well as beheading."

Harric nodded, and labored to heed the advice. Then it was Caris's turn to attack, and though it was the same move each time, she came on with such ferocity that Harric was instantly in retreat.

"The same thing goes for the parries, son. Grand motions like that are good for a stage, but not a fight. Sweeping parries overcompensate and leave you open for another attack. See? She got you. Only Gregan's Lie is meant to be a grand and sweeping parry, and it's meant for very unusual circumstances. Are you concentrating, boy? You're about as dull as a sheep's tail this morning."

"Sorry," Harric said. *I'm distracted,* he wanted to add. *I summoned a monster and might have ruined my life and afterlife, and every time I blink the spirit world flashes through a hole in my head.*

Caris raked her gaze over Harric, her chin high, cheeks flushed. There was triumph in her eyes, as if she'd proved a point or won an argument with him.

"Look, I'm just tired—" he began, but she turned away and spoke to Willard.

"Spar with me," she said.

Willard's eyes darkened as he studied her eager face. Harric thought he detected a kind of veiled curiosity in his look, but there was also real opposition and distaste. "Think you're ready for that, do you?" said Willard. Caris nodded. "Very well. You're out, son. But watch as we spar, and pay attention to my movements. Small. Economical. Just enough to get it done. Understand?"

Harric nodded—relieved, for he had bigger troubles to worry about. Removing the heavy helm, he sat back against the tower, and as Willard donned his gear, he closed his eyes.

The teardrop window hung high in his mind like the rosette in the gable of his chambers in Gallows Ferry. The sight of it sent a stab of fear through his middle. Memory of the hideous creature who'd put it there flashed through his mind, and he shuddered, opening his eyes to banish the image.

Is it any worse than your mother? he asked himself. *No. So be strong, Harric. You need this.*

He closed his eyes again, and forced himself to study the tear-shaped window. The thing wasn't as bright as it had been when he first awoke. The indirect light of approaching dawn appeared to dim it. But he could still see the vague movements of the spirit world beyond—horrifying, but also fascinating. It was, after all, a window into the mysteries of the Unseen. What treasures must wait there! It was the surprise of the thing that made it so bad last night. Once he got used to it, he might not be bothered at all. And perhaps next time if he could avoid staring into the face of the Unseen Moon—into the soul-blinding mystery of existence itself—if he could avoid doing that again, then he might use it to banish his mother forever, and even master the trick of invisibility.

Tentatively, he strained upward to get a better look through, and when he managed it, the sight awed and thrilled him. Vision was less distinct in the Unseen, because the numerous ghostly filaments drifting up from almost everything around him formed a kind of spiritual mist that softened lines and contours, and because the advancing dawn blacked out the subtler shades of spirit light, just as his normal vision darkened at the approach of night.

Nevertheless, Willard and Caris still blazed with silver-blue internal light, and from their forms rose sheaves of wavering filaments like columns of light to the sky.

The beauty and complexity of Caris's soul took Harric by surprise. It was bewitching. Hypnotic. She was the center of a spiritual bonfire, a spirit alight with ghostly blue fire. Stranger yet, it seemed she was enwrapped in deep black hoops, lightless and opaque. The hoops plunged into her breast and flared out behind her like circular wings, pushing and stretching and redirecting the Unseen strands that rose from her spirit.

In a moment of insight, he realized what this was: it was the magic of the triple wedding ring. *That means it's Unseen magic that makes Caris love me.*

The notion was astounding. Could the Black Moon hold sway over the forces of love? Harric licked his chipped tooth, pondering, trying to get his mind around the concept. In a way, it made sense. Matters of the heart were literally unseen, obscure, dark. Why not love, then?

New possibilities flooded his mind. Could he use his Unseen vision to help get the ring off?

"Wake up, boy!" Willard said. "This is for your benefit. It isn't nap time."

Harric opened his eyes, heart bursting with joy. He wanted to shout out what he'd seen, but he dared not reveal how he knew it. Instead he tried to hide his now-labored breathing and the dizziness he felt from holding himself so high in his mind for so long.

"Something funny about that?" Willard asked, mistaking Harric's gasping for laughing.

"No, sir," Harric said, feigning a cough. "I was just…thinking about what you said." He did not dare look at Caris.

Willard frowned, and turned to Caris.

"All right, come at me, girl. Let's see what you've got, and don't hold back because I look lame, or I'll clobber you to get you mad. Do your best. This is a test."

Willard braced himself on the crutch as Caris stalked him. She tested him at first, feeling his defenses and exploring his style with a practiced air. Even Harric could see that her form was superb. This was her element. She was as much a fighter as a cat was a hunter of mice; the sword was as natural in her hand as the claws in Spook's paw.

Nevertheless, Willard breached her defenses and gave her a good, loud smack with the flat of his blade. "You're not trying, girl. Give me all you've got."

Harric had to hand it to the old knight: he was fair; he seemed to *want* her to impress him.

Caris drew his attack with a feint, took his blade high with her shield, dropped, and swung at his unprotected legs. However, her stroke was intercepted by a quick move of the knight's crutch, and the next moment her helmet rang with the impact of his sword.

"That was the Thresher…" The knight laughed, breathing heavily and replanting his crutch. "You don't see that too often these days, I'll wager." Caris glared from within the helmet. "Don't give me that look. You aimed the Millstone at an old man's legs! You deserved it."

Caris flew at him anew.

Harric could not resist closing his eyes again to see her soul afire in the Unseen. He experimented with widening the window, and found he could do it by pressing more of his consciousness up and through the opening, but only with much exertion, and success brought with it an odd, detached feeling, which was not at all pleasant. His shirt clung to the sweat of his back, and his lungs began to labor as if he stood on tiptoes and with someone else on his shoulders. Gasping, he abandoned it and opened his eyes to watch in the Seen.

"It's all right, girl," Willard said to Molly, as she glared at Caris from the spot where Willard had picketed her, pawing up clods of earth.

Crows scolded from the branches of the fire-cones above.

None of this penetrated Caris's focus.

She changed tactics, circling away from his sword arm and leveling most attacks to his head, which made it difficult for him to riposte, since he was continually forced to readjust his crutch amidst the hail of blows.

The sound of steel on steel resounded off the ridge above.

Willard stumbled several times, and his breathing grew ragged. When his crutch faltered on a stone, he tottered sideways and Caris lunged for the opening. In the same instant the knight's control returned as if it had never been gone, and with a quick turn of his weapon Caris's blade spun from her grip. He placed his point lightly on her shoulder, his crutch set firmly.

"I've seen that one, too," he panted, eyes blazing. "But never from a novice. Pick it up! Show me again."

Something caught Harric's attention beyond the spirit window. Peering through, he realized it was Caris: despite the dimming effect of approaching dawn in the Unseen, her spirit had grown brighter. The looping black rings that bound her wavered, trembled—actually *smoked*, it seemed, like grass too close to a fire.

"Come at me!" she shouted to Willard. "Come on!"

"I can't, girl. I have to wait for you to come to me. As you know, I'm not very mobile."

"*You're not lame.*" Caris snorted. "It's a trick. To make me overconfident. To distract me and lure me in. Let's see you come at me. Come on!"

"I tell you, I have to wait for you to come in range."

"Bah!"

Large square teeth flashed behind Willard's gigantic mustachios. "Go ahead and wait, then. I can use the rest."

Caris lunged, engaging, retreating, rotating and lunging, circling and forcing him to turn to face her. Grass tore and flew beneath her boots. Willard kept the crutch planted and pivoted on his skinny legs, kicking the odd rock from beneath his footing. She tried a dozen feints and attacks in a dozen combinations and scored a few glancing blows against him, but she refused to count them in light of the solid strokes he'd landed on her.

Harric let himself become hypnotized by the steady succession of movements and themes, and marveled at this window to her identity. To watch her fight, Harric realized, was to watch the deepest fires in Caris, and it was profoundly moving. In that moment, he desired her more than ever.

Caris landed the final blow—a solid cuff to the knee. A heartbeat later, the sun peeked over the hill, and the window in Harric's mind vanished as if it had never been.

"Gods leave me, that felt good," Willard said. He stripped the helmet from his head, beaming. "I haven't had a good sweat like that in moons. I'm going to pay for this in pains tomorrow. Down to my last roll of ragleaf, too, but it might just be worth it."

As they caught their breath, Willard studied her. Caris's eyes glinted with stoic pride, and he frowned.

"Don't be smug, girl," said Willard. "Your disengage is over-large, and your eyes tell me where your next blow is coming almost every time."

Caris blinked in surprise. She opened her mouth, closed it, and before she found her voice, the old knight had turned away to face Harric.

"You're as wet as if *you* were the one sparring, son. Get fit. Set a practice dummy in the stable and practice what you've learned here. I don't say it's necessary for a valet-squire to carry a sword, but it would shame your blood not to." He indicated the green blood line on Harric's bastard belt with a nod. "Dawn again tomorrow. The both of you."

"Yes, sir," Harric said.

"Yes, sir," Caris mumbled, turning to the barn. Her hands rose to cover her ears as she strode off through the doors. Harric felt a twinge of embarrassment for her, even though Willard had already turned and hadn't seen her reaction. The old knight limped along the side of the tower, gouts of ragleaf smoke swirling in his wake. "I expect that tower stocked for horses by midday," he called over his shoulder. "Get it done before the day's heat."

Harric sighed, and followed Caris into the barn. He wouldn't approach her now, but he'd be near if she needed to talk. Rag nickered in greeting as they entered, her ears pricked and alert. Caris went to her, and Rag nuzzled her ear. Rag seemed eager for a run in a field. Indeed, all signs of her exhaustion had vanished, something he wouldn't have expected to see until after a week or two of rest.

"Looks like she's had a visit from the healer too," he murmured.

Caris disappeared behind Rag, retreating farther from communication. *Into the horse world*, Harric guessed.

He picked up a bucket to bring water into the troughs, and was just leaving when Willard's voice startled him from the yard outside. "Harric? You in there?"

"Here, sir."

The old knight appeared in the doorway. In silhouette, the incongruence of huge arms and torso over spindly legs seemed more absurd than ever. The knight's eyes found Harric, then scanned the barn from under bristling brows. "I suppose you think you're pretty smart setting me up against the girl." The eyes twinkled in a cloud of ragleaf.

Harric returned his gaze without expression. "Told you she could fight."

Willard snorted. "You did *not* tell me." His brows rose for emphasis. "You said she could 'fight.' You never said she could *fight*. Trying to get me killed?"

"No, sir."

Willard grunted. He scanned the barn again, then stumped back out the door.

When Harric heard the tower door bang behind the knight, he turned and peered into the darkness at the back of the barn. "Hear that?" he said, trying to locate Caris in the gloom. "I think that's as close to a compliment as you're going to get."

Caris stepped from Rag's stall, beaming. A laugh of shared joy burst from Harric's lips as he crossed to her and snatched her into a tight embrace before she could recoil. In spite of herself, she gave him a swift squeeze.

He let her go and stepped back. "He knew you were here, you know. I think you shocked him out of his mind for a while, and he had to wander off to collect his wits."

She blushed. "He made me so mad I had to come in here."

"That's as close to approval as you'll get, so savor it."

"I don't care. He said it, and now I know it." Her chin rose, but her gaze also softened. She seemed to want to speak or reach out to him, but didn't know how, so she stood there, brow pursed.

"You're welcome," Harric said gently.

She flushed, and nodded curtly.

"Girl!" Willard called from somewhere outside.

"Coming." She gave a rueful smile and left.

Harric watched, heart rising. He ran his gaze over the shapely shoulders under her clinging shirt, and the graceful hips no longer enfolded in steel.

"Fool," he muttered to himself as she disappeared. He turned back to brushing Idgit. "It's not her that wants you; it's the ring."

Rag glanced over and snorted.

"Not worth it?" Harric said, as if she had spoken. "Oh, I think you're wrong there."

By midday they'd filled the troughs in the tower and packed the hoppers with hay. Once they'd moved their saddles in, Caris climbed the stairs to rest in the gallery with Abellia and Willard, and Harric went to the barn loft, where he fell fast asleep.

He woke with Spook warm against his side, when the light in the hayloft window had dwindled to a faint gray square, and the teardrop hole had reappeared in his mind.

The sight of the hole turned his stomach.

Part of him had hoped it had been permanently erased by the morning sun. Maybe all he had to do to be clear of the whole mess was find the imp in the forest and return the witch-stone to him. The rest of him, however, knew all too well if he turned over the stone, he'd have no way to drive off his mother. And the thought of her continued haunting was unbearable. Anything would be better than that.

He'd find the imp that night, and use the witch-stone to drive his mother off for good.

Despite this resolution, however—or perhaps because of it—anxiety plagued him the rest of the day. He managed to engage in conversation with the others in the tower, and drank rather more of the honey wine than he intended, but none of it diverted his worries, and none of it sped the coming of night, when all would be asleep and he could leave the tower.

When Willard finally rose with a yawn from his seat at the window, Abellia had long since retired, and Caris was fast asleep by the hearth.

Harric masked his worry by echoing the yawn. "Dawn practice again, sir? I'll be there."

Willard grunted. He leaned out the tall west windows, frowning, then drew back in and closed them fast. "We'll close these up tonight, to keep out the damp. I'm a hen's ass if I don't feel a fog coming on."

It took a moment for this to sink into Harric's distracted awareness, but when it did, hairs on his neck stood on end, and he froze. "Fog? Here on the mountain?"

Willard crossed the room and closed the east windows with a noisy sigh. "Doesn't seem likely, I know. But after your second or third century you get a sense for such things." He winked at Harric as he limped through the door of the closet they'd converted to his bedroom. "Besides, I can see it in the valley, creeping up the slopes like a line of specters. Sleep well, son."

He makes a poor smith who fears sparks.
He makes a poor priest who fears death.

—Arkendian Proverb

32

Father Kogan Fills His Belly

Kogan stared at the signpost, chewing at his beard. There were letters on the sign, which made his eyes ache, and made him wish he had the Widow Larkin with him. She had a head for letters and would straight tell him what they said. The letters stood out clear, and there was a fresh painting of the crown in one corner of the placard, which meant it was the Queen's sign. But under the paint was a faded mark. A handprint, it was. What you see when a guard bids you stop.

"Like as not it says, *Turn back, Queen's land*," he muttered. He shifted the massive Phyros ax to his other shoulder, and took a long drink from his water skin. The water was still cold from the last stream he crossed, and tasted good in spite of the tang of the skin, which tasted like it once had wine in it. He'd been hiking without sleep since he left Marta and Miles. A day straight, that was, and he was dog tired. But no matter. He'd jog a while and get his blood moving.

He hadn't taken a step when he noticed the sound of hoofbeats from the wood he'd just emerged from. Many hooves, and near, by the sound of them. He hadn't noticed their approach because he'd been puzzling over the sign.

Stepping behind a boulder the size of a shed, he hunkered down on his heels, cursing the invention of letters and signposts. The deep thud of the hooves and the ring and clack of armor told him it was a company of armored knights on destriers; if he'd been spotted, it would be a short battle.

When the company of knights drew adjacent his position, the leader called out, and the hoofbeats quieted to the sound of blowing horses. He judged the nearest was so close a normal man could have stood where he was and spit on it, though he himself could likely spit on several, as he could spit farther than any man he knew.

He sank as low as he could between his heels, and leaned his back flat against the boulder. Intending to hold his breath and listen, he was halfway through a deep intake of air when a whiff of perfume struck him in the nose like an ax and he gagged on the foul stuff such that only the lucky approach of another thundering company saved him from being heard.

Two dozens of knights and retainers now, he judged. Holding the ax with one hand, he used the other to pull up a fold of his smothercoat to sift the air.

"Fire-cone pass," a man called back to the rear of the company. "Sign says no open flames, and no spitfires past this point." A dozen men laughed in chorus.

"Good thing we don't have spitfires," said one.

"Indeed. Dismount! We'll break for a piss and a drink. Fetch wine!"

Someone dismounted so near that their shadow in the early morning sunlight flashed across the dirt next to Kogan. Kogan reset his grip on the ax. *This is it.* The first to step around the boulder with his cob in his hand to piss would fall in two pieces. Then he'd make his stand against the boulder and wouldn't be satisfied until he took at least twelve with him, and he'd know when he lost count that he could rest.

"Hold!" the leader called. "Belay that order. Something stinks like a pig's ass here."

"Rot, you're right," said voice so loud its owner could be no more than a stride from rounding the boulder. "It rotting stinks to the moons. That Phyros piss?"

"No. If we find confirmation of Willard's passing, I'll send you with word to His Holiness. Saddle up! I'll find a spot that doesn't fist rape my nose."

Kogan ground his teeth. *Least I don't smell like a lady's pillowcase, ye silk-button cockerel. Wouldn't know a proper smell if I rolled you in it.* The company remounted and rode. When he judged the last had gone, Kogan shifted until he could see their diminishing backs in double file on the road. A shining company of oranges and yellows and one green, with lances and pennons flying. He counted them to twelve almost twice. Half were armored knights, the rest squires and grooms with heavy spitfires and crossbows balanced across their saddles.

Willard may have come that way, too. Gods leave me, I hope I haven't led them to ye, Will.

He sat back down against the boulder and laid the ax across his thighs. He wouldn't travel again until nightfall. No telling where the company would camp or leave spotters, or when they might send messengers back down the road.

He woke to the sound of creaking axles and the murmur of men's voices. By the sun's position, he guessed it late afternoon. When the source of the noise passed, he peered out and saw a cart full of workmen and another full of tools and great piles of hemp rope like they were going to a siege. It occurred to him then that Willard could be holed up in the very tower Kogan had set out to find. "I'll be a pig's ass after all." He chuckled. He toyed with the idea of following the troupe and causing mischief amongst their ranks. *Not that I owes you anymore, Will. But I might like it if you owe me one for a change.*

He waited till sunset and the Bright Mother rose, then set out hiking east on the road. As he chewed the last of the bread Marta had given him, he crested a ridge and got his first view of the fire-cone stand and its thunder-rod. He'd nearly make it there before sunrise, he gauged, unless darkness slowed him or he encountered a camp of knights.

He'd scarcely thought this when he heard a rider approaching from ahead. He hid in the trees in time to see a knight pass, heading back down the road with a message. Too late it occurred to him he might have waylaid the man to intercept the message and take the food in his panniers.

The next time he heard a rider's hooves, he stepped behind a tree and waited with ax in hand. Peering around the tree, he tried to determine if the rider were a knight or perhaps just a workman. He didn't want to take out a workman. Likely as not, they were good common folk forced into service by the knights. But the moonlight under the trees was broken and he couldn't get a clear look before the man got too close and he had to duck back. He could call out, "Who goes there?" but that risked revealing himself to a squire who could loose a crossbow bolt into his gut or spur past and alert the priest hunters.

Cursing, he'd resolved to let the man pass unmolested when the stink of perfume relieved all doubt of innocent workmen. When the horse's head passed the tree, Kogan grabbed the reins with one hand and swept the hapless squire from the saddle with the broad side of the Phyros ax.

The man crashed into another tree on the way down, and the horse went berserk. Kogan held the reins down and kept the beast's head low until it responded to his cooing and gentling and ceased to struggle. The man didn't move. Even the broad side of a Phyros ax left few survivors. He stroked the animal's nose, and spoke kindly, and soon he was able to loop the reins over a branch and leave it while he explored the saddlebags. He had a way with beasts that way. Never panicked himself, and they responded to that.

In the panniers he found cheese and bread and a flagon of wine, all of which he downed while the horse munched a handful of carrots. When he pilfered the rest of the food—a bag of dried beef and apricots—he set the horse free and left the squire his purse so it would appear he wasn't robbed, but thrown from his horse.

In a shard of light from the moon, the squire's dead eyes stared accusingly at Kogan.

"It's the gods' war," the priest said as he stepped over him. "In the name of Krato, you'd have done a sight worse to me."

Though life and well-being come only from the Bright Mother, and the Mad Moon
gives power to destroy, such is but the endless round of death and rebirth in this
sphere.
In the Unseen lies transcendence.

— From the banned Iberg tract "Void of Salvation," credited to
Lupistano Uscelana, Black Moon apologist

33

The Unseen

When the door closed behind Willard, Harric raced across the room and opened the shutters to peer into the forest, which was now splattered with the silver light of the Mother. No fog around the tower, but through the trees he caught glimpses of the valley below, which was bright with silver fogbanks advancing up its sides.

Harric buckled on his sword and flew down the stairs. Memories of the fog in Gallows Ferry made him tremble as he reached the bottom of the tower. Forcing himself forward, he laid his shaking hands on the bar securing the outer door, heaved it up, and opened the door. Nothing waited in ambush, but a mist seemed to exhale from the ground beneath the trees, where it made a ghostly haze above the roots.

Spook mewed, emerging from the darkness beside the stable, the fur of his neck spiked and bristling.

"Stay here, Spook." Harric drew sword with his right hand and witch-stone with his left, and sprang down the outer stairs for the trees. Up the path he sprinted, stumbling over roots and plunging through patches of darkness and moonlight until he reached the clearing where he'd summoned the imp.

As if he'd never left, Finkoklocos Marn awaited in partial darkness, hunched and bobbing like a grounded bat.

"Took you long enough. Where you been?" His voice was that of a lifelong ragleaf smoker, graveled and dry.

"In the tower. I wasn't sure you'd be out here."

"Where else would I be? I almost came looking for you."

Harric's first urge was to turn and run. The sight of Fink's needled jaws and plague-boil eyes sent pricks of terror up his spine. It wasn't enough to banish the thought of his mother's continued haunting, however. His second urge was to tell the imp his mother was on her way with an army of ghouls, and beg Fink for help. What stopped him was the possibility Fink might fear the fog spirits and abandon Harric to his fate. He had to allow that it was just as possible the imp would help without hesitation, but Harric couldn't risk it.

"Let's find a place farther from the cliff," Harric said, thinking of the fog spirits' attempts to cast him from high places. He tried to sound casual, but to his own ears it sounded like a squeak.

A thicket of needlelike teeth glinted silver in the moonlight. "Sure, kid."

Fink stepped into a patch of the Bright Mother's light, blank eyes turned to Harric, bulbous nose wagging. The creature appeared to be totally hairless, with skin like smooth black leather stretched over skinny limbs, and about the size of a seven-year-old child if you didn't count his peaked wings. The wings almost doubled his height when folded, and extended a fathom to each side when he flapped for balance, which he did often, as if unused to walking or standing on solid ground.

Harric started to move, but a movement behind Fink caught his eye, and he stopped. It seemed part of the forest began to move with them. Something huge was there, and very close.

"HE'S PRETTY." It was a grating basso voice, so deep it was hardly audible. Its vibrations set his guts thrumming, the hairs on his body on end.

An answering wind like a giant's whisper stirred beside it: *"Brighter than the last one."*

"Shut up, Sick, you're scaring him," Fink snapped. "Sere! Back off!" He turned to Harric. "Don't worry, kid. They're my sisters. Here to protect you."

Three gigantic muscled and breasted versions of Fink in varying degrees of deformity grinned down at Harric from the edge of the clearing. They stood at two or three times Harric's height. He almost gagged at the sight of them. Gaunt, hollow, starved. Eyes like spider eggs in dry sockets peering down at his soul through the aperture in the top of his mind. He felt naked and vulnerable—violated—and unable to stop them.

Here to protect me, the imp had said. Harric repeated the words in his mind, clutching desperately for their meaning, which eluded him in the face of what he saw. Even in that state of heightened fear, however, he realized his mother could be no match for them.

"Protect me from what?"

Fink shrugged matter-of-factly. "Seekers. Feeders. All kinds of things in the Unseen."

"You're open, sweet honey," said the third sister, a skull-and-bone horror with a soft and feminine voice. "Like a soft-boil' egg with a little open hole at the top."

"My—head? The hole. The—"

"Oculus," Fink provided. "How do you like it?"

"Oculus. Ah. Good." Harric quelled a morbid urge to push himself up through his oculus for a closer view of the sisters in the Unseen. Would they appear differently in the Unseen? Could they look any worse?

"Yeah, I give good oculus," said Fink. "The problem with a new oculus is that they're always stuck open. Sure, it closes on its own in daylight. That's just reflex. But you don't know how to close it when you want to, or bar it against intrusion, so any old sprite could reach in there and scoop you out like a dollop of custard. Till you learn to control it, my sisters are here to protect you. And believe me—that means you're safe. No one challenges my sisters."

Turning to his sisters, Fink clapped his hands. "Okay, show's over, girls. I got work to do, and you're a distraction. Take your last looks and get lost. Shoo!"

There was a nasty, hissing growl from the sisters. It seemed they swelled in preparation to pounce on their skinny brother. Then the air imploded with a concussive shudder, and they vanished.

"See? I take care of you," Fink said. "We'll have a lot of fun together, you and me. Now—let's go find that romantic, secluded spot you mentioned."

Harric felt like someone had removed the tendons in his knees. What in the Black Moon *were* those things?

Fink's face contorted. After a moment, Harric thought he recognized a twisted rendition of concern among the teeth and bulging eyes. "They upset you? Sorry, kid. Thought I'd be totally up front with you. Right from the start. No secrets. They scare the gas outta me too, tell you the truth. Lucky for you, they're with *me*, see. We got an understanding. And right now you need those three. Believe me. I'm not big enough to drive off a Harrow."

Harric nodded. *Fog spirits, either.* It was down to thirty paces' visibility. Empty faces formed and dissolved in the fog.

"Nice weather we're having," said Fink.

Harric followed the imp deeper into the fire-cone stand, gathering his nerves. Fink stopped in a small clearing fronted on one side with a boulder the size of a carriage. Harric put his back to the boulder, and tried to still his slamming heartbeat by calming his breathing. *You can do this, Harric. You need this.* The first matter he needed to clear up was the rupture in his mind, which the imp had created *without asking.* Harric had to reach deep beneath his fears, however, to find his anger. "You didn't ask if I wanted this oculus." His voice sounded tremulous in his own ears. "You just jumped me and poked it through my forehead."

Fink returned his stare, unblinking. "You want me to seal it up?"

"*Could* you seal it up?"

Fink's leer widened. "I like you, kid. Ask all the right questions. Yeah, I could seal it up; I'm not a Mad Moon tryst that only knows how to break things." He waited, one hairless eyebrow raised as if in amusement. "Just say the word, and it's gone forever. But then you give me my nexus stone back."

"That's not the point. I want to know why you did it."

Fink shrugged. "Maybe you wanted one. We don't have a contract yet, see, and some guys might like a little oculus to help them make such a life-changing decision."

A shiver of fear crept up Harric's spine. The stakes had clearly risen above anticipated levels. But there was excitement in that shiver as well, for the danger also validated the promise of power.

Visibility was down to twenty paces, and Harric saw whole figures moving in the mist. The imp stared at Harric, apparently unaware of the others.

"What decision?" Harric said. "What contract?"

Fink's grin widened. "The decision of whether you're gonna keep that oculus and my nexus stone. 'Cause I come with both. No middle ground."

"And the contract?"

Fink shrugged again. "Regular master-slave deal."

A short laugh escaped Harric's lips. "Ah, no. No master. No slave."

Fink's eyebrow rose and stayed raised. "I don't make the rules, kid."

Harric's anger at bastard slavery welled up from deep caverns within him. "No slave, and no master," he said, his lip curling involuntarily. "Not in my contract."

Something Fink saw in Harric's face caused the imp to step back in surprise. He studied Harric. His eyes narrowed, then he seemed to come to a realization that sent a flash of hunger across the grotesque face. "You mean, you want a *partnership?*" He said it slowly, as if defining a legal term. "As in, *equals?*"

A sneer was evident in Fink's tone, but he waited in silence for Harric's reply.

Harric bit back his impatience. "Yes. A partnership. Equals."

Fink shook his bald head, long nose waggling. "We don't do it like that, kid. The Iberg Black Circle sets the rules, and the Black Circle says *master-slave*."

"Well, this isn't Ibergia, it's Arkendia. And in Arkendia we don't have a Black Circle, whatever that is. And we don't have slaves."

The leer had frozen on Fink's face. When the white orbs of his eyes faltered away in thought, it occurred to Harric it was *Fink* who was the slave in such contracts, and that Harric had stunned him with an offer of *freedom*. A strange and wonderful vindication rose in Harric as he realized he had just offered that greatest of gifts to another. It felt nobler than anything he had ever done. What better foundation, too, for such a risky relationship?

To free a slave is to earn unstinting devotion, his mother's training whispered in his thoughts. *There is no truer ally. You yourself are proof of that.*

"Partners," Harric repeated, extending his hand. "Equals. No more poking holes in my head without asking."

Fink looked up, grotesque face unreadable. A taloned hand rose tentatively to meet Harric's, then drew back. Fink's long black tongue licked the hedge of needlelike teeth, his white eyes darting about. "You see my sisters around?"

Harric saw only trees, but shuddered at the suggestion of the sisters.

"Yeah, I know," Fink said. "Trade childhoods with me?"

"You wouldn't offer if you knew my mother."

Harric glanced at the thickening fog in the trees. For no reason he could see, it did not seem to enter the hollow in front of the boulder, leaving a clear space of twenty paces across, but now the figures in the fog were clear and plentiful.

"Um, actually, there's something I need to tell you," Harric said. "She's here. My mother, that is. This is her fog."

Fink shrugged. "So?"

"You *know*?" Harric stared in surprise at the imp's blank eyes.

"I been fighting to keep her away from you since you killed my master and snatched my stone."

"Is she what your sisters are here to protect me from?"

The imp hissed. "No, kid. We can't touch her. She has Right of Last Kin. It's the right of your last kin to protect you in the Unseen, act as your guardian while you're alive. It's an ancient rule that we can't touch last kin."

"*Protect* me? She wants to kill me!"

"Yeah. Ironic, isn't it? But rules are rules, kid. We can't touch her."

Harric blinked, dumbfounded.

"She isn't your everyday grave spirit, either," Fink said, waving a claw through the fog so it swirled between them. "This fog is new. She must have promised someone something for helping to take you down. Probably promised that nexus stone."

"*Someone?*"

Again the inscrutable hedgerows of teeth. A grin? A grimace? "Some*one*, some*thing*." Fink shrugged. "Important thing is, it's here, and it hides her and blinds us in the Unseen."

"What are they?" Harric said, pointing his sword at the shapes in the fog. "Why do they want to kill me?"

"They're spirits from a grave island, and it isn't them that wants you dead, kid. It's her. She probably forced them. Scared them, or promised freedom from their island if they helped."

"Grave spirits. You mean people?"

Again the lipless grin. "Sure. All you Arkendians bury your kin on islands so they can't protect you after death. They get real weak and helpless out there. Easy to push around." He made a hacking sound that might have been a laugh. "All except you, kid. You didn't bury you mother on an island. Bet you wish you had."

From the fog came shuffling and scraping of a dozen or more bodies.

Harric swallowed, and thrust the witch-stone before him like a ward.

Fink crow-hopped to his side. "Fight them with your sword, kid. They can't hurt you in the Unseen, so they'll manifest some kind of bodies in the Seen, and you can cut them down. You got the reach on them."

Harric stood ready. A face emerged from the edge of the fog. Mournful, hungry eyes racked with longing. It might have been someone's grandmother, only famine-gaunt and desperate, the skin torn and hanging from her face.

"Why do they look like ghouls?"

"That's how they translate into the Seen; their true form, mad and diseased."

Harric glanced at Fink, though he could not read the grotesque face. "Why mad? What made them mad?"

"Imprisonment on the island. You people starve your dead. Drives them mad."

More faces emerged, eyes wild with hunger. Whole figures followed— crooked, hunched, and clawed. They crouched, watching Harric like wild dogs stalking a faun. Harric shifted his feet, his hands sweating as he clutched the stone and sword.

"Here's how it'll fall out, kid. They'll try to knock you out or take that stone, so cut them down as fast as they come. Be fast. Then kill them in the Unseen, or they'll be back."

Harric's heart pounded in his throat. "How the Black Moon do I kill them in the Unseen? They're all—"

Shapes rushed from the fog, gaunt figures on swift and silent feet, bony hands extended like raptor claws. No time to think, Harric slashed, clipping hands and slicing skin, backswinging across the second rank of limbs and specters that howled and dissolved in snarling agony. Claws tore at his breeches and grasped at his ankles, nearly tripping him up, but he kicked them away. The sheer mass of bodies and limbs came so fast it threatened to overwhelm him.

A heavy blow glanced from the side of his head, sending flashes of light across his vision. He staggered back to win room to swing the blade, only to come up against the face of the boulder.

"Fink!"

No answer. The imp had vanished.

He hacked and jabbed, clipping skulls and jabbing ribs. To his relief he found the space before him clear, giving him more space in which to work the sword.

"Close your eyes!" Fink hissed, his voice weirdly distorted.

"Are you mad?" But the creatures before him had halted and retreated to the fringes of the surrounding fog, beyond reach.

"Close your eyes, kid! Cut the grave lines!"

Harric closed his eyes and plunged fully into the Unseen.

The immersion took him by surprise. Instead of peeking through a little window in the top of his mind, he stepped right through into blinding whiteness. In the Unseen, the fog was a wall of dazzling white encircling the little hollow. Before him, in that bleached and shadowless space, the spirits he injured now struggled to move away. Bent double, as if laboring against a violent wind, the spirits clung to taut, glowing lines that extended from themselves into the fog. Hand over hand they hauled themselves toward the dazzling mist, glancing back in terror at Harric. Harric felt no overwhelming wind, but the spirits strained away from him labored against some mighty force. For reasons he couldn't identify, they weren't blown back from him, but rather *drawn* to him in some awful and invisible tide.

"The grave lines!" Fink rasped. "Cut them before they reach the fog!"

"Wha—? With my sword? They're ghosts!"

"Iron cuts in both worlds, kid! Hurry!"

Harric leapt past the nearest grave spirit, unhindered by the Unseen force that pinned it, and swept his blade through its line. He felt a brief tug on the blade as the line severed, then the line vanished, and the spirit tumbled toward Harric—flailing, eyes wide with terror—as if dropping from some fatal height, but sideways at Harric, instead of down. Harric dodged, but the spirit's trajectory changed with him as he moved. Reflexively, he cast up his hands to ward impact, and the spirit vanished into the stone.

Into the stone?

Harric looked around for the spirit, and behind himself, but saw nothing.

The other spirits grew frantic in their efforts to escape. "Mercy!" they cried.

Harric had moved several paces to the side, and the invisible force that drew the spirits had shifted with him—the stone, he realized. Like the moon from which it drew its power, the stone in Harric's hand drew the stuff of spirit with its own peculiar gravity. To what end, Harric had no idea, but to judge by their frantic resistance, the spirits sensed it would not be a good one.

Weirdly, Harric felt absolutely no equal or opposite force tugging against the stone. Totally unencumbered, he waved the stone to one side, and the direction of the tug on the spirits shifted with it. *I haven't the faintest notion what I'm doing.*

"Have mercy!" the nearest grave spirit cried. It was the grandmother spirit, which had lagged behind the others in the bid to escape him. "Mercy! She forced us!"

"Cut them all!" Fink cried from atop the boulder. "Before they escape, or they'll be back!"

Some of the swifter spirits had escaped the well of tide in which the grandmother was snared. These had retreated to the edge of the fog had turned to watch. Their faces were those of people, not ghouls. Mothers and fathers, the odd child—famine-gaunt, faint, sorrowing.

"Forgive us," the grandmother said. "Have mercy!"

Harric lowered his sword and stepped back.

"He will *not* show mercy," said his mother's voice. "For mercy is *not* what I taught him."

Caris woke with a start. A noise had wakened her. She sat up, looking around the sleeping area in front of the hearth, to find Harric's mattress empty. She felt a twinge of annoyance. Was he off on the ridge again, where she'd found him the night before? What the Black Moon was he doing out there?

She stood and walked over to the door that opened onto the stairs, and found it shut. It might have been that door she heard, which would indicate he'd only just left. But the tall shutters over the east and west windows had also been closed, which was strange. Perhaps the shutters had blown closed, and that was what she'd heard?

She crossed to the west window, her bare feet scuffing the smooth stone floors, and pushed them open. What she saw below froze her breath inside her.

Fog. White mist had crept in around the feet of the tower, its fingers creeping up the ridge between the fire-cones. Harric had gone out to face his mother without her.

"Gods take you, Harric!"

She ran back to her bed and struggled into her clothes, cursing Harric's name all the while. She grabbed a lantern from the kitchen and dashed down the stairs, belting her sword as she went.

The Giants threw fire upon me
Ice-smiting hammers upon my skin.
In the War of Creation
Who could I pray to?
I found help in my own hands and eyes.

—Arkus, sire of Arkendian Independence,
in the heroic poem, "The First Making"

34

Without Masters

The Lady Dimoore stepped from the fog like an empress in state, clothed not in her old gowns, but in youthful glory—in gathers of her own spirit's strands, like a robe of glowing ribbons. In the Unseen she was magnificent. Ageless. Radiating confidence and power. This was not the mad mother Harric had known in the last years of her life, nor the mother that haunted his dreams. This was the mother he'd adored when he was young. And the vision took him aback.

Her eyes regarded Harric with a mixture of pride and cool determination. She spoke now in the calm tones of a master in her prime.

"The stone is evil, Harric. It devours your soul even now. See how it feeds on your strands? How it plucks them from the Tapestry of Fate?"

Harric's eyes followed her gesture to the sky, where indeed his own strands no longer streamed upward to the web of souls in the same abundance as the night before. Many of them bent downward and plunged into the stone clutched in his fist. "Thus it devours your future. I can no longer see your destiny."

"That's normal, kid," Fink said. The imp flapped down from the boulder to land beside Harric with a snap of leather wings. "And it's good, too, since it limits her getting her fingers in your strings."

Harric looked back to his mother, stunned by her beauty and power.

Beside her the imp was a scabrous crow.

How long had it been since she'd been so in life? When he was very young, perhaps. The last ten years of her life her visions had worn her into madness.

"As long as it devours your strands, you are a man without a role in the grand pageant. An unknown, without destiny."

"Like a wild card, right, kid? That's what you like—Jack of Souls, and all that."

Harric looked at Fink. "How do you know about that?"

Fink's grin flashed. "Had to learn about the jack that took my nexus before I offered him a contract. Nothing you wouldn't do yourself."

Bright strands flashed from his mother's arm, lashing toward the imp. Fink cringed behind Harric like a dog that knew beatings, and retreated to the top of the boulder.

"Away from him, you vulture!" She sent a strand snapping in the air between them. "This vile creature has invaded your dreams, Harric, hiding in that foul cat so I could not protect you. He is wicked. He is envious, and deceitful." She turned her burning gaze on Fink, as if she could pry into him with her eyes. "He needs you, Harric—I see that—but for what I cannot tell, for your fate is now obscured to me." She closed her eyes and rolled her head back, as she did when overcome by visions, only now she seemed not ravaged by the Sight, as she had been in life, but master of it. She frowned, as if frustrated at what she saw, then sighed and turned her gaze again on Harric. "This much I can read in the web: the imp wants you for more than your soul. You are a door to something he craves, and which only you can provide."

Fink hacked a kind of nervous cackle behind. "She's holding herself together pretty good, isn't she, kid? Bet you never saw her like this before. All sane and pretty? She's putting all she's got into holding herself together for this show. That's how bad she wants you as her little puppet again. But test her a little, and she'll crack. I guarantee it. And then hold on to your boots when she does."

Black fury rippled across his mother's features, but vanished as quickly as it came, and she laughed. The sound was a wonderful, musical tinkle that made Harric smile. "When the toad speaks, he shows his black heart."

This was the mother he remembered from his youngest years, before the madness had consumed her—a lady, in complete control of herself, unaffected by lesser beings around her. Aches and desires long buried in Harric rose to meet this. But it didn't match his memory of her in Abellia's chair, when she'd been half starved, as obsessed and mad as ever. *That's how she translated to the Seen,* he thought. How then could she be so whole in the Unseen?

"You must abandon this wretch," she said, with another flick of strands toward Fink. "*I* shall be your teacher, Harric. Free from my madness, I can be the mother and teacher I wanted to be for you. It will be as it was meant to be—as it was when you were small—I have seen it in the web! I have so much left to teach you. Come. Dig up my bones and take me everywhere with you."

The oldest of human needs ached in Harric's heart. If his mother were no longer mad, might she not reveal her true love for him, the love she'd always felt? Might she not explain the mysteries her madness had cloaked in riddles?

And it made him angry.

Every detail in the last ten years of his life clashed with that dream, and his heart rebelled against it. Anger blazed to fury, boiling up from his heart into his brain.

"You tried to kill me, Mother," he seethed. "How is that not mad? If you aren't as mad as ever, why the doom on my nineteenth birthday?"

Her eyebrows raised in surprise. "Must I explain? It should be obvious. It was to drive you out of Gallows Ferry, else you would have stayed there to rot, and wasted all I gave you."

He stared, expecting more. "That's it?"

"Need I more reason than that? You would have wasted all our labors in an idle life of bitterness."

"You killed my friends, Mother! You tortured them with prophecies and killed them in that fog. That was all part of driving me out? They had nothing to do with it."

She shook her head sadly. "They would have died that day regardless what I did. It was woven in the web. I simply dressed it in fog to put the fear in you. I assure you, I arranged for a much gentler death than what they would otherwise have experienced."

Harric's fury knotted in his throat as he remembered the misery of his friends. "Forget their deaths—you poisoned their last years with your predictions, Mother. You didn't have to tell them the day of their deaths, but you did. That was the worst of it."

She pursed her lips. "They vexed me. Silly boys."

"They were my friends!"

"But all of that was before my death, when I was mad. Surely you cannot hold such things against me. And my plan, after all, worked beautifully. Not only did it dislodge you from Gallows Ferry, but it did so in the company of your childhood hero, for which I should think I deserve some thanks."

"Horseshit, Mother. *I* chose Willard, and *I* made that happen. *You* meant to kill me, but you failed. I beat you, Mother, and now you're trying to cover it with a lie."

She laughed. The notes tinkled prettily. "Kill you! My dear boy, you make it sound so final. As if I would end your life in this world for all time."

"That's what *kill* means, Mother."

She sighed, gazing down at him. "What a monster you must think me. But your thinking is limited to the present, Harric, to *this* version of you only. I see the future, my son—*all* your potential futures and all potential versions of you. Like branches spreading outward from this point, I see them." She raised her eyes to the infinite web in the sky above them, where some of Harric's strands still rose to mingle and disappear among thousands of others. "Some of these futures are bright—some of these future Harrics are even glorious!— but others are foul and ignoble, ending badly." Her eyes snapped back to Harric's. "When I say I mean to kill you, dear Harric, I do not mean *all* your potential future selves, only those that do not lead to our best possible destiny. Right now, that means any future involving this vile, usurping creature and its soul-devouring stone."

Fink hacked out a laugh atop the boulder. "The stone doesn't consume spirit, lady. It *draws it* to the moon, which is where all mortal spirits eventually go. Natural, like the kid said."

"Lies," she hissed, eyes still on Harric. "Cast it away. I will guide your destiny to a glory far above what this wizened impit can offer."

Harric shook his head, his teeth bared in anger and pain. But as he'd listened, his anger had clarified his thoughts, burned away all else but the most fundamental truths of what he wanted, what he needed, and what he was. "You just don't get it, do you, Mother? You never did, and you never will. So let me explain it to you the best I can, once and for all.

"Sane or insane, you're still an egomaniac obsessed with redeeming your pathetic legacy in court, and as such you love only one thing: yourself. I know you, Mother. Did you think a pack of pretty lies and hopes would make me forget all the things you put me through? Did you think you could cast them in a rosy light? And there are a few flaws in your logic, Mother. First of all, if you can't see my fate as long as I have the stone, then how could you possibly know that my fate with the stone would be bad? You can't. It might, in fact, be glorious, but you can't see it either way."

"Would you gamble with your destiny when I can guarantee it?"

"I don't want your destiny, Mother! I don't want your glorious plan, and I don't want your help, which I can't tell from murder. The Old Ones are returning, the Chaos Moon is coming, and all you can think of is redeeming your stupid name. It's the only thing you love, Mother. So I'll serve the Queen my way, with *this…*" He raised the stone before him, and she recoiled. "No Arkendian courtiste has ever had the advantage of invisibility. None of the Queen's enemies would expect it! None could resist it! With that power and the skills you gave me, I will make a difference for the Queen. I'll accomplish more than the best courtistes that ever lived. *That* is a destiny worth seeking, Mother. *That* is the destiny I choose. I reject your lies. I cast you out."

He turned from her, but out of the corner of his eye he saw her stiffen and swell in fury.

"Ungrateful son!" Her voice cracked with rage. "Turn and look at me!"

He whirled upon her, his own rage tingling in his limbs, and spat. "There is nothing you can say, Mother. We are finished."

Naked fury now burned away her mask of calm. Strands of burning spirit writhed around her like the flames of a pyre. "I warned you," she hissed. "This black-hearted impit will fat you with lies, use you for his moon, and feast upon your soul. To destroy you now would be a mercy. And indeed, it is better to destroy my masterwork than let its flaws defame me." Her chin rose so she looked at him down her long, thin nose. "Goodbye, Harric. Your time is at an end. *Now.*"

The grave spirits charged.

Too late, Harric realized he'd left the protection of the boulder, exposing his back, and that while he'd talked, the grave spirits had encircled him and re-entered the Seen. They rushed from all sides, but not from directly ahead of Harric, where spirits to either side of his mother had given her plenty of space—all this he comprehended in a single frozen instant, along with his only possible course of action.

He, too, charged: straight up the gap, and straight at his mother.

The nearest ghouls blundered past him, groping like blind things, which, he realized, was exactly what they were, since they were in the Seen, and he was still in the Unseen. It seemed by entering the spirit world, he became invisible in the material world of the Seen! Equally clear, however, was the fact that the ghouls, though blind to him, could still feel him and hurt him when they found him, for they rushed the spot where he had been, claws extended for grappling. Harric dashed past them, stone thrust before him at his mother.

Discovering her mistake, she screamed. "Stop!" She backed into the fog, but he kept advancing, and the proud flames of her spirit strands bent and distorted. Several of the nearest strands sucked toward his stone and dove into its blackness like strings down a drain. She tried to escape, but the closer he got, the more forcefully the stone sucked her strands into its black mouth, until it had swallowed so many it dragged her backward out of the mist.

"Harric! Stop this!" she screamed. "You don't know what you do!"

Harric pulled, and she jerked toward him. Real terror seized her, and she thrashed. More and more of her strands succumbed to the tides, cascading into the stone until he seemed to have her by the hair, and the only thing restraining her from flying wholly down the vortex was her grave tether, a taut ribbon of spirit straining back through the forest to her Gallows Ferry grave.

In his right hand Harric raised the sword above her tether.

"Stop!" she shrieked. "You don't understand!"

"I don't have to understand. I know you, Mother. And you've played me for the last time." Harric gripped the sword tighter in preparation for the blow—tried to end it, to set himself free—but his anger somehow did not extend so far as the destruction of the mad soul before him. If anything, he felt pity.

"Take him!" she shouted to the grave spirits, who had re-entered the Unseen, and watched from beyond the reach of the stone. "If he slays me you will have no reward! What are you waiting for?"

The spirits only cringed further away, apparently fearing the stone more than her wrath—or perhaps they sensed their tormentor was about to be destroyed, and they watched in revenge. She cursed them, shrieking in humiliation, naked and stretched between stone and tether. "This is your doom!" she spat at Harric. "You have thrown away your destiny!" Whatever golden glory she'd appropriated for the night had abandoned her; she was now as gaunt and hollow as the grave spirits.

Harric's sword arm dropped to his side. He turned again to Fink.

"What are you doing, kid? Don't you want to be free?"

"I do. But not like this."

Fink stared with blank white eyes. "What do you want to do?"

Before Harric could reply, Fink's already horrible mouth distorted into a hideous snarl, and his mother's laughter erupted behind Harric. He whirled around and found her standing with both feet on the ground, her previous helplessness somehow overcome, or else faked from the outset. With a quick motion she gathered in a broad sheaf of her strands, looped them over his head, and twisted them into the fountain of strands soaring upward from his spirit. When he tried to free himself, his strands evaded his fingers like smoke.

Her laughter filled the clearing, no longer musical, but strident and cruel. "I knew you couldn't do it." With a sneer of disgust, she pulled her strands taut, drawing his along with them, and plunged them into the stone. One by one, the rest of his strands began to follow, whipping past his head into the stone, and the more strands that fell in, the more he felt the insistent draw of the stone in his hand. Very soon the force of the draw became so strong it was difficult to hold the stone away from himself without using both hands.

"Fink!" he cried.

"Hold on, kid!"

One of the plunging strands brushed the edge of Harric's oculus, sending a weird buzzing through his body, and all at once he exploded into the air. It seemed the strand had hooked his oculus and flung him from his body. Fathoms below, he saw his stunned body standing vacant in the clearing, mouth agape, as Fink pounced upon it like a crow on a carcass.

His mother's eyes followed Harric's progress upward, glittering in triumph. She reached out to the strand that had snagged him, and plucked it like a harp string. The vibration sent him whipping away along the strand like a bead on a string. Whirling, disoriented, he sped through ghostly fire-cones, farther and farther away from his body

He tried to scream, but he had no voice.

Then stillness.

He found himself standing in the fog amidst the silent trees. Caris stumbled past him, her soul as bright as a signal flare, sword and lantern in her hands.

"Harric?" she called. She tripped on a root, caught herself, and continued.

A violet strand from Caris swung past him, and suddenly he whipped along its glowing length, dodging fire-cone limbs, until he stood beside Willard in the tower. The old knight brooded at the west window, as if he'd been unable to sleep, sipping a mug of Abellia's honey wine. Abellia, too, had risen for a nightcap, and sat near him at the table.

"They are out making the kisses, I think," she said, shaking her head.

Willard grunted. "We hope to remove the ring when we reach the Kwendi. They put the enchantment into it, they can take it out. We hope."

Abellia nodded, her wrinkled hands gripping her cup of wine. The intense interest on her face was out of Willard's view, but it was clear enough in her voice. "Is Brolli showing how they put the magic in the witch-silver? It is a great mystery to my people."

Willard cast her an impassive look. She dropped her gaze, as if to hide her expression. "So I hear. I think you'll recall he said he doesn't personally have that art."

These aren't visions, Harric realized. *They're real. One of my strands is somehow connected to Willard—or one of his to me—and I see him as he is right now.*

A brilliant strand of gold touched Harric's head, and he spun off through the forest, over the ridge, and down into the valley, where the fog had thinned to nothing. This time he found himself beside Brolli, who hunched in the rocks above the pass. Below him the gatehouse fortress smoldered from some new fire in the remaining tower, which the defenders appeared to have quenched, for it still stood, with only a few dark points of flame yet flickering in the Unseen. Beyond the walls, several dozen knights and workmen had laid a camp behind a heavy timber siege tower at the far end of the turnabout. The tower had been mounted on crude wooden wheels and covered in rawhide. It appeared to be finished, and the workmen were packing their tools away in an ox-cart as if anxious to leave.

Bannus rode from the camp to the gatehouse. In the Unseen, he was almost painful to look at—a vision of violet fire, strands teeming to the sky, his Phyros a thing of light itself. He disappeared from view behind the parapet, but his voice boomed over the rock wall and cliff face. "Dogs! At dawn you will die. Do not surrender and make a mock of our labors. The only mercy you will know is to find death in battle."

Then a blue strand touched Harric's oculus and he flung across the world to Gallows Ferry. He stood again in his own garret apartment beside Mother Ganner as she stooped over his bed. A bowl of herbed water and used compresses stood on the bedside table. Worried and grim, Mother Ganner tucked a very pale and thin Lyla under the sheets.

"Sleep now, la," she whispered. "Time heals all. Every day a little better than the last. Harric'd be proud of you, la."

Another jerk sailed him over the forests to the foot of a lake, where a giant bearded man leaned against a towering stone and gazed at a V-shaped gap in a line of mountain ridges above him. He recognized the giant as the priest who had saved his life in the market. As he watched, the priest pushed away from the stone and hiked along the lake toward the mountains, and Harric recognized the road below the fortified pass.

His mother's laughter pierced the vision. Pain exploded across his head like a stave across the skull. The world spun. He felt a tremendous wrenching snap that knocked his senses reeling.

When he regained awareness, he found himself back in his body, in a tortured embrace with Fink.

"Cut her!" Fink cried, his horrible face only a hand's breadth from Harric's. "Cut her!"

Harric gasped, tried to orient himself, and gradually pieced together his situation. By tangling their strands, his mother had somehow caused his strands to follow after hers, cascading them into the stone until it had swallowed almost all of them, pulling him toward its vortex. The only thing keeping

Harric from flying down the black hole of the stone was Fink, who interceded, spread-eagled with one hand on Harric's chest, the other holding the stone as far from Harric as possible. Harric was helpless against the monstrous force, just as his mother was, but Fink seemed to be immune. It brought to Harric's mind a time when, swimming in the river, its current pinned him against a logjam and he'd been unable to lift a limb against its immense power, until Chacks and Remo had hauled him from its grasp.

Still stretched between the stone and her tether, his mother no longer struggled, but lay still, letting its current wash over her into the stone. "What will you do now, my lovely son? You must release me, or suffer the same fate."

"Cut her tether!" Fink cried.

"I can't!" Harric said, stretching the blade out and falling well short of the tether.

"Cut *her*, then!"

His mother laughed. "He couldn't do it then; he won't do it now."

"Harric?" Caris's voice echoed eerily nearby. "Harric, where are you?"

"Caris!" he cried. "Here! I'm here!"

Caris blundered into the clearing only paces away, sword bright as fire, lantern like a blot of darkness in a cage. She stared about through the fog, head turning all about. "Where are you?"

Like the grave spirits when they entered the world of the Seen, she couldn't see him. And she could see nothing of his struggle, or his mother or Fink, or the stone. Only paces away, she swept her sword through the fog, as if she expected to startle grave spirits from the air. Harric had no doubt her sword would cut him, or Fink, or his mother equally well in the Unseen. *Iron cuts in both worlds*, Fink had said.

"Now!" Harric cried, taken by an inspiration. "Strike, Caris! Strike! The Claxon!"

Her eyes widened at the apparent nearness of voice in the absence of source. Then she seemed to understand, and she executed a tentative Claxon.

"No!" his mother cried, as the blade cleft the air beside her.

Had Caris been a pace nearer, it would have severed his mother's tether to the grave.

"Again!" Harric cried. This time he grabbed Fink's arm and leaned to pull him one step to the side, which drew his mother's tether into Caris's path. "Claxon!"

Bewildered, Caris slashed her blade with a more forceful Claxon, and the tip passed cleanly through the tether.

His mother screamed in terror, and swept toward the stone like a fly in a drain. It swallowed her up to her waist, tearing most of her strands free of Harric's, and weirdly distorting her torso where she protruded from its surface. The few strands that remained entangled with Harric's proved enough to halt her descent, so she hung half in, half out, her arms flailing at her strands as if she'd climb them out of the hole.

The immense pressure drawing Harric into the stone ceased. He staggered back from Fink.

The thicket of needles flashed in Fink's wide mouth. "That was genius, kid."

The imp pressed the witch-stone back into Harric's hand, with Harric's mother eerily protruding from its surface, her ghostly arms grasping at his shoulders ineffectually.

More of her strands slipped from Harric's, falling back into the stone, and with each she sank deeper, until only her head and supplicating arms remained above. The rest of her distorted and collapsed into the surface of the stone.

"Harric! You cannot do this!" she cried.

"Is that your mother?" Caris said, eyes darting around the clearing for the source of the voice. She executed another vicious Claxon on the word *mother*, and then another, drawing perilously close to Harric.

"Yes! Stop swinging; you did it. I'm all right."

Caris jumped at the sound of his voice. She stopped swinging, but her eyes shone white with fear. "Why can't I see you?" she cried, backing away. "What's happening?" She raised her fists to her head, as if she'd cover her ears while still holding sword and lantern. She crouched, panting, teeth clenched.

"It's all right, Caris! You did it."

Fink crow-hopped to Caris's side. He stayed out of range of the sword, should she decide to use it, but she seemed near total collapse, kneeling and balling up, moaning.

"She needs her horse," Harric said, half to himself, half to Fink.

Fink quirked his head to one side, and did something with his claws in her strands. She went limp as a de-stringed marionette, and slumped to her knees, then to her side. Fink snatched the lantern from her hand, stood it on the ground, and met Harric's gaze with an inscrutable grin. "Asleep," Fink croaked.

Harric nodded.

"Look at me, Harric," his mother said. "There isn't much time." He met her gaze. Only her head and one hand remained above the rim of the stone. Her eyes peered into his face, soft and pleading, but Harric turned his attention to his few remaining strands that remained entangled with hers. He was dimly aware of her talking, as he wondered at the luminous ribbons that emanated from his spirit. He ran his fingers through them, and found they had a faint, soft physical feel, like the finest silk might feel in water. When she said something about "only testing him," and how he'd "passed again," he snared the last of her strands in his hand, disentangled them from his own, and held her out above the void.

Very quietly he said, "I wonder if I'll pass this test."

Her eyes flashed, and her face darkened. Was it doubt he saw amidst the rage? "You cannot do this." She pressed her lips and lifted her chin. "You won't."

"What are you waiting for, kid? Prove her wrong."

Harric shook his head. "You say you can't touch her. Because she's my last kin, or something. I take it that's some kind of spirit law. Okay. But what if I *ask* you to do it? Then could you?"

"Harric, don't be a fool," his mother hissed. "You mustn't waive your only protection. This is the very thing they crave!"

"If I pledge to negotiate the contract with you," said Harric, still ignoring her, "could you get rid of her?"

Fink had frozen. His milk-white eyes narrowed to shrewd slits. Very slowly, he nodded. "You've got authority to send her off. Give me the word and she'll never bother you again."

"He'll deceive you, Harric! He will steal your soul at the first opportunity!"

"I don't want her killed or destroyed," Harric said. "Can you just…put her back in her grave? Put her to rest, or something?" He was thinking of an impit tale of a peasant priest who returned lost spirits to their graves with a silver net and lantern. "I don't want her hurt."

Fink's grin diminished, but he shrugged his bony shoulders. "Up to her if she'll rest. But I can stick her in her grave. Nothing simpler. Just don't get in any trouble while I'm gone. I won't be back till tomorrow night."

Harric nodded. "Then I'm in." He turned to his mother, whose eyes remained wide with terror. "Remember what you used to teach me? Show mercy to an enemy, and she becomes your tool?"

"I never said that."

"You didn't? Huh. I guess you're right; I must have said it. Goodbye, Mother. Try to find your rest. I'll visit when I have a use for you."

"Harric!"

Fink brandished a particularly bright strand of spirit he'd gathered from the web, and advanced on her with a wicked glint in his pus-boil eyes. The grave spirits, which had watched the whole affair in horrified fascination, saw the look in Fink's face, and retreated as one along their tethers into the dissipating fog.

"You heard him, witch," said Fink, hauling her by her strands from the stone. "Show me how fast you can fly."

Without another look at Harric, she fled west through the spectral forest toward Gallows Ferry, with Fink close on her trail. In that eerie landscape she appeared as a flashing spirit, brighter than the stuff around her, and Fink a blot of darkness without strands. As his mother's cries of despair diminished in the distance, a wave of power and freedom thrilled through Harric's body. He found himself laughing, wishing Caris were awake to join him, wishing he could tell her all that happened.

The weight of the Unseen fell upon Harric like a fall of rocks. Fink, he realized, had carried the burden of the spell that had kept him in the spirit world during the entire exchange. Harric didn't try to keep the portal open, but let it close and expel him to the Seen, where he fell back to his hands and knees, gasping until his heart and breathing slowed.

When he'd recovered enough to look around, he shivered. Caris lay only paces away, so he crawled to her, and backed himself into the warm crook of her hips, where he could sit and watch her peaceful face in the gold light of her lantern.

Caris stirred. Her eyes opened, distant and dreamy, as if she were drugged. "Hey," he said.

Her gaze drifted his direction. "Did we get her?"

"Got her. She won't be back."

She closed her eyes and smiled. "Hooray for us."

"You were incredible," he said, twining a hand in hers. "I'll never forget it."

"Mmm," she said, and sank again into whatever oblivion Fink had devised for her.

The fog had fled, the Bright Mother had set, and the womb of darkness around them was complete. Once again, it was the hour between the setting of the Bright Mother and the rising of the Mad Moon—Jack's Hour—just as the hour he left Gallows Ferry (how long ago it seemed!).

Spook appeared beside him, green eyes wide and bright, a limp mouse in his jaws. Harric swept him into his arms, and Spook dropped the mouse on Harric's chest.

"Thanks, Spooky. This night just gets better and better."

Harric scratched the cat's ears.

The constellation of the Jack winked down through the branches. Most wonderfully, the seven stars that formed his head were missing. The Unseen

Moon had covered them with a perfect halo of darkness.

Harric laughed and took it as an omen of destiny.

Father Kogan trudged through the dissipating fog, one hand on the cliff wall to keep from stepping off the edge of the gorge. "Another ghost come near me and I'll cut it in two like the last one. Hear that, ghosts? Reckon you learned your lesson. Such a fog as I never seen, full of whispers and shapes. But I ain't no fool afraid of no magic. I'm a priest of Arkus and my heart and steel are sound, and it's a fool ghost that tempts me."

Almost like stepping through a door, he stepped from the fog and found himself on the road again, still angling up one side of a steep-cut granite valley.

The sound of a horse's snort drifted up from the valley behind him. He peered back into the receding fog, where the moonlight illumined shadows approaching up the road.

"Blood and brains," he muttered. The outcrop where he stood was exposed to the moonlight and free of cracks or boulders for hiding, and any moment the figures in the fog would emerge and see him. He dodged around the bend and sprinted fifty paces past to where a wrinkle in the cliff provided a crease of shadow that proved to be a deep crack in the cliff, and big enough for him to squeeze himself and hunker down with a view of the bend. Only heartbeats later, Sir Bannus himself rounded the bend, torch in one hand and an iron-bound horn at his lips. The immortal let go with a bone-rattling blast from the horn that nearly emptied Kogan's bowels. Phyros ax forgotten, the magnificent Gygon galloped past, followed by Bannus's shield bearer and pack horses in tow. The blast echoed again from the valley.

"That wasn't no ghost," he muttered.

When they were well past, he stood and watched the immortal's approach to the fort, where cheers from his army echoed in the canyon.

"Gods leave me, Will. I brought the monster right to ye."

Kogan started to run after them. "But I'll be there to finish my role, whatever may come. I owe ye that."

We succeed not because we are strong, but because we are not alone.

Attributed to Sir Willard after the defeat of the Old Ones.

35

Desperation & Despair

A bell sounded, clear and loud as a ship's knell in the dissipating fog.

Caris stirred. Her eyes opened. The bell rang again, and kept ringing from the direction of the tower. "That's Abellia's bell. Something's wrong."

Harric's jaw dropped. "Bannus…" In the triumphant struggle with his mother, he'd forgotten what he'd seen in his vision of Brolli at the pass: the siege tower was complete; Bannus would attack the gate at dawn.

"Bannus! Gods leave us!" Caris did not question how he guessed this. She jumped to her feet, hauling him up by the hand. They ran through the trees, the light of her lantern jogging crazily off the trunks. The bell clanged until they reached the tower, where Willard stood in the west window, hauling at the bell rope.

"Blast it, where have you been?" Willard shouted. "Bannus is in the pass and will breach the walls at daybreak."

"Are we retreating?" she asked.

"No, gods leave us. We should, but Brolli's still there. He sent Mudruffle to fetch us. The blasted chimpey thinks we can help hold the fort. He has no idea what he's fighting. Boy! Get up here and help me arm. Girl! Saddle the horses."

Mudruffle's horse walked out of the stable, his clay-and-wattle figure still buckled into the saddle. "My harness performed its function as anticipated," he honked, "but it requires certain adjustments I cannot perform in a timely fashion. Given the urgency of our situation and the straightness of my limbs, might I ask you to cinch up the buckle behind my back, Lady Caris? I—oh! Thank you," he said, as she tightened and tested the straps.

"You are going back to the pass?" she asked.

"Indeed so, lady. I cannot ride as well as you can, so let your master know I have gone, and that you will pass me shortly on the trail."

"I will."

Mudruffle rode off, jouncing ridiculously, and Harric and Caris ran to their separate tasks. In the tower, Harric found Willard struggling with the buckles of his breastplate, while Abellia set out sacks from the kitchen and fretted.

"This is food for some days," she said, laying the sacks by the door. "I am to be most sad you are going. I am hoping you come back."

"If we can, we will," Willard said. "In fact, we *must*; our horses aren't near enough rested."

Working quickly and silently, Harric armed Willard. When Caris rejoined them, he helped her as well. The three of them mounted and rode out hard, holding torches to light their trail until the Mad Moon rose; already the clouds in the east burned at his approach.

They passed Mudruffle before they reached the lake.

"Do not delay for my sake!" he called as they galloped past. "I shall catch up, and if you must flee into the wild, I will guide you with my maps."

By the time he disappeared in the distance behind them, the Mad Moon had cleared the eastern ridge and painted the landscape in blood.

In the hour before sunrise, the three reached the river at the foot of the lake and followed it down through the canyon above the fortress. The growing murmur of the falls drifted to them up the canyon, signaling they neared its end. They slowed their approach. Soon Harric recognized the pile of rocks from which he and Brolli had peered down on the back of the fortress on the first night Bannus roared at the gates. "This is it," he said to Caris, pointing out the pile. Almost at the same time, Brolli stepped from the shadows at the base of the rocks. They halted beside him.

Brolli's face was grim. "You could not come more near to the trouble. They wait only for dawn."

Harric expected Willard to explode in fury for Brolli's sending Mudruffle, instead of himself, away from danger, but Willard merely gave a curt nod. "What's the size and comportment of their host?"

Brolli stared at him, brow furrowed. Rather than ask for a translation, he beckoned. "Come see." He preceded them up the rocks to his viewpoint, but turned halfway up to grab Willard's hands to pull while Caris helped from behind.

The view of the scene below was much as Harric had seen it in his vision:

huge fires blazed beyond the walls of the fortress, illumining the completed siege tower that stood back from the walls, awaiting dawn. Torches burned on the tower's upper levels. Crossbowmen manned the top, watching the narrow ledge that ran across the cliff and into the fissure behind the leaning tower of rock above the turnabout.

Harric noticed the bodies of two defenders now lay on the ledge. The one he and Brolli had seen on their first night in the pass had made it two-thirds of the way to the fissure; the other, who had apparently tried the feat since then, had made it only halfway. Feathered quarrels jutted from his corpse like the quillions of a porcupine.

On the fortification wall below, there was very little movement. A few heads moved behind the battlements, but by Harric's count there would only be ten men left to defend it. Enough, perhaps, if Sir Bannus were not among the attackers.

"At dawn they'll overrun the place," Willard said. "I suppose you think we can stop them if we reach that leaning column of rock, but at that range those crossbows on the tower would pierce our armor and their spitfires would cook us before we got halfway across that ledge. I don't see how this could be done."

"*With magic*," Brolli said. His owlish eyes flashed. "Maybe I destroy the tower."

Willard ground his teeth as if biting back his anger. The muscles of his jaw bulged. When he spoke, it was in low, measured tones. "You put yourself in danger—you put us *all* in danger—to prove a point about magic?"

Brolli did not rise to the bait. "I am tired of running. Better we fight them. And my magic is certain."

"It is not certain! You said yourself *maybe* you destroy the tower."

"You misunderstand me. My magic may not destroy the tower, but it *will* knock down the bowmen. While they are down, we run to the rockfall." With his hands before his wolfish grin, Brolli pantomimed the rock tower toppling. "You see? If my magic destroys tower, good. But even if it does not, it knocks bowmen down and we run to the rockfall. You see?"

"None of this takes into account what Bannus might do, or how you employ your magic in front of a dozen magic-fearing Arkendian guardsmen on the wall. They might tear you to pieces before you got off your spell. Far too risky—not at all certain—"

Harric did not hear the rest. While they argued, he'd slipped back down the rocks and away down the dark road beside the river. Hugging shadows at the base of the rock pile, he slipped past his friends and ran, counting on their argument and the burning fires to distract them until he came to the stairs that climbed to the foot of the ledge. He found the first stair in the shadow of the fortification, cut into the cliff, and rose steeply under the cover of shadow for half its ascent. As he'd noted the first time he and Brolli came through, the builders had erected a low stone wall to hide the stairs from eyes below, providing plenty of cover for a crouching climber. Harric crouched and climbed.

Brolli's plan had seemed daring to Harric, but there was another way that Harric alone could accomplish, and without so much risk to the ambassador.

At the top of the stairs, some four fathoms above the top of the battlements, the cover of the wall ended. He stopped behind the last bit of wall to catch his breath, his thighs burning from the climb. Before him, the bare ledge forged ahead, rising slightly as it cut across the face of the cliff. It was just wide enough for a large man to walk without turning sideways, and stretched perhaps sixty paces to where it ended in the fissure. Halfway across lay the body of the first guardsman; beyond that, the second. The siege tower stood even with the second corpse, its top three fathoms below and its crossbowmen watching the ledge.

Harric drew the witch-stone from his shirt. Its slick surface felt cool in the palm of his hand, but sweat prickled on his neck as he contemplated what he was about to do. He'd only entered the Unseen without help once before, and in the brief time he'd been there it had sapped him like he'd run a mile at full speed up a mountain. Indeed, he'd passed out from it. Without Fink's help he feared he might pass out and fall off the cliff or suddenly become visible to the crossbowmen.

Far above him, a few high clouds paled with the approach of dawn.

It's now or never. Harric closed his eyes, and peered into the Unseen through the oculus at the top of his mind. The landscape lay before him like a dreamy, underwater reflection of itself. Filaments of spirit rose from everything around him, clouding the air with luminescent strands. So beautiful it now seemed. Had he feared it before? Once more he felt the strange sensation of standing on the bottom of a slow-moving river amidst a forest of wavering strands, like water grasses. Because of these filaments it was difficult to see beyond a hundred paces or so. A *slow, gloriously bright river*, he amended. In contrast, the fires of the siege tower made dense points of flickering blackness.

Harric strained his consciousness up at the oculus. He imagined he was climbing out through that high window in his mind. A thrill of danger shot through him as it began to open above him, and then pulled him through. He found himself standing fully in the Unseen, his body alight with pale filaments flickering into the sky.

The weight of his entrance into the Unseen staggered him. He gasped, felt himself growing faint. He tottered and threw his hands out for balance, but knocked his cheek against the cliff before he steadied himself.

I can do this. I have to do this.

He walked out onto the narrow ledge, eyes on the luminescent stone before him, hand on the cliff to his right. In three steps, his head was pounding with the effort. In ten paces he crossed above the battlements, his lungs heaving, burning as if he carried his horse on his back. Panic scattered his thoughts as he realized it was too difficult to maintain. *I'm going to pass out and drop into the Seen!* He staggered toward the body of the first guardsman, which lay midway between the wall and the siege tower. *Too far! I can't make it!*

Dimly he recognized how ironic it was that he should get no farther with magic than the first defender had without. His vision went black; the roaring became a high, hissing shriek, and he could bear it no more: his knees buckled as he fell into ringing blackness.

"Harric!" Caris called softly. She scanned around her, painfully aware of the fact that Willard would notice and become irritated. No sign of him around their vantage on the rock pile. Her gaze swept the road behind, where the horses stood hobbled. Still nothing.

"Where the Black Moon is Harric?" Willard grunted, craning his neck to check by the horses.

Brolli turned his huge eyes to the road behind, then again to where it approached the fortress. After a moment, he made a noise that might have been a rueful laugh. "There." He pointed to a distant point on the road below them.

Shielding her eyes from the light of the enemy's fires, Caris saw movement behind the fortifications. A dim figure jogged down the road toward the wall. Harric. He slowed, seemed to pause when he was almost to the fortress, then left the road, climbing up to the side and out of sight. Stairs? Yes. A dark line of stairs with a low wall as rail or cover.

"He grew tired of the old men arguing," Brolli said.

"Gods leave him," Willard muttered. "What the Black Moon does he think he's doing?"

"Making a look at that cliff ledge, I think."

Caris felt a stab of anxiety. Surely it was as clear to him as it was to Harric that running out on that ledge was suicide. He appeared again at the top of the stairs; the angle of her view had him silhouetted against the illumined cliff rocks beyond. Surely he would turn about soon and come back to report some new reconnaissance. She'd sensed over the last few days a desire in Harric to impress Willard—to somehow appear capable of more than dressing the old knight or buffing his saddle. Did he think this sort of spying was the way to show he was useful? *Gods leave him, why'd he leave without telling me?*

"I see him," Willard muttered. "He'd better not get any ideas of heroics. Girl. Get him back here. Take a shield," he added. "And I don't want you taking any risks, so stay behind cover. Keep that shield between you and the tower in case you're spotted. Understand? No heroics."

Caris clambered down the rock pile. She grabbed the tall shield from Harric's horse and set off at a trot, her armor clacking with every stride. With every boot fall, her anger at Harric compounded. *Why didn't he tell me? Did he think I'd stop him? Betray him to Willard?* The notion galled her, but in truth she knew she might well have stopped him, and the fact he was justified in his secrecy galled her even more.

When she reached the place where Harric had turned aside, she saw the stairs, but their protective wall was much too low to allow her to climb normally; she'd have to crouch almost double. Nor could she see the top of the stairs from the bottom, as the staircase curved around an outcrop. So she climbed. She took the stairs two at a stride, bent double in her armor. When she rounded enough of the bend to see the top of the stairs, she was breathing quite hard and sweating into her quilting. Worse, Harric was not in the stairwell.

Her eyes pried through the dark of the stairs, looking for where he might have hidden, but found nothing but the uniform lines of stair after stair.

Another stab of panic. *Where the Black Moon are you?*

She reached the top of the stair to find no sign of him there, nor on the ledge of the path across the cliff. She was certain she had not passed him on the stair, but was so baffled that she glanced behind her just to be sure. There was nowhere above her he could have gone, unless he'd fallen off the ledge.

Her breath hitched, and she swallowed a hard knot in her throat.

She could not look over the edge without revealing herself to watching crossbowmen, but if she did it quickly she could be back again behind the wall before they could aim and shoot. She looked back up the road above the pass to the pile of boulders where Willard and Brolli still watched. She could see their shapes in the dim light of the moon. Was one of them motioning her to return?

Gods leave you, Harric. Where are you?

He had to have fallen. She put her eye to a chink in the wall and took a good look at the siege tower. Three men with crossbows watched the ledge, talking in low tones. One seemed to look right at her, though he gave no sign he saw her.

Gripping the shield on each side, she held it before her. Then she stood up and stepped out just as Bannus's horn sounded in the valley.

She almost jumped from her armor.

Too startled to look carefully for Harric, she nearly forgot to look at all. She caught a hasty glimpse of fire-lit stone below, then someone cried out on the tower, and she lurched back, missed a step on the stairs, and nearly tumbled, catching herself as she slammed a shoulder against the cliff wall.

The words that came out of her mouth were not ladylike.

A crossbow quarrel clattered off the cliff at the top of the stairs and into the stairwell at her feet.

Pain woke Harric. Searing pain behind his eyes. *A bolt must have lodged in my brain.* Voices nearby, arguing. Something tickled his cheek. *A fly. There's a fly on my cheek.* He opened his eyes, to find something hairy lay directly in his face. It was the back of someone's head. Maybe a hair was tickling his cheek. The person lay beside him, unmoving. Something smelled like a dead cat.

A hissing bolt struck his companion with a sharp *whap!* His companion jerked stiffly.

Slowly, Harric pieced it all together. He was on the ledge. He'd passed out and fallen between the first guardsman's body and the cliff; the guardsman's body screened him from the crossbows of the tower.

"Dead," a voice said. "You're imagining things."

"I tell you he stood."

"You're drunk."

"I haven't had a drop, and I know what I saw."

Another quarrel raced in and hit the corpse's head with a sickening *thok,* jogging it into Harric's nose.

"It won't stand anymore," said a third voice. Laughter.

Harric had no idea how long he'd been out, but judging by the fact that the bowmen still shot at the corpse, it hadn't been long. Above him the high clouds turned pink with approaching sunrise. He couldn't afford to rest, or sunrise would catch him and he'd be thrust from the Unseen as he had been that morning, only this time with fatal results.

Careful not to raise his head, he craned his neck to peer up the ledge toward the fissure at the end of the ledge. He'd made it almost halfway. From here the crack looked as big as a smelter's chimney, wide enough even for Caris to enter. He could not see the resin charge, but it had to be there, he reasoned, since he'd seen no evidence of either of the slain guards bringing charges with them.

The second dead guard lay halfway between himself and the safety of the fissure. He knew he could not hold himself in the Unseen long enough to make it all the way to the fissure, but if he could get to the next corpse he could lie down and rest beside it before attempting the final leg.

He closed his eyes and peered out of his oculus into the Unseen, then opened them in panic as he realized he no longer held the witch-stone in his hand. *Moons!* He felt around between himself and the body, but found nothing. He searched with the other hand between himself and the cliff face, but again found nothing. Cursing, he spread his legs until they encountered the cliff on one side and the corpse on the other. No witch-stone. Then it rolled free from between his thighs, and he clapped his legs together just in time to catch it between his ankles.

Biting back more curses, he reached one hand down as far as he could reach, then curled his legs up and bent at the waist until he felt its glossy surface in his fingers. But as he grasped the stone, he budged the corpse, and another cry went up from the tower.

"There! See? His arm moved! Get that spitfire over here."

Harric closed his eyes and rose into the oculus. It was no easier this time, and when he entered into the Unseen the headache thundered behind his eyes, doubling as he climbed to his feet and staggered up the ledge. From the corner of his eye he saw the spitfire erupt from the siege tower. In the Unseen, it appeared as a black line of darkness, and as it streaked from the weapon it painted the landscape in weird shadows. He heard the resin wad splatter against the stone behind him, hissing as it burned.

Harric kept his eyes on the path and staggered forward to the second corpse, which lay even with the siege tower on his left. Gasping, he collapsed beside the body and let himself fall through the oculus into the Seen. Flat on his stomach, his head swam with roaring pain. Sweat soaked his shirt. It clung to his skin like he'd just emerged from a pool.

"Mother of moons, now that one's moving," said a voice just below him. "See his leg there? It just edged over."

A crossbow thrummed, and the corpse beside Harric jerked. "It's rats, then. He ain't breathing."

"Reload that spitfire. Time to roast another rat."

Get up! Harric cursed himself. *Now! Or it will be too late!*

He entered the Unseen one last time, but this time he could barely get his head through the oculus before his ears roared and his vision grew dark. He choked in pain, and let it go. *I can't do it!* he realized. *I have nothing left!*

The corpse nearest Caris burned and stank of singed hair and worse. The crossbowmen on the tower now took potshots at the second corpse. *Boredom?* she wondered.

Then she saw the boots. Four boot soles faced her on the ledge. *Harric!* She stared in disbelief, a combination of wonder and anger rising in her throat. He lay wedged between the second corpse and the cliff face. He must have crept out when the tower men had been distracted, but what could possibly have distracted them? There had been nothing she could recall. Had he crawled there on his belly, hugging the cliff and relying on the edge of the ledge to shield him from view from below? She wouldn't have thought it possible, but there he was, clear as day! She'd been too preoccupied with the tower and everything else to notice before.

A strange mix of admiration and fury warred in her brain.

A bolt hissed in front of her face and cracked against the wall beside her, startling her from her reverie. She jerked the shield up and crouched for cover.

On the ledge, one of Harric's boots twitched. His chest rose and fell as if he were breathing rapidly. Was he wounded? Panicking? A breath of fear tickled her heart. He hadn't moved since she'd been there. Why? A little voice in her head whispered a chilling possibility she took as truth: *because you called their attention back to the ledge.*

The scenario unraveled itself in her imagination like the ending of a sad ballad: the crossbowmen, lax in their duties, had allowed him to inch out there on his belly until she spoiled it by rousing the bowmen to watch again like hawks. Now Harric dare not move. *He's trapped, and I trapped him.*

She ground her teeth, rejecting the guilt that assailed her. *No, this is his fault. This is what happens when he sneaks off without telling me. None of this would have happened if he'd trusted me.*

She peered through a peephole at the tower. Four crossbowmen. Two of them watched her position; the other two continued their sport of sniping at the second corpse. Beside them, a spitfire knight reamed out his weapon.

Bannus's horn sounded again, louder. It seemed to come from just beyond the nearest bend below the pass. She shifted her gaze through the peephole in time to see a rider appear around the bend, followed by three others. The first was clearly Sir Bannus on his gigantic Phyros, Gygon. The next appeared to be his squire or some other knight. The last two followed on leads behind the squire, and, judging by their sagging posture, were captives bound in their saddles.

An answering horn rang out from the siege tower, and Bannus sounded his deep, harsh horn again. He rode past the tents and tower, into the roundabout. "My tor! My castle!" he roared. "You have done well!"

Caris felt her gut clench at the sight of him. On the gigantic, scarred Phyros he seemed truly a god among mortals. His dark violet skin was as scarred as his Phyros's hide, but to the point of mutilation—monstrous—over a frame three times the size of a knight, and muscled like ten men. In the segmented black armor he radiated divinity, invincibility. To see him even at a distance, Caris felt herself shrink to a little girl in armor.

"Wall men!" Bannus bellowed. He reined in before the gatehouse. "Your time is nigh!"

Atop the battlements, a few tiny heads appeared. He roared with laughter and turned to face his men, who had emerged from their tents, or climbed the siege tower to lean out from the timbered levels. The bowmen on the top, Caris noted, had stopped their sniping, though they still watched the ledge. She chewed her lip, hoping Harric would not choose this time to make a break for the fissure, thinking the bowmen were distracted.

"I bring you a sign!" Bannus cried. "A sign that the Old Ways have returned!" He gestured behind his saddle to a pair of baskets hung on either side. The basket nearest Caris appeared to be filled with human heads. One head wobbled on top of the basket, a young man's head, judging by the cut of the hair. Each of the baskets might have been big enough to hold a dozen such heads.

Gods leave us, has he slain all of Gallows Ferry?

Bannus reached back and grabbed the hair of the wobbling head and jerked it up.

And the face screamed.

He hauled it from the basket, and it appeared to be more than just a head, but she only glimpsed it, for Bannus simultaneously spun Gygon to better display his trophy to the wall men, blocking her view with his massive immortal body. A prickle of horror crawled up her spine. The basket had been too small to hold even half a body. She'd heard the tales of this. With Phyros blood they'd kept the boy alive. The Old One's greatest weapon was terror, and this their greatest use of it. Who would stand against them and risk capture, if this might be their fate? This is how they enslaved the land for centuries.

"Behold!" Bannus roared. "This is the fate of all who defy me! Is it not known? Have I neglected this land so long the tales have dimmed?"

Silence from the battlements.

Bannus howled with rage, and whirled Gygon to face his own men. Again Caris glimpsed his trophy—eyes rolling in fear, a simple shirt with fluttering sleeves—before Phyros's body obscured it. Is this what you wish?" Behold! I bring you an eastern bastard!" Bannus bellowed to his men. "Is this not a pretty piece of flesh?"

The men on the siege tower roared approval.

"Squires!" Bannus pointed to the ranks of men in the camp. "Come forward! He is yours!"

At first, the lines of men stood as if stunned. Then a trio of steel-clad squires strode from the ranks, pushing other squires before them. Bright yellow plumes bobbed from the helms of the trio, who must have been brothers. The trio shoved the others across the roundabout to the immortal, all grins and yellow-plumed swagger.

They converged on Bannus's trophy, and the immortal released him to their arms.

"Go!" Bannus commanded. "Let him lick clean your boots! Practice on him as you will."

Following the lead of the trio, the company of squires cheered, and crowded around their new pet. Caris glimpsed the young bastard's terror as they appeared to taunt him with pinches and jabs. When the trio took the prize for their own and bore him to the tents, the rest remained before Bannus, and cheered them on.

One of the smallest squires, however, stood apart from the rest. He didn't laugh, but stared in shock after the whooping trio.

"Boy!" Bannus' eyes fixed on the squire. "You have no taste for bastard?" He hoisted a head from the other basket, this one with long woman's hair and a fluttering shift—and slung her into the arms of the other squires. "Lay her out for him!" Bannus commanded.

The squires complied and stepped back.

"Come, boy! Take her here. We'll make you a man before these walls."

The lone squire stood petrified, abandoned by the others He couldn't have been older than twelve. His arms trembled. His head shook feebly as if to deny this was happening.

Caris clapped a hand to her mouth to suppress a sob, but unable to look away.

"Who brought this milk-rag to my battle?" Bannus roared. "He defiles this place! Take her, boy, or you shall be as she, and serve in our tents!"

A knight strode from camp, a pained grin plastered to his face. The boy's father? With a gruff hand behind the boy, he guided him to stand before Bannus. The boy clung to the knight's arm, and when he tried to bury his face in his side, the man struck him. They stood above the woman, whose face Caris could see in a gap between the watching squires. She had flopped on her back, and now panted. Hair stuck to her face, but she twitched it aside with a flick of her head and glared up at them.

She said something, and Caris realized she was laughing. Harsh, hoarse laughter.

"See what you've brought upon us!" she cried out to the watching knights. "All of you! See what he's done? And he'll do it to you! To your sons! See what your insane religion brings upon us?"

The knight kicked her, but she kept laughing, and the boy pulled away from his father, shaking his head. The father grinned for Sir Bannus and collared the boy, bending low to speak in his ear.

The boy looked up at Bannus. He swallowed. He dropped to his knees beside the woman, disappearing from Caris's view behind the wall of squires..

"Take her now," said Bannus, "or I will make you my toy."

Bannus's squire rode into the roundabout, his destrier's hooves clattering loudly in the silence. He still led the pair of horses bearing captives. Dirty, bent, strong: peasant men, Caris judged. Hands bound to the saddle.

"Sir Titus," Bannus called, his eyes never leaving the boy. "Bring my ax."

Bannus dismounted and loomed over the boy, opposite the boy's father, who stood motionless as stone. In the gap between squires, Caris saw the boy began to shake violently. The woman had stopped laughing. Her eyes grew soft, and she spoke gently to the boy.

Sir Titus drew up beside Bannus and handed him an ax. Bannus pointed to one of the peasant men on the horse behind Titus, and then to the ground beside the boy.

"I wish to show this cob warmer and his father the fate they have earned this day."

The father startled. "*The father*, Your Holiness? Me?" He stepped back from his son. "Surely not I. The boy, yes, but—"

"You sired this girl," Bannus rumbled. "You disgrace your steel."

Titus motioned to the camp, which had grown silent. Men watched impassively, or with fixed grins like that of the father. As Titus moved, his hood shifted and Caris saw the glint of the red mask covering his face. *The Faceless One*, she realized. *Just as Harric said.* Four knights emerged from the ranks beside the tower and hauled one of the captives from a horse. They dragged the man beside the unfortunate boy and father, and staked his limbs to the ground.

All the while, the woman spoke softly to the boy, and the boy nodded faintly in reply.

Bannus paid them no attention. He turned to his Phyros and made a quick incision in the beast's scarred neck. Dark blood gushed from the wound into a bowl he held underneath. Gygon made no movement, and the bleeding quickly stopped. Bannus handed the bowl to the Faceless One, who cradled it in both hands and took it to the side of the staked man.

"Wall men!" Bannus said, turning again to the gatehouse. "Behold, that you may know your fate of all cowards unworthy of the Old Ways." He picked up the ax, and made a show of aiming it at one of the staked man's arms. "Do not offer to surrender, wall men. Do not ask for mercy, for there will be none. When we enter your little fortress, you will beg for mercy, and receive none. Yet you will live, for we shall make shapes of you that men remember. When they see you they will say, 'There goes one who forgot how to kneel.'"

"Bannus!" Willard's voice rang out over the battlements, and the sound of it made Caris jump. "You pathetic dog raper. Do you yet live? Time I remedy that."

Caris switched peepholes and found the old knight standing on the battlement.

If possible, the silence that followed was deeper than that which Bannus had engendered with his horrors. The ax froze. Bannus's mutilated head tilted as if listening. He lowered the ax. He turned toward the gatehouse.

Willard had chosen a spot out of view of the crossbowmen, but in full sight of Bannus. To Caris he looked pathetically small and vulnerable compared to the swollen, rippling immortal.

"I would know that voice if it were removed a thousand years from my hearing," Bannus rumbled. "It is the voice of the Abominator. But I see only this pitiful old woman on the wall. Where is the Abominator? Let him show himself."

"You grow slow in your dotage," said Willard. "I am here. I do not fear your gaze."

Sir Bannus stepped toward Willard, and stepped again. It seemed to Caris, by his expression, that he was drawn to the aging knight as if to some horrible wonder. He stopped below Willard, and his laughter boomed from the walls. "Can it be true? He is aged! He has forsaken the Blood! This old woman is the great and mighty Sir Willard? No. I shall not let that stand. I shall not let you escape into death, Sir Willard, for you must pay for your crimes. When I take you I shall force the holy Blood through your lips and until you are reborn—a rebirth you never earned—then I will defeat you in equal combat and make a trophy of your trunk. You will spend eternity as an ornament in my hall, Abominator, the price of your treachery."

"The price of justice, that would be," said Willard. "But it is my choice whether I take the Blood, Sir Bannus, and I choose to die. As should you. This Blood—this borrowed divinity—mads you, though you call it holiness."

Bannus stepped closer, seething. "You never deserved your mount. I should have slain you the day you came begging to the Sacred Isle."

"Molly chose me. Do you doubt the divine judgment of the Blood?"

Bannus howled. The sound of it shocked Caris, and sent her ears ringing. "Speak not of the Blood!" he roared. With the swiftness of a striking snake, Bannus flung the ax. The weapon was nothing more than a blur and a clash of steel as Willard vanished from her view.

Roaring rose in Caris's ears as she stared at the empty battlement. Willard! Had he ducked? Had he been hit? If he'd ducked, why hadn't he reappeared? The roaring rose to a deafening volume. She put her hands to her ears to block it out, but it did no good. It never did any good. The roaring grew louder behind her hands and she felt the familiar darkness coming, terror rising and buckling her knees, driving her into a ball on the stairs.

Not now! You have to do something! Harric lives! Act! Move!

She staggered to her feet, shield in hands, and stumbled onto the ledge.

The sound of a large waterfall grew as Kogan jogged toward the final bend in the cliff road. When he stepped around the bend, he saw the end of the valley: a V-shaped pass only a half-mile hence, with a squat stone fort plugging the gap in the pass. Outside the fort walls stood a crude siege tower and the winking campfires of a small army. *Will must be in that fort.*

Kogan chewed at his beard. The report of spitfires drifted to him on the breeze. "So it starts," he muttered. "I wish you was here, Widow Larkin, to counsel me. I'm only one man against an army, but you'd know what to do. You got a head for puzzles."

Torches began moving down the road toward him. Two torches. Soon the sound of trotting horses drifted down the valley.

He cast about for a squat hole, but found that side of the bend bright with moonlight and bare of hiding holes on the one side, and too sheer a drop without ledges on the cliff side.

Two riders. He could take them, maybe. But since they moved at a pretty good trot, one could easy get away and sound the alarm, and that wouldn't do. The only advantage he had was the fact the enemy didn't know where he was.

He retreated around the bend and found a crease in the cliff with a pile of boulders at its base. Squatting in the crease, he made a little more room for himself by shoving boulders away onto the road.

"Ho, now, here's an idea!" he said aloud. "How if I make a little rock farm on the road, Widda Larkin, so them horses has to slow? Then I could pick 'em off as they slow, grabbing rats at a rat hole." He shoved another boulder out, then tossed another. He could hear no hoofbeats yet, but he wasn't sure the sound would carry well around the bend; they could make the turn with almost no warning. He tossed chunks of rock as fast as he could, spreading them out, and soon he had a goodly garden of the treacherous crop spanning twenty paces of the road. Pleased with himself, he returned to his squat hole and laid his ax across his knees. "Widda, you'd be proud. Using my noggin. And it ain't no small help to cut off Bannus's message lines. Widda sweet, I am Willard's rearguard surprise."

The riders reined up at the treacherous spread of boulders. "Careful," one said. "Bit of a rockfall."

Side by side, the two navigated the rocks, but it was slow work, and the horses balked at it.

"What the Black Moon's that smell?" said one.

Kogan pulled them over the backs of their saddles and slammed them onto the boulders. "That," he growled, as one drew a blade and slapped it against the knees of his smothercoat, "is the smell of *justice*, ye perfumed cob." He launched the blade wielder over the cliff with a shove of his boot. The other, dazed from his landing, flew after without struggle.

Kogan peered over the edge. Too far down in shadow to see where they landed. "Rearguard secure, Will." He frowned. "Wait a shake. That wasn't using my noggin. Shoulda pumped 'em first for information!" He slapped his head, then dismissed the criticism with a wave. "Bah! That ain't my way. The information won't get where it was headed, and there's an end."

He took a wine bottle from the saddle of one of the horses, and retrieved his ax from the squat hole. From the bend he peered back at the fort. No more riders.

He took a deep draft of the wine bottle. Then took another, draining it, and tossed the bottle after its late owners. Still no riders for the rearguard. But with Bannus there, the army would not be still. To be a useful rearguard, he'd need to advance.

"Ain't my way to wait for crumbs from the table, neither," he said, resuming his jog. "Rearguard advancing, Will. I aim to do you such service that this time it'll be you what owes *me*."

36

Sir Bannus

Harric heard the crossbows fire — two, three, four at once — and the sound of hissing bolts. None of them struck the corpse beside him or anywhere near him; they'd gone hissing down at some target near the head of the stairs to thump dully into wood or crack off the cliff.

"Run!" Caris yelled.

Harric twisted his neck to the side to see Caris crouching well behind him on the ledge, sidestepping in his direction with a quarrel-riddled shield held in both hands before her.

"Run!" she yelled. "They reload!"

A spitfire popped, and Caris dove forward to crash on her armored belly on the stone. A gout of white fire sprayed across the wall and ledge where she'd been. "Run!"

Harric ran. Five running strides — almost halfway to the fissure before someone on the tower cried, "There!"

He concentrated on placing one foot before the other on the ledge, for his legs felt so weak he feared they'd fail to respond quickly enough, and he'd stumble. Six, seven strides, and still the crossbowmen loaded their weapons. Then a bolt cracked against the wall only a handbreadth before his nose, spraying rock fragments into his mouth and eyes. He cried out in pain, blinded, and stumbled, his arm scraping along the cliff. His boot caught the stone and he fell hard to his knees. A bolt hissed by and slammed the rock above his head. He scrambled blindly on hands and knees. Tears flooded his eyes as he tried to blink out the shards.

Pounding boots behind him.

"Run!" Caris yelled, and the sound of her voice was loud in his ears. She bumped his back hard with an armored knee. He heard her grunt as a bolt hissed into a wooden *thunk* beside him. She shoved him in the back with her knee. "Run! You're almost there!"

Before him, the blurry fissure rose like a sanctuary. He scrambled forward and threw himself on his belly, then rose again onto hollow-sounding planks. As an eye cleared enough to see he'd made it, he dove into the farthest reach of the fissure.

A flurry of bolts clattered around the mouth of the fissure. One struck wood, and one struck metal with a dull *plink* as another ricocheted around the stone walls to land beside him on the planks. Caris piled over him and crashed onto the planking. An armored knee stove a plank in two, and her leg disappeared in the hole. A spitfire splashed the entrance of the gap with burning resin. Smoke filled the chimney, but none of the fire reached where they lay.

Caris was cussing like a raftsman. Tears cleared from Harric's eyes. He watched as she flung her crumbling shield aside and fought free of the hole in the planking. Staggering to her feet, she doffed her helmet and beat at one of her boots, which was on fire.

Harric propped himself into a sitting position and grinned around gasps for breath. "Gods leave me, that couldn't have gone better if we'd planned it."

Still cursing, she socked him in the arm, hard. "Yes, it could have."

He didn't even grunt. "Okay, maybe I deserved that."

She socked him again, harder, and this time he winced.

"Ow. Okay, I'm sorry. You made your point."

She pulled him up to his feet, fury contorting her pretty face. "Now it's their turn to panic." She strode to the edge of the gap and peeked out at the tower. No bolts answered the gesture. The men in the tower were in full flight down the ladders.

"Someone's won the gap!" they cried. "Move! Clear out or we all die!"

Harric looked about the fissure, searching for the resin charges. The space behind the tower of rock was narrow, with a plank floor above a deep wedge of space. At the back end of the chimney stood a tall ladder that reached to a higher, deeper ledge in the cliff above the leaning tower. *The escape route*, Harric realized. And through the gap left by the broken plank he saw where the resin charges had been laid—deep in vertical drill holes in the rock. Wax-covered fuses ran up from the drill holes to a box upon the plank at his feet. He opened the box, breaking the wax seal. Inside, a simple flint wheel rested in a nest of resin and fuse ends.

Caris peered over his shoulder. "Do it."

He raised an eyebrow. "You want to blow up with it?" He indicated the ladder. "When you're up, I'll light it and follow."

She hesitated, as if suspecting it might be another trick to abandon her, then evidently decided there was nowhere for him to go, and climbed the ladder. The rungs creaked under her armored weight, and the top rungs split, but she managed to put enough of her weight on her arms to keep it from breaking. Harric steadied the ladder as she reached the top and crawled over the rim of the bedrock.

Outside the fissure in the roundabout, men shouted and horses whinnied.

Bannus roared, "Cowards! Return to your posts!"

Sir Willard answered him from somewhere on the battlements. "Leave now, Bannus, and we will let you live. Take Gygon and return to the Isle of Phyrosi. This is your last chance. Your time here is done."

"He lives!" Caris laughed. "Harric, Willard lives!"

Harric grinned. "Let's give his words a little punch." He dashed to the box and turned the flint wheel with his thumb. The wheel spat orange sparks into the resin, which went up in a brilliant flash that lit up the chimney like lightning and sent spots through Harric's vision. The fire raced through the wax and disappeared down the drill holes.

"Shit!" Harric dropped the box and leapt onto the ladder. "Shit, shit, shit!" He climbed as fast as he could, his legs still sluggish from his time in the Unseen.

The sound of steel on steel from the roundabout. Men cried out in pain. "Back to your posts!" Bannus roared. "Bring me the milk boy! I will slay every coward among you!"

Two rungs from the top, the one Caris had split gave way. Harric caught himself, but the sudden jerk of his momentum sent the ladder sliding sideways, carrying him out toward the mouth of the crack and over the void.

"Harric!" Caris lunged for the ladder, but it slid out of reach.

Harric thrust himself up one more rung as it tipped, which brought him within reach of the ledge, even as the ladder tipped sideways out of the crack. Harric grabbed the rim of the cliff with one hand. Caris seized his sleeve. He had no strength to raise himself, but Caris did not let go. Grunting, she clamped her other hand on his wrist, got her knees beneath her, and hauled him over the rim of the bedrock.

Before his legs cleared the rim, a deafening concussion shook the cliff. The force of it flung Harric's legs up and dumped him onto Caris. He scrambled off, and then belly-flopped to the edge of their ledge to see the leaning tower come loose of its moorings and descend upon the siege tower and road with a titanic boom and backwind of dust.

When the smoke cleared, the siege tower was gone, buried in a pile of boulders the size of coaches. The trio of yellow-plumed squires stood staring in disbelief, their equipment and companions—their immortal leader—quite gone. Nor could they cross that stupendous rockfall. Not for a long time. The collapse left a treacherous wall between the road and gatehouse. To pass they would need charges and toolers to rebuild the road, and by then the Blue Order would have come. By then, the Queen would send reinforcements.

The trio mounted two horses picketed on the road, and galloped away. Absurdly, one blew a silver-throated horn in sound of victory.

A cry of triumph burst from Harric's lips. His ears rang from the blast, but he thought he heard faint shouts from the wall. Looking over, he saw Willard on the battlements with several cheering guardsmen. Brolli leapt up and down at the edge of the gatehouse, waving his long arms. Harric waved his arms back, and turned to Caris to embrace her, but she reflected none of his triumph.

"What's wrong?" He followed her gaze. "Willard lives. He is on the battlement. Look! We beat them."

Caris shook her head. "She's gone," she murmured, eyes still searching the rubble. "That woman, the one the boy was supposed to… I think she told him to be brave. I think she tried to encourage him to do what he had to do. In that horrible scene she was the only one with any guts."

Harric bowed his head. "We took away her suffering. She'd have asked for that very thing if she'd been rescued."

Tears streamed down Caris's face. She nodded. "Oh, Harric, it's happening again—the Old Ones. They're back. The Queen has to fight them. We all have to fight them."

"We will. We are."

She turned to gaze down at the wall. Willard and Brolli had disappeared. "What if Brolli's people go to war with us? What if Brolli doesn't trust the Queen, and recommends his people go to war?"

"How could he?" He touched the side of her face and locked eyes with her. "He just saw an Old One in action, Caris. An Old One in all his twisted, mad-brained horror. Brolli may not like our queen—she may allow hanging of witches and brutal justice—but that's nothing to what the Old Ones bring if she falls and they rise again. There's no way Brolli will recommend war. He needs the Queen to keep the Old Ones at bay."

A spark of a smile lit behind her eyes, as well as something else that might have been admiration. She nodded. "That makes it even more important that we get him back to his people, so he can tell them what he's seen."

Harric's face grew serious. "And we'll get the ring off."

She dropped her eyes, then glanced up again.

"Not that I don't want you to love me," he added. "But you never bargained for a love charm on your finger."

Caris's brow furrowed. She opened her mouth to speak.

"Girl! Boy!" Willard's voice drifted up the cliff to their resting place, startling them both.

"Lovers! Matings!" Brolli shouted. "You live, yes?"

"I'm a hairy pizzle if they both survived," Willard growled.

Caris blushed. She stood, and Harric rose beside her. They walked to the edge of the cliff to peer down to the ledge below them, where Willard and Brolli and several beaming guardsmen stood gazing up at them. Willard had not removed his armor to climb the stairs, and his face was flushed with the effort. So were the faces of the guardsmen, who likely had helped him every step of the way in addition to carrying a ladder between them. A fat roll of ragleaf jutted from Willard's mustachios. When he saw Harric and Caris, a flicker of relief passed behind his eyes.

Caris waved. "We're here."

"We did it," said Harric.

The guardsmen let out a "*hurrah!*" in unison.

"Ha-ha!" Brolli echoed. He turned to Willard. "You are a hairy pizzle."

Willard glared up at them. "You're bloody well going to pay for that little stunt," he growled. "The both of you."

"But we're bloody well glad for that stunt," Brolli added. He laughed his barking laugh, and Willard smiled in spite of himself.

"Glad you made it," Willard admitted. "I'm tired of losing squires."

The guardsmen brought the ladder forward and propped it against the cliff so the two could climb down.

When they stood again on the ledge, Brolli pressed himself against each in turn, with a strange no-armed hug.

Willard pointed imperiously back to the stairs. Harric examined the narrow ledge and the knight's protruding belly, which left no room for slipping past him. Willard, seeing his error, frowned. "I'll be waiting at the foot of the stairs."

"This is the thanks we get for destroying Sir Bannus?" said Harric, arms crossed.

Willard's brows shot up. A cloud of ragleaf gusted from his nostrils and set his mustachios to fuming. "You didn't destroy Sir Bannus," he said, not unkindly. "He and Gygon leapt from the cliff to avoid the rock." He grinned, square teeth flashing. "I thank you for that memory. But it takes more than a bad fall onto a boulder field to kill an immortal. You may rest assured that neither is terribly comfortable at this moment, but they yet live. And if it were not for the rubble now blocking the pass, we might expect them again this night."

As if on cue, a harsh horn rang from the depths of the canyon. Bannus's horn. It sounded again and again, the deep note reverberating from the ridges in chorus with the thunder of the falls. The guardsmen's faces fell. Willard sucked grimly on his ragleaf. "Time to move out. Best not be on this ledge if he returns."

As the guardsmen hoisted the ladder and turned to go, Harric noticed they'd both been staring. Harric caught the glance of the nearest, and the man ducked his head and muttered an acknowledgement. Harric blinked in surprise. It was awe and respect he saw there. Respect—for him.

The horn sounded again from the bowels of the gorge, and then, as if in reply, a shrill horn answered from the darkness of the road beyond the rubble.

Te-woot-woot! Te-woot-woot!

Their procession stopped. Six pairs of eyes pried into the darkness of the road beyond.

"What in the Black Moon was that?" said Willard.

"The same horn of your trio," said Brolli.

It was. Harric recognized it, and felt a jolt of panic at the thought of crossbows aimed from the darkness.

"But that is not a warring tune, yes?" He bent his owlish gaze into the darkness below and grinned.

Harric swallowed his panic. "He's right. It's 'Radish, Radish.'" Relief flooded him and he laughed. "It's a priest song."

Willard's mouth went slack. "Not…"

"The one about Father Muggin and the eating contest with the Old One—"

"I know the bloody song, boy, but—"

"It's him!" Brolli pointed to a shape now scrambling on all fours up the dark side of the rubble below them. It looked like a huge garl bear at first, or possibly a yoab, but as it approached the summit of the tumbled rock, three yellow-plumed helmets rose above it upon a spear into the light from the tower fires. The helms had been impaled through the eyeholes, and now swayed in the light like a grisly totem of battle.

Bannus's horn sounded from the deep, but before the note ended, Father Kogan belly-flopped over the summit of the rubble, planted the spear in a crack, and blew a mighty *TE-WOOT-WOOT! TE-WOOT-WOOT!* on the silver horn.

The men on the battlements cheered. Harric found himself cheering, "Radish! Radish!"

TE-WOOT-WOOT! TE-WOOT-WOOT! TE-WOOT-WOOT!

"All right, Father," Willard growled. "Even Bannus gets the point."

Kogan kept up his victory song until it seemed he might collapse, and then he did, as the rubble beneath him slid and cast him down in a cascade of stones. He jarred to a halt against a slab of stone, and remained there, shaking as if panting or laughing. "Oh, Will! You couldn't have writ a better ballad than this was."

"I shall write it myself," said Brolli. "'Sir Willard and the Tooting Priest.'"

To Harric's surprise, Willard smiled. "More apt a title than you know." To Kogan he called, "You are most welcome here, Father. I see you met Bannus's rearguard."

"Sped them on their way, Will. Good West Isle lads, they were. Let me borrow their hats."

"So I see."

Kogan flashed a crack-toothed grin. "Best of all, Will, now it's you that owes me one. And that's as it should be."

"Well, I'll be damned. So it is."

A clatter of chain and drawbridge erupted from the gatehouse as the bridge descended. A half-dozen guards on the battlement began a chant: "Ra-dish, Ra-dish!" A huge-bellied guard with a beard to rival Kogan's hoisted a keg to his shoulder and tapped it into his mouth in the traditional challenge.

TE-WOOT-WOOT! Kogan blew. "Arkendia!"

The men cheered, and the chant continued as Kogan discarded the spear and proceeded to scramble across the rubble on all fours. After a considerable number of falls and bruising slides, he reached a point near enough for the guards to throw him rope ladders that brought him over the rockfall. Dusty, and bleeding from a dozen scrapes, Kogan strode across the waiting drawbridge like a returning hero.

On the cliff ledge above him, Willard put a hand on the shoulder of the guard beside Harric. "Now that he's in, you get that gate up and lower the port. Keep a two-man watch for the night. *Sober watch.* You understand?"

"But sir—"

Willard seized his collars and pulled him close. "You think this a ballad? Ballads don't sing of limbless toys, do they? Of tortured boys? Do you forget what you saw tonight?"

"No, sir…"

"*Never* forget it. Bannus lives, and now he hates *you*." He emphasized the word with a hard jab on the sternum. "You are no mere guardsman now. The great Sir Bannus has plans for you and every man in this watch."

The guard swallowed. "Yes, sir. Two men."

Willard pinned the man with his gaze for several heartbeats, then released him with a nod.

"We owes you our lives, sir. There aught else we can do?"

"You can. Give this priest a place to stay."

The guardsman beamed. "It'll be an honor."

"It'll be a liability. Among other things, expect to run out of drink and meat."

"We'll send for more. Sure to get a garrison here when word gets out."

A cheer went up as Kogan blew another *TE-WOOT-WOOT* inside the gatehouse walls.

The procession on the ledge resumed its careful march across the cliff, but Harric took Caris's hand to stay her, and let the others go. He leaned his back against the cliff, weary, and drew her down to sit beside him on the ledge. Though the sky lightened in the east, the Jack remained visible above—cape flowing, hand extended to pick the Knight's pocket. Or was it to take her hand? And though dawn was nearly on them, Harric thought he saw the Unseen Moon remained perfectly aligned in its halo of darkness.

"Well, gods leave me," he muttered. "What are the chances of that?"

"What?" Caris said, following his gaze. "Chances of what?"

Harric turned to her and smiled. "What are the chances the stars will give us a minute of peace together tonight?"

If the growing light had allowed, Harric imagined he'd have seen her blush. To her credit and his great satisfaction, however, she didn't drop her eyes as she might have only a week before. She held his gaze and laughed.

"The stars have nothing to do with it. We're Arkendian. If we want something, we make it happen ourselves. Right?"

Harric tilted his head to the side to study her from the corners of his eyes. "If Willard had said that, he'd have been preaching. You make it sound like a proposition."

Mischief flashed in her eyes. Altering her voice, she made a very bad imitation of Harric: "I'm sure I have no idea what you mean."

"Oh?" He laughed. "Remind me to show you when we're alone."

EPILOGUE

Fink followed as she fled over hill and through forests to her grave. Her rapid retreat took most of the fun out of it. He'd hoped for more of a fight, but after only a few quick licks, she'd turned tail and made straight for Gallows Ferry and her burial cairn. When he finally caught her in that miserable cliff village, he found her waiting at the stones that covered her bones.

Crazy laughter tinkled from her lips, as if she'd just challenged him to a race and won.

The merry twinkle of her eyes sent a tremor of doubt through Fink.

"I see nothing good in your future, imp," she said.

His lips peeled back in a sneer. "How long have you had the Sight, lady?"

"How long have you had it?" she mocked, as if she knew damned well he didn't have it. She laughed again, secure in the Right of Last Kin, secure in the limits of power Harric laid upon him, secure in whatever it was she beheld in the web.

Fink bristled. Where'd she get that? Where'd she come by understanding of the Unseen most imps never had? The Sight alone was not enough to bring the depth of knowledge she displayed. Nor would it impart such moon-blasted confidence. He narrowed his eyes as if to better pick out clues in the wash of strands boiling upward from her spirit. Maybe she was a Spinner's pet. He could find no Spinner's mark upon her, but two of the three Spinners could be relied on to mark pets only subtly, and sometimes not at all.

That made him nervous. He didn't dare meddle with a Spinner. Not directly.

Her eyes laughed as if she'd read his thoughts. Her lips pressed together and raised her thin eyebrows. She cocked her head as if to say, "I'll never tell."

He had nothing to lose. Why not prompt her? "Where'd all your frenzy and wailing go?" he croaked, as if he knew the answer and wanted her to know he knew. "That was quite an act."

Her eyes brightened—she saw the feint coming a mile away. "I know what you want from him. I could have told him, but that would have skewed the futures. But I can tell *you* something: you won't get what you're after, imp. He'll outmaneuver you, as he did me."

"Yeah? Well, he knows all your tricks, lady. He don't know mine."

She laughed and watched him. "So speaks ignorance and pride."

Fink felt a prickle of irritation. At the same time he glimpsed the slightest hint of doubt behind her mask of certainty. If he'd looked away he would have missed it. She was that good. A kind of awed respect dawned in Fink even as the leer of triumph spread across his face. "Gotcha," he said. "Nice try, lady. But you can't trick a trickster."

The doubt was gone from her eyes, but now her laughter seemed forced.

His interest waned. "We're done here, lady. Get in your grave, or—"

She'd already gone.

He stood in silence, disappointed. *What a killjoy.* No begging and gnashing of teeth. No fun. She'd dodged all that.

But what game had she been at? He pondered their exchange, searching for seams. She seemed to have wanted Fink to believe it had been part of her plan all along for Fink to apprentice her son. That she'd had no intention of reuniting with Harric. But to what end would she do that? To save face? She seemed far too clever and complex for that. What, then? To put him off his guard? Off his guard from what? The kid?

It didn't make sense. But it didn't matter anymore. She was back where she belonged. He lifted the fallen capstone from the ground beside the cairn, and returned it to the top. Then he shook his head to clear it, the way a dog shakes after swimming, and dusted his hands.

"All right, kid. Now you owe me."

He turned toward the east, where, in the distant forest, the young Arkendian awaited his return. The kid knew nothing of the Unseen. He was a blank slate. There was almost no challenge to it. But the kid had said, *No contract. No slaves.* He glanced around for his snooping sisters, who would love to catch him in a misstep like that.

What was he playing at? Had his mother put him up to that?

Fink launched himself into the air and flapped his way eastward, thinking on the matter.

He could hear the kid out. He could put a truth geas on him to be sure no one put him up to it. And then what? Freedom?

Fink's jaws widened, and the wind almost purred between the thicket of needle teeth. Freedom. Now *that* was power. A surge of desire thrilled through him, and though the sky already grew pale in the east, he redoubled his efforts and raced back the way he had come.

Coming August 2015
from Tortoise Rampant

THE KNAVE OF SOULS

Book Two of The Unseen Moon Series

STEPHEN C. MERLINO

TORTOISE
RAMPANT

AUTHOR'S NOTES

Thank you for reading! While it's still fresh in your mind, please take time to leave a review on Amazon at http://amzn.com/0986267414 and on Goodreads at https://www.goodreads.com/book/show/23659310-the-jack-of-souls

For updates or announcements on the release dates for books two and three, *The Knave of Souls*, and *The Prince of Souls*, subscribe to my newsletter at stephenmerlino.com, and/or follow @stephenmerlino, or on Facebook, Stephen Merlino.

BACKERS

To the believers who backed *The Unseen Moon* trilogy, I owe an enormous debt of gratitude. When I first pushed the "launch" button on our Kickstarter campaign, I worried it might fail to reach even its minimum funding goal of Book One, but you people funded **all three** books. I am deeply grateful, and humbled by your support. Below, listed in order of backing, are your names — you, the people that made *The Unseen Moon* trilogy a reality, and made it possible for me to write, rather than fundraise, the rest of 2014 & 2015.

With all my heart, thank you!

Don Crowe
Rodney Taber
Kathryn Rogers
Craig Holt
Scott Merlino
Stone Gossard
Alex Anderson
David Dewine
Todd Floyd
Vikramaditya Prakash
Jane Tomlinson
Pat Perkins
Katherine Swenson
Lynn Rambaldini
Steph Judy
Norma Patterson
David Baugh
Brandy Coward
John Tomlinson, Jr.
Corinne O'Flynn
Matt Newland
Tracey Tomlinson
Rachel Gleeson
John & Danya Schwab
Renee Ruhl
Jo Eike
Lucas Virgili
Glenn Rotton
Brenda & Don Mallett
Niki Tupper
Pam Stucky
Stephen Specht
Dennis Reichenbach

Jim Rogers, Jr.
Marlys Gerber
Jules Hughes
Mark Hauge
Juliana Groisman
Lucinda Payne Santiago
Ryan Niman
Jeff Seymour
Sue Constan
Jodi Ryzowski
Amy Raby
Ace Forsythe
Charla Lemoine
Katherine Nolte
Anne Belen
Anne LaChasse
Alison Rambaldini
Kirsten Fitzgerald
Dick Vitulli
Charlotte Bushue
Katherine Van Slyke
Quinn Roberts
John Joynt
Heron Prior
Steve Viles
Brian Senter
Scott Maynard
Emma Major
Paul Hughes
Peter Bush
Gail Mitchell
Janka Hobbs
Kathrina Simonen
Fiona Robertson
Richard Sundberg
Ed Almquist

Steve Gurr
Kai Ichikawa
Lisa Floyd
Barbara Bender
Anthony
Betsy Lee
Mariann Krizsan
Stefan Marmion
Brett Frosaker
Gabriela Fulcher
Brainiac187
James Arnold
J.S. Elliot
Rob Rose-Leigh
Delaney Ruston
Thomas Cleland
Ross Bowen
Ricciardi Luc
Christy Shaver
Jim Tomlinson
Larry Couch
Arne Radtke
Cathleen King
Phoebe Copeland
Jim Naeger
Alan Hellie
Ashli Black
Rob H. Stevens
Joshua Haynes
Ian Wright
Brad Karr
Becca Morris
Jeff Miller
Deirdre Hancock
Nancy Katims
Brandon Smith
Evan Roberts

Roman Pauer
Stephanie Hahn-Wagner
Delaney Hancock
Tye & Ann Swiftney
Laura Yeats
Cole Krause
Rebecca Carr
Boo Edmunds
Michael Downey
Derek Freeman
Austin Warawa
Michael Frost
Jeanne McGuire
Alexander John
Aristotle Kimball
Tamara Towers
Brian Karr
John & Sue Tomlinson
Tyler King
Emily Woog
Kathryn Duffy
Amy Collins
AcceptablyPsycho
Patricia Gureski-Samyn
Jeanne Rea
Molly Roberts
Judith Karr
James Buckhorn
Gromm (Colby) 43
Levi Jette
Brian Lambert
Peter Lambros
Laura Matter
Kerry Morris

Continued on the next page

BACKERS

Continued from previous page.

David & Julia Marks
Roy Romasanta
Suraya Safavi
Laura Becht
Shaun Skelton
Nick Markham
Kerry Morris
David & Julia Marks
Roy Romasanta
Suraya Safavi
Laura Becht
Shaun Skelton

Nick Markham
Lisa Davis
Jerrie Carlson
Linda Kralowetz
Yankton Robins
Peter Polivka
Kate Parr
Chris Ocano
Karen Dubois
Andreas Gustafsson
Nathan Kitchner
Chad Bowden

Tyler Voiles
Stefan Fransson
Heather
Gabe Much
Michelle Stroyan
Justin Olson
Kathereine
Hernandez
Raghu Tirunarain
Daniel Barnet
Mary Kay
Thompson

Jennifer Wilkin
Penick
Celia Anderson
Andrea Lupien
Caitlin Bartlett
Mark Seidl
Cuong Treu
Joanne
SwordFire

ABOUT

Stephen C. Merlino

Stephen Merlino lives in Seattle, Washington, where he writes, plays, and teaches high school English. In 2014, his novel, *The Jack of Souls*, won the prestigious Pacific Northwest Writers Association award for fantasy, and the Southwest Writers award for fantasy. He now lives with the most desirable woman in the world, two fabulous children, one cat, and three chickens.

Follow him at:

Blog: stephenmerlino.com
Twitter: @StephenMerlino
Facebook: Stephen Merlino
Goodreads: https://www.goodreads.com/user/show/
25533231-stephen-merlino

Made in the USA
Middletown, DE
03 December 2018